I0760373

DIRTY TIES

PAM GODWIN

Editor: Jacy Mackin
Cover artist: Okay Creations

Visit my website at pamgodwin.com

The ache between my legs throbbed, intensely and obsessively. Sometimes I didn't think about him for hours, not the fluidity of his leather-wrapped body crouched on his sportbike or the strength of his hands around the grips. Often, I went an entire day without mentally tracing the muscle definition in his shoulders and thighs, imagining the flex of his ass, the thrust of his hips.

Today hadn't been one of those days.

I'd tried to confine my thoughts to merger proposals, senior staffing issues, and all the other initiatives that demanded attention under my leadership. But he was always present, fighting and twisting and charging into my mind, riding on his steel horse, and carrying my body beyond the edge of restless desire.

A man I'd never met.

Gah! Where was my damned dignity? I shut down the tablet displaying the new photos of him and returned it to my leather satchel. Who would've thought Chicago's favorite criminal would be spotted at a grocery store? Somehow, it made him more human. The media seemed to agree, buzzing excitedly about his public appearance on local television and papers. I didn't like that, didn't like sharing him with four million women.

Outside the windows of the company car, the mammoth columns and well-lit awning of the Trump Tower drew closer. I shoved my aching feet into the heels, the phone pinned between my ear and shoulder. "When these pictures were snapped, was he caught off guard?" My insides fluttered with foolish hope. "Anyone see his face before he got away?"

The ruffle of papers scraped through the speaker, followed by my personal assistant's husky, feminine voice. "Nope. He never removed the helmet."

Always masked, much to my despair, as well as every woman, journalist, and cop in Chicago. Everyone wanted a piece of him.

Thanks to online gambling, the web of criminals profiting from the underground racing syndicate enticed corruption from all over the world—investors, mobsters, and racers alike—turning my Chicago into a hub of dirty money. And at the forefront of this underworld was the undefeated racer himself.

Maybe it was his anonymity that held the city so captivated. Or the inexplicable way he invited death at 185 mph on narrow, potholed streets. Two years ago, one of the reporters at my company had coined him *Evader,* and the moniker stuck. Should've been *Invader*, given his persistent intrusion into my fantasies and the subsequent wet spot cooling in my panties.

I squeezed my thighs together. A rough fuck from one of my husband's hired playmates would be the second best way to spend the evening. The first being entwined with the notorious sportbike racer while straddling the vibrations of his inline-four engine.

The town car rolled to a stop, and I smoothed the skirt over my knees. "Did you send me the latest file?"

My standing order to receive those encrypted files was almost as risky as my appearances at Evader's dangerous venues. But Jenna couldn't open the files without the private key. She had no idea they contained the details for upcoming illegal races, information the police and media would love to get their hands on.

The file I was waiting on tonight held the map for the race that was starting in a few hours.

"Yes, Mrs. Baskel. Anything else?"

"That'll be all." I dropped the phone in my purse and grabbed the satchel.

The chauffeur opened my door. The din of honking and shouting carried me out, capturing me in the energy of the city. I vibrated with the rush of sensations, the scent of asphalt, the warm press of the evening wind, and the buzz of passing pedestrians, their voices rich in layered accents. At seven o'clock on a Thursday, the nightlife crush had just begun.

I strode the few paces to the dedicated entrance for residents of the Trump Tower, my heart beating with the pulse of traffic. Glass walls of modern architecture towered above, glimmering with the reflection of city lights. Behind those walls, people just like me accumulated millions of dollars through hard work, innovation, marriages…and lies.

While my own marriage was forged in deception, the heart of it resided in a deep friendship, nurtured by our families since birth. A smile twitched my cheeks. The stunning Italian genes Collin Anderson inherited from his mother were an added bonus.

My smile faded. Too bad the sexual chemistry was all wrong. It might've been the perfect marriage.

The breeze curled around my bare legs beneath the stiff skirt. Despite the toe-squeezing heels, it would've been a beautiful night to walk the four blocks from the Trenchant Media building. A beautiful night for a race.

Every cell in my body sizzled with anticipation. In just a few hours, I would be waiting at the finish line, straining for a stolen glimpse of him.

"Good evening, Mrs. Baskel." The attendant swept ahead of my brisk walk and held the exterior door open with a decorous stance, his attentive gaze awaiting my direction should I need anything.

My executive position at Trenchant Media, my renowned husband, and our moneyed lifestyle commanded superior service from staff and colleagues. But beneath the tailored power-suit and affluent family, I was a woman like any other with a need for acceptance, a connection to cling to, a passion to balance out the monotony. "Evening, Jimmy. Has Mr. Anderson received any visitors this evening?"

"Yes, ma'am. A young man arrived forty-five minutes ago."

Oh hell, yes. "Thank you." I shaped my mouth into a flat line to hide a giddy smile and quickened my gait through the marble foyer. In the elevator, the silver-haired attendant pressed the button for the eighty-eighth floor. A minute later, I strode into the foyer of the condo, pulling the pins from my hair and freeing the unruly blonde mess.

The hall on the left led to my suite, and the one on the right would take me to Collin's rooms. But I continued to the front like I did every night, magnetized to the wall of windows and its views of the lake, the river, the bridges, and the twinkling cityscape.

Dropping the satchel and purse on the suede armchair, I veered to the wet bar and poured a dirty martini, extra dirty.

The first sip awoke my throat and warmed my blood, instantly relaxing the twelve hours of tension that had accumulated at work. Pinpricks bit through the arches of my feet, but the heels would stay on a little longer. I needed the seduction of those five extra inches for whatever awaited in Collin's bedroom.

Lost to the glow of lights flickering eighty-eight stories below, I finished the martini, poured another, and removed the suit jacket. Drink in hand, I entered Collin's hall, hoping to catch him in a deliciously compromising position.

Strained grunts greeted me at the cracked door. I nudged it open with the toe of my shoe and leaned against the doorframe to absorb the sensual landscape.

The bed sat perpendicular to the door at the far side of the room. Collin lay on his back, lengthwise on the mattress, his legs dangling off the end. The cords in his neck stretched, every gorgeous inch of him bare. His fingers threaded through the dark hair of the familiar head bobbing between his spread thighs. Seth knelt on the floor, one hand kneading Collin's balls, the other pinching and twisting his dark nipple.

My skin heated from the inside out, and my mouth moistened. God, I loved watching Collin in the throes of pleasure. He gave so much of himself to his demanding job and family. It was liberating to see him take something for himself.

He rolled his hips, his trim body trembling, and his eyes caught mine. "Kaci." His fingers curled on the bed in a come-hither motion.

All of his lovers were bisexual, and this one was a regular. Perhaps too regular. Seth wasn't one of the hired escorts from the discreet service Collin used. He'd met this particular lover at a photo shoot, and while the dark-haired photographer had always tolerated me, his affections centered one-hundred percent on Collin. Like now.

"Fuck." Collin groaned. "The man knows how to give head."

Yeah, yeah, I'd heard it for years. Supposedly, a woman couldn't rival the sucking power of a man's lips. I set the martini on the dresser and sashayed toward the bed. "I do, too." Collin knew this, not because his cock had ever breached my lips, but because he'd been watching me blow guys since we were fifteen.

"Show him." Collin's long fingers tightened in Seth's hair, yanking the man off him.

Seth had fucked me a few times—my ass, my cunt, but not yet my mouth. He climbed to his feet and licked his lips. So blatant in the focus of his lust, he didn't spare me a glance. His gaze remained locked on Collin's erection as he shoved his briefs to his feet and kicked them away.

Seth might've preferred Collin, but he never seemed repulsed by my participation. Good thing, because Collin was *my* husband, and our unconventional marriage required a middle man. If Seth entertained any misgivings about his role in our relationship, I wouldn't have to show him the door. Collin would do it for me.

I approached the bed and unbuttoned my blouse. "Maybe he's intimidated by my tongue." I addressed my husband, but caught Seth's chocolate gaze in challenge.

Collin huffed. "Hell, *I'm* intimidated by your tongue."

Seth shifted from foot to foot, glancing between us and chewing the inside of his cheek. Somewhat boyish in his attractiveness, his appeal was most notable in his dark, brooding eyebrows and pouty lips. His lean physique matched Collin's. A runner's build, slim on muscle, but his long legs and soaring height gave him the illusion of strength.

Seth studied me for a weighted moment with a maddening mix of heat and hesitancy stewing in his eyes. What was he thinking? I held my breath and his gaze.

He blinked, gripped the back of my neck, and shoved his tongue past my teeth.

Alrighty then. A bit forced, but I welcomed the roughness, meeting his tongue thrust for thrust. His lips mashed aggressively against mine, his fingers digging into my neck. His other hand caught my laced-covered breast, squeezing with the same bruising pressure as his kiss. I liked it, perhaps a little too much.

I reached for his erection, and my hand bumped into Collin's fingers where he was unrolling a condom over Seth's rigid girth. The need thrumming from their shallow breaths fueled mine. In a few moments, I would be writhing beneath all their sweaty, aroused flesh. The anticipation spurred me to bite Seth's lips and grind against his hard-on while imagining a different body, a stronger, more powerful one encased in racing leathers.

Collin yanked his hand away before my groin made contact with his fingers. I laughed, breaking the kiss with a shiver. "Pussy."

"Skank." The look he gave me was as deep-rooted as our friendship, one that bore the same private smile and mischievous eyes from our childhood amidst dismal dinner parties and stuffy classrooms.

With a grace bred into every genteel fiber of his body, he rose to his feet. His expression, however, was anything but formal as he devoured the quivering movements of Seth's torso with his eyes at half-mast. "He's all yours."

Silly man. As long as he was in the room, his lover would never be all mine. I lowered to my knees, wrapped anxious fingers around

Seth's engorged cock, and licked the tip.

Just like that, my brain rushed through the images of the man who plagued me. He would have a thicker cock, perhaps uncut with veins pulsing beneath my fingertips. A hard, formidable mystery, a man who fought things that were deadlier, fiercer, and more uncivilized than anything in this room. For years, I'd stood alone, toe-to-toe against powerful men. How I wished to have an invincible man on my side.

As Seth pushed into my mouth, the funky taste of latex assaulted my tastebuds. I breathed through it. Either this or Oral HPV. No deliberation there, given the extensive number of partners we shared.

I fondled and sucked until the tang of rubber faded. Hollowing my cheeks, I worshiped him with hard pulls and a flicking tongue while pumping a fist at the base. Collin ground his own wrapped cock against Seth's hip, inches from my face. So damned tempting to curl my fingers around it and make him yelp.

His hands swept the other man's chest, abs, and ass in urgent strokes, their tongues battling together in an open-mouth fusion of masculine arousal.

Their combined musk charged my inhales, spurring me to suck faster, harder, until a visible tremor rippled through Seth's legs. He spread out his feet, revealing Collin's fingers thrusting in and out of his ass. Seth wouldn't last long.

I stood, wobbly on the heels, and unzipped the skirt. It fell to the floor. My blouse and panties followed. As I reached behind and unclasped the bra, Collin released Seth's lips with a teasing lick and nodded toward the bed.

My nipples peaked against the chill in the air, or perhaps at the sensual sight of Collin stroking Seth's dick. His strokes stopped with a tight grip, and his gray-blue eyes caught mine.

Christ, Collin was breathtaking. Midnight-black hair, damp from a recent shower, combed back in perfect, short waves. The slender bone structure of his face suited his refined public image, but his blunt, square chin better fit the man I knew privately.

A dimple appeared in his cheek. "You ready for him?"

Not 'Are you wet?' Poor guy refused to acknowledge the mechanics of a cunt, which made teasing him oh-so diabolical. "I'm dripping, throbbing, gaping—"

"All right. Enough." His tone was clipped, but the creases fanning from his bright eyes gentled his regal features. "Get your soft little ass on the bed."

"Always with the *soft* shit. Maybe I should shoot up testosterone and grow a beard." We shared a smirk, and he rolled his eyes to the ceiling, shaking his head. Then I glanced at Seth. "What do you think? Is my body too soft?" Was I fishing for compliments? Maybe. But I never had to question our other partners, their ardor distributed equally between Collin and me.

Because the others were *paid* to pleasure *both* of us. I shoved that thought away.

Seth seemed to be struggling to focus on anything beyond Collin's fingers fondling his dick. He jerked his hips and gasped. "Yeah."

Yeah? Bastard wasn't even paying attention.

Collin let go of him and stepped back with his hands on his narrow hips. Assessment narrowed his eyes. Protectiveness dominated his statue-like posture. Of course, *he'd* teased me my entire life, but one disrespectful twitch from Seth and the night would be over.

Seth snapped his head up, his eyes darting between us. "No. I mean…" He made a show of ogling me from tits to heels. "You're soft in all the right places, Mrs. *Baskel*."

I bristled at the inflection he'd put on my maiden name. "Baskel is my identity." I'd kept my name so I wouldn't *just* be the wife of the famous Collin Anderson. "Doesn't make us less married."

Collin rubbed his chin, his thumb moving over the deep cleft there, his disapproval clear in the juts of his sharp cheekbones. He lowered his hand. "Do you have a problem with this arrangement, Seth?"

A flinch lifted Seth's shoulders. "No. Sorry. I didn't mean anything by it." His arms hung at his sides, and his head descended toward his chest.

Way to go, Kaci. I climbed onto the bed and rolled to my back, propping up on my elbows. "It's fine." I raised a leg and rested the spike of the heel on Seth's thigh, nudging him. "I didn't kill the mood, did I?"

A moment of hesitation stifled the air. I met Collin's eyes and waited for him to ask for a night alone with his lover. But he wanted me there in his fucked up way. I could count on one hand the number of times he'd had sex without my participation. He sought my presence as a tangible form of approval, his own acceptance of his sexuality hanging on the intolerant opinions of his political party.

He glanced at Seth's hard-on, which jerked under his heated gaze. "Do you want to fuck my wife?"

"Yes." A thick inhale sharpened his answer. He gripped my ankle and used it to widen my legs, his other hand cupping the back of my opposite knee.

When his lips touched my inner thigh, I melted into the mattress and cupped my breasts, rolling the sensitive nipples between my fingers. His mouth trailed a warm path to the apex of my legs. *Keep going.* My thighs trembled, and the steel ring piercing my clit added pressure to the needy pulsations.

At the last inch, he swerved to the side, over my hipbone, and along my ribs.

I ground my teeth, but I refused to lower myself to demanding things he wasn't inclined to do.

His mouth moved up my body, and he brushed my hand from my tit to bite down on the nipple. Sharp, chilling pain shot through me, sparking a spasm along my inner muscles.

"Ahhh." My gasps cut off when Seth captured my mouth.

The quick, assertive kiss slid away as his lips tickled over my cheek and his cock pressed against my opening. The back of Collin's hand brushed my inner thigh, his fingers sliding up and down Seth's length.

God, I was so wet, so damned ready. He could slip right in, and in the span of a shuddering breath, he did. His thickness filled me with a burst of body-tingling pleasure. I searched his flushed face, and he seemed to be as aroused as I was, given the parted lips, stuttering breaths, and shiny eyes holding mine.

His intensity heated when a bottle of lube landed on the mattress. He thrust frantically at the sight of it, his gaze falling away to catch a glimpse of the man behind him.

I stretched to meet Collin's eyes, slipping my hands over his to help him spread the hard muscles of Seth's ass.

Collin watched me until the moment he thrust, his dark lashes lowering as his hips slammed against Seth's backside. I hated when he did that, when he broke eye contact to focus on the body between us. At the same time, it would've been weird as fuck to stare into his eyes as we got off. That just wasn't the nature of our relationship, and dwelling on it left me cold inside.

With Seth's entire focus on Collin now, my thoughts fled to a comforting place, forming images of Evader's sculpted body moving over me, his kiss-swollen lips, and the vicious stretch of his arousal. I imagined him making love to my body with fire and ferocity, his concentration on me, on my pleasure, and nothing else.

Collin's head fell back. The tendons in his neck rose against his flushed skin, and his body jerked into another ruthless plunge. Then he fucked me the only way he could...with another man's cock.

The weight of both men ground against my pierced clit. I flexed my hips, working toward that glorious edge. All I could think about was satisfying the urgent need for release with a man I'd never met. Greedy as I was, maybe I could reach it more than once before they finished.

Seth rose up, his back pressing against Collin's front. Their mouths collided in a frantic clash of tongues, and the sudden intensity of Seth's strokes propelled me to the cusp of orgasm. Collin pounded harder, each hard drive pushing Seth deeper inside me.

Collin's eyes squeezed shut. His body trembled. The pace of his pumping staggered, losing rhythm. He was close. So was I. We lunged together, pulled apart, ramming over and over. Three bodies rocked in sync, coaxing a blissful heat through my core.

Sweat beaded over my skin. My pulse thundered past my ears, and my muscles tensed for the rush.

On the next thrust, Seth fell out. Shit. I wriggled my hips, tried to nudge him back in, but he wasn't hitting my opening. I reached down to guide him, and my fingers met a sagging condom. What the hell?

I arched up and looked down my body. Seth's cock lay against his leg, the condom clinging halfway off. Motherfuck.

When I caught his eyes, he glanced away and worked the condom back in place.

And they thought I was soft? Might've been humorous if I weren't seconds away from kneeing him in the gay nuts. The fucking liar had banged me before without incident. But thinking on it, in the past I'd arrived after the foreplay. Perhaps the blow job had pushed him past his tolerance level?

Collin stilled, his hand wrapping around Seth's fingers, attempting to stroke him back to hardness. "What happened?"

"I don't know. Just give me a minute." Seth looked everywhere but at me, his eyebrows lowering as he jerked on his deflated dick.

I drew a deep breath, the awkwardness palpable, the mood soured. No need to ruin the night for Collin. I climbed to my knees and moved to their sides. With a palm on Collin's cheek, I turned his head and kissed the cleft on his whiskered chin. "I'm gonna go."

His pale eyes turned to glass, and his hands gripped Seth's hips as if to push him away.

I grabbed his forearm. "Finish." I softened my expression.

"Please?"

A tic jumped in his rigid jaw, and he glanced down where he was still seated in Seth's ass. If I lingered, my presence would only crowd his heart with more remorse. His guilt over our pressured marriage was so heavy in moments like this it pulled on my soul.

I grabbed my clothes from the floor and darted from the room without looking back, hoping like hell he listened for once.

As I walked the length of the seven-thousand square-foot condo, my bare feet echoed in hollow slaps along the two-story ceilings. Collin and I designed the interior of our five-million-dollar home, and we'd earned every damned penny that went into it. But sometimes the high-quality fixtures, the lush furnishings, and the full-service amenities were unwanted reminders that we were on a power-hungry path to becoming just like our parents.

Born three months apart with no siblings, we'd spent thirty-seven years bending to our parents' political agendas. The Andersons and the Baskels not only blackmailed us into marriage, they reigned over our careers from their high-backed chairs on the board of Trenchant Media.

I stopped in the kitchen for a glass of water and headed to my bedroom. We didn't give a shit about wealth. Collin hosted his political television program *The Anderson Angle* because he believed in his ideas. His fresh, forward-thinking commentary swayed fiscal policies and expertly guided decision makers on the nation's economy.

At the top of his company, I led the *Trenchant Times* division, overseeing the digital and print operations. For ten years, I'd stubbornly fought the board to deliver neutral, hard-hitting facts to the people, battling the self-fulfilling conglomerate because, dammit, someone needed to do it. Yeah, it was an arrogant undertaking, but not completely benevolent. My pursuit was personal; my vendetta fermented in hatred.

I threw the bundle of clothes into the bedroom closet, and one of the heels dented the wall with a satisfying thunk. When our parents discovered Collin's sexual orientation during the rise of his popularity, we were forced to sign a contract that kept his secret buried beneath Trenchant's conservative image. The contract stipulated everything from our marriage and careers to who we voted for and how we dressed.

If our parents knew what Collin was up to at that very moment—my fingernails dug into my palms—they would end our careers and wrongfully send Collin to prison with purchased evidence.

I would do what was needed to protect him, despite the painful shortcoming in our marriage. A marriage that left me yearning, night after night, for an intimate connection that couldn't be sated by a shared partner. God, I longed for a connection that was *given,* not bought, despite the risks. The kind of breathless intoxication I fantasized about with a faceless man on a sportbike and had no hope of obtaining at the end of Seth's limp dick.

Which was why I wouldn't miss the underground race that began in—I glanced at the clock on the nightstand—two hours, for a glimpse of something more. To glory in those almost-maybe tilts of that mysterious helmet in my direction.

A hot shower didn't wash away the disappointment that had followed me from Collin's room. The restless need for release—*for something*—pulsed through my body and fucked with my pulse.

I dropped the towel on the floor and paced around the oversized furniture in my unlit bedroom—the couch and chaise lounge, the king-size bed, the towering bookshelves lining the walls. Velvety fabrics, dark heavy wood, warm shades of red and brown, the decor was inviting yet…empty, the furnishings as unused as the day I moved in.

I spent my days in the office and my evenings with Collin or sneaking into races. But I slept here, in this cavernous space, isolated and hollow, and I hated it.

Fuck, I was in a mood. Attending the race would pump some vigor into my blood. I didn't even mind if I missed a glimpse of Evader. He was just a glamorous thrill that added to the experience.

Liar.

I brushed a hand down my belly, teasing the need running beneath my skin, and my fingers grazed the stripe of hair between my legs. I had two hours to wait. Two hours until I saw him again. I stretched lazily, recalling the way he thrust four-hundred pounds of torquey craftsmanship on oil-slicked streets. His dark silhouette as intimidating and elegant as his bike, he always ignored the crowd with bored indifference, like he hadn't just rocked their adventure-seeking world.

Sighing, I retrieved the tablet and lay on the bed. The e-mail from Jenna waited in my inbox, as promised. Tonight's race would begin near Bunker Hill, wind and turn through the back streets of downtown, and end at the intersection of State and Ninth Street.

The exterior wall of windows cast a silver glow over my skin. I placed my feet flat on the mattress, my knees spread and pointed to the vaulted ceiling, and traced the shadowy lines of my thighs with the pads of my fingers, shivering against the caress. The air brushed my flesh, like a soft kiss without judgment, and it felt uninhibited, freeing, but lonely all the same.

I tapped the tablet until last weekend's *Trenchant Times'* story filled the screen. Dozens of images had been captured during the illegal race through Lincoln Park, most of them zoomed in on a sleek BMW S1000RR sportbike and its undefeated rider.

Dressed neck to toe in black leather, the potent lines of his body molded to the sexy machine. His torso bent horizontally over the bike, following the sporty tail-up, nose-down design, mounting it like a lover. The way his thighs gripped the aluminum frame made me envious. I wanted to be that machine, to feel the strength of his legs while being ridden to the edge of death and back. Heat flooded my core, and a heavy exhale escaped my lips.

I swiped back and forth between the photos, searching for the best angle of his ass. There. The rear shot of him taking a sharp corner. His knee hovered inches from the ground, flirting with danger and sending a shiver to the best places.

Propping the tablet against my raised thigh, I slid my fingers along my slit and imagined straddling his lap, my wetness staining his leather pants. I'd grind against him and clutch his glossy black helmet with both hands, lifting it slowly, just enough to reveal his lips. I would lick them next, of course, and the stubble on his jaw—

Would he have stubble? Yeah, it would burn a trail of fire against my skin.

Dipping inside my opening, I wet my fingers, circled my clit, and flicked the piercing. My toes curled, and a breathless tremor sunk my body into the mattress.

His helmet needed to come off, stat. I mentally yanked it up, my body quivering in anticipation of his face. I strained to make out his blurry expression, so I reached for his hair, dragged him closer, peering up and seeing…seeing…what?

I scrunched my nose and dug through a collection of stimulating images in my finger vault, searching frantically for inspiration. Narrow chin? Too pompous. Freckles? Bleh, innocent. Long, black hair? Definitely not.

Fuck if I couldn't envision the right head shot. Screw it. Let him have his obscurity. Wasn't that part of the allure? He didn't need a face for me to fantasy-fuck him.

But what if he had a hairy mole on his lip? Or a unibrow? Buck teeth?

Another caress between my legs. "God, I'm shallow." I inserted three fingers, knuckles deep, reaching for the feeling of fullness.

"Not from where I'm standing."

I flinched and followed the soft timbre to the doorway. Collin leaned against the frame, clad in tailored, black boxers, his arms crossed over his bare chest like an underwear model. Shadows hid his face, but I could imagine the conflict tightening the skin around his eyes. I never left his bed unfulfilled, and he probably saw it as a failure on his part. No doubt he was here to rectify that.

Sliding wet fingers to my tummy, I closed my legs. "Tell me you finished before you sent him home."

"Yeah. I did." Each word caught thickly in his throat. He strode into the room and disappeared into the en-suite bathroom. A moment later, he returned, carrying my favorite vibrator with the fluttering clit stimulator.

When he reached the bed, gray light from the windows landed across his upper body, revealing drawn eyebrows and a grumpy scowl. Knowing Collin, he was anxious to clear the air between us and verbalize whatever internal war he was waging. Did it make me a sucky friend because I wanted to skip the emotional argument? "Collin, I'm fine. Let's not do this."

His face turned to stone. "Let's not do what, Kaci? Let's not communicate? Let's not talk about how I just fucked the shit out of a man who lied to us?" The vibrator dangled from the hand at his side. His other hand scrubbed roughly over his mouth. "I don't know if I'm more pissed at him for lying about being into you or at myself for not seeing through the bullshit. I mean, fuck, I'm *known* for my ability to read people."

That was mostly true. There was a list of powerful individuals who refused to be interviewed on his show because they feared he'd sniff out their secrets and expose them on TV. Strange how he didn't have the same intuition about the people closest to him, like me and our parents. "Seth isn't one of your political adversaries."

"Tell me about it. Soon as that hot little fuck struts through the door, my fucking brain scrambles." His hand flew angrily through the air, circling around his head. "He's turning me into a bottom."

"Did he fuck your ass?"

His eyes widened in appall. "No."

God, he had so many hang ups he couldn't fit them all in his ridiculously oversized closet. "The thing with Seth was bound to happen eventually." I kept my voice quiet, calming. "We're safer with the escort service anyway."

He sat beside my hip, facing me, and set the vibrator between my breasts. "I like him."

Oh. "You *like* him like him?"

His shoulder lifted. "I don't know, but I can't stop thinking about how badly I want to find out."

Which explained the turbulent emotions clouding his face. He didn't tolerate deceit, yet he liked Seth despite being lied to.

"Invite him back and punish his ass for lying to you." I poked him in the ribs, the same spot I'd been torturing since before his voice dropped.

"Arrgh." He grabbed my wrist. His lips twitched then descended into a sulky arc. "I'm not going to pursue a relationship that excludes you." His thumb stroked my palm, his gaze lifting to the windows. "It's fucking selfish."

I lunged up, and the vibrator and tablet tumbled to the mattress. "Fuck your guilt, Collin. If you enjoy sharing your partners with me, that's one thing, but it was never the arrangement we'd agreed on."

Seven years ago, we filled the headlines as the nation's most celebrated marriage amongst traditional conservatives. Privately, we vowed to take lovers, separately or shared. It didn't matter as long as our adversaries never found out.

"I'm not going to fuck around," he muttered, "if you're going to be in here by yourself, doing…" He waved a hand at my groin.

"Doing what?" I bit my lip to hide a grin.

He dropped his arm and gave me a pointed look. "Spanking the kitty."

"The kitty likes to be spanked."

He raised a brow. I released the smile and nudged him with a knee. "Explore this thing with Seth. Just be careful. The way he looks at you worries me. Hell hath no fury like unrequited love and all that. We don't need any more enemies."

His gaze didn't waver from mine. Stubborn and determined, he was thinking too hard, likely circling around how this potential relationship would impact me.

I met his eyes. "If I had my own man, a *straight* man, you would give me your blessing to fuck him without you."

He nodded, and the corner of his mouth ticked up. "*After* I ran a full investigation on him, of course."

"Of course."

He raked a hand through his hair. "*If* I continue with Seth"—he peered up at me—"I'll set better boundaries. But I will *not* leave you unattended."

Meaning he would continue to hire gigolos to get me off. Jesus, that sounded so pathetic. "I'm perfectly capable of finding my own companion."

He laughed, the ass. What the fuck ever. So I'd never arranged my own one-night stand. Only because I was terrified I'd sleep with a man who would expose our lifestyle. Collin went to great lengths vetting our partners with the help of the PI on his payroll. And he required a non-disclosure agreement before a single seductive glance was exchanged. I could do all these things myself. I'd just never needed to.

"I've got a man on a motorcycle." I pointed at the fallen tablet. "He's safe." A fantasy that would never be realized.

"Seriously doubt he's safe." He rotated the screen and stared at the photo. "What do you think he's hiding under all that leather?"

I lay back and picked up the vibrator, closing my eyes. "Something huge and stiff."

He groaned. "God woman, you need to work on your creativity." He shifted closer, stretching his legs toward my head, evidently settling in. "A man like that fucks like he rides. With intimidation, recklessness, and unharnessed energy. He's powered by adrenaline and takes what he wants without care."

I loosened my legs, parting my knees, as the warm rumble of his voice illustrated my thoughts. The danger surrounding the mysterious man captivated me. Did he take all that risk just for the thrill of it? Or was it the money? It was rumored he made millions on each race, betting on himself and accumulating enemies with every win.

A night in his arms wouldn't be that risky because he had more to lose than I did, right? Wouldn't he be more concerned about hiding his own secrets than unraveling mine? I was transfixed by that idea, longing for the only kind of passionate connection I could chance, one of shared anonymity.

I wanted to be claimed by a mystery who possessed a woman as ferociously as he protected her. I wanted a fucking pipe dream.

Collin swiped the screen on the tablet. "Bet he's built like a machine, his cock an iron piston. And you know those muscles in his ass aren't muscles at all, but carbon fiber over Kevlar. Aerodynamic and bulletproof."

A bulletproof ass? Ooookay, that was an interesting visual, somewhat bionic-man-like in the details, but it worked. My body primed for penetration, and the vibrator slipped right in.

His dirty mouth rumbled on, describing the various methods in which an unlawful daredevil would steal through the night, plundering unsuspecting holes and virginal crevices. With lightning speed, I reached the pinnacle, teetering on the peak of relief.

Collin flipped around, reclining with his head beside mine. "His ass would be so fucking tight, and he wouldn't give it up easy. I'd have to fight him, wrestle him to the floor. 'Course, I'm strong enough so he—"

"Do you mind?" I tightened my grip on the vibrator. "This is my fantasy."

"You can be there. Just bring a strap-on."

Considering my luck with men, Evader was likely gay or married. Probably both. "Trying to concentrate here. Go back to the iron cock part."

He rolled to face me, his head on the pillow and his breath tickling my ear. "It would hurt at first. He's too big, and he's not built to be gentle. But it's a good burn. The kind that stretches so deeply he wouldn't leave a single nerve-ending untouched."

My muscles quaked around the pulse of the toy. Right. There. *Don't stop.*

"He's fucked half the city so his experience is unparalleled, the madness in his strokes legendary."

Collin was so full of shit. Dozens of women claimed to have bedded Chicago's favorite bad boy, but my reporters had disproved every allegation, considering not a single one could believably describe that unidentifiable face.

Unless he fucked with his helmet on.

Collin drummed his fingers on his abs. "When he fucks, he doesn't just rip open your filthy desires. He alters them until all you feel is the velocity of his thrusts searing into every tender cavity, wrenching every hungry breath, for the rest of your cock-starved life."

I laughed as I plunged into the orgasm. Shock waves ricocheted over my skin, releasing the tension from my body with each sated exhale. When I caught my breath and collected my senses, I flicked off the vibrator and set it aside.

His lips brushed my shoulder. "I'm sorry about tonight."

"Don't." I turned toward him and pinched his chin, giving it a little shake. "I married my best friend. No regrets."

He closed his eyes. "You married a gay man who supports an anti-gay political party on national TV."

"And you married a breeder who leaves cum trails on your lovers' cocks."

He half-laughed, half-choked. "Jesus, you're nasty."

"You're one to talk. And quit whining about your political party."

He was in a perpetual orbit of turmoil, one that wobbled between the private man I adored and the right-wing conservative I begrudged. While we didn't agree on politics, his accomplishments made me proud to play the role of his conservative wife. And his audience loved him—an audience largely defined as religious, extreme in their traditionalism, and anti-gay. He was their voice and passionately advocated their beliefs. Well, all but one.

I rolled to my back and released a sigh. "You've *never* spoken against same-sex rights."

"Does it really matter? The nation's perception of me is its reality."

If he aired his secret, it would certainly change perceptions. And get him booed off television. Narrow-minded bastards.

"Sometimes I wish…" He rose to sit on the edge of the bed with his back to me. "I wish I could take care of you instead of pawning you off to every Tom, Dick, and Harry. If I were a little less gay…"

Oh, his guilt was in full force tonight. I snagged the vibrator and climbed off the bed. "You haven't stuck your dick in me in twenty-two years, Collin. And you *know* why." It was a tired discussion, but he needed the reminder. I flicked on the lamp and stood before him.

His gaze darted over my chest, my hips, and the strip of blonde hair above my clit ring. It was a cursory glance, much like the ones I received from women in the gym locker room. An appreciative look at my fit body, but not a twinge of sexual interest.

He hung his head. When we gave each other our *V*-cards at fifteen, his sexual orientation had been questioned but not yet explored. The reason we didn't connect in the bedroom, then or now, was because the romantic chemistry between us simply didn't exist. That said, he never slept with me or another woman again.

I strode toward the bathroom and said over my shoulder, "Don't forget five minutes with me scared you away from pussy for life."

"It was forty-five minutes, hooker." He followed on my heels. "You made a gay man straight for almost an hour." He caught my arm at the doorway and planted a kiss on my forehead. "No regrets."

No regrets. It was our mantra because we were both full of them. He wanted a relationship with a man he didn't have to hide. I wanted a relationship with a man who didn't have to fuck me through an intermediary partner. He wanted children *in vitro*. I wanted to conceive, *some day*, in the throes of passion.

We could lament all the things we couldn't have. Or we could focus on the one honest thing we did have. Each other.

I pinched his pouty bottom lip. "No regrets, and if we're done with the mushy crap"—I thumped him hard enough in the stomach to make his chuckle sound like a grunt—"I need to pee." I tossed the vibrator in the sink and perched on the toilet.

He turned on the faucet and soaped up the toy. "So you saw those new photos of your boyfriend?" He gave me a sidelong glance. "Public appearance at a grocery store?"

"Don't call him my boyfriend." He didn't even know I existed. "And everyone has to eat, Collin."

"Mm. I imagined he chewed bolts and drank motor oil."

Rolling my eyes, I flushed the toilet and stepped to the second sink.

Collin leaned a hip against the counter, his well-bred frame wrapped in golden flesh that had been bathed and beautified by a lifetime of expensive creams. He was a portrait of sophistication, blending seamlessly with the luxurious surroundings of the bathroom's imported marble and high-thread-counts. Yet the sight of his manicured fingers wrapped around the silicone vibrator represented the Collin few knew. The Collin who was well-versed in how to fit a dildo in a tight ass.

He dried it off and returned it to the bottom drawer. "When is the next race?"

"In one hour, according to my source."

The venues were officiated by anonymous coordinators. The map of each race was distributed in advance via an online network, where *friendships* were made by referral only using a sophisticated web of private servers to hide IP addresses. It was complex, well-funded, and ever-changing, making it impossible for the Feds to monitor the communications let alone trace identities.

My inability to gain access to the network hadn't deterred me, not when I had the best journalists in the country on my payroll.

Collin's lips pressed into a hard line of worry. "Still got that undercover reporter risking his ass for you?"

"Hal Pinkerton, and he won't find out it's for me." What I didn't know was if he used an informant or if he'd somehow become a trusted peer in the network of motorheads and moneyed gamblers. Either way, his intel was reliable, and I personally and anonymously rewarded his efforts, wiring money for each piece of information he posted on a secure site. My PA, Jenna, retrieved the details from the encrypted server. Details that would never grace the pages of the *Trenchant Times.*

Too much dirty money rode on these races, enough to permanently silence anyone who forewarned the police or media of the venue locations.

"Those bikers…" Collin's dark brows gathered over darker eyes. "They can hurt you. Badly."

Ironically, he was the one who introduced me to the world of bikers. He took me to my first Grand Prix race when we were eighteen. I was so enthralled with the speed and power of superbikes I bought my first one shortly after.

I glared at him. "I'm careful."

He stared right back, and I withered a little inside. He knew me better than anyone and studied me as if he sensed the whisper of discomfort that didn't belong. Did he know about the secrets I withheld from him? My suspicions about our parents?

His narrowed gaze pushed against me, prodding me to unload my heart. Which would only further burden his.

I bit down on my lip. "What?"

After a stubborn moment of volleyed glares, he shook his head and strode out of the bathroom. Releasing a soundless breath, I followed him then veered into the closet to pull on the leggings and camisole that went under my leathers.

When I emerged, I found him at the dresser, fingering the wedding ring I never wore. He didn't wear his, either. Legally, we were married, but emotionally, we weren't. Wearing the rings didn't feel right, and thankfully, the contract didn't require it.

His gaze focused inward as he returned the diamond band to its box and tucked it back in the drawer.

I leaned a hip against the dresser. "What's going on, Collin?"

A shrug. "Just one of those nights. Got shit on my mind."

My eyes narrowed. "Like what? Seth? The show?" I exhaled. "Us?"

"The show." The floor creaked as he paced my bedroom, updating me on everything that went wrong with tonight's filming of *The Anderson Angle.*

He spent his mornings writing each show and filmed the one hour segment at five o'clock every evening, which broadcasted at nine. He handpicked every guest, predicting what they would say in the interview, sometimes down to the last word. This gave him an edge, enabling him to formulate his counterarguments ahead of time. But sometimes he misjudged, like tonight with the CEO of Nationside Energy.

Standing in the center of the room in his Derek Rose silk boxers and frowning at his feet, he looked vulnerable, defeated. "Overall, it worked out." He nodded. "Yeah, I think we'll get away with it. But I won't be asking him back."

He lived and died by his ratings and would work himself into a frenzy until the numbers posted tomorrow afternoon. I squeezed the hand at his side and let go. He didn't want pretty words or warm hugs. He vented to me, I listened, and he moved on.

Which he was doing now, his swift strides carrying him to the door. "I'm doing a segment tomorrow on police brutality." He stopped in the doorway and held up a finger, tapping the air as if keeping rhythm with the thoughts in his head. "I'll get a cocky cop. Yeah. The power-drunk type with a short fuse." He scratched his jaw, pale eyes glimmering. "And he has to have a mustache."

With that, he vanished around the corner, presumably headed to his office on his side of the condo. I stared at the space he'd vacated, part of me wishing he'd stayed to keep me company. Maybe for just a few minutes of spooning until I left for the race. But I stopped thinking of him that way long before we married. Snuggling with Collin would be akin to cuddling my best girlfriend…if I had one of those.

His head popped back in, snapping me from my thoughts. "Be careful, hussy."

"Always—" But he was already gone. I sighed. "Punk."

He was right about the risk, of course. Attending the races was like walking into a secret biker bar without an invite or a gun. There was the threat of arrest and the defamation of my reputation to consider. But Collin's concerns had more to do with me being a woman, alone, amongst men who didn't respect boundaries or socially-accepted precepts.

Sure, I carried a gun and knew how to use it, but that argument only elevated Collin's blood pressure.

I shouldn't go. I had a long work day ahead of me tomorrow, and my eyes already burned with fatigue.

Standing by the bed, I placed my hands on the quilt, waiting for the soft, opulent fabrics to coax me in. Instead, the sight of the empty mattress produced a longing so intense it swelled against my ribs.

I was married to my best friend. I had his loyalty, his honesty, and his camaraderie. But I didn't have a man's arms around me while I slept. Didn't have a warm body to curl into, one that shared my bed and protected me from the things I couldn't fight alone.

That strong and persistent hunger buzzed through my bloodstream and tightened my insides. I walked to the closet, pulled on my silver leathers, and buckled my boots. I wasn't the kind of woman who could lie down and wait for life to *not* happen.

I braided my hair in a long tail and grabbed the silver motorcycle helmet and Kevlar gloves. A sense of control tingled through my body and filled my lungs with oxygen as I headed for the door.

The vibration in my balls amplified with the speed of the motorcycle, the four banger engine screaming with exertion. Only seven miles, five sharp turns, and two deadly intersections away from an assload of money. And the crazy French fucker on my ass? I *might* let him see the finish line…right before his face eats asphalt.

The rear-view camera in my helmet projected his distance onto my visor. Forty meters. Thirty meters. Ahead, the glowing stripe of red stretched to the horizon, not a single break in the taillights bottlenecking Michigan Avenue.

My heart thundered, my hands slick with sweat in the gloves as I surged to the finish line, fueled by memories of my mother. Growing up on the back of her motorcycle. Her patient instruction as she taught me how to ride my first sportbike. All the broken bones. Her loving care as I healed.

But it was always tainted by the terrible fear. Fear that pinned me to my hiding spot as I watched her killer clean his knife. Fear that saved me then but wouldn't save me now.

I shook it off and focused on the joyous moments of my childhood, on the passion she'd ingrained in me. Heat radiated through my chest, charging my blood with wild energy. Nothing beat this feeling, the grip of battle, the fight for supremacy, dominating with skill and lethal speed while straddling the kind of power few mortals could harness on congested streets.

God, what a rush. I flexed my fingers and pinned the throttle.

Chase vehicles zipped past, headed in the opposite direction, with mobile cameras mounted on the hoods. Enthusiasts chattered via two-way radio, using CCTV security cameras to channel the race on an underground network. The live feed bridged to the illegal web of electronic gambling, which enabled betting right up to the final mile.

The helmet's built-in police scanner added an incessant buzz to the noise. Miles behind us, cherry tops had two major disadvantages. They didn't know the layout of the racing grid, and squad cars couldn't touch the velocity of a hyper-focused sportbike. But if they located the cluster of racing fanatics likely gathering around the final marker, they could organize a barricade there. One I would find a way to hurtle if it came to that.

In this two-man race, one of us would win. The other would die—maybe not tonight, but wealthy gamblers didn't take to losing lightly. I drew in a determined breath and rolled my shoulders. I had this. Triumph was as easy as the whores waiting for me at the finish line. And a helluva lot more fulfilling.

Vernay Lebeau pursued my tail, gaining ground with each block. As rev-happy as he was annoying, his speeds through throngs of civilians while trying to lay me out might've spooked the shit out of anyone with a pulse. But his ham-handed desperation to win would ultimately cost him his dignity. And his life.

Twenty miles into the race and I had yet to max out the speedometer. Lebeau, on the other hand, took the hole-shot out of the grid and held the front door through the first half. I let him. Sportbikes malfunctioned at top speeds, just one of the numerous factors that could throw a race. Besides, I'd stolen the lead when he tried to whip a chain around my drive train.

It was a dick move, but that was the only kind he had. I grew up around bikes, lived and breathed in a cloud of exhaust, learning their inner workings until my heart pumped like a motor. Unlike Lebeau, who was just a street punk with his balls to the road and his eyes set on a six-figure prize. The French fuck didn't have a chance.

Holding steady at 150 mph, I stitched a line through the oncoming traffic and watched the readout on my visor. He closed in at ten meters. Five meters. Four.

The rumble of the approaching bike resonated with the purr of mine. Three meters. Two. Any closer and the frog-eater could stab a shank in my arm. Wouldn't be the first time I bled through the finish line.

One meter away, I jerked right and intersected his path on a tight left-hander. Rubber squealed behind me as the camera flashed images of his fishtailed swerve on the bottom edge of my visor. His lean angle dipped so low, his metal-spiked knee guard sparked pavement.

In the half-second it took him to recover, I opened the gas and broke through 185 mph. The engine whined, and the handlebars jerked back and forth, knocking my tucked knees against the gas tank. Following the helmet's navigation display, I slid around another sharp bend, dodging a fire hydrant, a crowd of wide-eyed pedestrians, and a row of parked cars. Over the sidewalk and through a red light, I careened toward a speeding SUV. Fuck.

Leaning all my weight forward, I squeezed the front brake. The back wheel rose off the ground, swung right, and missed the SUV's bumper. I released the brake. The tire hit pavement, rattling my teeth, and I bolted forward and out of traffic.

As a gust of air escaped my dry lips, the rear camera showed Lebeau pulling the same endo through the intersection. When his rear tire gripped the road, he burst across the second lane, causing two cars to skid. They missed him but not each other. The ear-piercing screech of metal on metal ricocheted off the buildings, a fucking collision that could've been avoided. And Lebeau was back on my ass.

Thirty meters ahead of him, I flogged it with a wide open throttle, pressing my stomach over the tank and relishing the surge of two hundred growling horses thrusting me down the long slab of road. I had five digits riding on this race, a wager I would quadruple when I won. If I lost, well, I'd have men a lot more ruthless than Lebeau chasing me.

The only rule in these races was to stay on the course, which meant I could draw the Glock that was strapped in my hidden shoulder holster and eliminate him. Guaranteed win. But no one would race a man who gunned down his opponents. No, the methods of winning required stealth. I preferred dexterity and technology over the barbaric snares many of the other underground racers depended on.

I tucked farther into the BMW S1000RR's vibrating frame, scanning the thermal images to avoid the high concentrations of red that indicated body heat. Civilians littered the streets, on foot and in cars, the deadliest roadblocks. Despite my violent reputation, my thirst for blood excluded innocents.

Sweat dampened my hair, and the tight space in the helmet overheated my cheeks. Indicators flashed across the anti-fog visor, calculating speeds, distances, rpms, and hi-tech analytics like facial recognition and live maps of approaching traffic and police hot spots.

A few more turns and another intersection later, I twisted around a hairpin and onto a narrow side road empty of traffic. The thermal sensor picked up a spark on the pavement ahead. What in the godhole was that?

Two things were certain. Someone had killed the street lights, and Lebeau was deliberately lagging behind. I gritted my teeth and spoke into the mic. "Night vision."

The helmet's interface switched from a kaleidoscope of color to hues of green. The shadowed alley illuminated, stretching out for several blocks and revealing a depth and clarity that couldn't be captured with thermal. Because the bright beams of headlights impeded the technology, night vision was limited but extremely precise in identifying details…like the spike strip blending into the dark, oily crevices of the street.

The zigzag of metal thorns stretched building to building three blocks ahead. The handy work of Lebeau's guys, no doubt. There had to be a way out.

My heart pounded, and my hands tightened on the grips as Lebeau screamed up from behind. Which way would he go?

A wall of trash cluttered a few feet before the strip. It stood as tall as the bike and twice as deep, piled against the building. Indecision tore through me, battling with the adrenaline heating my blood. Either the spikes didn't reach the garbage or the pile hid a ramp. Two blocks to go.

I angled toward the trash as Lebeau closed the three meters between us. Something flashed in the camera image. There. Metal reflected from Lebeau's hand where he clutched the handlebar grip. A knife.

He hammered down, accelerating between me and the building, evidently intending to lay me down before I reached the trash heap. I set my jaw and squeezed my thighs around the aluminum bodywork, tensing to dodge the impending strike.

Inches from my side, he swung, and the blade arced rubberside, aiming for my ankles. I yanked my leg up and braced my boot on the windshield, jerking the handlebars to avoid a lopsided manhole cover.

Too damned late. His hand connected with my leg, jolting a wealth of pain through my thigh. I wrenched my foot towards my body, bringing the other boot up to stand in a squat on the seat. The position protected my core against another strike, but it was a lethal test of balance at 150 mph.

Thrashing down the alley, seconds until impact with the trash, I steadied my feet on the narrow seat and reached down to grip the source of the anguish burning my leg. My gloved fingers collided with the knife handle protruding from my thigh.

Fuck, fuck, fuuuuck. My pulse sped up, and my teeth bared. I let the anger in, gloried in it as it flushed through my body. Anger had molded me at thirteen when I watched my mother's blood spray the walls. It strengthened me through my most vulnerable years in the children's home. And now, it kept me focused.

Lebeau was a dead motherfucker.

His front tire rammed hard and fast, the rubber burning against my frame slider, his gloved hand stretching for the knife in my leg. The son of a bitch wanted his blade back?

A churning smog as dense and black as the night sky enveloped me. My muscles heated, and my stomach hardened into a furious knot of muscle. I wanted to pull the blade free and stab him through the visor repeatedly. I wanted to watch him horizontally park against the building and explode on impact. I wanted to smell his burning flesh polluting the air as I rolled to the finish line.

In that feral moment, in the space of a seething breath, my mother's lifeless eyes filled my vision. They told me to be patient. To be smart. To avenge with precision and cool detachment. To save the butchering for the families I was after.

My front tire hit the trash pile, Lebeau hanging right at my side. With my hands on the grips, I kicked out my aching leg and slammed my boot into his helmet. Blinding pain burst stars across my vision. No way could I leverage enough force to flatten him, but the impact sent his bike screeching along the side of the building, slowing him enough to give me the lead.

A sudden incline whipped my head back to the road. Shit, a ramp hid in the heap after all. A steep fucking ramp.

I dug the toes of my boots into the seat. Tightened my fists around the grips. Slipped the clutch. Lifted the front tire skyward into a wheelie. My pulse spiked as the rear tire hit the end of the ramp then spun out.

Behind me, Lebeau wobbled back on my trail as I pitched forward, tires first. The bike's four-hundred pounds of wet weight shot through the air and over the spike strip. I clung to the grips, toes hooked on the seat, my body and the frame vertical with the ground.

Adrenaline quickened my breath and soared through my bloodstream. Ah God, the thrill was electrifying. I landed shiny side up, but the collision of rubber against concrete jarred the steel in my thigh, spreading sparks of agony to every inch of my body.

On my tail, Lebeau made the same jump. Goddammit. I tasted blood and unclenched my jaw, releasing the gouged skin inside my cheek. Christ, my leg was fucking wasted. I coughed through a parched throat and dropped my boots to the foot pegs. "Thermal."

Full color returned to the visor display, the finish line blinking on the map. Two more blocks.

I ripped it up, bolting out of the alley, skirted around an oncoming truck, and stretched out on the final block. No surprise, Lebeau was still vertical and ten meters behind me, gobbling up pavement.

And fuck, the pain gripped me by the balls. The fire heaving from the wound felt like it was seconds from scorching my leg right off my hip.

The wail of police sirens rang out in the distance. Up ahead, traffic lights blinked in an intersection, bracketed by two walls of bikes. Dozens of engines revved and sputtered, growing in number but ready to scatter the moment the heat showed up.

I focused on the blinking red lights. The finish line.

In the lead by twenty meters, I could rush forward, claim the win, and collect my money. But as the hole in my leg stabbed like a vindictive bitch, soaking my favorite leathers in crimson, I couldn't smother the fury simmering in my gut. My mother taught me how to ride, how to win, and when she died in a river of her blood, she taught me how to hate.

A block from the finish line, I squeezed the binders, spun the bike to face Lebeau head on, and skidded to a stop. He rose from his tucked lean, seemingly surprised, but didn't slow.

On the two-lane street, a smart man would've passed in a wide arc and hauled ass to the finish line. Lebeau was a dumb fuck.

He approached on my left, close enough to clip me, probably his intention. At the last second, I leaned right with the bike, yanked the knife from my leg, and returned it in kind. I only needed to point the sharp end in a firm grasp, holding my arm loose as to not dislocate my shoulder. His momentum took care of the rest, the blade piercing his chest.

It happened so fast, he didn't see it coming. Arrogance caught him. Shock teetered him. And the bite of the steel jerked his shoulders, the flinch careening his bike to the side.

He countersteered, but both wheels lost grip, refusing to regain traction. Might've had something to do with his hands releasing the handlebars to grab at his chest. The frame slipped out from beneath him, and the velocity of his forward motion sent his body pavement surfing until his helmet crashed into the curb.

Road rash was the least of his problems. His limbs tumbled to a stop, twisted at awkward angles around his unmoving torso. Dead or alive, it made no difference. The mobsters who bet on him would see that he never ate another croissant or frog or whatever he shoved in his prissy mouth.

Sirens grew in proximity and volume, and my GPS alerts blared in my ears. The cops were four blocks away. I thrashed the throttle, pivoted the bike toward the finish line, and shot forward. The rear-view camera showed several guys dragging Lebeau off the street and into a waiting getaway car. Probably the same asshats who threw the spike strip and who would probably help him flee the country and the target that was now on his back.

Unlike Lebeau, I didn't need a team of people to hold my damned dick. I wore the most hi-tech helmet in existence. Binocular-wide field-of-view, voice-activated, powered by Bluetooth controls on the bike, and wired to the Interwebs, the head-up display kept my eyes on the road, and the 9mm plating protected my skull. The U.S. military would cream themselves if they discovered my warehouse, my intel, and the engineer who worked for me.

As I rolled beneath the traffic light, a notification popped up on the visor display, alerting me that my winnings had been deposited in one of my offshore accounts. I gripped the wound on my leg and drew a deep breath through my nose. I might've smiled if my jaw wasn't locked in a teeth-grinding grimace of pain.

Speculations on what I did with my winnings were as satisfying as they were inaccurate, some theorizing the lavish lifestyle of a playboy, others romanticizing the philanthropy of a heroic outlaw. I fed the rumors, planting seeds of embellishment that disguised the truth.

Destroying Trenchant Media, the most influential entity in the nation, had been my mother's crusade. Killing the two prominent families behind the conglomerate was mine.

Motorcyclists and pedestrians invaded the street, fleeing in all directions to circumvent the nearing sirens. I savored the chaos. It kept me aware, focused, searching for my exit.

I motored through the exodus, held up by the mass of scuttling people, and maintained my trademark silence as the shouting echoed off the buildings. *Evader! What's your real name? Where did you learn to race? Show us your face. Take me for a ride, baby. Did Lebeau cut you?*

Could they not see the wound seeping all over my leg? Leather-clad women pressed their tattooed tits against my arms, begging for a ride, their glimmering eyes promising a wild ten minutes against an alley wall or a dirty hour between motel sheets.

I shoved at their wandering hands and gunned the bike through the crush. If I wanted to ambush someone, trick him, and learn his identity, I'd do it while his pants were around his ankles. So yeah, I didn't fuck the women connected to the race. My paranoia prohibited it. And at the moment, so did the hole in my leg.

Didn't stop me from scanning the frenzy for a silver Ducati Testastretta. She wasn't always here, but when she was, she lingered on the outskirts, always alone, eerily still and watchful. I probed the mob of bodies, searching for her seductive curves sheathed in metallic silver leathers.

Seriously, who went to the trouble to custom match their wardrobe to the paint on their fairings? Someone with too much money. Someone who didn't belong in this scene.

The fat-wallet investors in this business didn't ride, and they certainly didn't attend the races in person. Who the fuck was she?

Helmets and hair of every color and style spread out above the thinning horde. Maybe I missed her? I held my breath and headed for my escape route, seeking her signature braid, the thick rope of blonde hair that snaked from her silver helmet, curling around her chest and teasing her waist. I wanted to use it to bind her wrists while I fucked her.

Which was the most irrational fucking thought I'd had all night. Must've been the lingering adrenaline. I needed to shed my racing persona, find a willing body, and fuck the energy out of my system. First, I needed to kick dust and find a doctor.

Red and blue lights reflected off the glass building a block away, the piercing sirens rising above the rumble of scattering motorcycles. Out of time.

I revved the throttle and spun out the rear wheel with the front brake locked, a fast way to scatter the masses. Then I bolted through an opening and gagged it the hell out of there.

The thermal sensor flashed red as I rounded a blind corner. I shifted left to avoid the oncoming bike and blinked. The silver Ducati.

My heart thumped, and my muscles twitched to flip a U-turn and pursue her.

Her bike wobbled, and her helmet jerked in my direction, whipping her blonde braid across her slender back. I slowed but didn't turn my head. I didn't have to. The rear camera showed her decelerating, her head rotating to watch my retreating backside.

I didn't know what was more enthralling, knowing she was here for me or *not* knowing the reason why. She rolled in on too much money to be a reporter or undercover cop. The aftermarket upgrades on her bike alone cost fifty times more than the average bike here. She didn't engage in the rowdy shit talking, wasn't scantily dressed, and never flashed her tits like the women who frequented the races. Hell, in the nine months since I first noticed her, I'd never seen her remove her helmet.

She stood out like a sparkling jewel amidst the cesspool of thugs, gangsters, and bikers who arrived in groups. She came alone, watching the finish line from the seat of her flashy pasta rocket. No license plate. No apparent weapon. She might as well have waved a sign that said *Rob me, rape me*. She was either stupid or I was missing something crucial. Both notions fucked with my head.

A squad car swerved in behind me, blocking my view of her, and a man's voice bellowed over the loudspeaker. "Pull over and step away from the bike."

One of these nights, when I wasn't bleeding all over the fucking place or hightailing it from the boys in blue, I'd follow her, corner her, then…what? My cock jerked in answer.

Caning it down State Street, I carved the next corner with a horizontal lean. Six blocks later, the flashing lights dimmed to tiny blurs in the backdrop. I veered onto the entrance ramp, merged onto 290, and opened the throttle.

Last thing I needed was a fling with some well-to-do, danger-seeking fangirl. She was probably just a bored housewife, looking for the kind of hard fuck she wasn't getting from her uptight husband. And there I was, lollygagging after every goddamned race, flirting with the five-O on my ass in hopes of seeing her. A dangerous distraction.

My mother's death had instilled a sense of purpose in my life. As much as racing channeled my anger and breathed life into my memories of her, the money I won funded her purpose. *My purpose.*

When my mother died, she had no money, no family, and no gurgled final words to offer her only child. What she left me with was knowledge. Dangerous knowledge of buried scandals, corrupt corporations and politicians, and their hushed victims. Victims like her.

I weaved through interstate traffic, the anguish in my leg clawing through my body as the engine exerted max power. But I was free *and alive* to see another sunrise. To finish what my mother had started.

Kathleen Baskel glowered at me from across the boardroom table. Ugh, that look. It twisted with the same disgust she used to give my scuffed sneakers after I'd spent an afternoon chasing Collin along the banks of the Outer Drive Bridge.

I straightened my back in the stiff leather chair and offered my sweetest smile. She didn't always look at me like she wanted to ship me back to boarding school. Sometimes, her dark blue gaze touched my face with warmth and approval. Didn't it?

Who was I kidding? My mother was a cold-hearted bitch.

She smoothed a hand over her dyed auburn hair and gave the bob an extra pat at her jawline. Her fingers lowered to tap the armrest of her chair, and she blew out an irritated huff. Then she huffed again as if annoyed by the fact that *I* had caused her to expel a noisy breath. "Stop being so difficult, Kaci."

A flush crept up my neck, brought on from her nasty tone and intensified by the unwavering scowl of the man in my periphery. The man I had yet to make eye contact with.

I folded my hands on the table. "I'm not being difficult, *Mother*. I'm merely stating facts you refuse to hear."

Her lips formed a stern white line. "Collin—"

"Is not trying to vilify the Chicago PD."

She flared her nostrils, the only bits on her Botoxed face that moved. "Interviewing Officer Dipshit on *our* television broadcast is—"

"Daniel Wyatt has twenty years on the force."

"—a childish way to raise ratings." She sat back and set her jaw. "Not to mention the upheaval it will cause among our supporters."

There it was, the driving force behind this meeting. Whatever alliances our parents had built over the years controlled every goddamned thing at Trenchant.

I stared at the woman across the table, her slender frame showcased in a black pantsuit from the latest Chanel collection. The ostentatious diamond on her ring finger cost more than the average annual income in Illinois. She had more money than she could spend in a lifetime. What the hell did she gain from her *supporters*? Special favors? Popularity in her haughty clubs? Influence and attention?

She stunk of greed and decay. Problem was, I couldn't prove if bribery, subterfuge, or anything unlawful occurred within these alliances. When they ordered me to shred documents beneath their watchful eyes, they had reasonable justification. Their subtle manipulations, like slanting Collin's show and erasing numbers on financial statements, seemed to be within the realm of the law.

Legal, yet erratic and ambiguous, like pieces of a big, ugly secret I wasn't privy to. It didn't feel right, and I sure as fuck didn't trust them.

Exhaustion pulled on my shoulders. God, I didn't want to deal with her at eight o'clock in the morning. My morning dose of vitamins and caffeine hadn't kicked in, given the constant urge to yawn and the overwhelming need to face-plant right on this table and steal a nap. Wouldn't my mother love that?

When I'd crawled back in bed last night after the race, sleep had never come. My brain was in a permanent state of unrest, my body quivering on a tight-wire, longing for things so far out of my reach I was turning myself into a miserable tragedy. And I had five more meetings and a budget summary to evaluate before I could attempt another night's sleep.

I rested my elbows on the table and leaned forward. "Collin hosts personalities on all sides of the debates. It's what keeps the show *honest.*"

Another huff. She stood and gathered her tablet and phone. "I don't have time for this."

Of course, she didn't. Mrs. I've-got-asses-to-kiss-and-lives-to-ruin didn't have time for anyone with a net worth below nine digits. She glanced at the silent presence at the head of the table. "Trent."

Collin's father lifted his chin but didn't move his eyes from me, his gaze a phantom stroke over my face. "I'll take it from here, Kathleen."

My insides filled with ice. Fuck that. I jumped to my feet to follow my mother's escape.

"Sit. Down." His command thundered through the boardroom

and wobbled my knees. The same tone he'd used when he caught his son in bed with me and another man.

I dropped in the chair and looked to my mother, hoping for the miracle of all miracles that some kind of maternal instinct would spark inside her frozen heart.

She paused in the doorway, her sapphire eyes a colder reflection of mine. They lowered to my featherweight wool dress, and her over-plumped lips tipped down at the corners. "If you want to succeed, start with the way you dress."

The fuck? I fingered the square neckline at my collarbone, brushed a hand down the unwrinkled indigo fabric, and tugged at the knee-length hem. I was wearing a modest Armani classic for Christ's sake.

The door clicked behind her, and the automatic lock engaged, shutting me in with the last man I wanted to share air with…alone.

He stood, one hand in the pocket of his designer gray slacks, and approached with a nonchalance that ratcheted my shoulders to my ears. He trailed his fingers over each chair back he passed, his sharp hazel eyes laser-locked on mine.

My nerves caught fire, and my fingernails dug into my palms. It was shameful how easily he reduced me to the little girl who'd always fumbled in his presence, like when I'd spilled punch on his white carpet and chipped Collin's tooth with a badly-aimed tennis racket. Like when I walked in on Trent banging the nanny.

When he reached my side, my ribs compressed as panic expanded my lungs, but I kept my breaths quiet and steady.

He lowered in a crouch and swiveled my chair to face him. "How are things with my son?" His knuckle grazed my knee. I jerked away, but he caught my thigh beneath the hem of the skirt, his fingers clenching in a bruising grip. "Is he…satisfying you?"

My stomach roiled at his taunting tone. I grabbed his wrist and shoved, but my strength was no match for his. He was a physically fit, youthful-looking sixty-five-year-old, with thick blond hair, polished skin, and barely a crinkle fanning from the corners of his yellow eyes. He must've spent a fortune on cosmetic surgery, hair plugs, and personal trainers.

I wanted to look away from him because his proximity made me sick. But he did this thing with his eyes, flickering them in a stare down meant to intimidate, to make me vulnerable. He thought he'd shackled me in a sexless marriage and assumed, in my desperation, I could be seduced by his vile attractiveness.

Acid simmered in the back of my throat. I'd been deflecting his inappropriate touches since the first buds of breasts swelled on my chest, and I liked to think I could continue to stave him off.

But his advances were growing bolder, becoming more frequent and making me hyper-vigilant, jittery, and fucking terrified to come to work.

I shoved harder against his hand, but the more I resisted, the higher his fingers climbed. He wanted a struggle—I could see it glimmering in his eyes—and I refused to play his sick games.

Funny that, seeing how the contract forbid me to cheat on Collin, the initiator of the whole damned arrangement encouraged me to break it.

I released my grip on his wrist. I'd avoided him as much as I could over the years, but he was part of my family, my employer, and he was malicious enough to hurt me, or kill me, if I refused a direct order.

Still, I had my limits. I would never willingly spread my legs for this man. It was the unwilling part, however, that corkscrewed my stomach every time he cornered me. I had threatened on multiple occasions that I would file charges if he assaulted me.

How long would that threat ward him off? Would anything stop him? Certainly not my parents. Their allegiance was, and always would be, with Trent Anderson and Trenchant Media. As if they were part of a feudalist system, where lords and ladies offered their daughter in marriage in return for the king's protection and power.

As his thumb stroked the crease between my clenched knees, graphic thoughts of castration strengthened my backbone and raised my chin. "If you want Collin to make changes to tonight's segment, tell him yourself."

"That's what I have you for, darling." His other hand joined the first, his palms inching up my thighs and taking the skirt with it. "He listens to you, and you listen to me."

I pressed against the seat back and squeezed my legs even tighter as sweat gathered between my breasts. "If you don't remove your hands, you'll regret it." It was a hollow threat, but I would *not* give him the sobbing kind of fight he wanted.

His quiet chuckle prickled goosebumps across my arms. "Naïve girl. You forget who I am. Who my friends are."

He was wrong about that. His powerful friends were the reason I hadn't followed through on my murderous imaginings. And to call them powerful was an understatement. Often, I eavesdropped on snippets of conversations between Trent and my father in the den after dinner. Supposedly, he and my father met up with their secret fraternity of prominent CEOs, former U.S. presidents, oil barons, and royal families. They gathered in an undisclosed location to partake in heavy drinking, collared sex slaves, and bizarre rituals while hashing out their plans for the future of the world.

Rumors. Fucking hearsay without evidence or verification. I knew better than to entertain that shit.

With a deep breath, I clenched and relaxed my fingers. Me against whatever egos stood behind Trent would not keep Collin out of prison. Nor would it stop our parents from manipulating his show.

I closed my eyes and bit out the words he was waiting for. "I'll speak to Collin about tonight's segment."

His hands retreated, straightening my skirt. "I know you will." He rose and towered over me, an embodiment of antediluvian cloaks and secret guilds, dressed to deceive in modern Gucci threads. "There's another matter I need you to handle."

I met his cold gaze, holding my face as passive as possible, while my insides trembled with dread. These behind-closed-door requests prodded me to resist, flee, do something that didn't make me feel like his accomplice. But the consequences chained me to the chair.

"I want you to obtain access to that underground racing network. Find out everything you can on the racers, the dates, and the maps of each race, and report back to me."

What? Why would he—? Oh God, did he know about my involvement? My feet itched to move. I fought it, digging my heels into the carpet. "I…I don't—" *Stop stuttering, dumbass.* "I wouldn't even know where to begin."

What were the signs of lying? I held my head still and kept my eyes on his, blinking slowly and naturally.

He pivoted and strolled along the length of the table. "You have the resources on your payroll. Use them."

I swallowed quickly and schooled my breath while his back was turned. "Who cares about a gang of irresponsible bikers?"

Grabbing his phone from the table, he shifted to face me and swiped the screen. Swipe. Swipe. Tap. He stared at the screen and swiped again.

Good grief, was he already bored with this conversation? I folded my arms over my chest, my neck aching with tension.

His finger stilled. "The police chief cares."

An undercurrent of suspicion sifted through me, not an unusual reaction to the cryptic shit that fell from his mouth.

I chewed the inside of my cheek. I could give him everything he wanted on the races right now, tell him I had the information because I was running an undercover story. It was only a matter of time before he got what he wanted anyway.

My insides cringed at the thought. A foolish reaction, but I felt more loyalty for an outlaw biker I'd never met than I did for our parents. "Why don't you just call one of your *friends* to dig up the info? They're probably VIP investors on the network."

He didn't lift his head from his phone, but his eyes rolled up and locked on mine. "My friends don't engage in the primitive interests of commoners."

Did he really just say that? I bit my tongue. Considering my *primitive interest* in Evader, maybe I should've been offended. But hey, if I died knowing I was nothing like Trent Anderson, I'd consider his comment a fucking compliment.

He dropped the phone in his pocket. "If you want that promotion, you'll adhere to the contract and do as you're told." He hit a button beneath the table to unlock the doors and ambled out without a look in my direction.

Dismissed like a menial office worker.

He vanished around the corner, and I released a heavy breath. My career was far from menial. Next week, I would be the CEO of a Fortune 500 company. *If* Collin and I continued to comply with their demands, remained married, and didn't commit adultery. I sighed. *If* we didn't get *caught.*

God, I needed that promotion, the title I'd busted my ass for. MBA in leadership and organizational development from Yale. Certified public accountant with a BA in accounting and economics from Georgetown. Twelve-hour workdays and not a single vacation in fifteen years. Damn right, I'd earned it.

Next week, Trent would hand off his CEO position to me. Then I would have control of the entire conglomerate. Transforming our families' company from a self-fulfilling entity into an unbiased, trustworthy news source was an aspiration bigger than myself. I could do it, but that wasn't why I needed it.

What ruled my every breath was the legally binding contract Collin and I had been forced to sign. And that contract had a loophole.

See, the CEO of Trenchant Media also reigned as the chairman of the board, and the chairman had the voting power to appoint and remove board members. Trent had thought of that and included a clause in our original twenty-one page contract that nullified this policy.

He must've thought I was a fucking moron or that I was too spineless to try to deceive him, because the pompous prick never checked the final draft of the contract. Never noticed I'd rephrased that clause, only slightly but just enough. Enough to slant its meaning into vague nothingness.

I needed the CEO position to appoint myself head of the board. So I could remove him. All of them. Strip their rights the way they'd stolen mine. Without their power base at Trenchant, Collin and I could fight them, maybe get our freedom back. *Marry who we wanted.* Just thinking about it made my heart thump.

Until then, I had to play along with their demands and fill the role of dutiful daughter.

I tugged my phone from my purse on the way out, dialing as I walked down the hall toward my office.

"Morning, love." Collin's voice brushed against my ear like silk. "Everything okay?"

He knew about his father's threat, about the purchased evidence that placed him at the scene of an unsolved murder. He had no alibi, no proof of innocence, and no defense. Outside of that, he was in the dark about what I did for our parents, what I planned to do.

I hated keeping things from him, but I didn't do it to betray his trust. If Trenchant found itself caught in a scandal for its unethical business practices, his ignorance would protect him. That was what my dishonesty gave him. Blissful ignorance.

"Yeah." I tried to put a smile in my voice. "Everything's fine. I was just thinking about your police brutality segment tonight. Do you remember Dave O'Neil?"

"Leon, dammit, where are you going? Hang on, Kaci." The phone muffled. "Why didn't you turn back there? We're going to get caught in traffic—"

Judging by the sudden silence, he'd covered the mouthpiece to yell at the limo driver. I grinned. God, he was a horrible backseat driver.

Scratching sounded through the speaker, and he said, "Dave O'Neil? Was that the cop who escorted you undetected from a race a few months back?"

I'd been pulled over that night. Trying to flee the scene at 150 miles per hour. Detained by Officer O'Neil, who I'd paid off to let me go without mentioning my name in a report. "Yeah. I kind of owe him, and I know he'd shit himself to be on the *Anderson Angle*."

"You want me to interview him instead of Daniel Wyatt?" His voice lowered, his words drawn out with reservation.

"I'm sure the makeup crew could give him a real-looking mustache." I strode into my office and shut the door.

"Funny." He sighed. "I don't know, Kaci. I don't know anything about the guy, and I only have a few hours to write the script."

I'd had Officer O'Neil investigated after that night to cover my tracks. Five kids, clean record, never shot a man while on duty. Exactly the kind of officer my mother's right-wing supporters would approve of. "A five minute phone call with him, and the great Collin Anderson will be able to infer what toothpaste he uses and what his favorite sports team is."

He groaned, but ten minutes later, I'd convinced him to switch the interviewees. I ended the call and lowered into the chair behind my desk. My insides felt hard and cold, foreign yet becoming more and more familiar. I'd manipulated my best friend. Again.

Every time I did this—deceived him, managed him, gave into our parents—something broke inside me, and another piece of who I was fell away, altering me into something, *someone*, I despised.

The difference was I loved Collin. Hard to believe his parents shared that sentiment. What kind of people would sentence their own son to prison? Their only child? The heir to their empire? These were the same people who nurtured his career, granted him a celebrity position within the company, and elevated him higher and higher to ensure the success of his career.

It came down to control. They controlled him the same way they controlled me.

The phone on my desk buzzed, and *Reception* displayed on the ID. I hit the speaker button. "Jenna?"

"Your nine o'clock meeting is about to start."

I released a breath. "I'll be right out." I gathered my laptop and cell phone and treaded toward the door.

Thirteen hours later, I dragged my aching feet through the condo and down the hall to my bedroom, stripping my clothes as I walked. Nude and exhausted, I freed my hair and stared at the empty sheets on the bed.

Just like that, the cold feeling inside me returned. I was terrified to be alone, to spend the rest of my life alone. I was terrified to not be alone, to fall for a man, knowing my situation didn't allow that. I was terrified to fall for a man who fell for me, because I wanted that more than anything.

As I stared at the bed, swaying with fatigue, I couldn't do it. Couldn't climb into the lonely void and tell myself everything was okay. Not tonight. I needed something…real. A hug? A warm body? Collin.

I pivoted and headed to the other side of the condo, my gait quickening along the unlit hall to his suite, my bare skin prickling against the chill in the air.

He was probably asleep. I would just sneak under his covers and wrap my arms around him. Maybe entwine our legs. He liked his space, but he'd hold me. Collin never turned me away.

The door stood open, his bedroom dimly lit by the cityscape beyond the wall of windows. I crept to the bed and stopped, straining my eyes through the dark.

The blankets rose over a wide man-sized mountain in the center of the mattress. Two dark heads rested on the pillow, bodies twisted together, and breaths whispering in steady rhythms of sleep.

My eyes burned and tears rose up. Why the fucking tears? I swiped at my cheeks and backed out of the room. I caught myself on the doorjamb, my knees wobbling.

What was my problem? Was it shock? He'd never had a man stay the night. Neither of us had. But I'd told him to pursue a relationship, and I was happy for him. I was. My best friend had a real chance at…something more.

Then why did it feel like there were claws in my chest, scratching and digging and hollowing out my insides?

I forced myself to stand taller, face the room, and accept the view before me. The claws in my chest dug, dug, dug, swelling a burning lump in my throat. Maybe this was jealousy? Not of Seth but of Collin, of what he had. A man to hold, to cuddle, to wake up with.

God, I was a selfish, wretched friend.

Heat coiled up my spine, chasing the climb of release. *Pert, round ass spread over the bike.* I reached for it, my balls drawing closer to my body with each pump. *Blonde braid around my fist.* Another drive of my hips. *Ahhhh!* I exploded in a muscle-gripping orgasm. Semen burst from my cock, and my thrusts slowed, my back bowing. A groan ripped from my throat as tremors coursed over my skin.

My cock twitched in my fist. I leaned a shoulder against the shower wall and reached for the faucet to adjust the temperature. Cool water pelted my overheated body, diffusing the riot of sensations, the peak of pleasure gone as quickly as it had come.

I wanted a do-over. Hell, I wanted the real thing.

It had only been two days since I got laid. Didn't matter. The faceless woman I'd met at the bar hadn't been *her*. My body was singularly focused on silver leather painted over hourglass curves, my mind refusing to move past it. Until I discovered who she was. Until I fucked her.

It should've annoyed me, this unreasonable fixation, but I didn't care. The next race was a week away. If she showed, I'd confront her. I was done waiting. I needed to fuck her out of my head because, God help me, I had more important things to concentrate on.

I finished showering, carefully washing around the one-day-old stitches on my thigh, and slipped on a pair of jeans, a t-shirt, and black Converse. Then I strode through the yawning space of my sanctuary, the glow of the indirect lighting leading the way to the kitchen area.

The usual chill brushed my skin as I walked the length of the functional, uninviting space. Red brick deadened the walls. Steel beams reinforced the cathedral ceiling. When I'd converted the hundred-year-old church into livable space, I'd left it as one open room, adding only a bed, a couch, kitchen counters and appliances in the corner, and an enclosed bathroom.

I designed it to be spacious enough to hold all sixteen of my motorcycles, *if* I ever had a need to move them from the basement.

The simple lines and hard surfaces conformed to an industrial aesthetic that said, *Don't sit down. Don't get comfortable. There's work to do.* But the absence of windows and neighbors was why I chose this structure. Privacy was, in my case, freedom.

Horizontal oak wall panels surrounded the kitchen cabinets. A cosmetic facade. I reached above the refrigerator and punched a button. The panels beside the fridge rolled up like a garage door, revealing the elevator shaft hidden behind it.

I stepped into the lift, tapped the code in the keypad, and descended below ground.

The lift bounced to a stop. As the steel doors opened, the screams of an overworked engine slammed into my chest, the clamor reverberating off the walls of the confined space.

"Benny?" I shouted over the racket and weaved around tables and waist-high piles of junk. Circuit boards, flickering computer monitors, miscellaneous motorcycle parts, and greasy tools cluttered the gymnasium-sized basement. "Benny!"

Where the hell was my scatter-brained engineer? I passed Benny's gaming area, a gaudy purple couch, and six widescreen TVs on the wall, but no Benny.

The rumble of the motor blasted from the enclosed garage at the far end. Didn't mean Benny was in there, and I really didn't want to make the damned walk to find out, the stitches in my leg pulling with every step. But I refused to limp. Refused to show a hint of weakness, even in the privacy of my home.

Heading that way, I grabbed my helmet from the center workbench, the one I always wore during races. As I turned, the toe of my Chucks kicked a— What the hell? Was that a fucking grenade?

I eyed it warily as it skittered over the floor, my heart grinding to a stop. Before the bouncing green shell collided with the wall, I sprinted into the three-bay garage, slammed the steel door behind me, and waited for the world to detonate.

The explosion didn't come. Not that I would've heard it over the pealing motor enclosed in the room with me. The roar was so goddamned loud it rattled my teeth and stabbed my brain. Good thing the garage was a room within a room, two-stories below ground, constructed with hi-tech soundproofing.

With a finger plugged in one ear and the helmet dangling from the other, I zigzagged through the rows of motorcycles and approached the rear of the revving bike.

The MTT Turbine Streetfighter was a new prototype, one I hadn't raced yet. Suspended a foot above the floor on a mechanically swaying stand, the tires spun freely and the frame swung side-to-side as if simulating turns. The engine grumbled at peak torque thanks to Benny's hand on the grip, holding the gas open.

My nostrils burned, and my eyes watered from the fumes. Surely the ventilation system was working?

Benny stood on the bike, bent at the waist, balancing as I had done in the last race, but perhaps with a bit more grace. Her brown creeper boots angled in a pigeon-toed pose on the seat. Sheathed in tight army-green pants, her skinny bird legs were capped with yellow plastic knee guards.

She rocked with the tilt of the frame, hands on the grips and ass in the air. A gun holster fastened around her thigh. Frowning, I leaned down for a closer look.

I blew out a breath. Just a toy pistol, thank Christ. I never knew what to expect. Like the grenade, I might've overreacted, but there had been too many explosive, near-death accidents over the years. What I did know was Benny with a loaded firearm would be a face-palm of apocalyptic proportions.

My gaze fell away from the back of her thighs. Wait, were those—? I glanced back and angled my head. Yeah, those were ruffles on the ass of her pants.

I walked around to the front of the bike, scrutinizing the leather jacket I'd never seen before. Clearly tailored to fit *me*, it draped her small shoulders.

Another prototype engulfed her head—the helmet she'd been tinkering with for several weeks. A rainbow of wires snaked from it, connecting to square patches along the sleeves of the jacket.

The helmet tilted up, leveling with my face. The opaque visor shielded what I guessed was a crazed expression highlighted by glittery makeup.

I narrowed my eyes and mouthed, "What are you doing?"

The motorized stand oscillated the bike to the right, shaking the frame as well as the crazy woman balancing atop it. She let go of the grips and rose to her full height, arms stretched out to her sides. Then she lifted a boot, pointed it behind her like a warrior ballerina high on methanol fumes, and squealed over the screech of the motor.

Amidst her harebrained stunt, the bike shifted, and her upper body toppled forward, likely weighted down by the helmet. I reached out my free hand to catch her arm, but she slapped it away. Her back straightened, her fists whipped through the air, and she hopped off.

She was either fucking around or testing a new design. Who knew with her? I'd stopped trying to keep up with her antics years ago.

I turned off the bike and the motorized stand, and blessed silence blanketed the room. She removed the oversized helmet, ripping the wires as she tossed it and the jacket on the table beside her.

Fire-red hair covered her head, a stark contrast from the prior day's silvery white. It spiked every which way around the black sweatband on her forehead.

She jabbed her fingers through the shoulder-length strands, swooping them away from her neck. "Wassup?"

"Tell me that's not a live grenade on the floor out there, waiting to be kicked."

Green eyes glimmered beneath the fluorescent lighting. "Did you kick it?" Her gasp rolled into a laugh. "God, you should see the look on your face." She bared her teeth and scrunched her nose, hissing noisily.

Was her feral opossum act supposed to be an imitation of my expression?

"So yeeeeah, if you happen upon *another* grenade"—she bit her lip—"don't kick it."

Which meant I would spend that evening sweeping the warehouse of all things fragile, flammable, perishable, combustible, chemical, or potentially hazardous.

She hopped up on the table and swung her legs. "Your unbalanced forces issue is resolved."

"What unbalanced forces issue?"

Gold dust shimmered on her fluttering lashes and thickened into swirly lines at her temples. "We're not just dealing with the force of gravity pulling downward and the normal force of the ground pushing upward." Her voice sped up, her hands flying through the air. "If the engine applies two-thousand Newtons of force—"

And this was where I tuned out. In her exuberance to nerd all over the shop floor, she had a tendency to forget we met at MIT, that my test scores were only slightly lower than hers, and the only reason I transferred from the physics and engineering departments to the business school was to broaden our skill set. Because by then, I knew MIT's top graduate would become the nerdacious half of our two-man team.

"—creates equilibrium and, thus, state of motion." Her black tank top clung to her chest, her tiny breasts having zero state of motion as she bounced on her butt and talked with her hands.

I was pretty sure a pimply-faced, Cheetos-eating teenage boy lurked beneath the glam boots and angel glitter.

One that hacked technology already in existence and altered it beyond the boundaries of the law to fit my needs.

One that also didn't know when to shut up. "The friction exerts a rightward force upon the leftward-moving bike and—"

"Benny." I scrubbed a palm over my face.

"An analysis had to be done to determine if the forces acting upon—"

"Benny!" I pointed at the broken wires twisted around the helmet and jacket beside her. "Get to the fucking point."

She fisted her hands on her hips. "Fine, grumpy jackasshole." She cocked her head. "Since you're so keen on standing on your bike at 167 miles per hour, I designed a balance system. With wireless sensors in the sleeves of your jacket, the helmet will beep when equilibrium is lost and calibrate the acceleration and velocity vectors of your body. The digital gauge will tell you when, where, and how far to lean. Happy?"

"No." I pinched the bridge of my nose. Just what I didn't need, more alarms flashing in my face. At least, now I knew how she'd stayed balanced on her rigged contraption. "I know how to lean my damned bike."

She stared at her boots and mumbled, "Contentious, menstruating, fun killah."

"What was that?"

She sniffed. "Nothing."

I held out the helmet in my hand. "I need a modification on this by Saturday's race."

Her pale cheeks rose in color. "But I just gave you the Best. Mod. Evah."

I spun the helmet between my hands, flipping it upside down and revealing the rows of buttons along the inside panel. "What I *need* is"—for lack of a better term—"x-ray vision."

Her chin sawed side-to-side, scraping her teeth together and making my ears bleed. "Like radar detection? Through-the-wall imaging to map the layout of a building?"

"No, more like the ability to selectively see through a smaller object"—like a silver helmet—"as if it were translucent." Combined with the facial recognition software, I would be able to identify what I hoped was a fuckable face.

For an exasperating moment, she regarded me with one of her bizarre expressions I didn't have a chance in hell of interpreting. Then she bent over her knees and roared with laughter while slapping her thighs.

I set my jaw. What the shit was so damned funny?

Eventually, she sobered and snatched the helmet from my hands. "Don't sell your soul to Big Brother, he'd said." Sliding off the table, she tossed the helmet between her hands as she paced a circle around me. "Join me, and we'll decimate evil and transcend conventional morality with technology, he'd crowed. You'll have enough freedom and money to delight your little futurist heart, he'd promised."

Yeah, okay, she was paraphrasing the pitch I'd given her in grad school. When she was approached by a branch of the government—one that claimed some cloak-and-dagger crap about having no name or existence—I'd offered a sweeter deal. So what? I hadn't over-promised.

I crossed my arms over my chest. "What are you saying? You want a raise?" Fuck, her salary already exceeded two million a year.

She paused in front of me, the spikes of her hair several inches below my chin. Tilting her head back, she squinted up at me. "Did Superman use his x-ray vision to sneak peeks at Lois Lane's undies?"

I stiffened. No doubt my glare bulged my eyes out of my head.

"No. He didn't." She shook her finger at my face. "He used his powers to honor ethical codes and social mores." She tossed the helmet at my chest.

I caught the costly piece of equipment before it hit the concrete floor and set it on the table. "What the hell are you going on about?"

"Don't play dumb with me, Logan Flynt. This x-ray business reeks of Eau de Miss Ducati." She drew the plastic gun from her thigh and pressed the barrel against my forehead. "Who, like Lois Lane, is a scrotum fister. A flaunter of coy curves. A show stealer…"

I stopped listening. Christ Almighty, why had I mentioned her to Benny? *Huge* lapse in judgment. I squared my shoulders, shoved my head against the gun, and gave her my most intimidating glower. "We're done here."

The corner of her mouth curled up. "Aw, maybe that's the problem." A full grin pulled her lips from her teeth. "Maybe you *need* a good scrotum fisting. I know a girl—"

"Yep, we're done." I clamped my hand over her smug smirk and raised my eyes to the toy gun digging against my brow.

She squeezed the trigger, and fuck me, the obnoxious *pop* made me flinch. Goddammit, I was not in the fucking mood for this. I dropped my hand and scowled.

"So much anger, you angry angry angriphile." Poking a finger through the trigger guard, she twirled the gun in the air.

I dropped my head back and closed my eyes. If she weren't so fucking brilliant, I might've had her committed by now. Well, there was also the fact that she was my only friend, the sole person I trusted with my life.

She seemed completely oblivious to my growing frustration as she aimed the gun, mock-shooting limbs off my body. When her eyes locked on mine, I bit out, "Add the modification. That's what I'm paying you for."

"You're paying me to save humanity from Trenchant Media." She blew on the muzzle and holstered it on her thigh. "Which is so much more poetic than *x-ray*ted panties," she sang in a melodic yet condescending voice.

I ground my teeth, impatience sharpening my breath.

She glanced at her watch-free wrist. "Oh, look at that. I'm late for a date with Solid Snake."

Solid Snake? Probably had something to do with her costume. She called it cosplay. I called it delusional.

She struck a pose, one hand on the butt of the gun, the other punching the space between us. "I make a foxy Meryl Silverburgh, yeah?"

"Yeah." I had no clue. "So I'll assume x-ray vision is a technology beyond your skill level, then?"

"Pfft. Hardly." She strutted to the secondary elevator at the rear of the garage and raised the metal gate. The only external passage to and from the underground warehouse, it was wide enough to transport six bikes at a time.

She lowered the gate and peered at me through the bars. Despite her childish outer layers, what stared back at me was profound, organically-evolved intelligence, albeit off-the-grid and not always identifiable. But that only added to her lively spirit, and my irritation notwithstanding, I found it endearing.

I envied her carefree nature, how she was able to roll between her animated mischief and bleeding-edge innovations. To be able to shut things out and goof around was something I'd always wanted the freedom to do, but I couldn't.

She turned away and faced the back wall, her voice quiet. "You can always find a Ducati if you're looking for a distraction, Evader Man. But in matters of revenge, looking for distractions often signifies a change of heart."

The keypad beeped, and the lift ascended. When the concrete shaft swallowed the top of the elevator, she folded at the waist and grabbed her ankles. Her upside down smile flashed between her boots as she wiggled her fingers at me. "Toodles."

I stood there for a moment, rankled and defensive, with no one around to engage in the argument I itched for. I spun, strode across the garage, and stopped before the coal furnace in the wall and the newspaper article framed above it.

The clipping featured a photo of my mother crouched on her Honda CB750. Blue eyes shining, brown hair pulled back in a messy ponytail, she smiled with pride and vivacity and heart.

I was thirty-two now, so the article was printed…nineteen years ago. Long damned time without her. That morning was my last joyous memory of her. I'd stood just outside the frame of the picture, dazzled and stupefied as the cameras clicked.

My eyes lowered to the text, scanning the words for the millionth time as an achy burn tightened my throat.

LA resident, Maura Flynt, was inducted into the Motorcycle Hall of Fame after a trailblazing career as a pro superbike racer, Hollywood stunt rider, and exhibition daredevil, rivaling the likes of Evel Knievel.

My hands fisted at my sides. That night, she was murdered in our hotel room while I hid beneath the bed. That night, my thirteen-year-old dreams morphed from racing in the World Championship Grand Prix to filling Hell with the gutted targets of my revenge.

In matters of revenge, looking for distractions often signifies a change of heart.

Benny didn't know revenge. It didn't claw at her underbelly and wake her in a feverish sweat at night. But she knew *me*, and she subscribed to justice and family. I was her family as much as she was mine.

We'd worked side-by-side in this garage since we graduated from MIT eight years earlier. Her, developing and expanding on my ideas. Me, following my mother's leads and…revenging.

My first kill was the assassin who'd sliced my mother's throat. Took me five years to hunt him down and thirty seconds to open his neck the way he'd butchered hers.

I placed my hand against the incinerator door and let the heat soak into my palm. Eight more bodies had joined his fiery grave. I killed killers, rapists, career criminals, all of them named in my mother's diary. All of them tied to Trenchant Media. And I wasn't done.

But we needed money. We always needed money. Especially the way my sole employee raped my wallet.

A grin tugged at my mouth. Benny was worth every dime. To fund my endeavors and her salary, she'd designed the underground racing network and the untraceable technology that protected its secret society of gamblers, thus giving Evader a profitable platform.

Of course, no one knew who launched and maintained the network, but because the winner always advanced to the next race and I'd never lost, Evader had become the racing icon.

If I lost? Well, besides evading death at the hands of pissed-off gamblers, I'd lose my income stream, my high-paid employee, and the resources needed to finish what I'd started.

My attention flicked back to the newspaper clipping. I wasn't looking for a distraction, and I sure as hell hadn't had a change of heart. Revenge wasn't an emotion. It was my inheritance, the acting force that lived in my blood and sustained my balance. It was my equilibrium.

Revenge.

I raced to finance it.

I evaded to protect it.

I killed to attain it.

I planned everything.

Once Trent Anderson announced his replacement as CEO of Trenchant Media, I would be there, donned in a suit, staring into his eyes, and smiling as I accepted the offer.

Then I would gut him, all of them, from the inside out.

Six long days passed, my waking hours spent in the office, spurts of sleep coming only when I forced it. But finally, I shed the miserable heels and the creep of Trent's fingers, if only for a fleeting night.

I weaved the Ducati through convoys of bikers, my skin heating beneath the tight mold of my custom leathers. Hundreds had gathered around the finish line, the sputter of exhaust pipes resonating with the wild pumping of my blood.

A potluck of young men with crew cuts and athletic physiques reclined on enduros, sportbikes, busas, and zooks in a colorful array of fairings and racing leathers. These were the guys who longed to race but would probably never find the balls to throw down against a competitor like Evader.

On the other side of the street, tattooed, bearded brutes and their voluptuous women straddled choppers and cruisers. As I passed, their fuck-off vibes and explicit banter strained the chilly air and crawled down my spine.

The distant sirens, the flash of knives and guns tucked in waistbands, and the general paranoia innate to an assembly of criminals created an atmosphere that pulsed with danger. An ambiance where the country's worst crime rate met its soul mate.

Flasks in hands, engines growling, cigarettes drooping from lips, and fingers groping exposed cleavage, this was how the roughnecks partied. A far leap from the social graces and black tie affairs I'd spent a lifetime stifling yawns through.

I should've been terrified. Maybe I was. Adrenaline-induced fear was part of the appeal, after all, and my body buzzed with a heady mix of excitement and caution.

Ironic how this was the world I felt most comfortable in. Here, the danger was predictable, tattooed, and armed with bullets. Unlike the office, where the threat hid behind calculating smiles and opulent charity events.

My senses on high alert, I maneuvered through the outskirts of the commotion until I spotted an empty street a couple blocks from the finish line. Evader would tear through the finish line any moment. I wouldn't be able to see him take the win from two blocks away, but I promised Collin I'd always lay low and out of sight.

With a regretful sigh, I motored away from the crowd. I carried a Springfield .40 cal wedged in my waistband, the comforting steel warming my tailbone. I'd removed my license plate a few miles back. And I never took off my helmet, never let my visor linger on any one person. Even with these precautions, I'd fended off bikers more times than I cared to count.

It wasn't like I couldn't afford to hire a security team—wouldn't that have been cool?—but armed guards would ruin the whole minimize-attention-while-living-rebelliously thing I was going for.

I passed an alley close to the crowd, but it held deep, unoccupied shadows. A much better viewpoint of the finish line. Would it be safer than the open street farther down? Probably not, but dammit, I came here for a reason. To escape work. To escape Trent hounding my ass and fucking with my mind. To escape the emptiness of my bed. I came for a glimpse, for a fantasy to materialize in the flesh.

Screw Collin and his lay-low promise. I wouldn't be front and center for the finish, but I wouldn't miss it, either.

Backing the bike into the alcove, I lowered the kickstand and switched off the engine. Hidden and silent. A glimpse through the mob confirmed no one was looking at me, their focus locked on the race and each other.

The steel supports of the surrounding bridge rattled my bones as one of Chicago's 'L' trains zoomed overhead. But this position would give me the perfect glimpse of him when he broke from the horde, his shoulders squared with aggression and his body pressed so close to the bike he might as well be fucking it. God, the man was a fearless, panty-soaking badass in black leather.

The rowdy hoots and cranking throttles escalated, followed by the distinct purr of his 999 cc inline-4. My thighs tightened around the frame of the bike as I strained my neck, searching for a gap in the press of chrome and leather.

Something shifted at the edge of my periphery. My hackles raised, and I jerked my head.

A hand swung out from behind and caught my throat. A huge, calloused hand with jabbing fingers, clamping down, threatening my airway.

My pulse spiked as I grabbed at my neck and lunged to the side, jerking away. But the hand held me immobile, tightening. I gasped, clawing at the fingers. Fuck me, this couldn't be happening. Shock chilled my blood as my gaze flew to the key in the ignition. I reached for it.

"Don't move." A masculine voice to match the strength of his grip.

Keep your cool. Don't freak out. My chest rose and fell with the heave of my lungs. I was freaking the fuck out. "What do you want?" A squeak.

His hand clamped harder as he shifted to stand before me. Wrinkles indented his bald head. Sleeveless leather jacket, rugged jeans, and faded ink on his neck and arms, he sported the standard uniform for this scene.

His soaring height and broad shoulders blocked my view of the street. His cryptic smile drained the blood from my face, leaving a tingling chill in my cheeks.

The gun in my waistband grew heavy. Could I draw it and flick off the safety before he disarmed me? I lowered my fists to my lap and swallowed around the vise of his fingers. "Let me go."

His hard gaze flicked over the Ducati, my leather-clad legs, and lingered on my visor, squinting as if trying to see my face through the shield. "Nice bike. Titanium parts, programmable electronic sequential gearbox, carbon fiber gas tank? Shit, you've got what? A couple hundred G's in upgrades alone?"

So he wanted to rob me. A relief really, considering the alternatives. *If you survive this, buy a cheap damned bike and dress like a felon.*

My muscles trembled to hand over the bike. But rage drew my fingers around my hip, reaching for the gun.

His grip squeezed painfully hard and closed off my air. Blinding agony spread through my throat, burning my lungs. I grabbed with both hands, trying to pry away his fingers, my bulky gloves hindering my ability to latch on.

He raised his free hand and scratched the stubble on his jaw with a vicious-looking blade.

Oh God, I was in deep shit. "Help." My shout roared through my head, but it escaped without breath or sound. Time slowed as I focused on my laboring heartbeat and my desperate need for air.

Surely, he wouldn't kill me. I couldn't die silently, right here, where hundreds of people gathered just yards away.

But my hiding spot was too deep inside the alley, smothered in darkness. *So damned stupid, Kaci.*

The crowd was engaged in the race, screaming and cheering, with their backs to us. Not that they could've heard me over the thunder of all those engines and the passing trains above.

Black spots swarmed my vision. My helmet grew heavy, constricting, my feet kicking the pavement.

He glanced over his shoulder and back to me, deep grooves rutting his bald head. "Scream all you want. No one will hear you." He loosened his grip but didn't let go.

I sucked in rapid, painful breaths, my fingers gripping his, and choked, "I'll step off the bike." *And reach for my gun.* "Key's in the ignition. Take it." *So I can put a bullet in your skull, motherfucker.*

He stepped back to give me room, but as I slid off the seat, he didn't release my neck and instead used it to shove my back against the wall of the building. "What's a rich little thing like you doing in a place like this all alone?"

The sirens grew louder, closer, and I clung to that sound with my pulse in my throat. "Cops are coming." I kicked out a boot and collided with his shin.

He grunted, and in a blink, we became a kicking, shoving tussle of arms and legs. I yanked at the fingers on my throat and reached for the gun at my back. But he pinned me with his weight and trapped my hand between my back and the wall.

I whipped my helmet forward and crunched his nose. He roared and slammed a knee into my thigh, forcing my legs apart. I wound up pressed against the wall, one hand yanked high up my back and the cold steel of his blade against my throat.

My free hand wrapped around his wrist, trying to stay the weapon that was an impulse away from cutting me. Police sirens rang out one maybe two blocks away. I closed my eyes, opened them. "You're out of time, Baldy."

He laughed. "The cops have enough going on out there"—he nodded to the street—"to keep them occupied for a while."

Fuck, he was right. Soon, they would be chasing bikes all over the city. How long would it take for a squad car to shine a light into this alley?

Too long. I bucked beneath him, screaming and thrashing uselessly, panting with noisy breaths. *Jesus, calm down.* I loosened my hold on his wrist and relaxed my fingers. Deep inhale. Exhale.

"We're going to walk toward that door." He thrust his chin toward the back of the alley.

A door? The realization had been there, but now it bathed my core in ice. He wasn't here for my bike. Fear gathered in my throat, and it felt way too much like a sob. Not good, not good, oh holy fuck, not good.

The growl of passing motorcycles ricocheted through the alley, but I couldn't turn my head to look at the street. The race must've ended. Everyone was fleeing.

My exhales came hot and fast, stifling the interior of the helmet. "Where does the door go?" A crowded bar? A secluded hallway? *Please let it be a bar.*

He ground his pelvis against my hip, his erection shooting my pulse into overdrive. "A garage. My car. Let's go."

My hands shook, one wrapped around his wrist, the other pinned to my back, inches from the gun. If he disarmed me and I stepped into his car, I was dead. I twisted against his weight, each jerk sliding the blade over my throat.

The rumble of another passing bike sounded close, really close, but I still couldn't turn my head. The burn of steel cutting the vulnerable spot beneath my chin watered my eyes and gritted my teeth.

My knuckles grazed the butt of the gun. Would he shove the blade in if I moved my arm? I would have to be quick. I jerked my hand.

A fist shot out from my left, slamming into Baldy's jaw and dislodging the knife.

My hand went for my throat, the other for my gun, as he sprawled across the ground and cupped his nose. Blood spurted between his fingers, his wide-eyed glare locked on the blur lunging at him again. A blur of long, lean, enraged masculinity.

The owner of the unerring fist moved with lethal ferocity, black leather encasing the hard lines of his body. A body I'd recognize anywhere.

I didn't blink, didn't breathe, afraid I'd miss the black helmet, black boots, and lightning-fast fist that was now pounding the ever-loving shit out of Baldy's face. I was dreaming, and oh sweet Jesus, what an exquisite dream.

Wake up.

I shook myself from the paralyzed stupor and drew the .40 cal from my back, flicked off the safety, and strode toward the wrestling bodies.

Sirens screamed past the alley, the roar of motorcycles vibrating the ground and bellowing in my ears. Baldy lay on his back, swinging his fists and nailing shots on Evader's stomach, ribs, and throat.

My pulse rushed past my ears, and the gun shook in my hands. I lined up the sights and aimed the barrel at Baldy's bloody face. "Hands above your head."

I cringed at my quivering voice, but I *did* know how to use a gun. Collin and I shot targets at the range a few times a year. And fuck, I *wanted* to apply what I'd practiced.

Baldy raised his arms and interlaced his fingers on his head. Yeah, he'd done this before.

Evader knelt over him, his strength visible in the stretch of the jacket over his back and shoulders. His helmet cocked, angled in my direction. "I had this."

Oh my God, his voice. Okay, it was definitely synthesized, his timbre humming with an electronic overlay, but it was deep and gravelly and so goddamned sexy.

Pull yourself together, Kaci. He was far more dangerous than the man who just attacked me.

"Get out of here." I nodded to the street behind me, and as if on cue, another squad car zoomed by. "I'll hold him until you're gone."

What was I saying? I didn't want him to leave.

I thought I heard a chuckle, but couldn't be sure with the whine of sirens and exhaust pipes. He looked back at Baldy, swung an arm, and knocked him out. Damn. Okay, that worked too.

I lowered the gun. "You won the race?"

"Of course." He rose and erased the distance between us in three strides.

My nerves shivered, overloaded and amped up, and oh God, he was just standing there, heating the air around me, staring at me. What did he want? I opened my mouth to spew a gushing *thank you.*

He snatched the gun from my hand.

What the? "Give that ba—"

He lifted my chin and stroked a gloved finger over the nicks on my throat. Each caress irritated the cuts, but I didn't want him to stop. He raised the finger in front of my visor, blood soaking the leather tip. "Have you learned your lesson?"

His voice reverberated through me, and my knees weakened. Even with the electronic distortion, he sounded pissed.

My heart panted, and a throb swelled, hot and needy, between my legs. All because of a pissed-off synthesized voice? I might've just swallowed my self-respect, but I couldn't help it. My body had one mission, and that mission vibrated against me like he wanted to tear me in half. Damn me to hell, but my inner muscles clenched at the thought.

I touched my throat and flinched at the bite of pain. "It's just a scratch."

The reflection of my helmet in his visor wavered as he shook his head. He gazed down on me as if he were…considering something? God, I wished I could see his face, his eyes.

His finger returned to my throat, trailed a path beneath my chin, lifting it and catching on the edge of the helmet. He tugged it, like he wanted to rip off the shield and see my eyes, too. "Get on your bike, sweetheart."

He flicked the safety on the gun and gripped my shoulders, turning my body to face the bike. Both bikes. His and mine side-by-side. Oh, how I loved the sight of that.

His fingers touched my hip, slipping beneath my jacket to stroke my bare skin. I trembled against the brush of his glove, until he opened his mouth. "This is your last race."

The temperature in my helmet rose by ten degrees, and my cheeks inflamed. I glared at him over my shoulder. "Excuse me?"

Smack. A stinging jolt of fire rippled over my ass, and I shuffled forward. He fucking hit me! I placed my hands on the bike's seat, and unbidden, a grin took hold of my face. He fucking *spanked* me.

His hands returned to my hips, lifting the hem of the jacket. Then he wriggled the gun beneath my waistband. "Go."

More sirens filled the street. Shit. I hurried onto the bike and started the engine. Beside me, he straddled his BMW S1000RR and fired it up.

I rolled forward to the mouth of the alley and looked back. He hadn't moved, his helmet pointed toward me, his body upright and still.

My chest tightened. I wasn't ready to say good-bye. What if this was the only encounter we ever had?

"You coming?" I shouted over the pipes. The image of him *coming* curled my lips into an immature, hopeful, and probably goofy-as-hell smile. Good thing he couldn't see it.

He studied me for a heated moment then lowered into a tuck against his bike and yelled, "After you. You can count on it."

My smile stretched so far across my face, it hurt. I mirrored his lean, opened the gas, and squealed into the street.

Blue and red lights filled my vision on all sides. Most of the cops were in the process of detaining bikers, but several cruised up and down the perimeter. Like the one that just pulled in behind us.

I gave it more gas and tore away, Evader right on my tail. The Ducati had a faster top-speed than his BMW, but I didn't have the balls to push it over 200 mph. Even now, our 160 mph speed scared the bejesus out of me. I half-expected him to pass me, but as the flashing lights faded behind us, we fell into a steady clip with me in the lead.

Adrenaline surged through my bloodstream as we blew through red lights and zipped the wrong way on one-way streets, weaving around traffic and narrowly missing oncoming cars. Breaking all these laws might've exploded my heart if I were alone, but having him with me, trusting he had my back, it was crazy liberating.

In fact, I kind of hoped he would try to pass me so I could show him the top speed of my bike.

A few minutes later, I veered onto the freeway. Figured it was the best way to escape the traps of downtown streets.

But where to now? Would he follow? Hope fluttered in my belly, and my limbs tingled. I didn't know what I was hoping for exactly. To see his face? Fat chance. To hear his voice again? Yes, please. To fuck with our helmets on? Awkward, but I'd take it.

Watching his headlights in my side mirrors, I stayed on 290 until Ashland Ave and turned north toward Union Park. Plenty of baseball diamonds, tennis courts, unlit corners in the playground...yeah, unlit corners.

I swear, I hadn't smiled this much since that time Collin secretly filmed Donny McKnight, my high school crush, taking a shower in the locker room. Damn, that boy had a tight ass.

When I reached Union Park, I slowed to a stop in an empty parking lot beside the basketball courts. Evader slid in beside me, and I struggled to keep my breathing at a normal tempo.

His long legs braced on either side of his bike, and his gloved hands rested on his knees. He didn't speak, simply watched me from an arm's length away. It was surreal to be this close to him. How many people saw him outside of the races? Who was he when he wasn't shrouded in black and straddling a bike? And the question every woman in the city wanted answered? Was his face as viciously sexy as his body?

He rolled his neck on his shoulders and flexed his fingers. "Got a name?"

God, that voice. I bit the tip of my tongue as heat bloomed between my legs. "Yeah. You?"

"I've got a couple." He lifted a boot, resting it on his frame slider, and perched a forearm on his knee. The movement brought his helmet so, so close to mine. "Why are you here, rich girl? All alone with a known felon? What do you want?"

The better question was, why would he follow someone like me? What did *he* want? I should feel him out, play the brazen hussy I was sure he was used to dealing with.

I leaned over my bike and propped my elbows on the gas tank, stretching out my body for his eyes. "I pegged you for a fuck-first, ask-questions-later kind of guy."

His low, digitized chuckle sizzled my pleasure centers as he leaned his head back, revealing a shadow of stubble beneath the strong lines of his jaw. When his helmet lowered, he reached out and trailed gloved fingers along the back of my thigh, around my ass, my hip, then repeated the caress, slowly, torturously.

The angle of his helmet followed the shape of my body and the movement of his hand, the exploration lighting up my insides with an electric buzz. Did he like what he saw? My breath quickened. Did he want to see more?

He leaned closer, hooked a finger under my chin strap, and dragged my helmet toward his. "Show me your face."

I shivered at the demand in his deep, electronic voice. "You first."

As a hunted man, he had a lot more riding on the safety of incognito than I did. *If* he was willing to trust me with his identity—a big desperate *if* here—I'd return the favor. He didn't know where I lived and probably wouldn't recognize my face.

But what if he *did* recognize me? Seeing how he avoided the media and how my family owned the largest multimedia conglomerate in the world…yeah, those technicalities wouldn't win me a hard ride on his cock.

He released my chin strap, and for a dizzying second, I thought he would reach for his helmet. But his head jerked toward the street, and his back straightened. In the span of several heartbeats, the warning chirp of a police siren pierced the quiet.

Fuck my life. I clutched the grips, ready to jet, but he grabbed my thigh and squeezed. He stared straight ahead—at the tree line?—the heat from his hand seeping through two layers of leather. What were we waiting for?

When he let go of my leg, he rattled off detailed directions, which streets to take, which ones to avoid, an ass-backward way to return to the interstate. "Do not deviate. Do not slow." He smacked the back of my helmet. "Go."

"What about you?" Jesus, did I sound desperate or what?

"Right behind you." Promise silkened his tone.

I took off, veering between two squad cars, and followed his directions. His headlights bobbed in my side mirrors, but after several blocks, he fell behind. My heart thudded dully in my chest, disappointment creeping around my throat. He stayed with me until the freeway, but after a few miles, I lost him to the flow of traffic.

The achy weight of rejection sank in my stomach. I didn't want to acknowledge it. Just because I couldn't see him, didn't mean he'd slipped away.

Patrol cars filled the freeway, zipping by in both directions, sirens blaring. Dammit, I'd forgotten to put my license plate back on. I hunched my shoulders and maintained the speed limit.

With every mile I put behind me, I glanced less and less at the side mirrors. The hard knot in my gut told me he wasn't back there and hadn't been for a while.

It was better this way. I could go home, hide in my room, and figure out how I was going to explain the cuts on my neck to Collin. I needed to confront the *could've's* and *would've's* surrounding the attack in the alley. I needed to face the possibility that tonight was my last race.

But not because Evader had spanked me and issued that order.

A wave of heat tingled through my thighs. Okay, that was totally why.

I inhaled deeply. I was *not* going to go home and obsess about him. He'd asked me what I wanted, and I would've said *him*. But for one night? What about tomorrow? And the night after that?

A twinge pinched my chest. What I wanted I couldn't have. The wife of a well-known commentator shacking up with a well-known felon? That had scandal written all over it.

Fifteen minutes and several laps around Trump Tower later, I was certain he hadn't followed me. I swiped my security badge at the garage entrance and parked in my designated spot two floors down.

Shuffling toward the elevator, I removed my gloves, tucked them in my pockets, and reached for the buckle on my chin strap.

A hum vibrated the air, growing closer, louder. Reverberations crackled over the concrete and shook my legs. I knew that sound, could feel its familiar growl liquefy every cell in my body.

The world slowed down as the glossy black fairings of a S1000RR emerged at the top of the ramp and stopped. Engine idling, my pulse skipping, his black boot lowered to the ground.

Crouched low, shoulders forward, he rolled gloved hands on the grips. An electric charge gathered around him, galvanizing with expectation, as his dark helmet locked in my direction.

My breaths rushed out, thrilled and delirious. He'd followed me.

I stopped breathing. Oh fuck, *he'd followed me.*

How? Shit, how had he raised the secured garage door? A shiver tore up my spine. Now he knew where I lived.

Oh God, what have I done?

The rev of his motorcycle split the air, the throaty growl rendering me immobile. Its echo ripped through the cavernous space of the garage, muddling the indecision gripping my muscles. The thrilling prospect of him being here tingled my face even as fear thundered through my veins.

Run? Wise choice. He didn't know my identity, didn't know which floor I lived on. About a dozen running steps and I could slip into the elevator before he made it down the ramp.

But my boots stuck to the concrete as the glare of his helmet bore into me, drowning me in his intention to chase. I stood in the cross-hairs, grateful to be standing really, considering how badly my legs trembled.

Of all the gorgeous women in Chicago, why me? Why would he pursue one faceless woman? I mean, sure I kept my body in shape and I knew how to tear up a street on the Ducati, but for a guy as secretive as he was…what was he here for? Maybe it was the chase that got him off?

Widening my stance, I raised my chin and met his stare head on. I wanted him to see I could handle him. Wanted him to lean on the throttle and burn away the distance between us. I wanted him to pursue me for all the irrational, menacing reasons that should've had me drawing the gun from my back.

The gun he'd placed there with bold, seductive fingers.

What kind of man follows an armed woman home and breaks into her secured garage?

The kind who fucked as dangerously as he lived.

I shuddered, and a warm pulse awoke between my legs. Evidently, my self-preservation had reached an unrecoverable level of failage.

Another rev of his engine, and he zoomed down the ramp. The

sudden bolt of the bike unlocked my feet. I shuffled backward, toward the elevator.

He parked beside the Ducati and killed the engine as my back hit the elevator doors. My hand crept over the wall, half-heartedly seeking the up button.

Guards monitored the security cameras. Any moment, a resident could motor by. Maybe they'd recognize him all decked out in his racing leathers. Maybe they wouldn't. He didn't seem to care.

With silent steps, he stalked toward me. I might've given up my search for that button. I was kind of distracted by the way his leathers stretched over his thighs and cupped the very masculine bulge between his legs. The way he slid off his gloves, finger by finger, and tucked them into the pocket of his jacket. The way his helmet never shifted its focus from me.

His casual gait radiated control, the kind of effortless power that breathed around confident men. His aura was potent and far-reaching, apparently, because I had a heck of a time breathing through its effects.

A few strides away, his altered voice reached my ears. "—not having this conversation. Three feet now. Do you have her RFID?"

What did RFID mean? I shook my head. "What are you talking about?"

Reducing the final steps between us, he spoke so low I had to concentrate to hear him. "Cameras down?"

My gaze flew over the garage ceiling. Yeah, there were cameras, but what the hell? He wasn't holding a cell phone. Was he talking to himself?

He slid a thin flashlight into his pocket. Where had that come from?

I deserted my search for the button. Going up was no longer an option, not if he planned to join me. "Who are you talking to?" I asked, more like a command.

His approach didn't stop until his chest bumped my helmet and my back pressed against the elevator doors. "Good. Hang tight." He reached up and pushed a thumb against the underside of his helmet.

I narrowed my eyes. Was his gear James Bondified with a comm device? Did that kind of technology even exist? "What did you just touch under there?" I reached for his helmet.

His hand caught mine, skin-on-skin, and guided it to the button on the wall. No amount of tugging could deter him. On the heels of the attack in the alley, I should've been screaming and kicking, but this man had protected me. He was a law breaker, but I didn't think he'd shove a blade against my throat.

When our fingers pressed the beveled edge, I let my helmet rest against the doors. "What are you doing?"

"Going up."

"No, you're not." For so many reasons. One, he was a criminal. Two, he'd recognize Collin. If my association with the media didn't make him run, my marriage status would. Three…well, I forgot what three was, but four, *he was a criminal.*

I inhaled a steady breath to clear my flustered head. He could step into the elevator, but he didn't have a key card to make it move. Mine was zipped inside the pocket of my jacket, next to my phone.

Leather creaked as he shifted closer, and holy shit, he was hard all over. Like carbon-fiber-muscles hard. Electricity thrummed where the pillars of his thighs bracketed my legs, where his huge hand enclosed my fingers, and where his granite chest pinned my helmet to the doors.

Damn, Collin had been on to something. The strength surrounding me felt superhuman.

Those charged points of connection glued us together in a way that went beyond physical contact. They reached deep, stirring a feeling I'd always hoped existed but had never experienced.

The lub-dub lub-dub slam of my heart pulled me beneath the tide of reason where I floated, for just a moment, in whatever this was. Maybe his heart was as disoriented as mine? I wanted to remove the helmet, lay my cheek against his chest, and find out.

This was attraction. That was all. Long, pent-up, sexual attraction.

Ding.

The doors opened, but before I fell through, he hooked an arm around my waist and backed me in. I didn't fight him, way too curious about what he'd do next. And stupid. I should have my head checked.

The garage elevator never had an attendant, and the lift was empty. The doors shut, the walls closed in, and my pulse spiked. Christ, it was a small space, and he was so very *not small*, crowding the tiny enclosure and hijacking the air.

He hadn't looked this big on his bike. Not that he was body-builder big, but his shoulders mantled mine, and his torso curtained my vision. Strong, too, given the unmovable arm around my waist. Time to flip out.

I'd rather climb his tall, dark, and deadly frame and hump it like an animal. I bit my lip. *Real classy, Kaci.* My mother would be so proud.

He released my waist and removed a metal card from his pocket. Without the arm lock, I still felt restrained, pressed into the corner of the lift by his mere presence. Probably a good time for a reality check.

I closed my eyes, envisioning my usual elevator rides. Cold, empty, unfulfilled journeys to nowhere. When I glanced up, the man I'd mentally fucked for nine months was still there, in the flesh, staring down at me.

Dark and motionless. Goddamned unnerving.

Hard to breathe.

Still staring.

My chest constricted.

Tighter.

No air.

Shit.

"Why did you follow me?" Good lord, that came out breathy.

"We weren't done." He pivoted to face the panel of buttons.

Wow. Okay, that sounded delectably elusive, full of promise while telling me absolutely nothing. And what was he doing with that metal card? Wait. Important questions first. "Are you gay?" Because really, the odds had not been kind to me.

He lowered his hand and glanced back at me. "Are you?" He returned to the panel. "I can work with that if your girlfriend has an ass like yours."

Such a pervy, straight-guy response. My reckless heart rejoiced. "Married?"

His body froze from shoulders to shit-kickers. Uh oh. "If I were married," he bit out without turning around, "I would be at home, fucking my wife."

I frowned. My God, he was *offended.* The way he'd said it—*fucking my wife*—shoved a familiar ache against my ribs, the one that starved for his brand of aggressive, protective, fierce devotion. *And sexual attraction.* Damn him.

"What about you?" he asked. "Married?"

"No." Not in the intimate way, which was the only way that concerned him. It wasn't like this encounter would lead to dates at the opera and Christmas dinner with the family.

A rasp billowed through his helmet. "What's your deal with the races? You get off on bikers attacking you in dark alleys?"

I didn't like his accusing tone and didn't hide the snark in mine.

"Nah. It's just a complicated farce to explain my choice of evening wear." I gestured to my helmet and leathers, not that he was looking at me.

His head dipped toward the panel, revealing the tanned skin of his nape. My gaze followed the strong column of his neck to the shock of hair peeking out of his helmet. It was longer than a buzz cut but didn't reach his hairline. A shade between light brown and blond, the ends glinted with copper hues. Stunning.

Soundlessly, I stretched out a hand to brush my fingers against the strands, but before I made contact, his visor swiveled to look at me. *Interesting.*

Leaning around his broad frame, I watched him shove the metal card in and out of the card slot. "I don't know what you're trying to do, but this building has top-notch security."

Could he lock down the elevator with that thing? To keep us from being interrupted? Or was he trying to go up? He'd need my card to do that.

A foolish flutter took flight in my stomach. He'd followed me. He was clearly doing something to the elevator. Why wasn't I freaking out about this?

His hips shifted, and leather creased around the flex of his butt, outlining hard handfuls of muscle. I shouldn't have stared, it was rude, but I was spellbound. I loved the way his pants contoured his ass, embodying every fantasy I'd ever had. He only had to stand there, all tall and muscular and arrogant enough to keep his back to me, knowing I had a gun.

I liked the view so much I couldn't tear my eyes away. My fingers tingled.

"Are you staring at my ass?"

Jesus, did he have eyes in the back of his head? "What else am I going to look at?"

Abandoning the card slot, he turned and leaned his back against the wall. His wide stance and the lounge of his upper body tilted his pelvis just right. Leather molded around the raised ridge of his cock and strained to contain the brawn of his thighs.

My brain screamed *look away* while my body melted into a gawking blob of liquid heat.

He reached out and hooked a finger under the collar of my jacket, tugging me right up against the focus of my attention. He was so hard and thick I didn't just feel his length against my thigh. I felt his arousal everywhere.

His legs were long but so were mine, and our hips met in a grind of mutual need, verbalized by our simultaneous exhales. There wasn't a cell in my body that didn't shudder with thrilling pleasure.

The elevator had yet to move, but it grew smaller, the walls pushing me closer to this mysterious, tempting man. My breath rushed out in sharp bursts then quickened as his hands came down on my ass. The hard smack became a painful squeeze, one he used to force my body impossibly close to his.

His grip was neither gentle nor tentative. He held me against the steel trap of his body as if I had no say in what happened next. With a hand clenched against the crease of my butt and thigh, his other caught the back of my neck. His hold on my body was dominating, the aggressive stab of his length against my clit so damned erotic. Confident. Unapologetic. Perfect.

"Tell me, Miss Ducati"—the drag of his voice vibrated deep inside me—"will I find your pussy as tight as I've imagined it?"

I closed my fingers around his shoulders, struggling to control myself, the clenching between my legs unbearable. And he wanted to know how tight my pussy was?

Caged in the *V* of his thighs, his back to the wall, a hand on my neck, the other clutching my ass, I was restrained by muscle. His rock-solid grip wasn't letting me go anywhere, not that I wanted to.

The top of my helmet tapped his chin guard as we moved in a slide of leather. The sensual roll of his hips and the grind of mine built into the most torrid dry hump I'd ever experienced.

The fluorescent lights reflected off his black helmet, making his visor even more opaque. I had no idea who he was under there. Maybe that was part of the allure. A seductive mystery.

I slid my hands to his chest, the leather of his jacket surprisingly soft and thin, like velvet over brick. I traced the carved dips around his pecs, each muscle etched from stone, my fingertips buzzing with sensory-overload.

"If you're going to feel me up"—the hand on my neck slid to the snap at my collar and tugged roughly—"take off your jacket. It's only fair."

So fucking tempting. I wore only a thin shelf-bra cami underneath. I glanced at the panel of buttons, wondering if someone would call the elevator, hoping they wouldn't.

"Elevator's not going anywhere."

So he'd done something to it. Would the guards notice it was jammed and come to investigate? "How—"

"Invite me up." He yanked the zipper from my throat to waist, and his hips froze.

The sudden chill peaked my nipples against the fabric, his visor reflecting the curves of my cleavage. His hands clenched around my ribs, and his eyes… Good thing I couldn't see them because if they were smoldering, I might've internally combusted.

As it was, my skin inflamed, and my hand twitched to punch floor *88*. Invite him up? If he recognized Collin, discovered I was married, how would he react? Would he understand or use it against me?

Or I could text Collin, tell him to disappear, then sneak Evader into my room.

Ha! I dropped my helmet on his chest. How had I gone from responsible adult to slutty teenager in the blink of a few minutes? "I can't."

His hands wandered from my ribs to the gun at my back. I stiffened, breath caught in my throat, until he moved the gun to the pocket of my jacket. "You won't invite me up. Won't give me your name. Won't remove your helmet. What are you hiding?"

"Same things you are."

"I doubt that." He traced a finger along the front of my waistband, lingering on the button. A frustrating linger. But the best kind of frustrating. "Who *are* you?"

Oh, I'm only an executive at the largest multimedia conglomerate in the world. Is this a good time for a front page interview? "You mean, where does my money come from?"

"Sure."

I pushed his back against the wall, and his hands flew to my waist, dragging me into the bracket of his legs.

I reached for the zipper at his neck and slowly lowered it. "I lure notorious men into elevators and fuck them unconscious, all so I can steal their clothes and hock them as collector's items on Ebay."

"That so?" Despite the electronic dubbing, his voice had deepened into a graveled rumble.

"Mm hmm. How much would this jacket fetch in an auction?" I slid the zipper down, down—Oh God, no shirt, no chest hair—and lower still. I reached the end and pulled the jacket open, exposing a long stretch of naked torso. All that flesh so smooth and cut… Jesus, I wasn't sure how I'd walk away without smelling it, tasting it.

"Might have blood on the sleeve." He held up his arm. Sure enough, a dry stain darkened the cuff. "Increases the value, right?"

A reminder that he injured, maimed, and often killed during the races. *That* was the kind of man I was rubbing up against. But temptation was carved into his sexy-as-fuck body. I couldn't back away, couldn't fight it.

He was the only man who could arouse me and scare me in the

same breath, who could make my pulse thunder so ferociously I felt carelessly drunk. "Is that *your* blood?"

"Drago Carrara's."

The Italian racer he'd beat tonight. I followed his waistband from abs to spine, the pragmatic part of me looking for a gun or a blade while the throw-my-panties-to-the-wind part savored the feel of every muscled indentation that carved his hips. "Are you hiding a weapon?"

He grabbed my wandering hand, spun us until the wall caught my back, and oh my God, his grip pressed my palm against the steel bar between his legs. "Am I?"

I had no words. No, I was operating in a haze of lust. His fingers abandoned the button of my pants, traveled up my ribs, and before I realized his intent, he ripped my cami from neck to waist.

My breasts fell free, nipples hardening beneath the gaze of his visor. Then his hands were everywhere, a frenzied caress of skin on skin, of heat and want. He cupped and stroked, tracing every curve, his cock driving against my palm, his breath rushing out in sharp exhales.

Every touch, every thrust of his hips, made me even more needy, my mind fuzzy, lost in the feel of him. His fingerprints branded my skin, and the temperature in the elevator spiked from hot to atomic. I never wanted this moment to end.

How far could we take it? I didn't have condoms with me and doubted he'd carried any to the race. Didn't stop my mind from rushing to the desired conclusion. "STDs?"

"Presumptuous about where this is going, aren't we?"

I traced the curve of his erection, molding my fingers around its impossibly hard girth. "I'm holding some pretty damning evidence, Evader."

His hands curled around my neck, his thumbs trailing gently over the cuts. He held me like he wanted to kiss me. The kind of kiss that lasted for hours, the kind that would leave an eternal aftershock.

The kind of kiss that would unveil his eyes. Were they green or brown? Dark blue like mine? More importantly, would they give me a window into the man behind the mask? The man who'd risked his ass to save mine.

I swallowed against his touch, wanting that kiss. "I want to thank you for helping me in the alley." I reached for the strap beneath his chin.

He caught my hand and pulled it between our bodies, his other hand still wrapped around my neck. "Thank me by inviting me up."

Could he feel my pulse beating against my throat? I felt it everywhere, slamming through my arteries and jolting a throb through my clit. Heaven help me, I wanted to fuck the electronic vibrations out of his voice. I shook my head.

His body stiffened, his tone deepening. "Got someone waiting upstairs?"

Collin was probably seven inches deep inside Seth right now. Definitely not waiting. "No."

He relaxed, melting his weight against me. "All right." His thumb stroked the hollow of my throat. "We both have our secrets. Invite me up. We'll keep the lights off. Hell, we can keep our helmets on."

This man, my bed, in the dark? I'd let him blindfold me just so he'd remove his helmet. My hands would be my eyes, exploring his face, his mouth, every tantalizing inch of his chiseled body. I smoothed my palms over the ridges of his chest, stretching my fingers upward, past his collarbone.

His broad shoulders rolled against my touch, his skin warm and soft over packs of muscle. So much power in his arms, his sculpted chest and strong hands. I'd seen it all in the photos, barely confined by his leathers.

He wasn't a man women said no to. The way he carried himself, the way he fought. Built like a warrior, he knew how to manipulate torque and power between his legs. He knew what he could do with it, his killer instincts and quick reflexes, his silhouette so sleek and intimidating on his bike, now all hard and demanding pressed up against me. He knew how to get what he wanted.

"Let's go up." With a flick of his wrist, he freed the chin strap on my helmet.

Shit. I slapped my hands on top of my head to hold the helmet in place. "Sure, Stranger McDanger. I'll just give you the security code to my alarm while I'm at it and let you watch me while I'm sleeping. That sounds safe."

His hand swept down my throat, along my breastbone, and squeezed my tit. "You won't be sleeping." He pinched my nipple, hard enough to make my eyes water and my thighs tremble. "Think you're safer here than in your condo?"

"Nope. That's why silly innovations like security cameras are such a waste of money." With my hands on my helmet, I pointed a finger at the ceiling of the elevator.

"We'll do this here, then."

"This?" I mean, I knew what *this* was, had fantasized about it for months, but the elevator wasn't the place for a secret liaison.

"This." He shifted, his boots bracketing mine, and cupped a hand between my legs.

The squeak that left my mouth tumbled into a full-body moan as his fingers circled the clit piercing through my pants.

I rocked my hips against his hand as electric sparks lit up my body. I wanted it, wanted him, so very badly. His powerful shoulders, wide chest, the quickening of his breaths, the aggressive roll of his pelvis, the burnish of highlights glimmering his hair. All of it once a mystically-wrapped package now exposed and offered. I could take it, right now. Except… "Cameras."

"They're offline."

"That's…" I shook my head, my mind swimming through the unbelievability of it.

Was he lying? Not just anyone could walk into the Trump Tower and bring down its security network. It was too much. Like super-hacker, the government's-beaming-mind-control-rays-past-my-tinfoil-hat too much. Yet I knew he had something techie going on inside that helmet of his. While that added even more sexy to the whole growly-badass thing he had going on, it also meant he wasn't working alone.

"You were talking to someone in the garage. About the cameras?" I envisioned a van waiting outside on the curb, filled with a team of e-crime cyber nerds wearing headsets and thick-framed glasses. "Who?"

"How did you get access to the racing network?"

My throat closed up. Crap, I hadn't expected that question. As an executive at Trenchant, I knew too much about the races. I could broadcast the details, the grids, the racing times, all of it, and bring down the entire syndicate. How many people would try to kill me before that happened? How did I know there weren't people on my payroll who were members of the network? Watchers. Guardians.

If Evader discovered who I was, would *he* turn me over to the underground network? How loyal was he?

God, I sounded like a conspiracy nut, but I'd rather be paranoid than dead.

Actually, I'd rather be coming, because right now, his fingers were still rubbing my clit with maddening skill, making it damned hard to think. "I probably shouldn't tell you this, but I'm your next competitor, the racer you haven't defeated yet. Scared?"

A chuckle vibrated through his chest, the bionic accent giving it a dangerous edge. "There's no one I haven't defeated yet. But you race without clothes on, then yeah, you got a good chance of winning."

I released a soundless breath, thankful he hadn't pressed for the truth. He really did seem content with letting me keep my secrets.

Fingers slipped beneath the tight grip of my helmet. "Tell me your face is as intoxicating as your body." He wedged his hands around my jaw, his thumbs sweeping up and coming together on my lips. "What are you…twenty-five?"

Unsure how to answer, I lifted my shoulder, holding tight to my helmet. The compliment both warmed and worried me. I hadn't been twenty-five for twelve fucking years, and now I really didn't want him to know my age.

"Full lips," he murmured as a thumb pushed past my teeth and held down my tongue.

It was a dominating grip, an act of ownership, but not malicious. Which fit him well. Erotically so. Like the mold of his leathers.

I didn't release the hold on my helmet, but my God, this felt…right. How many men had I been with over the past two decades? Too many. Yet none had touched me, aroused me, or controlled me like this. And he did it with the pressure of his thumb.

The salty flavor of his skin fused with the scent of leather from the gloves he'd removed. He thrust in and out of my mouth, simulating the flex of his hips.

I sucked his thumb with hollowed cheeks, swirling my tongue and teasing a delicious moan from deep in his throat. Desire swelled between my belly button and spine, building into a knot and spreading low, lower, until my inner muscles ignited in mini-spasms.

I no longer gave a shit if he was lying about the cameras being down. I only cared about his fingers and where he would put them next.

"Fucking hell, that mouth." He moved his hands, closing his fingers around my neck. "What are you trying to do to me?"

I followed the *V* cut of his abs to the waistband of his pants. "Nothing near what I want to do."

He didn't stop me from freeing the button, didn't stay my hand as I grasped the zipper. His fingers mirrored my actions, yanking my pants to my thighs, only to find another layer of clothing.

In his hurry, he knocked my hand away from his zipper and gripped my leggings, the snug fit of cotton reluctant to slide past my hips. He seemed to give up on stripping me, his fingers shoving beneath the fabric, and with the absence of panties, sliding directly over my clit and the steel ring that adorned it.

"Jesus. Are you serious?" His modulated groan penetrated my chest as he worked his fingers. "Had it in my head you were a soulless Stepford bitch, sneaking away from a boring husband in the middle of the night. But this?" He pinched the piercing and used it to drive pressurized circles around my clit. "You're not a cookie-cutter rich girl, are you?"

I stifled a flinch. "Wow, I hope not." Some of what he'd said cut too close to my sensitive self-image. "You're kind of a dick for thinking it."

He laughed, and the complex sound magnified the tremors ricocheting through me. My legs turned to rubber. I fumbled for his zipper, bumping his erection and making his hips jerk against my hands.

With one arm braced on the wall, his head dipped toward me, knocking our helmets. We both groaned in frustration.

I reached into his pants, and the back of my hand brushed a trim patch of hair. I closed my eyes and breathed through my nose. Commando. Of course, he was. "Still won't remove your helmet?" I lowered his zipper and swallowed my next breath as his length jutted into my hands.

"Fuck." He leaned closer, trapping me, his fingers slipping inside me. "Yours first."

His touch swirled through my folds, slow at first, dragging along my inner walls. Then he accelerated his movements, sharpening into a savage pounding of fingers and flesh. Unyielding, intense, almost angry. I felt his reach so fucking deep. Waves of pleasure crashed through me, the wildness of it pouring from his skin and clipping his breaths.

The vicious thrusts of his fingers drove my back against the wall and my need way past go. His sturdy frame wrapped around me, his unfettered strength teasing my release closer, faster, then pulling back, only to start again.

My arousal slicked over his hand and down my inner thighs. My spine arched, and I closed my eyes, focusing on keeping my feet on the floor.

He fingered me to the edge of oblivion, over and over, arousing images of my knees on the ground, his fingers around my throat, and his powerful thighs bracketing my body, caging me in, controlling me.

Goosebumps rose across my chest, and a hum shook beneath my skin, trembling deeper, coiling inside me. Was it fear? Hunger? A collision of the two?

When I looked up, the answer was there. I felt it sliding over me, all six feet and endless inches of dark mystery and sexy confidence. The passion, the fire, the *something more* I would do anything for.

His hand slipped from my pants as I dropped to my knees, eye-level with his arousal. His wide length as glorious as it was intimidating, the broad, circumcised head drawing me closer, rushing saliva over my tongue. I placed a hand on my visor, a *fuck it all* away from shoving off my helmet.

If I kept my head down, loosened my hair around my face, would he see my features? If he did see me, maybe he wouldn't recognize me. Collin had the famous face, and unless Evader followed televised politics, he wouldn't know who I was. But without an investigation and a signed NDA, it was risky. He could blackmail me or leak our affair to the media, to my parents. Would he do that?

His fingers curled around the underside of my helmet. If I didn't remove it soon, he'd probably do it for me.

He used the grip to hold me an inch from his erection. "Do you want to stare at it or suck it?"

I held onto my helmet. "I don't know." I did, more than anything, but I hadn't thought this through. "I— I have a…career to protect."

"A career, huh? Beyond auctioning stolen merchandise?" His head jerked toward the metal card in the slot, and in the next heartbeat, every button on the panel lit up.

Blood drained from my face. "How did you—" Oh my God, he had access to every floor. "That's how you got through the garage door?"

"That was luck. Slipped in behind a Bentley."

Yeah, that didn't make me feel any safer. I started to stand, but his hands came down on mine, holding my helmet, and my body, in place. My heart pounded. "What are you going to do?"

He swiped a finger over his jaw—or along the edge of his helmet?—the movement done with blurring speed. "Yes."

"Yes? That's not an answer. Who are you talking to, dammit?"

His warm hands squeezed mine, using his hold to tilt my head back. "You want to wrap your mouth around my cock?"

The hard, heavy weight between us brushed against my exposed neck, coaxing a breathy rasp from my lips. "Yes."

"You want to keep your face hidden?"

"Yes."

He looked at the panel, his hands restraining the motion of my helmet. The floor dug into my knees, and my nerves volleyed between worry and excitement. He seemed to be waiting for something, and as the seconds passed, my worrying was winning out.

"What are—"

The overhead lights powered off, as did the panel of buttons. Pitch-black flooded the elevator. I blinked, shock locking my limbs as my breaths tumbled noisily through the dark.

"Does this resolve our dilemma?" His voice echoed around me, shivering my insides.

"Yes."

"Yes. The answer to all of life's problems." Despite my grip, he yanked off my helmet and dropped it beside my knees.

Cool air tingled my cheeks as I jerked my chin to my chest, my shoulders bunching around my face. With the total absence of light, he couldn't see me, and I couldn't see him, but sweet Lord, I could smell him. Leather, a hint of soap, and the natural scent of his skin guided me toward his straining cock.

I kept my head down, gripped the hard muscles of his bare ass, and rubbed my cheek against his arousal. Pulsing heat gathered between my legs as my face and lips explored the steel of his cock wrapped in warm, satiny skin.

His hands slapped against the metal wall above me, his length growing harder, hotter against my mouth. With an eager lick, I swirled my tongue around the tip, the salty drip of pre-cum smearing over my lips.

He groaned, low and guttural, and his legs trembled beneath my arms. "Look at me."

How did he know where I was looking? And why did he care? So he could turn the elevator back on? Or shine some kind of lamp— Shit! Didn't he have a flashlight in his pocket?

Head down. Don't look up. I curled my fingers around his length and drew him into my mouth. After a few teasing suckles, a nip of teeth, and a caress of his heavy balls, I dug in my nails and squeezed his sac.

He shouted, but it was thick with arousal and rumbled into a moan as I swallowed the full length of him. When he hit the back of my throat, I balled my left hand, squeezing my thumb, a trick to disable my gag reflex.

How long had it been since I'd done this without a condom? I didn't care. Hell, I wanted to drag my tongue over every inch of his unwrapped body. I wriggled my head back and forth, rubbing his cock against the back of my throat.

His body shook, and his ass flexed in my hand. I fucking loved it, loved that I could affect him as much as he affected me.

Jesus, he was so thick, the head of his cock cut my air, watering my eyes. My throat wanted to convulse, but I tightened my fist, eased back a little, and breathed through it.

The sounds of his sharp, uneven inhales surrounded me. I sucked harder, faster, letting saliva trickle out so I could slide my fist through it, pumping with a tight grip around the head and lapping at the tip.

"Goddamn, I can't…ff-fuuhh—" His words garbled into something inaudible, smothered by gasps.

He grasped the base of my braid, slid his hand to the rubber-band, and looped the tail around and around his wrist. The follicles bit at my scalp when he ran out of hair, his hold tightening against my head.

Bucking his hips, his movements staggered. He was close. I renewed my efforts, sucking with hard pulls, bringing him closer, closer, but I wouldn't let him come. Not yet—

He yanked my head back by the braid. His cock slipped from my mouth, and I stared up into the dark expanse above me.

His breathing stopped. His body went rigid. The silence was deafening.

Dread crawled over me. I couldn't explain it, but something was wrong.

He untwisted his wrist from my hair, yanking in his haste to disentangle it. "Put your helmet on." His biting tone sped up my pulse.

"What's wrong? What happened?"

The sound of his zipper reached my ears with painful finality. A lump crept into my throat as I fumbled for the helmet. When I found it, I shoved it on and climbed to my feet, righting my pants. Had I done something to piss him off? Maybe he heard someone on the other side of the doors?

As I retraced the last few seconds, the lights flickered on and the doors opened.

No one was waiting in the garage. He removed the metal card and darted out as if he couldn't get away from me fast enough.

No explanation or good-bye. Not even a backward glance or a *fuck you.*

I zipped up my jacket, my chin quivering with shock and rejection.

Maybe I stupidly hoped he'd come right back. Or maybe I wasn't ready to confront the emotion burning up my cheeks, but I reached for the button to hold the doors open.

That was when I noticed it, one button in particular, the only one lit up.

88. My floor.

My face caught fire, and my fists clenched. All that time, he had access to my condo? Not only did he know where I lived, he had a fucking key to get in.

My heart stopped, my breath strangling. If he knew my floor, did that mean he knew who I was?

I did the only thing I could. I ran after him.

10 LOGAN

If Benny would've wired x-ray vision in the helmet like I'd asked, I would've discovered Kaci Baskel's identity in the alley. I would *not* have followed her, wouldn't have resorted to night vision *after* her mouth was wrapped around my cock. Fuck!

Anger fueled my steps, and my fists burned to smash something. What the hell was I thinking? I'd been clumsy, careless, and now…

My teeth slammed together. I was so goddamned hard. My dick throbbed in its leather trap, aching to punish her deceitful mouth until she choked, to pound her ass until she couldn't walk.

Losing control, dickhead. Pull your shit together.

"Speaker on." My quiet command unmuted the cellular connection with Benny. So much easier than pressing the button beneath the helmet. "Need an update."

"First off," she growled through the speaker, "I wasn't done configuring the settings on the master key before you ripped it out of the elevator."

My fists clenched. Yeah, I knew my mistake as soon as I'd removed it and the single button for the eighty-eighth floor lit up. Benny had warned me about that, since the device replicated the nearest key card, but I hadn't been thinking straight. Still wasn't.

Tension tightened my face, pulling on my jaw. Dammit, I hadn't wanted Miss Ducati to know I could sneak into her condo, not before I knew who she was and certainly not now that I knew she was Kaci Baskel. I also didn't want to explore *why* I'd intended to trespass. "What else?"

"Trump security just found my hack on an encrypted channel." She groaned. "Crap, cameras are back up."

Shit. Benny dominated cryptography, but even the best hackers could be bested. She was just one person, working alone, so she relied on technologies already developed, hacking and cloning them. Like the facial and license plate recognition software. Casinos had been using that shit for years. She simply borrowed it. Same way she'd remotely borrowed the codes on the RFID key card in Kaci Baskel's pocket.

Goddammit, it all made sense, the reason she wouldn't show her face or give me her name, why she wouldn't invite me up. Thankfully, I'd muted the connection in the elevator. Benny hadn't been able to hear or see just how close I'd come to fucking Kaci.

I lengthened my strides, zipping up my jacket and pulling the flashlight from my pocket.

"Logan, you're coming up on a—"

"I fucking know where the cameras are." I aimed the flashlight, shining the beam at the eye of the lens mounted on the ceiling.

The high-powered light would blind the camera's sensor as I passed. The helmet concealed my face, but my attire was recognizable. I didn't need an outbreak of surveillance footage advertising Evader's visit to Trump Tower. And now that I knew who lived here, I definitely didn't need Evader associated with Trenchant.

My stomach hardened into a painful knot. She was no longer the mysterious Ducati woman I looked for after every race. She was one of *them*. A top executive. Daughter of murderers. *Wife* of the enemy.

Venom tunneled through my gut. My blood boiled, and my lungs labored for air. I'd never felt anything like this…this overwhelming surge of emotion, but it was undeniable, sinister, fucking cruel in its assault.

She'd let me stick my fingers in her cunt, my fucking dick in her mouth, and she belonged to another man. Sweat gathered beneath my jacket and slicked my hands. *Not just any man.*

Collin Anderson was the celebrated face of Trenchant, the son of a powerful family. Did that mean he was as evil as his parents? How could he not be strategically tied to their corruption?

I had no evidence of his guilt or his innocence, which angered me as much as the notion that she would slide into bed beside him tonight wet with arousal that had been stimulated by another man. *By me.*

"Seriously, Logan," Benny grumbled. "What were you thinking?"

"Piss off," I snapped, jerking the light at the next camera, my head dizzy, my jaw locked.

All I could see was a thick braid of blonde, bright eyes, and an ethereal face. A face that had threatened to bring me to my knees in the elevator. I hadn't needed to look at the photo that flashed on my visor, didn't need to read the name displayed by the facial recognition software.

The moment the night vision illuminated the arches of her cheekbones, the gentle slope of her nose, her heart-shaped lips, I knew. I knew every graceful line and curve etching her features and framing her huge, devastating eyes. Eyes that had blazed green through the infrared scope, but under a normal lens were vivid blue, as rich and complex as sapphires.

I'd tracked her public appearances on the Interwebs for eight years, watched those eyes mature with age, darken with secrets, and harden with lies. Her hair always smoothed back in a pretentious coil on her head, her curves hidden behind prim suits and high necklines. An effigy of sexy, untouchable wealth.

The online photos hadn't come close to capturing what I'd gazed down on in the elevator. Even with her hands on my ass and her mouth hovering over my cock, she had the kind of regal allure that couldn't be replicated in magazines or on screen. When she'd stared up at me, her braid had been an unraveling mess of seduction, her beauty bare of make-up, staggering, haunting.

A headache erupted behind my eyes. I passed another camera and angled the flashlight as Benny's voice crackled through the speaker. "Tell me you didn't put your dick—"

"*My* dick, *my* fucking business." The malice in my tone whipped through the garage, but I didn't want to hear her goddamned ragging or the pangs of truth in it.

I wasn't ready to regret the full-body bliss that had been Kaci Baskel. Her sharp wit, the heavy weight of her tits, the grip of her cunt, her sinful mouth, all assets in her seduction that'd had me demanding an invitation to her bed. I would've fucked her with my helmet off, my mouth on her lips, my cock jerking inside her, entwined in the dark.

Stupid, knowing her connections, but I still ached to fuck her. And *that*, I would regret. I could never forget who she was.

My pulse elevated and my ears roared as the stunning, blonde source of my anger pounded the concrete ten feet behind me. I needed to erect some un-fucking-friendly walls by the time she caught up and keep all the other shit locked down until I got out of there.

Holding the beam on the final camera, I stepped between the

bikes and removed a button-sized tracking device from my pocket. Same tracker I slapped on her helmet in the park. The one I peeled off when I removed her helmet in the elevator. I hadn't wanted to lose her when we bolted from the park, and I didn't want to lose her now, though the reasons had changed.

Shifting my body to block her view of my hand, I wedged the tracker between the windshield and dashboard of her Ducati. I snapped my hand back just as she was sweeping past me.

She slammed to a stop on the other side of her bike and bent over it, likely checking to see if I'd tampered with it. Her leathers were straightened and zipped, but I knew what was beneath. A ripped tank top. Hard nipples. Drenched panties. Fuck.

Her visor locked with mine, no doubt hiding a glare to match her rigid stance. "What did you just do?"

Something I should've done years ago. I'd never thought to track her, had always been focused on her parents. She was the second phase of my plan. The part where I would walk into Trenchant, force them to hire me, and name me the new CEO, all in order to oversee her activities, as well as all the other dirty ties at Trenchant Media.

I didn't give a shit about the job, but the top-level access would make it easier to string together all the loose ends. Until then, I didn't know if Kaci was included in my plans to destroy Trenchant. It wasn't like I was gunning to destroy her, but I couldn't help but lump her in with the rest of her vile family.

Flashlight aimed in one hand, I straddled my bike.

She moved to my side, fists on her hips, helmet cocked at the beam of light. "What are you doing with that?"

"Ignore her," Benny barked.

I held the light and shoved my key in the ignition, attempting a brush-off, but my mouth moved anyway. "The light washes out the cameras."

"Good." Kaci lowered her arms and nodded. "That's good."

Yeah, wouldn't want her husband to find out she was a cheating, fucking whore. I fired up the bike, the engine spitting a growl between us.

"Wait." She held out her hand, palm up. "I want that metal thing."

"Need to go, Logan," Benny said with urgency. "Guards will be checking on that elevator any minute."

I didn't respond, didn't want Kaci to question, *again*, who I was talking to.

"I don't know what happened back there." Kaci shoved her raised palm an inch from my chest. "Or what made you run, but you can't have a key to my condo." She shook her hand at me. "Whatever that thing is, hand it over."

That *thing* was an RFID reader, and from three feet away, it transmitted the security codes from her key card. Codes that Benny hacked to control the power in the elevator. And this wisp of woman was out of her mind to think she could demand anything from me.

"No." I raised the kickstand with my boot and backed up the bike.

She walked alongside, her hand reaching out and gripping my bicep. "Why?"

Her voice was soft, almost too soft beneath the din of the bike, but I'd been listening for it, fucking straining to hear her. Worse, I couldn't bring myself to jerk away from her touch.

"Logan," Benny shouted. "Slap the bitch and burn rubber."

I slammed my teeth together and stopped the roll of the bike. I'd forgotten Benny could hear both sides of the conversation.

Keeping the flashlight leveled, I reached up, hit the button, and killed the connection. To Kaci, I said, "I'm not giving you shit."

Her hand tightened on my arm. "I meant, why are you acting like this? What did I do?"

Seriously? I clamped my fist on the handlebar's grip. She should be asking her husband that question. Of course, she didn't know I knew she was married. Hell, maybe she didn't care. Fidelity wasn't exactly a trait that ran in the family.

She straightened her back, standing taller beside me. Her helmet tipped down, her thick rope of hair curling around one breast, taunting me.

I needed to shut her down and deliver a direct punch that would persuade her to forget all about Evader. "You give lousy head."

Her hand jerked away and clutched at her stomach. "Liar."

Christ, the hurt in her voice tightened my chest. I should tell her to go fuck herself and convince her I was a belligerent asshole. Which I was. Because her mouth had damned near destroyed me. She didn't just know how to suck my cock, she'd fucking owned it.

And she knew it.

What she didn't know was, during that dark, heated moment in the elevator, I'd seen her face. I knew her identity, her family, and all their dirty little secrets.

Without warning, her hand shot out and gripped my balls, her thumb pressing against the stiff proof of my lie. "The truth, Evader." The sad desperation in her tone clashed with the angry clutch of her fingers.

"Remove your fucking hand." *Grip me. Jerk it hard.*

She tightened her grasp, shooting a flood of heat through my cock. She had me by the balls, and in what was clearly a moment of insanity, I fucking loved it.

I hated her for that, for making me want her, which inflamed the urge to demean her, to call her a slut, to tell her I knew she was an unfaithful wife. She deserved the full wrath of every searing thought, every pound of forbidden pleasure she'd ignited.

But from her standpoint, Evader didn't know who she was, and it would stay that way. I didn't want her questioning how I knew or anything about the technology I used. I needed her to forget about Evader altogether.

I grabbed her wrist and used it to force her back. "Guards are coming."

As she looked around the empty garage, I tucked down, hit the gas, and gave it full stick. Bolting forward, I shot up the ramp, the tear of the engine vibrating my fury.

In the rear-view cam, she stomped her boot, her tits bouncing beneath the jacket, her hands balled at her sides. Then she raised an arm and flipped off my back.

Fuck her anger. She had no right to be pissed. I slammed my fist against the handlebar. Fucking whore.

Two guards lifted their heads as I zipped around the corner. I shined the flashlight in their faces, which was absurd. They'd seen me. At least they didn't have me on video.

The garage door rose, its sensor picking up my approach. I darted beneath, and as I merged into traffic, the nauseating plunge of regret crashed in. The shaking in my hands. The erratic thump of my pulse. The image of her body beneath her leathers. The knowledge that I'd touched another man's wife. I shifted my ass on the seat, unable to dull the discomfort between my legs.

I would see her again. Soon, in fact. But not the way I'd seen her tonight. Next time, there would be no helmets, no spark of recognition on her part. She wouldn't even know my voice.

Really, I had no idea how our next meeting would go. I'd collected enough evidence to turn in her family. And maybe I had enough money to fight their team of crooked lawyers and put them behind bars.

But they didn't deserve the justice of the legal system.

What about her? What was her involvement? Her access to the

racing network was spectacularly unnerving and unexpected. What did she gain from it? Did she know who I was, how I was connected to her?

Impossible. Very few people knew Maura Flynt had a son. Not even Trent Anderson. But he would.

In five days, we would meet for the first time. He expected a meeting with Logan Smith, an interview candidate for some VP position with a resume of fake experience.

But he would get Logan Flynt, a ghost from his past with a satchel full of blackmail.

11 LOGAN

Soulless. Not that a building was capable of deep feeling, but everything about this place, from the cold marble and fancy lighting to the wrinkle-free cushion beneath my ass, aspired to impress. And failed.

The modern display of wealth chilled the fucking air, stiff and lifeless like the puppets who wandered the halls. The entire executive floor seemed to be waiting for my next breath so it could suck the moisture, the taste, the goddamned effervescence from my being.

Even Trent Anderson's pretty assistant, Alicia Murphy, gave me the heebie jeebies. Her painted-on smile and straight brown hair were flawless. She sat behind a hunk of imported wood, she and the desk polished to a glossy shine. The kind of shine that tried too hard to hide the imperfections beneath.

Was the pretentious decor a representation of the real Kaci Baskel? Tedious, predictable lines to match her tightly-wrapped hair and rigid suits?

Well, that was why I was here. To break down Trenchant's mighty walls and determine what her role was within them. To do that, I was prepared to put up some repulsive pretenses to act in the company's best interest. Didn't mean I had to like it.

The easy route would've been to take out the entire family—Kaci and Collin included—from a safe distance. But if they were clean? I flexed my hands. Destroying innocent lives would make me as evil as the ones who destroyed my mother's.

I leaned back in the chair and forced my fingers to relax on my thighs. What I really wanted to do was tug at the necktie and free the button strangling my throat.

Meeting Trent wasn't what had my nerves buzzing and my hands sweating all morning. It was the possibility of seeing her, breathing her in, and pitching head over feet into memory, drowning in the sweet scent of her cunt on my fingers, the velvet lilt of her voice through the helmet, all the lingering sensations from an encounter that had chased my thoughts for five days.

Every detail about that night had been unexpected. She was a wild card, and that fucking terrified me.

I drew in a steady breath, recalling what my mother said when I broke my arm the first time. When I cried like a sissy and demanded she sell my sportbike. When I threatened to never ride again.

She grabbed my helmet, my arm flopping painfully at my side, and growled through her teeth, "If you don't wake up every morning scared out of your mind, you aren't working hard enough, you aren't fighting, and you aren't *living*. You *will* get back on that bike."

She'd been right. Arm in a cast, I was on that bike the next day and every day after, welcoming the fear with each new climb of the sun.

The phone on the desk buzzed. Alicia snatched the handset before it completed the first note of the ring tone. "Yes, Mr. Anderson."

Her eyes sparked, a curious change from the lazy, wanton looks she'd rolled my way for the past ten minutes. "No. There's one more appointment before lunch. He's waiting now." A pause. "Thank you, sir."

Returning the phone to the cradle, she rose and sliced her gaze to me. "Mr. Anderson will see you now."

I took my sweet-ass time gathering my messenger bag, rising to my feet, and strolling toward her, all the while hoping and dreading I'd pass Kaci in the hallway.

Alicia watched my movements, her eyes hardening when they landed on my Converse sneakers.

Fuck her. I refused to own a pair of loafers, couldn't imagine shoving my feet into something so pretentious. The suit was bad enough.

When she raised her eyes, I winked. Her breath caught, her judgment scattering into flushed surprise.

"Right this way, Mr. Smith." She turned on her strappy heels and sashayed down the hall. The deliberate swing in her hips was all for me. Maybe I would've ogled her ass under different circumstances, but she worked for Trent and given what I knew about his employees, I suspected that ass had been spread for him more times than I cared to think about.

The corridor behind Alicia's desk led deeper into Trent's wing. Kaci probably reigned over her own wing on the other side of the building. But if she were meeting with Trent, our paths could cross.

At the end of the main hall, I followed Alicia through heavy double doors. No Kaci. I refused to examine why my chest shrunk with disappointment.

The oversized name plaque on the wall was coated in glossy lacquer and reeked of arrogance. Much like the extravagant real estate that made up Trent's office, the bold cityscape beyond the wall of windows, the leather couches, the wet bar sparkling with crystal tumblers, and the man perched behind the monstrous desk.

This would be my office as soon as tomorrow, and I despised it. Despised him.

He didn't bother standing, simply waved a hand at the armchair across from him without looking up from the screen on his phone. "Have a seat."

I lowered into the chair and straightened my suit jacket as Alicia slid a folder before him.

"Mr. Anderson," she purred, cocking a hip beside him, "this is Logan Smith. Candidate for the Senior Vice President in the Technology Division." She tapped the folder. "His résumé, sir."

He flicked his eyes to her, one brow lifted. "I don't conduct interviews, Miss Murphy. What is this?"

Benny had been right about Trent not preparing for meetings. Evidently, he didn't even look at his schedule.

"It…it was on your calendar." Her chin lowered, her fingers twitching against her tight skirt. "I should've checked with you, sir. I apologize for the error."

It was on his calendar because Benny put it there.

I cleared my throat, effectively capturing their attention. "Miss Murphy, please collect the other board members. We have some family business to discuss."

Her eyes widened at my audacity, and Trent's shoulders stiffened. The skin around his thin lips tightened, his phone lowering to the desk.

He and I sat at the same height, yet he managed to look down at me, his hazel eyes tapering over the sharp line of his aristocratic nose. "What's your name again?"

Not a hint of recognition in his unblinking gaze. Not that I expected it. But he knew something wasn't right. Perhaps I wasn't the first person to walk into his office with retaliation on the mind.

I reclined in the chair and propped an ankle on the opposite knee. "Logan." I traced my bottom lip with my finger, slowly, deliberately. "Flynt."

He didn't gasp, didn't twitch a muscle. Kudos to him for mastering a stone expression. Bet his stomach was churning though, boiling up some serious denial under that rigid facade.

"Flynt," he repeated, his bored voice giving nothing away.

"Yep." I popped the *p,* rubbing my chin, methodically. "Flynt like the young stunt woman, Maura Flynt." I cocked my head. "She used to talk about you. Said you were her biggest fan."

No finger wriggling under the collar of his tie. No squirming in his chair. Nothing that telegraphed discomfort. He simply jerked his chin at Alicia, his tone businesslike. "Call in the other members, Miss Murphy. Set us up in the boardroom."

Just like that, he gave into the threat? No back-and-forth conversation to convince him just how serious I was? It was a sign of guilt, not that I needed more proof. He thought I knew he'd murdered my mother. Wouldn't he be surprised when I pretended I didn't?

Alicia's footsteps sounded her retreat, followed by the click of the doors closing.

Heavy silence settled around us. He regarded me as I studied him. His meticulously-styled blond hair, the inelastic skin around his eyes, the stern set of his posture, all of it frozen in reticence.

If he was trying to intimidate me, it wouldn't work. He didn't know shit about me, but I knew him, knew his secrets. I held the upper hand.

The leather of his chair creaked, breaking the tension straining between us. He crossed his legs at the knees. "You're not here for an interview."

But I would be walking away with a job. I gave him my most charming smile.

He pressed his lips together. "How are you related to Maura Flynt?"

I held his unflinching glare with one of my own. "We'll get to that."

A muscle bounced in his jaw. "I'm a busy man, Mr. Flynt. I don't have time for games."

Very few wrinkles marred his face, and not a strand of gray in sight. He looked twenty years younger than sixty-five. Maybe his assistants found him attractive, but his mouth was too small, his forehead too big and, the more he stared at me, the deeper his beady eyes sank into his skull.

I challenged his glare for another heartbeat before reaching into the messenger bag and removing a folder of papers. The first eight pages were newspaper clippings. Eight murders.

Spreading them over the desk in front of him, I watched his blank reaction. This could go a number of ways, most of them ending with an assassin on my tail as soon as I stepped outside the building.

I was prepared for that.

He glanced at each article, briefly and dispassionately, and leaned back, found my eyes. Smart bastard. When hiding guilt, reserve was the best response.

But I was only getting started. "We both know this isn't the extent of your crimes. Just a sampling of the ones I've linked back to Trenchant."

He laced his fingers together on his stomach and rolled his tongue behind thin lips, his eyelids hooded. "Mr. Flynt, most of these articles are over twenty years old. You're wasting my time."

I hadn't been as successful as my mother at digging up his crimes. Most of what I had on the families came from her notes. For the millionth time, I wondered how the hell she'd uncovered what she had.

Bending forward in the chair, I placed a transcript of a phone conversation over the article of the murdered Illinois woman. "Kelli Nelson. The assistant you raped five years ago. She threatened to file charges. You had her killed."

No reaction. Not even a flicker in his ratlike eyes.

"How much did you pay the sister to destroy this phone recording?" I gestured to the transcript, the phone call between Kelli and her sister the night Kelli was murdered, depicting the rape and Kelli's fear of Trent.

She'd explained to her sister in incriminating detail how she knew he was going to kill her. The fact that she'd recorded the conversation supported that. And while the transcript wouldn't hold up in court, the witness testimony would.

He sighed. "Are you done?"

"Not feeling it yet? Don't worry. You will." I covered each of the eight articles with documents the FBI would've loved to get their hands on.

The Trenchant accountant who discovered the board's money laundering. Stabbed. The reporter who was too good at his job, so good he'd uncovered a negotiation between his employer and Chicago's largest mob family. Shot in the head. And the security guard who was simply at the wrong place, overhearing the wrong conversation. Strangled in bed while sleeping beside his wife.

There were four other murdered assistants, each one prettier than the last, each with witnesses who could vouch for the women's willing affairs with Trent. Affairs that were cut off when his assistants grew too needy.

I'd bought Kelli Nelson's phone conversation from her sister. And Benny had hacked countless home computers and private servers belonging to crooked cops who had been paid off. Cops who had been bribed to hide evidence. A lot of evidence had been destroyed, but some nuggets remained tucked away on hard drives. Insurance policies, perhaps?

As he scanned the documents without touching them, I wished my mother's murder case was included, along with the written confession of her assassin. Just so I could see his reaction. But I couldn't play that card, couldn't reveal my true purpose, that I was here for revenge.

My heart thumped painfully against my ribs, my face chilling with fevered anticipation. I wanted revenge so badly. He was sitting right there, and the blade strapped beneath my slacks was so close, sharpened with lethal purpose.

Denying myself such an easy kill, the ultimate kill, fucking hurt. I wanted to bleed this pain, his blood, my memories. God, it would feel so good. Swinging the blade. Sinking it deep into his heart. Watching his life drain. A mind-numbing vibration of an open throttle. But Trent hadn't worked alone. I wanted to take down all of them.

I slouched low in the chair and sprawled my legs in front of me. "Five dead assistants, Trent?" And those were just the ones I knew about. "You've got some powerful connections to make something as repetitive and obvious as serial murders go away."

He smirked. "You know why conspiracies are so documented, researched, and resourceful?"

I didn't bother answering. He and I both knew I wasn't there under the premise of a *theory*.

Resting his elbows on the scattered papers, he leaned in. "Because they aren't backed by eye-witnesses. Conspiracies are like religion, boy. When you find something you don't understand, you fixate on an omnipotent being"—he laughed—"then you dig and obsess, regurgitate some *official* quotes from the Internet, and sell your story to rally supporters to join your cause. Why? Because it makes you feel less delusional, brainwashed, or willfully ignorant."

"Mm. That's all very fascinating, Trent, but I'm not interested in selling a story. I want to be a part of it."

A flinch snapped through his shoulders. Finally, cracking that hollow shell.

"Time for you to retire, old man. You can offer me your job now or after I meet the family. Either way, I'm walking out of here as CEO of Trenchant Media."

Crimson flushed his cheeks, and his eyes flashed. "You're out of your fucking mind. You're a goddamned nobody. A nutjob off the street."

I tossed a large orange confidential envelope at him, the final hammer dropping on his desk. I waited as he ripped it open, my body buzzing as he read through every paper.

When he finally raised his eyes, shock and fear strained the edges. His mouth opened, closed. Tongue-tied? Definitely dazed.

A heaviness settled in my chest. I expected to feel…lighter, but giving him the documents I'd held close for nineteen years hadn't changed a damned thing. "Now you know."

Now he knew my secrets. Well, all but two. He didn't know I knew who killed my mother. And nothing I gave him linked me to Evader and the underground racing syndicate.

The phone on his desk lit up. He pressed the speaker button, and Alicia's voice piped through the room. "Sir, Mrs. Anderson and the Baskels are waiting in the board room."

Super. Time to meet the families. I had folders for them, too. If Kaci and Collin were with them, maybe I'd have my answer about their involvement.

"Five minutes." He disconnected, his eyes still locked on me. "And if we don't meet your demand?"

"I have digital copies, of course, of all of this, of everything you've buried over the span of your careers." Some my mother had collected, the rest hacked, purchased, and bribed thanks to Benny's expertise. "Recorded conversations, coroners' reports, DNA evidence, statements given by *eye-witnesses*."

His face paled. Yeah, that kind of leak wouldn't be a conspiracy or a scandal. He was looking at a six-by-eight-sized future with a bedmate named Bulldawg.

He held up a page from the orange envelope and angled it so I could see it. "I take it this is your real résumé? Top honors at MIT?"

I'd included it to prove I was more than qualified to handle the legitimate aspects of the job. I nodded. "You realize if anything happens to me, I've got a trigger man waiting to press *send.* You can guess what that recipient list looks like."

Benny would broadcast every piece of evidence to Trenchant's multimedia competitors, local law enforcement, the FBI, and the families of the murder victims.

Neither Trent nor I wanted that. Of course, he didn't know I planned to kill him instead, so I needed to make damned sure he understood my fictitious motivation. "I want the same things as you. Power. Money. Women. But most of all, I want security."

Vertical lines appeared between his eyebrows.

"I want the protection that comes with the connections of a powerful family." I propped my elbow on the armrest and leaned my chin against my closed hand, all casual and contemplative. "Has there ever been a murder attempt against you or yours?"

"No one would dare." He studied me, something shifting in his narrowed eyes.

Was he remembering how he'd orchestrated my mother's death? Or was he berating himself for not knowing she had a son? Granted, she'd hidden me from the world, but if Trent had looked, it wouldn't have been hard to find me.

He was still studying me, his gaze ever-calculating. "What are you saying?"

"I'm here"—I stretched out my arms, indicating the expanse of my soon-to-be office—"to take advantage of your wealth, your connections, the reputation you've built, and the respect you command. But most importantly, your protection." Blah blah, bullshit. I lowered my hands, hardened my face. "No one will ever hurt someone I love again." And now he had my fake motivation.

The dickhead grinned. "Fierce. I like that."

Just wait, motherfucker. You haven't seen fierce.

"I wonder..." He returned the papers to the envelope. "Who this *someone* is you love?"

Of course, he'd want to know who his blackmailer loved and how he could use them as leverage. I would do everything possible to keep Benny out of his sights. As for the other *someone*, the truth was harmless. "Someone I haven't found yet. But when I do, I will not lose her the way I lost my mother."

He held up the orange envelope filled with secrets. "And this is why you chose Trenchant to be your *security?* Why you chose me?"

I'd hoped the contents of that envelope would make my motivation believable, make him *want* to trust me. But I knew, as soon as I walked out of here, he would investigate me, try to dig up whatever he could to use against me. I also knew he'd come up empty.

I smiled. "We understand each other." Not even close.

He leaned forward and tossed the confidential envelope in my lap, his eyes watching me with their unnerving scrutiny, analyzing my play. "There's one problem with your proposal."

I returned the envelope to the messenger bag with a calmness I didn't feel.

"The position has been contractually offered to my daughter-in-law."

My stomach dropped. *Kaci Baskel.* "Then contractually *un*-offer it. Sic your lawyers on it. Not my problem."

That smirk reappeared. "As CEO, everything is your problem. And she wants this job, *passionately*. Enough to fight for it. And she'll stir up a goddamned media circus on her way to the courthouse."

I gritted my teeth. Fuck, I hadn't seen this coming. Last thing I wanted was a publicized legal dispute.

How far would Trent go to avoid that? It seemed he was willing to deal with the scrutiny that would come with a new CEO with no experience in running a media corporation over ignoring my threats and giving the position to a family member who had been molded for the position since birth.

He stood and gathered the remaining papers. "The contract has a fidelity clause."

My throat thickened. "A what?"

"The contract is void if she cheats on my son."

12 LOGAN

Back in the mortuary-like lobby on the executive floor, I sat in a hard-ass chair, waiting to be invited into the boardroom, surrounded by stainless steel shelving and side tables, monochromatic wall art, and Alicia's lifeless personality where she sat behind her desk ten feet away. My palms grew hot, my jaw locked, and my veins thrummed with restless energy. *Fucker kept me waiting.*

When Trent led me to the lobby, I gave him the last of my folders. Documents that held all the unsavory evidence against his wife, Nicola, as well as Dalton and Kathleen Baskel. When he'd snatched them away, he ordered me to stay like a damned dog and strode off toward the boardroom.

Adding to my annoyance was the babysitter who arrived seconds later. A burly guy with a piece holstered at his hip, big arms crossed over a barrel chest, his suit-clad back holding up the wall beside the elevator. For twenty minutes, his tough-guy stance and watchful eyes broadcasted, *Just try to get past me.*

Fuckever. I said I wouldn't leave without the CEO position, and if the board wanted to pow-wow behind closed doors, so be it. In the end, they'd offer me the job.

Right about now, each of them was likely paging through his or her own personalized folder, scouring the brief but detailed accounts of their criminal histories. Arbitrage, laundering, insider trading, commercial bribery, embezzlement, harassment…murder.

Which brought my thoughts back to Kaci Baskel and Collin Anderson. How far did the apples fall? Their criminal involvement was purely speculative on my part, their activities hidden behind Trenchant's firewalls. I didn't have portfolios built against them because I hadn't been able to mine anything beyond a few suspicious transactions. Were they merely pawns? The next generation of

Trenchant corruption? Or were they kept in the dark?

I wanted to assume they were innocent based on the non-evidence, but I didn't trust my investigative skills. Most of the shit I had on their parents came from my mother, and I knew it was only a small fraction of their crimes. How much more was I missing?

The contract is void if she cheats on my son.

Memory flooded my body, her lips on my cock, her cunt clenching around my fingers, her sassy comebacks, the way she defiantly demanded I hand over the RFID reader. I couldn't decide which was hotter, when she melted in my hands or when she chased after me with an iron backbone.

My pulse elevated, and pressure swelled in my groin. Nine months of build-up, watching Miss Ducati from afar, had led to a landslide of desire and abandon. Hot, reckless temptation tainted with regret.

Regret of not finishing what we'd started. Regret of deceiving her the way she'd deceived me. Regret that she was married.

The surge of hunger evaporated, and instant anger took its place. Was her pussy so loose her family had to tie her legs closed with a contract? Why? What made her cheat? Was it a genetics thing? Like mother like daughter?

Nausea curled my stomach, and a sour taste filled my mouth. The damned contract was already void. Kaci had fucking cheated with me.

Scratch that. She'd cheated with Evader. She hadn't met *me* yet.

I glared at Alicia until she jerked her attention from my mouth to my eyes. "Where's Kaci Baskel today?"

Her curious gaze bounced over my face, down my chest then skipped away. A little too curious for my taste. No doubt she was wondering what was going on. She'd find out soon enough.

She tapped on the keyboard. "Off-site meeting until this afternoon. Would you like to leave her a message?"

Oh, I had a message for her. *You were right. I lied. You suck cock like a pro. Too bad you're an unfaithful slut. By the way, you won't be getting that promotion. As your boss, I'm amending your job description. Every task is now prefaced with "On your knees..."*

My stomach coiled with acid and excitement. I shook my head. "No message."

Fuck, maybe I wasn't being fair. Adultery was one thing, but this bitterness wasn't new. I'd judged Kaci Baskel long ago for the crimes of her parents.

The existence of the contract nagged at me. Why would she have to negotiate anything? Was it her idea, a way to secure her promotion? Or the board's requirement to ensure she remained faithful? Why did they care? Hell, infidelity was a minor infraction compared to her family's crimes. If she were a member of their dirty club, the CEO position would've been hers without stipulation.

No, that wasn't true. She could be a willing disciple, and they could be using contracts as a means to control her under the guise of testing her loyalty.

Alicia stood, figure-eight swishing her hips around the desk. "They're ready for you."

In short order, I had my empty messenger bag in hand, walking in step with her through a maze of halls and into a vast meeting room. There, I set my bag on a side table and stood before the Trenchant Board for the first time.

The door shut behind me, locking me in with the four pairs of flinty eyes. Shoulder to shoulder, they sat in their chairs, facing me with the table between us. Pinched lips, spineless backs at rigid attention, all in a fancy row of designer suits. Designed to make me feel like a man before a firing squad.

Little did they know, I would be the last one standing.

Revenge wasn't my only aspiration in life, but if it was the only thing I accomplished, if it resulted in my hometown free of my mother's murderers, it was enough for me.

I was just one of countless others who wanted to take these people down. In their race for power, they'd left so many victims in their wake. Victims who had families. Those left behind might not have known who killed their husbands, daughters, sisters, but I would give them that knowledge, along with proof that punishment had been served.

Justice. To wake up every day knowing I rid Chicago of its worst white-collar crime family. To fall asleep every night knowing one less assistant would be raped, one less whistle-blower would be dumped in the river.

To fill my lungs with peace, knowing I avenged my mother.

I burned for that. Just thinking about it ignited a fire in my blood.

"Before we begin," Trent said, catching my attention, "I looked up Maura Flynt while you were waiting. I'm sorry to hear about her death. I was a journalist years ago. That's how I met her. I interviewed her on the set of *Race to Midnight*."

The interview part was true. That movie had been her debut as a stunt double. A year before I was born.

I swallowed the anger and grief that tried to climb up my throat. He didn't know I knew the truth, and I needed to keep it that way in order to get close to him.

I nodded. "She had some crazy fans. They said her murderer had been stalking her for a while." Somehow Trent had pinned my mother's death on Edward Carthill, who later served time for a string of murders. I lifted a shoulder. "He died in prison a few years ago."

Without a flicker in his expression, he scrutinized mine, no doubt trying to determine if I believed the shit about Carthill.

"But that's not why I'm here." I prowled the length of the boardroom table and stopped behind the chair across from Dalton Baskel, Kaci's father.

Wire-rimmed glasses perched on his nose, and silver streaked the temples of his thinning brown hair. "Logan Flynt." The blue bow-tie at his neck bobbed with his throat. "I'm Dal—"

"Let's skip the formal introductions." I rested a forearm on the chair back. "I trust Trent gave you the packets I brought?"

"Yes, well..." Dalton's hand clenched on the table. "I'm—"

"The technical brain behind Trenchant Media? I understand you've transformed this print shop into the leading innovator in digital media."

The corner of his mouth bounced.

I tilted my head. "Too bad you can't publicly beat your chest about your biggest innovations."

He opened his mouth to interrupt, and I talked over him. "Computer trespassing, tampering with evidence, hacking, forgery, cyber defamation. My favorite is the hoax tweet you issued from Senator Roland's Twitter account. Remember that one? The destructive announcement that accused Newswide Corp of slander?"

He grimaced. "Mr. Flynt—"

"That was a two for one, right? A liberal senator's plunge in ratings *and* your biggest competitor suffering a four-hundred-billion dollar removal from the S&P 500 Index."

Kathleen Baskel slammed a fist on the table, her red-dyed hair as witch-like as her pointy chin. "Who do you think you are?"

Watching them get all worked up filled me with satisfaction. I slid my hands in my front pockets and shifted to stand before her. "Well, Kathleen. Since appearances are your thing. What do you see?" I shrugged and flashed my most charming smile. "The CEO of Trenchant? Do I fit the image?"

Her blue eyes blazed, the only feature she shared with her

daughter. But beneath the anger was appreciation, her gaze sliding over the musculature I busted my ass to maintain. She drank in my chest, my shoulders, and stalled on my lips.

I shifted toward her, lengthened my spine to accentuate my full height, and subtly expanded my muscles to exude an imposing, confident air. "Everyone in this room knows you like a pretty face. And a prettier bank balance. Charity parties. Rubbing elbows with the rich and sexy. Gets you wet, doesn't it, Kathleen?"

Her fingers went to her throat, her mouth gaping. Dalton turned a furious shade of constipated.

"Hey, I'm not judging." I absolutely was. In the years I'd tracked her, she'd slept with numerous billionaires, before and after she accepted their donations, all in the name of philanthropy for organizations that never saw a dime.

"This is bullshit, Trent." A seething whisper from the woman who had yet to speak.

A twinge lit behind my eye. Collin's mother, Nicola Anderson, was a piece of work. Her stunning Italian features did little to hide the ugly, vindictive creature inside. She might not have killed my mother, but she had been the voice in Trent's head. I didn't need hard evidence to prove it. I had my mother's diary, Trent's retinue of ex-lovers, and their personal accounts of just how sharp Nicola kept her claws.

I angled my body to face her. "You're careless, Nicola. I can smell you from a mile away, and jealousy smells a whole lot like fear."

She gripped the edge of the table, leaning in, elbows out. "Fuck you." She spit, actually sprayed a mist from her mouth. Thankfully, it didn't have enough momentum to reach my side of the table.

"My God, Nicola." Kathleen scowled. "Control yourself."

Trent placed a hand on his wife's arm. "Congratulations, boy. You've successfully demolished any chance you had at winning our cooperation." The subtle catch in his voice betrayed his lax posture and dormant eyes.

I nudged the chair across from him with the toe of my Chucks, sliding it out of the way. "No one has asked how I know what I know." I glanced at Kaci's father. "Maybe Dalton's figured it out?"

He adjusted the glasses on his nose. "Hacking. We made a call while you were waiting, verified your undergrad in Computer Science."

"And I'm just one of thousands of hackers. Thousands who could be investigating you right now." Lowering into a side-perch on the edge of the table, I folded my hands around my bent knee, one foot planted on the floor. "I didn't come here as an adversary. My intent was to show my appreciation for the underblubber of Trenchant. I've seen all your unattractive parts, the dirty weight you strategically keep tucked away from ignorant eyes. You're not America's most wanted. You're America's best. Kept. Secret."

Man, the atmosphere was pissed off now, stretching tighter with every second, pulling on my skin. But if I'd walked in here shooting rainbows up their asses, they would've chewed me up and spit me out. Assholes respected assholes.

I stifled a smile. "I don't give a shit what you do. I just want to profit from it." The lies had rolled off my tongue, but now I told them the truth. "I'm not having coffee with the FBI. I haven't friend requested the CEO of Newswide."

The air strained, oxygen thinning, unleashed breaths ready to snap.

"I'm here instead, accepting the job—"

Kathleen jumped to her feet, her eyes afire. "We will not—"

"—you *will* offer." I leaned forward. "Because you don't want an enemy with my skill set. An enemy that knows what I know. You *need* me on your side." I glared at her until she snapped her trap shut and lowered into the chair.

A sharp pain pounded through my head. From this bullshit act I was putting on? From the rot I was breathing in? I needed to get the hell away from these people.

How could Kaci willingly work here? Because they're family? Hard to believe that was the reason. She could nail an executive job anywhere. It didn't make sense. She had to be involved.

But I needed to be sure. The CEO's security clearance, the level Benny hadn't been able to hack, would give me unlimited access to Trenchant's internal network, personnel files, e-mail accounts, every employee's every mouse click, if I wanted it.

The only reason I hadn't shared my evidence with the world was so I could find out who all the players were—Kaci Baskel? Collin Anderson? Whomever else—and take them all down together. "I'm waiting for the offer."

Looks were exchanged, communicating in whatever silent language sick fucks used. Then three heads turned toward Trent.

Since these people were well-acquainted with risk, they were probably considering making me wait a day or two while they determined if they could contain the damage of my threat. So I upped the stakes. "If anyone tied to the evidence dies—eyewitnesses, bribed cops, relatives of the victims, *me*—the documents will be automatically distributed."

Trent tapped a finger on the table, watching the movement, his expression a blank canvas. Without lifting his eyes, he said, "There will be press releases to prepare, a company-wide announcement, the standard HR rundown of compensation and benefits. Your security clearance will take time—"

"You're forgetting the other matter," Dalton said with a sigh.

Unbidden, my neck stiffened. "Your daughter's contract."

Trent flicked his gaze to mine. "We'll handle it."

What the almighty fuck did that mean? It took everything I had to maintain my relaxed pose on the edge of the table. Christ, if she was a victim in this, if they killed her— "Is she an outsider? Or have you let her into the *family business*?"

A smile slithered over Trent's face. "She's our little darling in training. She does what she's told. You don't need to worry about her."

Darling in training? Jesus, that made her sound really fucking nefarious. Did she aspire to be like them? I stole a glance at her parents, and their smirks turned my stomach.

I dug deep, gathering my most agreeable voice. "I'm her boss now. I need to know what I'm dealing with."

Trent narrowed his eyes. "She's eager but naïve. Keep her on a short leash."

Christ, I was even more confused about her involvement than before. It was clear the marriage between her and Collin created a wholesome brand for Trenchant's right-winged supporters, but… "Naïve? You mean she's still learning how to"—*Cheat? Steal? Murder?*—"not get caught."

I waited for someone to correct me. No one did. Maybe I'd given away too much, revealing that my investigation of their children had slammed into a brick wall. But the lack of evidence could be owed to the fact that Kaci and Collin didn't have the twenty-to-thirty year crime history their parents had.

I glanced at the woman most concerned about appearances. "The contract ensures she doesn't do something stupid and drive Trenchant into a scandal?"

Kathleen nodded. "Precisely."

In return, it promised Kaci the CEO position, a promise that wouldn't be realized. Stealing the job from her didn't feel right, but that feeling was fed by my very strong desire to find her innocent *while* I took down her family.

I blanked my face. Fingers slack. Voice steady. "Okay, so you're going to set her up, lure her into an affair. And if she doesn't bite?"

Trent stacked the papers in front of him and stuffed them in the folder. "She'll bite. I'm sending her to The Watch tonight on an errand, so I'll see it done then."

So messed up. He'd plotted the ruination of his son's marriage with less deliberation than he would give a menu at a restaurant. And he'd intentionally mentioned the club she would be at so I'd what? Volunteer for the job?

I wanted to close my eyes and consider what was happening here, but if I did that, I'd imagine her with another man. No, I'd imagine her with me because picturing her with her husband or with a stranger set my fucking chest on fire.

Was it too hopeful to think her encounter with Evader was…singular? That she was a good person, and cheating wasn't commonplace for her?

Pull your head out of your ass. You need this contract negated.

But I *could* volunteer to be the bait, the tempter. *The other man.*

Fuck, I needed to shake this goddamned whatever that had my heart racing. She was never mine, would never be mine. For all I cared, Slutty Ducati could go where no slut had gone before. If she was weak enough to cheat on her husband, fuck her.

"Assuming the contract is a non-issue…" I stood. "When do I start?"

Trent rose as well, strolling my way, and the other three followed suit.

He held out his hand, and when I grasped it, my skin recoiled against the dry scrape of his fingers.

"You start now." His grip tightened, his tone frigid. "Welcome to Trenchant."

The murmur of voices drifted around me, melding with the clink of champagne flutes and the deep, lonely notes of a saxophone. The acoustics in The Watch dispersed noise with subtlety, tricking the ears to disregard individual sound while luring the soul to fuse with the collective whole.

I traced the stem of the martini glass, the aroma of alcohol tingling my nose, the soft laughter of a nearby couple caressing my skin. Maybe I'd be laughing too if Collin were here, but he was still at the studio. And as usual, Trent's order had been nonnegotiable.

Eight o'clock sharp. Wait at the bar. Accept the delivery. Don't ask questions.

Typical shady bullshit. What would it be this time? A nondescript envelope? A flash-drive? A whispered message of cryptic nonsense?

Sometimes I thought he contrived this crap just to test me, to see how I would maneuver assignments shrouded in I-could-tell-you-but-I'd-have-to-kill-you, like some perverse rite of passage. Other times, these tasks seemed a little too authentic to discredit, like the tiny hairs raising on my arms.

What if I was unwittingly meeting with mobsters? Aiding in felonies? I didn't know the nature of Trent's dealings.

But hey, in a couple weeks, I would be CEO. Which meant I could fire the board, clean up the company, and never ever participate in shady shit again. I filled my lungs with a deep inhale.

Until then, I didn't have a choice. Follow his directive or sentence Collin to prison.

So I sat on the last stool at the *L*-shaped bar and made the best of it. God knew I'd needed to let my hair down. Literally. It hung in thick waves around me, warming my back and tickling my elbows. The rest of my senses tuned in to the retro-festive surroundings.

I loved The Watch the first time I came here with Collin. Loved it now. The live jazz, the waitresses in fishnet stockings, the pre-prohibition furniture, the energy, the eccentrics it attracted. This nightclub was straight-up sexy.

A low snap sounded from the stage across the open room. *Click. Click. Click.* Steady, patient, the snapping fingers set the beat.

The murmurs waned. Heads turned. Bodies leaned. The foot of the older man beside me tapped in time. Then the saxophone joined in, breathing each note with a heavy soul. Slowly, the crowd angled toward the stage, listening, swaying, losing themselves.

I felt it, too. Deep, rich, and devastatingly bold. Like the eyes of the man at the other end of the bar. He was just a silhouette in my periphery, but I didn't need to look. His gaze was palpable, tracing my face and burning my cheeks, demanding I answer his silent query.

I was too damned nervous to flirt or mingle. *Wait at the bar. Accept the delivery.* The courier would come to me, unlike the man with the unnerving stare.

The bartender glided from counter to counter, taking orders and mixing drinks. When I caught his eyes, I threw back the last of the dirty martini and held it up. *One more.*

God, that searing stare. *Make it stop.* My breaths shortened, and my palms grew slick. I fought not to meet it, afraid if I did, I'd engage. Then what? Too risky.

I kept my attention on the bartender, who flitted around in his dapper vest, suspenders, and fedora as if he were serving up bootleg in the back of a speakeasy during the Woodrow Wilson administration. His outfit, the dim lighting, black velvet curtains, and deep shades of red all played into the vintage vibe.

My own throwback to the by-gone era was a blood-red rockabilly dress, empire waist, flared skirt, and thigh-high stockings topped with black bows. An outfit that had fetched numerous compliments when I walked in, which made this ol' thirty-seven-year-old feel right at home amidst so many gorgeous young ladies in short skirts and towering heels.

And after a survey of the sharply-dressed crowd, I was pretty sure every gentleman in Chicago with a penchant for cabaret was in the room.

Evader could be one of them, donning suspenders and sipping an elixir with a girl on his arm. He didn't know my face. I didn't know his. My chest tightened. It was tragic really, but I refused to let his douchery ruin my fantasy of him.

My one night with him might've pissed me the fuck off, but it had also added luminance to that achy place I burrowed every time I thought of him.

And I thought of him a lot. Goddamned always.

Maybe I would never find out what had spooked him, but part of me didn't want to know. He'd given me an erotic memory, one that breathed life into all that hard muscle beneath his dark leathers, and I wouldn't give that back. And despite the way he ran off, I bet I'd given him something comparable.

The bartender dropped off the martini, and unguarded, my senses flooded back to the man at the opposite end of the *L*-shaped bar. Before my brain caught on, my eyes snapped up and collided with his.

Trapped in the unblinking grip of his gaze, a swallow hung in my throat. My breath suspended. My entire body reacted. The shadow of stubble on his jaw made my skin prickle. The fullness of his lips sent a tingle through mine. Brown hair, trimmed on the sides and a mess of sexy on top, begged for my fingers, to rake and pull and not let go. I balled my hands in my lap.

Separated by a good twenty feet with the scurrying bartender between us, I couldn't make out the color of his eyes, but boy, were they smoldering. The heat they emitted raised the temperature in the room, stoking a trembling fever through my body. Who the hell was this guy? And why was I responding this way?

Five nights ago, I had the same intense reaction to a different guy. Ugh. I wasn't some shallow slut in pursuit of carnal pleasures. I didn't let my attentions flit randomly from one man to the next. I didn't *want* multiple men. What was going on with me?

His chin was tilted down, his gaze angled up beneath hooded lids. Combined with his stern jawline and the slight arch of one brow, he looked oh-so arrogant, broody, destructive. Sweet Jesus, he was so fucking gorgeous it was insulting, like a slap in the face to every man in the club.

And he was looking at me like I was the only woman on his radar.

My heart panted as I squeezed my thighs together, trying and failing to dull the throb between my legs, every sensation magnified by the buzz of alcohol coursing through my blood. The nightclub faded away, and the air between us charged.

He leaned forward, his hand reaching up to trace the lip of the pint glass in front of him, his eyes never leaving mine.The slow movement of his finger sent a shiver through me, hardening my nipples, as if he were trailing that fingertip around the curve of my breast. I sucked in my bottom lip and bit down on a shaky breath.

The corner of his mouth crooked up, replacing the broody look with a confident half-grin. I wished he wouldn't have done that, because holy mother of God, the lift of his right eyebrow was still there, fixed in place. Which meant he wasn't just insanely handsome. He was insanely handsome with a natural, lopsided arch in his brow.

As if that wasn't enough, I greedily drank in his body. He wore a white collared shirt that stretched tightly over his broad chest and thickly-muscled arms. Definitely a man who worked out. Virile. Strong. Probably in his late twenties. Couldn't be younger than that since the age limit at The Watch was twenty-seven and up.

His hands were big, rugged, relaxed on the bar top. And no wedding ring. Though I didn't wear one either.

When I returned to his face, his eyes narrowed, locked on something over my shoulder.

An arm reached from behind me and slid over the bar. A black sleeve. A man's hand. Holding a watch.

Hot breath stroked my ear, snapping my spine straight. "Tell Mr. Anderson," he whispered, "*Time's up.*"

As I turned, the man's lanky backside slipped into the throng of people and disappeared. I blew out a breath. Well, that was weird.

Twisting back, my attention caught on the watch beside the martini. A Timex watch with a fake leather band, the dials frozen on October twenty-seventh, eight o'clock. A month from today.

I glanced across the bar, and my ogler was no longer ogling, his gaze on the dark draft cupped in his hands. My stomach dropped. Had he lost interest? Maybe he was just giving me privacy?

Reaching into the clutch on my lap, I removed my phone and pulled up the text screen.

Me: still at the studio?

The response came back instantly.

Collin: Leaving shortly. Everything okay?

Me: meeting's over. gave me a timex to give ur dad. does trent have a cheap watch collection I dont know about?

I'd told Collin I was meeting someone for Trent, because I did that a lot, handling dinners with big clients and schmoozing with investors.

Collin didn't need to know tonight's meeting hadn't been a meeting at all. He didn't need to know about the shady shit I did for his father. It would only add to his guilt about our situation. He'd ask questions, and the answers would make him an accomplice. Like me.

An accomplice to what I had no fucking clue.

Collin: Well you are at The Watch. Maybe it's a joke? What did he say?

Me: time's up

Collin: LOL. Probably something to do with his odd bohemian fraternity buddies.

I wasn't so sure. My gut told me something significant was going to happen on October twenty-seventh at eight o'clock. I slipped the watch into the clutch. Tomorrow morning, I'd have one of my trusted engineers in the I/T department check it for chips before I turned it over to Trent.

Collin: You headed home?

Was I? I glanced across the bar and locked onto a pair of moody eyes. We exchanged a look, but I had no clue what it meant. He glared at me like he wanted to eat me. Or hurt me. Maybe both. Yet he hadn't moved a single sinewy muscle to make that happen.

Maybe he was married. Or assumed I was.

Or maybe he was aggravated because I was giving my phone more attention than I was giving him. I grinned, and his scowl deepened.

Me: a man is staring at me. hard.

Collin: Not bald and holding a knife is he?

Ugh. He was never going to let me forget that. Not that I could. He'd made me swear on his life and the lives of the children we would never have that my Evader days were over.

As much as it sickened me, I agreed. The races weren't safe. Didn't stop me from having a little meltdown in the privacy of my room, complete with pathetic farewell tears for the underground racing world.

Me: not funny

Collin: No it's not. So is he hawt?

Hot? He had the bearing of a medieval warrior. Thick forearms, broad shoulders, strong jaw, heavy brow, battle-ready glare. My body itched to move, tensing, leaning forward. I wanted to go to him, touch the scruff on his cheeks, fold into his side, and smell the skin on his neck.

Me: scorching

Collin: What are you wearing?

Me: rockabilly red

Collin: Damn. No wonder he's staring. He's probably not the only one. You look like a pin up girl in that dress.

Oh, Collin. A smile warmed my cheeks. I hadn't realized how much I needed that effortless compliment. It invigorated me, like the unpredictable notes of the saxophone, soothing away the notion that I wasn't enough for my husband, that the underground racing would go on without me, that I had a menacing watch in my purse.

The guy with the glaring problem didn't seem very thrilled with the smile I gave my phone. If he squeezed his pint any harder, it might break.

Collin: Garters?

Me: of course

Collin: In that case, I won't expect you home anytime soon. Don't break too many hearts.

What did he think I'd do? I didn't have sex without Collin choosing the man and running the background check.

Except Evader. I would've fucked him. Right there in that elevator.

Me: I need a Seth

Collin: Yeah, you do. He's incredible.

Oh sure, rub it in. I returned the phone to my clutch and set it on the bar.

The older man beside me slipped off the stool and wandered into the crowd, leaving a vacant seat. An opening for another man. My pulse fluttered. I glanced up, and he was definitely staring. Just not at me.

A curvy woman leaned her hourglass hip against his knee. Little black dress, platinum hair, bright red lipstick, the red forming a crimson sheen as she licked her pillowed lips.

He reclined against the stool back, his gaze following the fingernail she trailed down his chest, around the shirt buttons, disappearing beneath the counter. His eyes flicked to hers, his lips parted.

I slammed back the martini in two gulps. Dammit, I should've gone over there. I still could.

God, all that perky cleavage on display. And her youthful smile so full of sass. She could have any man in the room. I couldn't blame her for choosing the most attractive one.

Her mouth moved, no doubt seducing in sultry tones. I didn't have a chance at stealing his attention back. Nor should I try. Picking up a stranger at a bar without a background check? Too much risk for a selfish night of pleasure.

He caressed his knuckles over her bare shoulder, down her toned bicep, and wrapped long fingers around her elbow, yanking her close. My stomach clenched, but I couldn't look away as he dipped his head. He angled his mouth near her ear, moved his lips in a whisper.

Her body tensed right before he removed her hand from his lap and used it to spin her away. Then he dragged his stool closer to the bar, gave her his back, and downed his beer. Dismissed.

Ouch. If that had been me… Fucking hell, I couldn't handle another rejection. It had been fourteen days since Seth went limp inside me. Five days since Evader yanked my mouth off his cock and zoomed away.

My confidence with men had plunged into no naked touching, tasting, holding, kissing. Okay, it had only been five days, but was it an indication of the weeks and months to come? A future of going to bed alone while listening to the laughing moans of Collin and Seth? Fuck that.

"Been waiting for that fossil to leave." A deep voice interrupted my pity party. "Finally moved his old ass from this seat."

Charming. I dragged my attention from the man across the bar and met arctic blue eyes inches from my face.

He sat, facing me, and bracketed my stool with his long legs. "Name's Holden."

Holden radiated sex appeal. It danced in his eyes, glowed in his cheeks, and tumbled through his voice.

His boyish charisma brought a smile to my lips. "I'm—"

"The finest lady to grace this club. Don't freak out, but I've been watching you since you walked in." He looked me over from my lips to the bows beneath the flare of my short dress. When his eyes came back to mine, he shook his head, grinning. "So damned hot, girl. There's not a guy in this place who doesn't know it."

I was either desperate for compliments tonight or that was a really good pick up line.

He angled his blond head, holding that All-American smile with an ease that seemed involuntary.

"You're not so bad yourself." I held out my hand. "I'm Kaci."

His happy expression didn't flicker with recognition as he grasped my hand and placed it on his hard thigh. He was too young to connect my name to my face. He'd probably never even heard of Collin Anderson.

Why did it matter anyway? I wouldn't be leaving with him.

Fifteen minutes later, we'd covered the standard pleasantries, agreed on the underlying subversiveness in the retro decor, disagreed on the quality of the Chicago Bears quarterback. Basically, avoided all things personal even as the way he looked at me grew more and more intimate.

He bent in, his nose so close he could smell my breath. "Come home with me."

Oh wow, that was forward. I pulled my hand away, even as my needy insides tightened at the inviting curl of his plush lips and the glimmer in his lusty eyes. He was undeniably good-looking yet dimmed in comparison to the sexy broodiness I'd recently acquired an attraction for.

"No." My gaze swept across the bar and landed on the stool that had been empty since Holden showed up.

Holden reached for my hand, and I yanked it back. "Kaci, I

promise—"

"Take a hike." An unfamiliar voice dripped over me, low and rich like syrup. A voice that could only belong to—I shifted around, and oh my God—haunting green eyes. Or were they yellow? Definitely smoldering.

He bent at the waist, resting his arm along the back of my stool, the overhead pendant light illuminating his daunting expression and the complex hues of his eyes.

Golden irises, ringed in green, fastened on Holden. "Find somewhere else to put your dick. She's married."

She's married.

I sank deeper into the barstool and closed my eyes, realization landing like a brick in my gut. He'd stared at me all night because he recognized me. I was certain those weighted looks were sexual in nature, but apparently knowing I was married had discouraged him from approaching.

I sighed. It was for the best.

"She never said she was married." Holden's voice was low, frustrated.

A warm hand gripped my thigh. Way too big to be Holden's hand. I snapped my eyes open as the man, whose name I didn't know, leaned into Holden. "My wife doesn't have to tell you shit."

My thoughts froze, every cell in my body zoomed in on that syrupy voice. His wife? So he didn't know I was married? A tangle of relief and confusion sifted through me.

Had he said it to mark his territory? Stake his claim? Kind of a strange way to go about it. Strange in a really sexy way.

Which pinched my stomach with guilt. Letting him believe I was available made me feel horribly dishonest. But why? I wasn't married in the conventional sense.

Holden glared at the hand on my thigh and blinked up at the intimidating man's scowl. "Your wife? Then why have you been sitting over there eye-fucking her all night?"

My *husband* slipped his hand beneath my skirt, spiking my pulse as he traced a finger along the strap of my garters. "We're having a little fun tonight. Role-playing our first date." He slid me a smile that was so disarmingly hot I felt it in my panties. "Isn't that right, baby?"

For a moment, I let myself imagine that, to forget I didn't know this beautiful man, to simply enjoy the unexpected pleasure of his game and his warm hand against my leg. "Mm hmm."

Holden stood, his earlier grin replaced with flattened lips. "It was nice to meet you, Kaci." He glanced at the other man then strode toward the entryway.

My lungs released a breath then seized again when the gorgeous stranger grumbled, "Kaci."

If there was recognition in that expression, it was eclipsed by his dark brows and overall growly disposition.

I narrowed my eyes, every molecule in my body gravitating toward the fingers caressing my thigh. "And you are?"

He lowered onto Holden's stool without removing his hand, his legs sprawled around me, his heavy gaze in full force. "Logan."

I nodded. The name fit his serious, rough-hewed edge. I wanted to ask about the hand still touching my leg, but I didn't want him to remove it. "Why did you tell him we were married?"

"I didn't like the way he was looking at you."

The impact of his glare and the deep rumble of his timbre spread warmth through my body, no doubt reddening my cheeks.

He tilted his head, his hair all kinds of sexed-up as if he'd mussed it with aggravated fingers. "I heard you tell him *no*. Should I call him back?"

"No," I said a little too desperately. "Not interested."

"What about me?" The possessive hand on my thigh clenched. Relaxed. "Are you interested?"

Oh, let me count the ways. And each one led to heartbreak. I glanced at his forearm, where it disappeared beneath my skirt, his hand on my thigh coaxing a low-burning flame in my core. I should've shoved it away, but I liked it too much where it was.

I looked up into his golden-green eyes. "Is that really what you were doing all night? Eye-fucking me?"

"No."

No?

He wedged his fingers between the crease of my thighs and gripped the edge of the stool beneath. His body blocked the view from prying eyes, but the position was dubious. I squeezed my legs around his wrist, both trapping and hiding his hand, as if that would stop rumors.

With his grip on the seat, he dragged the stool across the wood floor, wrestling his hand free when my knees brushed his denim-clad groin.

Perfectly-fitted denim, as if it were cut exactly for his build and molded to outline the size and shape of the man beneath. Damn. The way the material stretched over his formidable bulge was offensive. Revealingly, erotically offensive.

The nightclub had a strict dress code to match its retro-classy women and eccentric gentlemen. Logan's collared shirt was crisp and white, the top button undone, framing the thick column of his neck. But his dark jeans bordered on not-allowed. Didn't matter. No one would turn him away. With his moody disposition and pensive eyes, he had the kind of look that craved a smoky room in the red-light district, longing for the bluesy rhythm of ragtime piano.

He was a dark poem, a sexy attitude, the epitome of rebellion. He was The Watch personified.

And God, those eyes. Gold with a thick emerald outline that seemed to burn brighter the longer he studied me. He was even more handsome up close, his beauty thrumming with masculinity.

But it was his intense focus that held every cell in my body in breathless captivation. He stared at me as if there was a distressing question trapped behind his lips. As if he could find the answer in a deep, hidden part of my eyes.

I raised my chin. "Just ask it."

"Ask what?" His right eyebrow, an arch of temptation, didn't move.

I wanted to touch it, follow the compelling curve with my finger. Could I? There was a grumpy twist on his lips, but would he bite? I could only hope.

I slowly raised my arm, focusing on his face, waiting for a snap or a snarl. He just sat there, spine straight, hands on his thighs, palms turned toward my legs between his, not quite touching, but from a distance, it might've looked that way.

Something in his stillness, his hesitancy, had my hand pausing in its ascent. He didn't make me feel unsafe. More like he was tightly restrained, like whatever he tamped down was vibrating beneath his skin, waiting for something.

He didn't twitch when my finger made contact with his eyebrow. In fact, I wasn't sure he was breathing. I stroked the strip of tiny hairs, gliding along the strong bone beneath. "Do you trim this to shape the—?"

"Fuck no."

I choked on a laugh. Collin was an obsessive plucker, and this guy was sooooo not Collin. I retraced the arch from the vertical indentations above his nose, up and over his eye, and lingered on his temple. "So it does this on its own? Naturally curves higher than the other one?"

"It's a fucking eyebrow." His eyes flicked between mine, the rest of him intensely still. So serious. "Why are you smiling?"

I shrugged. "It's a sexy eyebrow." When his jaw stiffened, I smiled wider. "And the surly thing you've got going on? That's sexy, too."

He closed his eyes, his nostrils flaring. Maybe I was annoying him, but the reprieve from his glare spiked my confidence. I *wanted* to flirt with him, to touch him, to get to know him. He was simply too good-looking, too intriguing to let go.

With my fingers at his temple, I curled in my palm and cupped his cheek and jaw, indulging in the day-old stubble that roughened his warm skin. He was real, not some ideal that could never be attained like Evader.

He leaned into my hand, only slightly, his eyes drifting open and falling on my mouth. I parted my lips and released a shaky breath, delighted with the catch in his inhale.

His eyes swept over all the blonde hair dangling around my arms. Thank God I'd worn it down. He seemed pleased by it, staring thoughtfully at the wavy length. Like he wanted to touch, pull, restrain me with it.

A ripple of heat shivered between my legs, and my chest heaved. I shifted my hand from his cheek to his hairline, sliding my fingers through the thick, brown strands. His eyes jumped to my throat, and I swallowed, relishing the flare in his blistering stare.

By the time he returned to my face, nothing in this world existed but him and me and the sensual language we exchanged with our eyes.

Come closer, his said, his legs separating from mine to spread wider.

How close? I stared back, sliding off the stool to stand and leaning my hips into the *V* of his thighs. *Like this?*

Gazes locked, he glided his hands up the backs of my knees, pausing on the tops of the stockings, fingers pressing into the skin above. His eyes flashed. *Closer.*

With him on the bar stool and me in five-inch heels, we were the same height. This worked in my favor because his arms wound around my back, his hard chest pressed against mine, and his groin cradled my hips. As I gripped his shoulders, his body heat, the smell of his shampoo, the molten gold of his irises, all that was him wrapped around me.

And wrapped in Logan was a toe-curling pleasure trip. So much so, I lost myself in it, in him, in the waves of need spiraling through me. I melted into the hard dips and ridges of his body, my arms looping around his shoulders, my hands running over his nape and through his hair. My lips, hovering an inch from his, separated, my tongue on my teeth, my breaths noisy, desperate.

The hands beneath my dress moved, his long fingers curling inward, gently stroking my inner thighs along the edge of my stockings. Each slow caress against my skin sent a jolt of electricity up my legs. My pussy swelled with heat, dampening my panties.

But none of those sensations compared to the intensity of our unwavering eye contact. I'd never been so caught up in someone's gaze that every breath, every touch, every needy throb depended on that visual connection. Heavy groping would've shattered it. Seductive words would've only gotten in the way. Watching him watch me was the best foreplay I'd ever experienced.

His thumbs hooked around the garters on the backs of my thighs. "That"—his lips moved a kiss away from mine—"was me eye-fucking you."

The thick rasp of his words melted through me, leaving me boneless and spellbound as I tried to decipher all the emotions swirling in my belly. This closeness, the intimacy, whispered all the things I hungered for. Mutual desire. Unguarded passion. Promise of more.

He slid his hands down my thighs, reversed the direction, and ran them up and over the flared skirt. He reached my ass and paused, circling his palms, squeezing. When I flexed my glutes beneath his hands, he leaned in and pressed his lips against my throat.

Oh God, I loved that. The heat of his breath, the bold possession of his hands, the slight lift of his hips as he nudged his erection against my heated center. The hard proof of his desire set my nerve-endings on fire and my heart into a rapid flutter of anticipation.

His hands continued their journey upward, along my spine, curled around my neck, and sifted through my hair. He made a fist in the strands and used the grip to tilt my head to the side. His face slanted the other way as he pulled my mouth to his, stopping just before our lips touched, holding me in a state of torment, where the only thing that separated us was the clash of our quickening breaths.

My hands fell to his shoulders, clinging to that hardness, fingers digging in. The wait was an aching forever, but so fucking worth it when his tongue darted out and touched my mouth.

Tremors rippled through my limbs, and my lips opened instantly.

Then he kissed me, his mouth a hot prison, one I blissfully fell into. And the fall was deep. Stretching the jaw, deep. Coil through the belly, deep. Spasm between the legs. *Deep.*

The entire cosmos narrowed until the only things that mattered were him and me and this kiss. His tongue rubbed against mine, his lips moving with aggression and demand. I tightened my grip on his shoulders, my knees wobbling, my face burning against the scrape of his whiskers. Oh God, what a burn. It shimmied over my skin and liquefied my insides.

The kiss strengthened, grew bolder, his tongue fucking my mouth with angry thrusts, the hand in my hair tightening until the follicles screamed in delicious agony. His other hand spread over the rise of my ass, pulling me against his arousal.

I rocked my hips, licking his mouth, our tongues tangling in an intoxicating dance. He tasted like Guinness, a hint of toothpaste, and something warm and exotic and all him.

My fingernails scratched over his shirt, gouging into his shoulder blades. Tingles raced up and down my legs, weakening them. But the arm around my waist held me tight, dizzyingly close, his cock a hard, heavy weight behind his zipper.

My inner walls contracted, aching to be stretched. I wanted to fuck him. Right now. Right here.

Right here.

In a public place.

Fuck! I tore my mouth from his, and we stared at one another, panting for air, lips wet and swollen. The fist in my hair released, lowering to my waist. I dropped my hands to his chest and blinked rapidly. "Fuck."

A satisfied grin danced at the edge of his mouth.

Goosebumps rose on my arms, my body fevered from arousal and nerves. I leaned back, glanced around the bar, feeling spectacularly exposed, naked, and on display.

The saxophone was no longer playing, but the crowd was gathered around the stage, a buzz charging through the packed bodies.

No one was looking this way, not a single eye watching the make-out session at the bar. I let out a tiny relief of air, hoping my ridiculous paranoia was just that. Ridiculous.

It was just a kiss, and the adultery clause in the contract was specific. There had to be proof of intercourse.

Christ, the way his tongue had fucked my mouth, it sure felt like

I'd broken the contract.

Feet shuffled over the stage. Men in bow ties weaved around the piano, drums, and the upright bass. The band was setting up. But it was the face behind the mic that explained the crowd's fascination.

The lights lowered, and I turned to Logan. "Been here before?"

He twisted at the waist, looking around. "No."

"Then you're in for a treat." I nodded at the stage and glanced over at him, the strong lines of his face etched in confusion, his eyes taking everything in.

Standing in the *V* of his legs, I leaned a hip against his hard thigh and rested an arm around his shoulder, angling us toward the stage. "Richard Cheese is making one of his impromptu appearances tonight."

His head jerked back. "That's his name? Dick cheese?"

Oh boy. I grinned. This was going to be a blast. "He does rock and hip-hop covers. *Lounge*-style. Really naughty songs crooned in a jazz voice. It's fucking awesome."

His left brow dipped low. He didn't look convinced.

"If you haven't heard *My neck, my back, lick my pussy and my crack* bellowed by a white guy with a heart full of soul, you haven't lived."

"Definitely need a life then." He smiled, and I felt it everywhere, surging my pulse with excitement.

The banging of the lowest piano key strummed through the room, followed by a series of high keys. As the tap of the hi-hat joined in, the crowd cheered.

I grabbed my clutch off the bar and waved it at the bartender. He skidded over, and I tossed it to him. "Hold this behind the bar?"

"You got it."

Logan gripped my waist, turning me to face him. "What are you doing?"

The horns kicked in, and Richard Cheese's "Ahhhhhhh" rose in crescendo.

Logan widened his eyes, his tone incredulous. "Is this *Welcome To The Jungle*?"

Nodding, I spun out of his grip and strode toward the crowded floor by the stage, a dance floor Collin and I used to tear up ten years ago. Back then, I danced to woo the crowd. But time had changed me. My desires had changed. I didn't want the attention of an entire room. I only wanted *his* attention.

I sensed him following me as I crossed the club, my gait seductive, confident, the length of my legs leading, giving the illusion of dragging my toes through each sensual stride. Hips rolling with the beat, I stretched my arms heavenward and melted into the music. My body loosened with each step, my hands roaming my shoulders, the outer curves of my breasts, the dip in my waist.

As the drummer tapped the crash, I stopped, looked over my shoulder, eyes downward as if watching my ass shake with each *tap tap tap*.

Lifting my eyes, they landed on Logan. His chin down, gaze up and locked on mine, he prowled toward me, stalking me, as he rolled up his sleeves.

Was he going to dance? My heart raced, and my skin heated. I curled my finger in a come-hither, swinging my hips and walking backwards. A backwards walk during which I never removed my eyes from his, never wanted to for fear he might disappear.

I glided over the dance floor, moving in time, my mind replaying our kiss, the heat of his mouth, the skill of his tongue, and I knew it wasn't enough. I wanted more with this man.

Maybe I wasn't as competent at hooking up as I used to be, but dammit, I was still attractive. Evader had rejected me for reasons other than my looks, considering he'd never seen my face.

The contract was what discouraged me, time and time again. Well, time was running out. I wasn't getting any younger.

Screw Trent and screw my sexless marriage. Because right now, avoiding the empty bed at home seemed a whole lot more important than dancing around a contract.

I deserved one night. One fuck-all, live-it-up, the-contract-doesn't-exist night.

Tonight, I intended to rock Logan's world. On the dance floor. And in his bed.

Melding into the sway of undulating bodies, with my hair down and a gorgeous man studying the move of my body with lust in his eyes, I felt weightless. Growing up, I despised the dance lessons Collin and I had been forced to take, but this, *this* I missed.

The stresses of my career, of Collin's career, had stolen this. But tonight, I took it back.

As the horns slowed in tempo, I held Logan's eyes and dragged the backs of my fingers from my chin to my ears, flicking my arms out on a cymbal bang.

He laughed and shook his head, standing on the edge of the dance floor, hands in his pockets.

The pound of piano keys set the rhythm of my walk as I strutted toward him, ankles dramatically crossing one before the other, bending my knees in a rolling bounce.

He slid his hands from his pockets, his stance loose, sexy, *ready.*

As the snare hit a trio of bangs, I whipped my chin from shoulder to shoulder with each crash. Then I pivoted, sidled my back up to his front, and rocked my ass against his arousal.

His hand circled my bicep and lifted my arm, hooking it behind his neck, his body curling around me in an erotic grind. He trailed a knuckle from my raised elbow to the side of my breast, leaving a trail of shivering flesh in its wake. His other hand flattened on my stomach, holding my back flush with his chest, our bodies moving with the rapid kick of the drums.

The song ended on a long blare of horns and a room full of applause.

I turned in his hold as the *snap snap snap* of fingers brought in the next tune, quickly accompanied by the pluck of the bass and Richard Cheese's sing-songy "Do you feel that? Ohhhhh shit."

Folding into his irresistible body, I wrapped my arms around his neck and lay my cheek on his chest, following the sway of his hips, letting the slow melody flow through my lungs.

When the beat sped up, I knew he recognized the song because he threw his head back and laughed. Then his eyes lowered to mine, crinkling with a smile, as he mouthed the depraved lyrics to *Down With The Sickness,* jazz-style.

The chorus broke in, and mischief lit up his expression. He angled his lips to my ear. "Foxtrot."

Before I could respond, his hand was in mine, the other sliding around my lower back, and we were twirling across the dance floor.

With our joined palms raised up and out, he swept me away from the entwined couples in our path, leading the steps with shocking ease. My free hand clung to his shoulder blade, my two-step gliding with fluid memory.

He held me close, closer than one should to pull off a foxtrot. But his feet stayed clear of mine, our movements synchronized, our chemistry out of the fucking stratosphere. When he brought our hands between us, holding mine against his chest and the confident glide of his body guiding me over the floor, the sum of all my desires surged through my veins like liquid fire. *This* was the sexiest dance in existence.

The thump of his heart beat against mine as our chests and thighs slid together. God, he looked great, smelled great, and when he spun me in an underarm turn, I never wanted the greatness to end.

But the song was coming to a close. Would he dance through another? Would he leave me with a parting kiss?

I searched his face, and he stared back with a burning glow in his eyes. If that wasn't an answer, the dip of his head and the crush of his lips was. Our tongues tangled, our bodies heated with perspiration, our hands grabbing and stroking and yanking.

I pulled back. "I'll get my purse."

He captured my face in the grip of his hands and kissed me again with a ferocity that left my head spinning and my pulse thundering. "Gotta grab my jacket. I'll meet you outside."

He headed to the coat room while I raced to the bar. There, I zipped a text off to Collin.

Me: leaving with him

Collin: Mr. Scorching?

Me: too risky?

Collin: Does he know who you are?

Me: don't think so

Collin: Be careful hooker

Me: always punk

Collin didn't judge me. He never did, but we lived and worked in a society of double standards. Very few would bat an eye at a man who crawled from one bed to another, because *Oh, men are just horny. They need to fuck and spread their seed.*

But what was the general perception of a woman who sucked a man's cock and five nights later went home with a different man? A skank? A whore? A shallow slut?

How many of those so-called sluts were simply lonely? Searching for a meaningful connection in a smile or an embrace or an orgasm? How many were hoping to find a *forever* connection?

It took courage and confidence to put yourself out there, to swallow the rejection and hurt that would undoubtedly come, then go right back out there and try again.

I wanted to be one of those brave women with the whole of my heart, but my circumstances were snarled with restrictions. Even if I found *forever* in a one-night stand, I couldn't keep it.

I held that thought at the surface as I strode through the exit. But the moment I stepped outside, the ugly seed of insecurity lodged in my throat. What if he changed his mind and left? Or never planned to wait at all?

It was unseasonably warm for September in Chicago, and I hadn't brought a coat. As I turned to glance down the street, a soft suede jacket was slung over my shoulders.

His gorgeous face filled my view, haloed by the glow of the streetlights. Relief settled over me, curling my lips.

He gripped my hand. "Let's roll."

His long-legged strides ate up the sidewalk, and I struggled to keep up with him.

"In a hurry, Logan?" My feet burned in the heels, but I jogged to catch up to his side. "Where are we going?"

With his hold on my hand, he tugged me into the next alcove and pinned my back against the stone veneer. He braced his elbows on the wall on either side of my head. The weight of his body pressed into mine, shooting my heart rate from zero to ninety.

He lowered his head, and his lips traced my jaw, lingering on the sensitive spot below my ear. A shiver ran through me. The good kind of shiver that relaxed my muscles and returned me to my prior state of blissful attraction.

His tongue circled my ear lobe, drawing it into his mouth. He sucked on the diamond stud Collin had given me, lapping and biting, and released it before I gave into a fit of ticklish laughter.

"We're going to a hotel." He nodded his head at the door beside me.

The sign above it read *The Bells Hotel.*

Oh. It took me by surprise. Maybe because I didn't know a hotel was here. Maybe because I assumed we would be going back to his place. "Do you live—?"

"I'm just passing through for the night."

Another surprise. But thinking on it, we hadn't talked, hadn't shared any personal information. I glanced up into his stunning eyes. "Where are you from?"

He shifted his weight to one leg, his body surrounding me, his expression unreadable. "Look. You're…" His eyes drifted over me from my lips to my legs, his pupils dilating, his jaw clenching.

"You're fucking gorgeous. Sexiest damned woman I've ever met."

My chest filled with warmth even though I knew there was a *but* coming.

He rubbed the back of his neck. "But all we've got is one night. And I don't want to spend a second of that time talking. Can you handle that?"

I wanted to laugh, but that would've been self-deprecating and pathetic. My sexual history was a compilation of one nights. One night was all I would ever have.

Hooking a finger in his belt loop, I dragged him to me. "I've got this."

My voice sounded certain. My rational mind wasn't so sure.

15 LOGAN

My head pounded, my thoughts growing heavier with every step toward the hotel room. Somewhere between my *All we've got is one night* declaration and the short elevator ride, the mood had shifted. The charged attraction that had pulled us together in the club agitated into an abject hum, straining the inches between us as we walked. She was nervous.

I picked up the pace, flipping the key card between my fingers, every cell in my body gravitating toward her. She hadn't spoken a word since we entered the lobby, her silence a hulking, awkward presence, which was crazy after the effortless way we'd melded on the dance floor.

Was she on the verge of changing her mind? If I touched her, took her hand in mine, would it push her over the edge? Make her run?

She'd said she wasn't interested in that douche—What was his name?—Holden. His smarmy smile screamed male escort, which would've been an easy solution for Trent. Maybe she'd picked up on his phoniness. Or maybe she wasn't in the habit of picking up men.

Except she didn't seem to have any reservations about sucking a man's cock in an elevator. I clenched my teeth. Evidently, she was good at not getting caught.

So was she worried about being seen in a hotel with a guy who wasn't her husband? But I'd already checked into the room earlier that evening, and we hadn't passed a single person in the small, empty hotel.

She had to be stewing about something else. General nervousness about sleeping with a stranger? Reservations about cheating? Or worry that one night wouldn't be enough?

All of the above scrambled my own head. My palms slicked, and my stomach hollowed with turmoil, curdling with the enormity of what I was going to do. The setup, the cameras, the betrayal that would be delivered to her father-in-law tomorrow.

The betrayal that would be in her eyes when she found out.

My skin tightened, and a burning lump swelled in my throat. I didn't want to be in this position. Christ, I didn't want to hurt her.

As I walked beside her, seeing my jacket smother her slender frame, a fierce protectiveness simmered through me. Trent had forced my hand, gave me no choice but to go against my ethics to help her commit adultery, all because I couldn't stomach the thought of anyone else doing it.

Another feeling tunneled through me, a hunger pulling at my insides. I wanted to lead her to the room under different circumstances, where there were no secrets, where I could explore her without pretense and get to know the woman on the Ducati.

That was the feeling I latched onto, the one my mind and body wouldn't fight. I ached for her, wanted her more than I'd ever wanted anyone, and for one night, she was mine.

"This is it." I stopped at the end of the hall, swiped the key card, and held the door open.

She stood on the threshold and stared at the room behind me. I'd left all the lights on, and now the illumination cast a glow over her beautiful face.

Despite the oversized jacket swallowing her shoulders and trepidation radiating from her pores, she looked startlingly mature, so smart and sexually confident in her vintage dress. The fabric followed her curves, classy not skanky, the high neckline tastefully concealing what I already knew were perfectly-shaped tits.

She was so unlike the uncultured, attention-seeking twenty-somethings I fucked and forgot. Her current uncertainty aside, she was an accomplished woman, with the education and experience to match her million-dollar salary. Combine that with the vibrant blonde hair tumbling over her shoulders, the creamy smooth skin of her angelic face, her knock-out figure, and she was staggering in her beauty.

And hesitant. I glanced back at the yellowing wallpaper, the dated bedspread, and the worn maroon carpet. Maybe this place was too low-rent for her affluent tastes?

No, she didn't strike me as the kind of woman who cared about that shit. Not like her mother. But what *did* she care about?

Her hands slid down the front of her dress, pressing against her flat stomach, the curves of her chest heaving against the fabric, stretching it. She nibbled on her bottom lip, her blue eyes focused inward, so deep and full of thought they sucked me in, made me want to learn everything about her for reasons that had nothing to do with her family.

She glanced down the uninhabited hall. The quaint hotel had three floors and maybe twenty rooms total, and the clerk had mentioned I had the third floor to myself this evening. She could scream my name through the walls, and no one would hear.

My God, just thinking about that wrenched my gaze to her mouth. A sinful mouth that had haunted me since that night in the elevator.

As I watched her, everything I wanted to know—including things I never knew I craved—stretched out in the depth of her gaze. Her worries, her desires, her painful beauty swirled in a mesmerizing dance of complexity, one I had no hope of untangling in the short span of a single night.

Her eyes shifted back to the room, connecting with mine. "I know talking isn't on the agenda, but I…" She drew in a breath, released it. "I need to tell you something."

My heart skipped. Tell me what? That she was married? Shit, maybe she would expose something crucial, or maybe—if I was really lucking up here—she would unload everything, and I could skip the whole CEO charade.

I held her gaze with a patient, open expression, even as logic told me she would never reveal her secrets to a stranger.

She stepped into the room, just enough for me to close the door behind her, and stopped against the wall, her looming disclosure buzzing between us.

Slipping my jacket off her shoulders, she set it and her purse on the chair beside her. "Okay." She turned to face me, her shoulders squared and head tilted back. "I'm just going to say it."

Christ, the way she looked at me, so many layers working in her eyes, none of which I could read, but whatever she was thinking, I knew it centered on me. My body tingled with expectation.

"I like you. I mean…" Lips parted, her half-lidded eyes swept over my body and returned to my face. "God, I love the way you watch me, the way you touch me." She leaned against the wall, tucking her hands behind her back, arousal flushing her pretty cheeks. "Your mouth, the feel of your tongue against mine, your kiss."

I licked my lips, my cock swelling with each husky word. "It's all yours. All night."

Her ravishing smile reached deep inside me, pulling me toward her with shocking force. My feet closed the distance, my body covering hers, my arms braced against the wall, trapping her.

She reached up and fingered the buttons on my shirt, not freeing them, just fidgeting, tormenting, her smile waning. "I don't do this sort of thing without…" She cleared her voice and forced her eyes to mine. "For reasons I won't get into, I always require an investigation and non-disclosure agreement."

My gut clenched, but with an incredible amount of effort, I kept my face relaxed and impassive as I stared down at her. She just admitted she slept around and did so with a contract. Evidently, her romp with Evader had been exempt from paperwork since she thought I couldn't see her face.

I wanted to believe our moment in the elevator had been significant to her, that whatever it was crackling between us was unique. Her non-disclosure bullshit crushed that notion, which made what I was about to do a hell of a lot easier. Her involvement at Trenchant aside, she was here by choice, cheating on her husband by her own free will.

She flattened her hand over my tense-as-hell chest. "Tonight…*this*…is really impulsive for me, so I'm… I guess I'm asking for your word that you won't ever use it against me." She swallowed, her voice small and unsure. "Please."

My mouth dried. She assumed I didn't know who she was, and of course, she knew there was a good chance I'd figure it out down the road. I could recognize her photo somewhere and sell the sordid details of our affair to the tabloids.

I couldn't fault her for being cautious, even if it wouldn't help her this time.

The sour tang of guilt hit the back of my throat. I swallowed it down with memories of my mother, her warmth and patience, her easy smile, and her tough love.

Kaci's family had taken her from me, left me without a single living family member. The boys' home hadn't been terrible, but Jesus, I'd missed her. Still did.

I needed to stop Trenchant Media from destroying any more lives.

Smoothing the guilt and grief from my face, I leaned down and kissed her cheek. "Don't care who you are"—I pressed my lips to her other cheek—"or what you're hiding. I just want to bury myself inside you for the next however many hours."

She sighed beneath my train-wreck of falsehoods and truths.

When this was all over, hopefully I would walk away with some semblance of integrity still intact.

I bent my knees and flexed my hips against hers, tracing my nose along her neck and filling my insides with the honeyed scent of her skin. "Tonight is our secret. You have my word."

The lie burned my throat like acid, but it evaporated with the softening of her body against mine. No matter how much shit I fed her tonight, I wouldn't lie to myself.

It was impossible to deny the way she affected me. The rawness in her smile, the intelligence in her eyes, her undeniable beauty—Jesus, even the erotic way she rode her bike—made her the essence of my every fantasy.

I trailed my fingers over her lips, dipping between them with each pass to wet the tips. How many times had I jerked off to the memory of her mouth in the elevator, the warmth of her lips against my fingers beneath the helmet, and the stroke of her tongue on my cock as I held her in place by her braid?

A surge of need throbbed between my legs, tightening my balls. My pulse barreled through my veins as I shoved my hands in her hair and angled her face, closing the gap between us. Her quickening breaths brushed my lips, and naked desire glazed her eyes.

I slammed my mouth against hers, chasing her tongue with aggressive strokes and biting her lips with a ferocity that made my ears roar. Her body trembled against me, her hands clawing up my back and fisting my shirt.

She tasted clean and sweet, but felt so goddamned indecent. That only made me want her more. A delicious shiver raced up my spine, my cock stiffening at the wrong angle against the zipper.

Without releasing her lips, I untangled a hand from her hair, adjusted my hard-on, and reached beneath the front of her skirts. Following the strap of the garters, I traced the edge of her panties between her thigh and pussy. The push of my knees against the insides of hers widened her stance, opening her for my fingers.

The first caress between her legs intensified the achy throb between mine. I broke the kiss and dropped my head against the wall beside hers, my fingers sliding along the indentation of her lace-covered slit. "So damned wet." A groan vibrated my chest. "Such a fucking turn-on."

She ground against my hand, her fingers digging into my back, pulling me closer. She looked up at me with hazy, heavy-lidded eyes. "Please, Logan."

My cock jerked, my self-control unraveling. I gripped the front of her panties and yanked hard. The strings at her hips ripped. I tossed the scrap to the floor and shoved my hand between her legs.

As my fingers brushed her clit piercing, I paused deliberately, as if I hadn't expected it, and let her hear the catch in my breath. I wanted so badly to grip that ring and circle it around and around until she came, to finish what I'd started five nights ago. But I'd have to use a different technique, one she wouldn't associate with Evader.

Capturing her parted lips with mine, I ate at her mouth while rolling the piercing up and down, pressing with teasing flicks. She moaned into the kiss, her hips bucking harder with each push and pull of the tiny steel ring.

"Is it sensitive?" I nipped her bottom lip.

She shook her head. "It heightens the sensations."

I was still blown away *and insanely aroused* thinking about her hiding clit jewelry under her expensive, stuffy suits. "Did it hurt?"

"Ahhh, that feels good." She half-laughed, half-groaned against my mouth. "It's a hood piercing, not as painful. God—" Her inhale cut off as I gave the ring a hard tug. "It was so long ago I barely remember."

I stretched my fingers, absorbing the wet, velvety feel of her pussy in my hand. "It's incredibly hot," I whispered at her ear. "Filthy." I pushed two fingers deep inside her.

She arched her back, her arms tightening around my ribs. Then she rocked her hips, fucking my hand, head rolled back, lips glistening from my kiss, tits bouncing in the cincture of her dress. Wild. Dirty. Stunning.

I scissored my fingers inside her with each thrust, my knuckles slamming against her soaking flesh, my thumb massaging her clit. Her inner muscles convulsed a second before her body tensed.

The gasping, glorious moan of her release filled me with a surge of satisfaction. I intended to ruin her, for her husband, for any man who signed her vulgar NDA.

Removing my hand, I spun her away from the door and smacked a heavy palm on her ass. "On the bed."

She glanced over her shoulder with a flushed yet startled look on her face. Well, shit. If she wasn't thinking of Evader before, she was now.

Screw it. Lots of men spanked their lovers, and I wanted her ass a blistering shade of red. Let her explain the marks to her husband.

I slammed my hand against her other cheek, thrilling in her husky gasp. "Bend over the mattress. Face down. Feet on the floor. Legs spread."

I was attempting to remove the intimacy, but as she threw back the bedspread and so easily obeyed my order, a chill licked up my spine. My lungs panted, and my cock ached in the confines of my jeans. I'd never been this hard in my life.

I stepped behind her and drank in the arches of her heart-shaped backside, the red skirts of her dress stopping just below her bare pussy. "Keep your eyes forward. Hands on the mattress beside your head."

She did as told, her voice breathy with her own command. "Condom."

Crouching behind her tight, curvy legs, I dragged my overnight bag across the carpet. Under the guise of digging for condoms, I removed the phone from my back pocket and opened the app that controlled the wireless cameras.

I'd set up the tiny eyes at every angle, hiding them in the headboard, the picture frame on the wall, the overhead light, and under the counter of the dresser behind me. Hi-tech proof.

Once the cameras started recording, I intended to keep her nudity as hidden as possible. Who knew what Trent would do with the footage? If her only crime was adultery…

I raked a hand through my hair. No way around it, this would be a humiliating, potentially-scandalous sex tape, but it didn't have to be titillating. After I merged and edited the videos, removing all shots of my face, the final clip would show the breach of contract, nothing more.

All I had to do was hit the *on* button on the camera app.

All I had to do was ignore the guilt tugging on my attraction for her. I wanted to hate her for that, for seducing me so thoroughly.

"Logan?" Her ankles wobbled in the sky-high heels, her fists bunching in the bedding beside her head.

My jaw clenched painfully as I moved my thumb and powered on the cameras. *Don't think about it. Just enjoy her.*

I dropped the phone on the bag, grabbed the box of rubbers, and tossed them on the bed in front of her face. Then I knelt behind her. Shifting closer, close enough for her to feel my breaths on the back of her thighs, I examined her delectable legs from her feet to her ass.

Sheer black stockings stretched over her skin, ending above her knees and held up by the garters that peeked from beneath the hem of her dress. If I lifted that hem, I'd find her swollen flesh saturated with her arousal. Her bent position and wide stance would also give me a glimpse of her anus, one of the many holes I intended to lose myself in for endless hours tonight.

The impatient burn between my legs ignited with a swelling burst of lust. I gripped her hips and slid my tongue over my bottom lip, wetting it, then slowly brushed my mouth along the inside of her knee, over the top of the stocking, and up her inner thigh.

The skirt gathered on my forehead as I licked from her piercing to the pucker of her ass, dipping deep along her slit with each swipe and lapping up her sharply sweet flavor.

The muscles in her legs flexed and quivered as her ass rocked against my face. I felt her need in every aching organ in my body and gave it back with a frantic tongue, a scrape of teeth, and the ruthless thrust of my hand.

Christ, I couldn't have kept my fingers out of her if I tried. She was so damned tight, so silky and warm. If I could've formed a coherent sentence, I would've told her so.

Instead, I used my lips to show my appreciation, licking and sucking, swirling my tongue around the clenched rim of her ass as my fingers drove harder, deeper inside her cunt.

The stubble on my face was sloppy wet, every inch of my hand drenched with her juices. I fucking loved it. So much so, it was easy to forget there was a man waiting for her at home.

Keeping her face forward and her hands on the bed like I'd ordered, she screamed as I fingered her through her second orgasm. As the convulsions along her inner walls relaxed, she grew quiet. In fact, she seemed to draw into herself. Her arms wrapped around her torso, hidden beneath her body. She pressed her face into the mattress, and I wasn't sure she was breathing until a muffled sob reached my ears.

My stomach sank. What the fuck?

I climbed up her trembling backside, straddling her waist, and pulled her arms out from beneath her. "Kaci?"

She turned her head, blue eyes wide and glistening, her cheeks glowing from her release. The most beautiful sight I'd ever seen.

"God, that was…" She rubbed a hand over her face, swiping at unshed tears. "Ugh, how embarrassing."

I pushed a lock of hair behind her ear. "Don't be embarrassed. Was it too much?"

"No." A smile quivered at the corner of her swollen lips. "It's just…" She closed her eyes and released a breath. "It's been a long time, Logan."

Something shifted inside of me, a tingly, restless sensation, floating through my limbs and lightening my body. "A long time…?"

"Since a man went down on me." Her eyes snapped open, locking on mine. "Years." Shaking her head, she laughed, but there was no humor in it.

So Collin Anderson didn't eat out his wife. Okay, not a reason to cheat on him, but seriously? What a putz. I was tempted to ask when she'd had sex last, but just because he didn't go down on her didn't mean he wasn't jerking off inside her three times a day.

A helpless burn tried to invade my chest. I refused to think about her with him, didn't want to crush the floaty feeling that had settled through me moments earlier. I'd given her something she needed, and while I shouldn't give a flying fuck, I couldn't stop myself from caring with the entirety of my being.

"Not gonna lie." I leaned in and pressed my lips against her soft neck. "I'm pretty damned happy I was the guy to break that dry spell."

A lustful sigh pushed past her lips. "Me, too."

Did she really feel that way? Did she feel connected to me at all, a guy she just met? Maybe I didn't want to know, didn't want to think about the part of me that sensed something deeper, something I desperately wanted reciprocated.

I ran the pads of my fingers across her lips, making her breath quicken. Then I leaned back, sitting upright with my knees on either side of her ribs. Struggling to pace my own breathing, I reached beneath her skirt and pushed a finger inside of her, careful to keep the material in the way of the cameras.

Her arousal coated my hand, her body still ready, wanton, so damned sexy. Thank God because the ache in my dick had raised my body temperature to unstable, my need to fuck her simmering beneath my skin.

I tried my best to not attack her like an animal as I bent over her head, grabbed a condom, and put my mouth at her ear. "Eyes forward. Don't move."

"So bossy." She smiled and turned her head to stare at the wall across from the bed.

A moment later, I had my painfully-hard cock wrapped in latex and positioned at her opening. With my hands curled around her tiny waist and my Chucks planted on the floor beside her heels, I pulled her hips against mine and slammed her onto my shaft.

My eyes rolled back into my head, my breath caught, and my muscles shook with the need to move. Hot, snug, liquid heaven. But in that euphoric second, buried deep inside Collin's wife, I knew it was wrong.

My father was an adulterer. God knew how many lives he'd ruined. Would this ruin Collin? Should it? What excuse had she given him tonight? How would she explain where she'd been? Why the fuck was she cheating on him?

My vision clouded, and my pulse raced. An edgy twitch crawled through my body, magnified by the clamp of her muscles around my cock. Seething heat coiled around my neck. I wanted to use her, punish her, make her swallow my anger.

I drove my hips, dug my fingers into her waist, and pounded into her with all my strength. She cried out, her hands scrambling over the bed. I gripped her harder, pinning her, and fucked her without mercy, without restraint, without technique. Pull out, slam in, out, in. No gentle caresses. No finesse. It was crude, angry, thoughtless.

I fucked her with the kind of hard-hitting savagery I'd longed to unleash on a woman but never dared. I fucked her until her voice strained from her screams and her body tensed in pain, and right before I reached the edge of orgasm, I pulled out.

I couldn't come. *I wouldn't.* Not like this.

With shaking fingers, I straightened her skirt and sat on the edge of the bed beside her hip. My muscles burned with exertion, my breaths rushed out in short bursts, and my head spun as I came to terms with what I'd just done.

"Logan." A demanding whisper, despite the rawness that scratched through it.

Guilt filled my stomach with lead, but the thing was, it was inconsequential. Because the moment I met her eyes over my shoulder and glimpsed the glassy look of pure wonderment on her face, I realized *she* had just fucked *me.*

She wasn't shrinking in fear or whimpering like a virgin. Her smile told me I'd just fulfilled a very naughty fantasy, one that featured a volatile asshole with the gall to claim her, shove her face into the mattress, and bang her with a furious temper. The lazy roll of her hips said she could take what I had to give all goddamned night, that she wanted my brand of piss and fire, wanted to be wrecked over and over by my pent-up anger.

Shocked to the base of my nuts and painfully turned on, I looked away and squeezed my dick, attempting to slow the raging pump of blood that throbbed through the length. I'd shown her the violence and furor inside me, let her see it in all its bitter glory. Hell, I'd slammed it into the back of her cunt. And she'd taken it, thrown it back at me, with her ass in the air, a smile on her lips, her hypnotic eyes begging for more.

She was a dangerous distraction, exactly what I didn't want. Yet she was everything I never knew I was searching for.

I was so fucked.

I bent down, as if unlacing my Chucks, and grabbed the phone from the bag, holding it on the floor where she couldn't see it.

She nudged my thigh with her hip, her breathy rasp tumbling over my shoulder. "I don't know what that was or why you didn't come, but you're not finished."

The job was done, but she was right. I wouldn't ever be finished with her. "I haven't even begun, you greedy slut."

What we just did…that had been for the cameras. For revenge. Maybe I was a selfish bastard, but the rest of the night was for me.

I tapped the screen and shut down the recording.

Boneless and light-headed, I wavered in my heels, bent over the mattress with my face in the bedding and the nerves beneath my skin buzzing from the proximity of the man beside me. The man who had just fucked me to delirium and back.

An ache pulsed between my legs, perpetuating the burn he'd left with his thrusts. The muscles at my waist twinged from where his hands had held me down. My throat burned from the strain of my vocal cords.

But my chest felt lighter, my mind clearer. The rest of my body drifted between languid contentment and anxious waiting.

I haven't even begun, you greedy slut.

God, he'd said it in such a biting tone my lungs had filled with ice. At the same time, I shivered with delight. He'd delivered the same dark promise in his glare from across the bar. I should've heeded it. Maybe I had. Wasn't that the reason I'd risked my career and Trent's threat against Collin's freedom to come here? To spend the night so lost in this man I'd forget about the consequences?

And to think I had stood in the doorway of the hotel room, trembling on the threshold of indecision. I'd almost backed out. I would've missed out on the most intense sex I'd ever experienced.

His arm bumped against my leg, his bicep flexing with whatever he was doing.

I hadn't gathered the strength to move from my face-down position, but I angled my head and drank in the teasing view of his backside where he sat on the edge of the bed. "So I think my screams might've reached Chicago Avenue. I'm surprised the neighbors haven't come knocking."

He didn't raise his head, but his chuckle was warm and delicious. "Evidently it's a slow night at The Bells Hotel. We have the floor to ourselves."

Folded at the waist, his chest over his lap, he appeared to be taking off his shoes. The narrow *V* of his lower back contracted and moved, but his shirttail concealed the muscle definition.

He still hadn't removed his jeans. Hadn't refastened them either, given how the waistband hung loose around the bend of his ass. I'd be ogling the top half of his crack if his shirt wasn't tucked in.

I couldn't see the front of him, which left me to imagine all sorts of lustful things about his cock. Was it hanging out of his zipper? Stiff and dragging over his hard stomach while he untied his shoes?

I squeezed my thighs together. I still hadn't seen him orgasm. I hadn't even seen him naked, but I had a good sense of his size, had felt the depth of pain and pleasure from his ramming length. And because I *was* a greedy slut, I needed to know if he was still aroused, if his cock matched the rigidness of his posture.

Pushing up on my arms, I backed off the bed and swayed dizzily to my feet. He raised his head at the same time, as if he'd been waiting, tuned in to my movements.

He straightened his back, black Converse in one hand, his erection in the other. The pound of my pulse filled my ears, in sync with the throb between my legs. He was incredibly stiff and thick, jutting from the open zipper of his jeans. His fingers curled around the base, clenching unapologetically, the condom still coated with my wetness.

I'd thought his shape was formidable beneath the mold of denim, but seeing him exposed and swollen and filling the huge grip of his hand—my God, no wonder I ached from my thighs to my belly button.

He tossed the shoes to the side, and the density of his golden eyes landed on me, pinning me in place. His desire was brazen, arousal dilating the pupils and weighing down his lids. But there was something else rotating there, a turbulent emotion sharpening the corners of his eyes.

The fierceness of it curled around my chest, warm and smothering and secure. It felt right, like I'd found myself, perhaps discovered everything I'd wanted, right there in the hostile intensity of his gaze.

What did that even mean? That I wanted to be owned or controlled or taken viciously? That I had a deep-seeded hankering to be hate-fucked? Why would he hate me?

No, that wasn't it. His passion was what spoke to me, his fire and venom. It was feverish, bold, and full of fight. All of which I welcomed, if only for one night, to fill the emptiness in my chest.

"If you're going to stare at me, do it with your clothes off." His voice was smooth and deliciously sexual, just like the slow slide of his fist as he twisted it over his length.

The next stroke took the condom with it. He dropped it on the floor then proceeded to rub himself, harder, faster, rocking his hips and fucking his hand, his eyes never leaving mine.

The erotic sight heated my skin and sank deep into my bones. He was so damned sexy it was arresting. The stubble on his jaw glinting a coppery hue beneath the overhead light. His thick lashes lowering as he broke eye contact to watch the slide of his fist. His lips separating on a ragged exhale.

Lips made for murmuring dirty words. Strong legs built for balance and speed. Hands meant to inflict pain and manipulate pleasure. A thick cock for stretching—

The slap of his hand on my ass sounded in my ears, and a smarting bolt of heat burst across my backside. Shock stole my breath, and I teetered in the heels.

He caught my elbow and used it to haul me chest-down on his lap, yanking up my dress.

"Wait. What are you—?"

Sharp, searing pain spread across my ass with another whack of his hand, and my startled yelp tumbled into a moan. I bucked through yet another smack, tensing, sighing. Then the real spanking came, the rapid whip of his hand striking every inch of my exposed backside and setting my skin on fire. With one arm braced across my back and his hard thighs pressing into my torso, he beat my ass without reprieve.

The anticipation of each strike stoked a maddening burn through my body, but I fought it, fought him, just to see if he'd fight back. To find out how badly he wanted it, to see if I was worth the effort. Even more thrilling was the intensity of his gaze on my face. I could feel him watching my reactions with total focus. If I didn't want this, he'd stop.

My smile belied the thrashing of my body. He wrestled me with one arm while swinging the other, all the while keeping my chest locked against his lap. But my arms were free, and I used them to jab my fists and shove at his ribs, laughing and—*Sonofabitch, that was a hard hit*—groaning as his strikes grew stronger, faster.

That's it. I angled an elbow and slammed it as hard as I could into the prodding erection at my side.

"Arrrgh, fuck!" He jerked back, hands on his cock and his knees drawing up as I scrambled off his lap. His face pinched with pain, and his eyes tapered into sexy slits. "What the hell was that for?"

I sidled out of his reach, kicking off the heels and rubbing my poor butt. "*What was that for?* My fucking ass is on fire!"

The pinched expression twisted into a diabolical smirk. He stood, vibrating with dirty plans, and unbuttoned his shirt. "Told you to take your clothes off."

Now I knew what to expect when I ignored an order. Biting down on a grin, I backed up. He stepped with me, his stern expression and fluid slide of muscle all prowly and growly.

I thrilled in the chase, my stomach tightening and my hungry skin burning for his touch. A few feet from the wall, I halted in my retreat and tilted my head. "Make me."

He launched, his arms hooking around my back and his chest slamming into mine. We stumbled backward. His hand caught our fall on the wall. But he kept coming, his heavy body plowing into mine, fencing me in with the unmoving surface at my back. With a hand on my ass and the other flat on the wall, he dipped his head.

The moment our lips collided, something snapped between us, an explosive release of restraint. And sweet Jesus, we surrendered to it. Our tongues whipped together, our bodies grinding. My hands flew to his hair, holding him to me as I inhaled the heavy breaths rushing past his lips.

Nothing compared to this, to him. Because he didn't just kiss. He fucked with his mouth, stretching and owning, dragging his tongue, wrenching every wanton part of me from my chest, and drawing it past my lips.

He kissed hard and deep and furiously possessive. He kissed like he was never letting go.

"Get this off." He pawed along the back of my dress, searching for the hidden zipper as his mouth overtook mine.

His hands went crazy, scratching and digging. I grinned against his lips, didn't lift a finger to help him. His urgency fueled the fire blazing through my veins.

Finally giving up on the zipper, he gathered the skirt and dragged it up and over my head. Our mouths separated as he tugged and stretched the material, forcing my arms in the air to pull it free.

He stepped back, and the dress fell from his hand, the sight of him untamed and painfully exquisite. His brown hair looked more blond in this light, with maybe a shimmer of red, the ends standing up in tousled spikes from my hands. His shirt hung open, framing the chiseled strength of his hairless chest.

His jeans hung precariously low on his hips, the zipper spread around the beautiful jut of his cock. He curled his fingers around it, stroking lazily, as his eyes roamed over me.

There was something so wickedly arousing about watching a man touch himself, and Logan took it to an illicit level. I leaned against the wall for support and licked my tingling lips.

"Jesus, Kaci. Look at you."

I glanced down at my body, at the red lace bra, black satin and rhinestone garter belt, and sheer thigh-high stockings. When I returned to his eyes, mine narrowed. Look at what? The expensive lingerie? Or my rapidly-approaching-forty physique? I crossed my arms over my belly.

He crouched, eye-level with the naked apex of my legs, and skimmed his hands over my skin, touching everywhere but not committing to one spot, like he couldn't decide where to start.

The caress of his fingers heated my inner thighs, the dip in my waist, and along the ridges of my ribs. His eyes followed the trail of his hands, his back rising and falling through heavy breaths. The muscled indentations in his wide shoulders twitched through the movement. He focused on me with every part of his body.

No one had ever looked at me like that before, like nothing had come before that moment and everything after would pale in comparison.

A strange feeling constricted my throat. I didn't know what to do with that, and whenever I was flustered, I said stupid shit. "I'm not twenty anymore."

He dropped his forehead on my mound and breathed out a groan. "Thank fuck for that."

That surprised me, which made me wonder… "How old are you?"

"Thirty-two." His whiskers scratched as his mouth pressed between my legs, the only warning I had before he bit down on the piercing and tugged with his teeth.

His assault might've been unbearable, but that tongue, holy hell… With a few well-placed and toe-curling licks, he brought me to another orgasm so fast my head spun.

Gasping and shaking from my release, I looked down. "Jesus, Logan. No more. I can't."

The irresistible arch of his eyebrow twitched. In the next moment, his hands were everywhere, frantically wrestling off the bra and garters as he walked us to the bed. The stockings went next.

During his fight with my clothes, I managed to strip off his shirt. I was still struggling with his jeans when he gripped my waist, lifted my body off the floor and flung me.

I landed on the bed, and he followed me down, shoving and kicking off his boxers and pants.

Finally naked, his hips rolled over mine, one hand sliding up my ribs, fingers latching onto my nipple. The other grappled with the box of condoms.

Chest-to-chest, skin-on-skin, the hard weight of his body felt excruciatingly perfect. His cock prodded my entrance, his pelvis grinding with urgency.

He fumbled with a foil package, bringing it to his mouth, his teeth tearing into it. “Fuck, baby. I need inside you so badly it hurts.”

I grabbed the rubber from his hand, and reaching between our sweat-slicked bodies, I rolled it on and positioned him. The instant I pulled my hands away, he thrust.

Our foreheads came together, and we groaned in unison. Deep and merciless, the drag of his cock stretched me open and filled me up, the friction of his thrusts shooting sparks of pleasure down my legs. I rolled my hips into each drive of his, but when he found his rhythm, all I could do was hang on. He moved fast and achingly wild, his attack mindlessly animalistic as he pounded into me over and over.

The mattress creaked with his thrusts, his ass flexing beneath my hands. With his forearms beside my head, holding up his weight, and his body stretched over mine, he caged me in. Shoving harder, deeper, his hips pushed my body up the mattress until my head touched the headboard.

It was brutal and unhinged, the bed frame banging against the wall and my insides twinging with each stabbing plunge. But this time was different. It felt more intimate than the first, like the only thing between us was…acceptance.

He held my face in his hands, showing me with the heat in his eyes how incredible it felt. The stroke of his thumbs along my cheeks told me how much he enjoyed my body. And when he captured my mouth, his fervent licks expressed exactly how much he wanted me.

Something warm and needy and hopeful pinched in my chest. He hadn’t been hired to make me feel this way. His salary wasn’t dependent on his performance. And he certainly wasn’t here to please Collin. He was here for me alone.

But I couldn't have *forever*. Hell, I couldn't even hope for more than one night.

I closed my eyes, opened them. He was a hot guy in a bar. A hard cock to massage an ache. And this was sex, raw and beautiful fucking. Nothing more.

And I would savor every second of it.

The kiss grew more insistent and feverish, the piston of his cock bringing me to that glorious edge. My hand tangled in his hair as heat shivered up and down my legs. My back arched, my nipples hardened, and my nails dug into his skin.

When I reached the peak, a piercing moan tore my throat. My body jerked as the orgasm pulled through me in violent waves. The implosion melted everything inside me, caving in my chest and taking him with me.

Fuck if it wasn't the most amazing thing I'd ever encountered, feeling his body shudder above me and watching the swollen flesh of his bottom lip roll inward as he bit down. His gaze clung to mine as he released that lip and opened his mouth in a grunting shout. His muscles shook. The cords in his neck stretched tight, and he pounded his hips, relentlessly, milking his release until the very last drop.

The scent of sex tinged the air. Perspiration slicked our skin. And despite the exhaustion of energy and arousal, we couldn't pull away from each other, couldn't look away, as if we were hanging onto the moment for as long as possible.

Lowering his head, he touched his mouth to mine, sliding his lips in a long, tender acknowledgment. I felt his gratitude in the swirl of his tongue, his wonderment in the weight of his breath, and a plea in his parting nibble.

He rolled off me, his gorgeous body sprawling over half of the bed, his chest still heaving with exertion. One hand stripped off the condom and dropped it on the floor, the other reached for my fingers, lacing them with his. Palms together, he pulled our joined hands against the hard bricks of his abs.

I tried not to think about how that simple connection made me feel and instead focused on the heavy rasps of his breaths and the soothing caress of his thumb across my knuckles.

As our heart rates slowed, I waited for him to fall asleep. Would I wake him before I left? Or skip the goodbye and sneak away with my composure intact?

His breathing changed, and his weight shifted beside me. "Break time's over."

Break time? I laughed. "You've got to be kidding."

He jack-knifed into a sitting position, gripped my thighs, and pulled my body between his legs. Then, with my knees hooked over his shoulders and his hands suspending my hips in the air, he buried his face in my pussy.

I didn't think it was possible, but he made it happen. He took me there, kicking and panting and moaning my release.

As the shuddering faded from my limbs, he lowered my hips to the bed, swatted my ass, and rumbled in a syrupy voice, "Your turn."

And so it went. I took him in my mouth, and he took me against the wall. Then he took me on the bathroom counter, bent over the dresser, and doggie-style on the floor. When his finger prodded my anus and I pushed against his touch, he took me there, too.

We guzzled all the bottled water in the mini-fridge before, after, and during. He might've only had two or three orgasms, but the man was a fucking machine, his stamina outrageously inhuman.

No matter how bone-weary and replete I became, it only took his insatiable kiss to coax me again and again. Our lips remained fused for so long the malt and mint flavor of his breath embedded in my tastebuds. All I could taste was him.

Hours passed, days, a lifetime. With my body draped over his, strong arms around my back, and his fingers combing through my hair, time didn't exist. Nothing existed outside this room.

But as soon as I had that thought, it made everything real. My job. My gay husband. Our contract. Time.

I glanced at the clock beside the bed. *3:36 AM.* Time to pull away from this dream and walk out that door. *And never see him again.*

I slid my cheek from his chest and blinked into his heavy-lidded eyes. "Stay another day, two, whatever. Just stay."

The hand in my hair tightened. He yanked, jerking my head back and bringing my face to his. As he stared at me, the gold in his eyes oscillated with a million thoughts. Was he considering it?

His fist tightened. "I asked for one night, Kaci. You said you could handle it."

A swallow hung in my throat. I'd meant what I'd said, with a tiny amendment. "I don't want to be your one night. I want to be your best night."

His sculpted face, shadowed with whiskers, softened. "You already are."

His response incapacitated me as the hand in my hair loosened, lowering to brush a wayward lock behind my ear. The caress trailed over my jaw and lingered on my lips. Not in a seductive way but in a final way.

Unspoken words shifted through his eyes. But their depths locked down, preventing his thoughts from escaping, shutting me out. Everything not said formed a black hole between us, dense and unknown and inevitable.

Time to go.

I swallowed down the clinging lump in my throat and climbed off the bed. Without analyzing, without peering over my shoulder, I collected my phone from the chair by the door and sent a text to Collin.

Me: Send a car. The Bells Hotel.

I hated waking Collin, but he knew which driver would be the most discreet about retrieving his wife from a hotel at this hour. A moment later, his message popped up.

Collin: 15 min

I dressed in silence and, thanks to my shitty willpower, stole glances at the bed.

Logan lay on his back with the sheet gathered around his waist, his eyes tracking me. His arms folded behind his head, the curvature of his biceps on mouth-watering display. Even now, exhausted and sore, I couldn't help but trace the bunching muscles in his abs with my gaze. Committing them to memory.

Something I'd never done before. My usual post-coital awkwardness was a naked walk back to my room, avoiding the feel of the man's gaze.

But standing here, dressed and anxious with my purse tucked beneath my arm, I searched his unreadable eyes for…something. Anything.

In a mesmerizing glide of masculine nudity, he rose from the bed and closed the distance between us. Cupping the back of my head, he touched his mouth to my lips, my forehead, and kissed the part in my hair.

"Unforgettable, Kaci." He leaned back, a small smile creasing his gorgeous face.

I nodded and returned his smile as a desperate plea crawled up my throat.

One night…Can you handle that?

I bit down on my tongue and stepped away from his hold.

My insides fluttered as I walked to the door. My gut twisted as I shut it behind me. By the time I crossed the empty lobby and stepped outside, my stomach roiled with the ugly pangs of goodbye.

My gait quickened at the sight of the shiny, black limo waiting on the curb. The passenger door swung open as I approached, and a familiar hand reached out for mine.

Collin tugged me inside and closed the door. As the limo rolled forward, his arm looped around my shoulders and tugged me against his side.

I set down my purse and rested my hand on his thigh. "You didn't have to come."

But I was glad he did. We could gossip like schoolgirls all the way home about the dirty things I did with a totally hot stranger. I let my head relax on his arm.

His denim-clad legs sprawled in the aisle, and leather house-slippers covered his feet. "We were still awake."

We? I leaned up and squinted at the shadowed end of the limo. Sure enough, there was Seth with his head back and eyes closed.

My insides constricted. Collin trusted him, but my gut didn't. It was one thing to sleep with a married man, but to witness his wife crawl from another man's bed? He knew too much about our lifestyle, and he could make a killing off the sordid details.

Collin pressed his lips to my temple. "Don't worry about him. I wore him out." He leaned back to look at me under the flicker of the passing streetlights. "You look pretty worn out yourself."

For the first time in hours, I considered my appearance. Tangled hair, wrinkled dress, smudged mascara, no panties. Hickies and swollen lips.

The backs of my eyes burned with an achy sense of loss. I had dreamed about a night like this so many times, had longed for a man like Logan for so long. A man exactly like him, in fact, with a dark helmet and a commanding presence. And now that it was over, now that he was gone, I wasn't even sure it had been real.

Collin cupped my cheek, his thumb swiping over the whisker-burn there. "You look lovingly worn out." He grinned. "Tell me everything."

Even at four in the morning, the short waves of his midnight hair were combed to perfection. His blue eyes glimmered with excitement as he settled into the seat and waited.

I wanted to let it all spill out. The dancing, the lack of conversation, my insecurities, Logan's stamina, and the ache that now plagued my stomach. I glanced across the limo, and a flashing headlight illuminated the whites of Seth's eyes.

Motherfucker. He was Collin's lover, not my best friend. I couldn't share the details of my one-night stand in front of him. Yet one more way he'd wedged himself between Collin and me.

I flattened my hand on Collin's thigh, staring at it. "It was nice."

His arm stiffened around me. He knew I wasn't going to talk, and he knew why. When I looked up at him, he was staring at Seth with a pensive expression. He lowered his lips to my ear and whispered, "Fair enough. But I want to hear it all when we get home."

I nodded then narrowed my eyes at the strange look on his face. "What?"

"Bet you didn't think about the races once tonight." He rubbed the cleft on his chin. "Or about your sexy elevator ride with Mr. Mysterious."

He was right about that. Logan had successfully owned every part of me, all the way down to the thoughts in my head.

"No, I didn't." I glanced at Seth, and he shut his eyes, a smile curling the corner of his mouth. I really didn't like him knowing about my run-in with Evader.

Collin slouched deeper into the seat, pulling me against his chest with an arm around my back. "Sounds like tonight might've soothed that ache you've been nursing."

A testament to how well he knew me. Not once had I mentioned my anger after the encounter with Evader. Hell, I could barely acknowledge it myself.

Evader. Just thinking his name sent a shiver through me. And that was what confused me. When I thought of Logan? Same damned shiver. I refused to pine for two men. I didn't want two men.

I wanted one. *The* one. A companion, a lover, someone to hold me at night and kiss me awake in the morning. Someone to fight with. Someone to fight *for* me.

I wanted legendary love. Love intensified to its highest power. The kind that would fill the vacancy in my heart with a simple touch, a thought, a broody glare.

But my circumstances didn't allow that kind of relationship. So I filled the emptiness with sex, with the hope that maybe it would bring…something more, like a one-night stand with fire and fight.

Which I'd found with both Evader and Logan. But did either of those nights soothe the emptiness? I was pretty sure I just traded one ache for another.

The next morning, I tried to keep the limp out of my strides as I stepped off the elevator on the executive floor. The Timex watch was a heavy weight in my hand, and my toes pinched in the godawful heels. But I was hiding much more than that. Like the hickies around my nipples, the red marks on my ass, and the soreness between my legs. A very good soreness.

Smiling to myself, I rounded the next corner with a straighter spine and a raised chin. My gait relaxed, my poise smoothing into confident professionalism.

The cute, blonde assistant, Alicia, gave me a smile and a "Morning, Mrs. Baskel," which I returned as I entered Trent's wing. Despite the pangs in my body and the dragging weight of no sleep, I felt remarkably alive, my skin zinging with wild energy. Once I delivered the watch, maybe I'd leave for the day, take the bike out, and embrace this invigorating attitude at a hundred miles per hour.

I'd like to embrace Logan at that speed.

Oh wait. I kind of already did.

But if I really let myself fantasize, the man beneath Evader's helmet would be Logan, and the hundred-miles-per-hour embrace would be on a BMW S1000RR. I sighed.

At the end of the corridor, I knocked on the pretentious double doors and stared down at the watch in my hand, its mystery still locked inside. I'd just left the I/T floor, where Raj Kannan told me in his heavy Malayalam accent, "Metal fused together, Mrs. Baskel. I open it and casing will break."

And Trent would know I'd tampered with it. What kind of message did it hold? My God, what kind of message needed to be delivered in such a cryptic way?

I checked my watch, adjusted the phone where it sat out of sight in my bra, and knocked again. The bastard better be in there. He'd told me—*demanded*—a ten o'clock meeting.

The door swung open. Inside, the noble Chicago skyline emblazoned the back wall of windows, creating an ironic backdrop for the slithering smile that greeted me.

"Right on time." Trent's gaze roamed my body, like the slimy journey of a slug.

Shuddering, I held up the watch and snapped, "You're welcome."

His fingers lingered on mine before he pocketed it in his gray slacks. "Was there a message?"

I stepped back to put space between us. "*Time's up.*"

His smile didn't move, but his eyes flickered.

My shoulders itched to curl forward, to protect my core from the insidious aura that clung to him, but I held my back as relaxed as possible. "What happens on October twenty-seventh?"

Hands in his pockets, he glanced at his overpriced loafers and returned to my face. "On October twenty-seventh, McDonald's will sell six million hamburgers and increase the global fat scale by another basis point. And statistics say the population will improve with the deaths of twenty-five more gang-bangers. And who knows? Maybe that will be the day an earthquake wipes out some third-world country no one gives a shit about."

Jesus. My fingers clenched at my sides. "You're disgusting."

"Lighten up, Kaci." He shifted further into the office and gestured inside. "Come in. We were just getting started."

Right. A meeting. Probably with my mother. Actually, I was feeling spunky enough today to enjoy her presence. I'd chosen her least favorite dress—tight around the chest, flirty at the knees—because *fuck her*. She wouldn't know her poor little celibate daughter was highly sexed this morning. But I'd love to shove my well-loved glow in her face and watch the Botox harden with envy.

With that energizing thought, I followed him in and turned the corner.

And everything froze. My feet, my breath, my heart.

The last person I expected to see glared at me from across the room. Wide shoulders encased in a black suit. A strong neck that didn't belong in a thin tie. And beneath the white shirt, I knew there was an eight-pack of polished, hairless abs.

My stomach dropped, and my lungs slammed together.

Hands behind his back, legs in a wide stance, Logan stood behind Trent's desk like he owned it. His face was cleanly shaven, but a shadow darkened his features. A dissonance of unreadable emotions furrowed his brow and shaped his jaw into a cinder block.

My mind raced through all the possible reasons he was here. Did I forget my driver's license? Did he search me out because he decided to stay? Or was this all a coincidence and he was just as surprised to see me?

He didn't look surprised.

My blood began a slow trickle downward, chilling everything between my face and my feet.

Trent shut the door behind me, locking the three of us in, and slipped in beside Logan behind the desk.

Logan seemed disinclined to step back or shift his stance in any way. They were the same height, but Logan's surly bearing dwarfed the man beside him.

"This is Logan Flynt." Trent lowered into the chair, his eyes calculating. "But you already knew that."

Sweat formed on the back of my neck. What did he want? What had he told Trent? Maybe not everything, which meant I needed to measure my response no matter how desperately I burned to attack him, to scream and demand answers.

I caught him looking at me, his eyes creased with tension and something else, something I hadn't seen last night. Whatever it was, it explained nothing and hinted at everything.

Pushing that to the back of my awareness, I softened my face into what I hoped was a cordial expression. "Logan."

His lips formed an angry line, and his eyes turned to golden glass.

Not good. I cleared my throat and said to Trent, "We met at The Watch last night." Damn that quiver in my voice.

Trent leaned forward, his fingers clicking over the keyboard on the desk. "You did more than meet."

The plasma screen on the wall beside me blinked on. My heart raced, and a sick swirl of nausea curdled in my gut.

I glanced at Logan. The sudden rigidness in his body shoved my thundering pulse past my ears.

The mouse pointer wiggled on the big screen as Trent maximized a video window and clicked play. I knew it was coming before I saw it. I felt it like fire on my skin and ice in my veins, right before it burned into my eyes.

The horrifying aftermath of my decisions, magnified on fifty-five inches of hi-def resolution, played out across the screen. My body bent over a bed. My mouth gaping in ecstasy. A blurry-faced man standing behind me. His cock ramming like there was no tomorrow.

The betrayal stabbed a jolt of pain through my chest and tunneled through the emptiness there, stretching it wider, deeper, hollowing me out. I let it spread through my body, absorbing its soundless devastation, like the video on the wall.

All of it captured with various camera angles. Cameras that had been set up in advance. Premeditated. Everything about last night had been planned.

My stomach erupted, angry and vengeful, forcing its misery up my throat. I fisted my hands, fighting it down. Goddammit, I fought to breathe, and when my lungs finally released, my anguish vented in a seething whisper. "Turn it off."

When the screen blanked, the blunt ache of relief tried to push me to the floor. But it was nothing compared to the gravity of Logan's gaze.

I locked my legs, refused to give him my eyes. Not until I pulled myself together. As much as I wanted to bloody my knuckles on his fucking face, that would solve exactly nothing. And I needed something. Answers.

The other dick in the room watched me the way he always did, his leeching gaze attaching and feeding. His unruffled posture reeked of satisfaction. He showed no signs of anger about my contract violation. No surprise by the content of the video. He'd arranged this.

Nausea simmered through me, fevering my skin. "You hired him."

"No," two voices answered. Though Logan's was louder and punctuated by the aggressive lean of his body and slam of his hands on the desk.

Trent glared up at him until he straightened and stepped back. Then Trent looked at me. "I hired someone else. You remember Holden."

The man I'd turned down. My only coup in a night of mistakes.

The shooting stabs of failure burned the backs of my eyes. My promotion. Collin's freedom. And the excruciating knowledge that I was *fucked* by a man as part of some plan.

"Why did you set me up?" I asked Trent, struggling to keep the pain from pitching my voice. "Because you didn't want to pass your CEO title to me?"

"Yes."

God, I felt the waste of my career in the depths of my soul, but there was another, more harrowing ramification. "Collin…"

He glanced at Logan and back at me. "We'll discuss that privately."

Sweat formed on my upper lip, and chills racked my body. I breathed through it, gathered my backbone, and forced all my energy into blanking my face and straightening my stance. He couldn't send him to prison. How could anyone do that to their own son? And why would he want to?

I dragged my eyes to Logan. He glared back with his chin angled down, his jaw set in warlike belligerence. What was his role in this? He had moved in and replaced Holden in the club. If he wasn't hired by Trent, he had his own agenda.

Dismissing him like a piece of furniture, I turned my attention to Trent. "What does he want?"

"Your promotion," Logan answered, his voice a corrosive abrasion across my nerves.

When I met his eyes, the slight arch of his right brow made my nails dig into my palms. Who the fuck was this guy? "Trent would never agree to that."

Logan bent over the desk, arms bracing his upper body, his suit jacket stretching to contain the angry flex of his muscles. "He already did. I'm your *boss*."

At Trent's nod, my rage exploded. Venom coiled around the line of my spine, propelling me forward. When I reached the desk, I matched Logan's lean, bending over the wide surface to shove my face in his. "No way in hell I'm working for you. I quit."

Fifteen years I busted my ass for this job. All of it gone. And Collin's freedom dangled on some unknown thread. Because of this man, who had given me his word in a hotel room, who had looked at me and touched me in ways that couldn't have been faked.

He used me, used my need for connection against me. He couldn't have hit me in a more vulnerable spot. And I let him. Which only made the hurt more nauseating.

Bile rose through my chest, gnawing at the back of my throat. My lungs cycled air without nourishing my body. I was going to be sick. But I locked it all inside. Emptied my face. Swallowed the pain. And stood tall.

"Kaci." Trent's voice pushed against my shivering skin. "The unsettled matter with Collin is contingent on your cooperation. You will remain in your position and report directly to Logan."

I sucked in a breath. So basically, I had to swallow my pride to keep Collin out of jail. "Are you serious? Jesus, Trent. I fucking hate you. Why in the fuck would you want me to work here?"

Maybe it was one of Logan's demands? Though knowing Trent, he was dangling the threat just to torment me.

Trent rose from the chair, his expression morphing into something I'd never seen on him before. Hard as stone, flushed with anger, and seconds from detonation. "You naïve little bitch."

Logan's entire body flinched, but Trent kept talking. "There is shit going—" He rolled back his shoulders and inhaled slowly. "There is more to running a Fortune 500 company than budget meetings and marketing proposals. Do *not* question me."

Everything about that diatribe made me question him. And he knew damned well my job was more than budget meetings and marketing proposals.

Logan stepped back and leaned against the wall, arms crossed at his chest. Why would Trent hand off the leadership to *him*?

I backed up, my mind swimming. But as I took in Logan's confident coolness and Trent's unraveling composure, the answer was glaring. "Logan blackmailed you."

Trent returned to his chair, his vacant expression the only answer I needed.

Blackmail meant they shared a secret. But Trent didn't trust Logan enough to discuss his threat against Collin, the only reason I was still standing here.

Well, I was done with secrets. I met Trent's eyes. "If you go through with your plan to frame Collin for murder, I will fight with everything I've got."

Logan didn't flinch, but the pensive shadow over his face deepened. "What is she talking about?"

Trent ignored him. "You'll lose. I have powerful connections, Kaci."

He sprawled in his chair, lazily stroking the armrest as if it were a throne in an invulnerable fortress. Maybe his claim to power held some legitimacy, but it was also arrogant and overreaching. Everyone had a weak spot. I didn't know what Trent's was, but it seemed Logan had found it.

"If you fight me," he said and nodded at the blank screen on the wall, "I'll leave you with nothing but a ruined reputation."

The sex tape. Yet one more thing to use against me. The impact of that slammed into my gut. Logan seemed to be surprised by this, his eyes widening as he pressed a fist against his side.

So he hadn't recorded us with the intention to share it with the world? Why did he care? It was *my* face on the video. The wife of a right-winged celebrity. It would destroy any chance I might've had at starting a new career.

Though none of that mattered if Collin went to prison.

I was trapped, thrashing against an immovable web of ties, and the deeper I got, the tighter they cinched around my throat.

My knees buckled, and my lungs heaved. I couldn't hold it in anymore. All the hurt and shock and helplessness that had manifested in my stomach rose up. As it boiled through my chest, I darted across the office, lurched into the private bathroom, and emptied my stomach into the toilet.

The misery rushed out so violently and for so long my eyes watered and my fingers locked painfully around the bowl.

The bathroom door clicked shut behind me, and approaching footsteps raised the hairs on my nape. I spit, dragged the back of my hand over my mouth, and climbed to my feet.

Trent held out a towel and leaned a hip against the counter. "One month."

I stared at the towel, waiting, for what I didn't know.

He stood between me and the door and tossed the towel on the floor at my feet. "You will work here, and you will not tell Logan Flynt my son is gay. In one month, you and Collin are free to do what you want, to divorce, I don't give a shit."

I met his eyes, my pulse pounding in my head. "October twenty-seventh is in one month. What's happening on that day? Who sent the watch?"

"That's not your concern. Just do your job and tell Logan *nothing*."

Was he positioning Trenchant Media for a merger? Keeping secrets to avoid a scandal? What kind of corporate negotiations were communicated via cryptic watches? I sidled around him, inching my way toward the door. "If I refuse?"

"Then Collin will be taking it up the ass in an orange jumpsuit."

My cheeks burned with disgust. When it came to degenerate dads, as in I-fucked-my-kid's-life, big-time degeneracy, I couldn't help but stand in awe of the all-time prizewinner.

One month. Just a flicker of time. Hell, I'd give Collin a lifetime if it kept him out of prison. "The only reason I'm standing here is because *I* care about what happens to your son."

"You're here because you're a whore." The coldness in his voice penetrated my bones. "This"—he cupped me between the legs—

"was supposed to be mine."

My stomach heaved with a long-buried memory as someone opened the door behind me. I shoved Trent in the chest, stumbling backward into Logan's brick chest of heat and rigid tension. His hands gripped my arms, and I jerked away.

Fuck him. Fuck both of them. I shouldered past Logan and his narrowed eyes and the anger radiating from his tie to his Converse sneakers.

In the office, I slowed my strides and rounded the desk. Strands of hair had tumbled from my bun and hung in my face. I swiped them away as I found what I was looking for.

Wrenching the flash drive from the computer, I shoved it in my bra and straightened my dress. Of course, there were copies of the video, but Trent wouldn't be jerking off to this one.

Logan's vibrating presence heated my back, the intensity of his gaze dripping down my spine. I shivered, hating him, hating how much I was attracted to him. Which was salt in the deepest wound. The pain rose to the surface, pressing beneath my skin, trying to escape.

"We need to talk." His voice pushed me into a quiet place, the eye of the storm.

I turned slowly to face him and gave him the eye contact we'd shared last night. I put all my backbone in it, let him see that I was hurting but not ruined. "I don't want to talk…or do anything with you. Can you handle that?"

His eyes closed. When they opened, I pulled back my arm and swung with every ounce of my strength. My fist landed across his cheek, and his face flew to the side.

He could've dodged it. I realized that as he looked back at me, his jaw loose and posture stooped, as if waiting for another punch.

So I hit him again. Same spot on his cheek. My fist throbbed, and not surprising, that second punch didn't make me feel any better than the first.

Resignation dulled his eyes, and his arms hung at his sides. Arms that had braced me against a wall and pinned me to a bed. Arms I had wanted so desperately to hold me to sleep last night.

My throat ached, my composure wavering, made worse by the threat standing in the bathroom doorway, watching us.

I brushed my sweaty hands over my dress and pivoted toward the exit. Fixing my hair as I walked, I was confident in my outward appearance by the time I stepped into the corridor.

Strong, even strides carried me to the elevator. I held my chin up and my face relaxed when I reached the ground floor lobby. But when my heels hit the sidewalk and the cool wind brushed my face, the trembling started, in my legs, my hands, my lips.

Stepping into the heavy flow of foot traffic, I removed the phone from my bra and dialed Collin. Voice-mail answered. I hung up and dialed again. Voice-mail. *Goddammit!*

I let the pedestrians lead me away from Trenchant as I dialed and texted Collin over and over, watching the sidewalk blur beneath my feet. I really didn't want to be alone with my thoughts right now.

Hindsight was a brutal bitch, and I wasn't just thinking about last night. If only I'd had the foresight to tell our parents to go fuck themselves the day I completed grad school, before I'd signed a marriage contract, before I'd been sucked into their dirty affairs.

What would it be like to have a mom to talk to, who would listen with understanding and love? Who wouldn't judge me for the mistakes I'd made or the hurt I felt? Who would never have forced me into a hopeless situation?

But I had Collin.

If he would answer his damned phone. I dialed again. Voice-mail.

I trudged on for blocks, aimlessly walking. Surrounded by people. Alone in my head.

And my head was stuck on Logan. I ran over all of his expressions and reactions from last night to now. I knew I was seeing things that weren't there, and I tried to parse the facts from the bias, but I kept coming back to the look on his face when I hit him.

It was possible that he regretted betraying me.

Not that it changed anything.

I stopped at a crosswalk and dialed again.

Finally, Collin picked up, his voice rushed. "Where are you?"

I glanced up at the street sign. "Corner of Michigan and Ontario. Where are *you*? Why weren't you answering?"

"Okay, I see you. Turn around."

I did, just as the limo pulled up beside me. The door swung open, and Collin jumped out, his arms open and his eyes wide with worry. He knew.

"Your dad called you."

He caught me in a hug and lifted me on my toes, cracking my tightly restrained emotions. "Yeah. He told me everything."

Probably not everything, but I'd rehash it when I was ready. Right now I just needed... I looped my arms around his slender shoulders and held tight. God, this was what I needed. The power of a hug. It invited me to let go.

My spine buckled, my breath slipped from my lungs, and my eyes closed, trapping the rising moisture. "Is Seth in the car?"

He shook his head. "Just us."

And the tears escaped, hot and silent, down my cheeks. His hand on the back of my head, his arm supporting my back, Collin's embrace bore my pain.

18 LOGAN

What was the price of revenge? What would I pay to exact atonement for all the wrongs done to me and others like me? When my hands were stained with blood and I dumped my first kill into the incinerator, I thought I knew what it cost me.

Standing beneath the cover of an awning eight blocks from Trenchant Tower, I watched Collin Anderson hold his wife across the street. That was when I felt the real price constricting my chest and siphoning my air. It was too much.

The trembling in her shoulders as she clung to him was too much. Her arms wrapped so tightly around his neck as if afraid he'd let go was too much.

The stream of pedestrians parted around them. Collin spoke in her ear, and her fingers slipped into the hair behind his, her head nodding against his neck.

It was hard to watch and impossible to look away. Whatever her reasons for sleeping with me, she loved *him*. It was too much.

I rubbed my chest, tried to massage away the resentful awareness. I resented Collin for having her. I resented hurting her. But most of all, I resented feeling this way. It was a foreign, unexpected emotion, and I fucking hated it.

The voice of reason told me everything about her was calculated, from her reserved poise to her sexy-as-fuck heels. She was Trent's protégée after all.

But the seething *I fucking hate you* she'd said to him stabbed my chest with doubt. Trent had a hold over her that was deeper than her greed for money and power. Did she even want those things?

When Trent played the video, I'd braced for a flinging string of spit, a scourge of insults, and a major-league explosion of drama to fit the treachery I'd committed against her. Instead she'd held her chin high, her eyes open and dry, and calmly punched my face.

I prodded my cheekbone, tracing the swelling. It twinged beneath the touch, but nowhere near enough.

She should've kicked my balls to my stomach and ridiculed my performance in bed. She should've threatened my life with venom in her eyes. That was what I expected going in. *That* I could've handled. Anything would've been easier than the quiet, lonely hurt that had shattered beneath her brave expression.

Amidst the flux of traffic, standing beside his fancy, black limo and comforting his wife, Collin lifted his eyes and aimed them directly at me. I leaned away from the building, straightening to my full height, and stared back.

He wouldn't know who I was, wouldn't be able to differentiate my face from the dozens of others moving between us. Yet he looked at me for a deliberate heartbeat, one that extended into endless more. Too long to be cursory. Too pointed to be unintelligible.

He knew.

Knew who I was? Knew I'd fucked his wife? Whatever he knew would not inspire an introduction with handshakes. I flexed my fingers at my sides. My muscles heated and bunched, ready for an ugly confrontation.

I wasn't sure what shocked me more. The fact that he picked me out of a crowd or the sight of him turning his back to me and pulling her into the limo.

My eyes blinked rapidly as the limo motored forward and merged into traffic. What the fuck? I rubbed my neck beneath the strangling collar. Had I just imagined all that?

I must have, because if I were her husband, I would've beaten her lover into the sidewalk until he stopped breathing.

As I walked back to the Trenchant Tower, it niggled. While I sat on the couch in Trent's office—*my* office—lots of things about Collin Anderson niggled.

What had he done to incite his wife to cheat on him? Not that he was to blame, but why would Trent frame him for murder? Was it an empty threat or did he have legitimate proof?

It was a strong enough threat to convince Kaci to stay on as my direct report. Which worked to my advantage. I needed her employed so I could monitor her activities.

Trent's moving crew scurried around me. Trent had left for the day and evidently wasn't keen on leaving me alone with his equipment. My burly babysitter from the day before stood by the door, eyeing every twitch of my finger.

He stepped to the side as a younger man rolled out a cart loaded with Trent's computer equipment. When I'd given Trent the video, I'd watched him move a copy of the file from the flash drive to his laptop. But I'd embedded a logic bomb in the video file. Twenty-minutes ago, the time-activated malware destroyed every copy except the one that remained safely hidden in my warehouse.

A sex tape scandal was one threat Kaci didn't have to worry about and one of the many reasons I wanted to talk to her when she ran out.

I pinched the bridge of my nose. Christ, my head pounded with so many unanswered questions.

When I'd walked into Trent's office unannounced this morning, he'd greeted me with his palm out and a sleazy smile on his face as he said, "Give me the video."

Of course Holden had contacted him, but how did he know I'd gone through with the trap?

But what bothered me most was the scene in his bathroom. It wasn't just the tension between him and Kaci that had set my teeth on edge. It was the way they were standing, his body too close for a man with his daughter-in-law. Was he in the habit of harassing her? Did he touch her, force himself on her?

My hands shook, and my ears pounded. If he fucking hurt her, I wouldn't just kill him. I'd kill him slowly and painfully.

I spent my first two days as CEO of Trenchant Media ruminating on this shit between introductory meetings with department heads. Kaci didn't return to work after she left with Collin, and Friday morning, she called in sick.

The GPS tracker I'd wedged behind her windshield turned me into a stalker. She took the bike out Thursday and Friday night. The app on my tablet showed her hitting top-speeds around the outskirts of the city. For two nights, I watched that red dot move over the map like a man possessed.

Like now, sprawled on the couch in Benny's gaming area, I couldn't bring myself to look away. There was comfort in it, knowing she was out riding her bike rather than at home riding her husband.

I ached to jump on my bike, chase her down, and demand answers. Hell, I had a key to her condo. I could barge in and fuck the truth out of her.

I pulled on the collar of my t-shirt, a desperate knot hardening in my throat.

Which was why my ass was on this couch. I needed to cool off as much as she needed to nurse her wounds. I'd give us both until Monday. *Two more days.*

Benny stretched out beside me with her laptop balancing on her stomach as she stalked Kaci on Trenchant's internal network.

Using a clone of my top-level security profile, she dropped sniffers on servers and desktops tied to the network while disabling action-logging to hide her trail. These wire-taps were a lightweight hack, a simple way to monitor Kaci's online activities, so I was surprised as hell when she told me an hour later she'd found something.

She leaned up and twirled one of the dozens of blue braids covering her head. "Jenna Greer."

I hadn't met Jenna yet, but I knew who she was. "Kaci's administrative assistant."

She gestured at the activity log on her screen. "Yeah, so she picks up these files from an encrypted server every day and e-mails them to Kaci."

I raked a hand through my hair, unable to drag my eyes from the moving dot on my tablet. "What files?"

"Don't know. They're encrypted."

And she'd need the private key to open them. The app on my tablet chirped, the dot moving north, Kaci's speed reaching 160 miles per hour. My heart raced as I pictured her in her silver leathers, her braid whipping around her back, risking her goddamned safety at that speed. I wanted her straddling *me,* bent forward and ass up, her thighs gripping mine like her life depended on it.

Benny leaned over my shoulder. "No matter how long you stare at that dot, it's not going to sprout an ass and tits." She tapped her chin. "Though I could code a modification for that. Think about it. An x-rated GPS navigator that guides you to your destination with a naked avatar and a bedroom voice." She tilted her head back and drawled a ridiculously low moan, "Take a *hard* right, baby. Yeah, right there. Drive harder."

I sighed heavily and turned off the tablet. "Jenna sends encrypted files to Kaci. And…?"

She rolled her green eyes and turned back to her laptop. "I checked out the activity on the server. The only other users logging in are Hal Pinkerton and Trent Anderson. Hal drops files. Jenna and Trent pick them up."

Who the hell was Hal Pinkerton?

For the next two hours, we hacked public and private records. Hal was a reporter at Trenchant under Kaci's chain of command. He paid property taxes on a Hayabusa sportbike, and two months ago, his father was released from prison on a legal technicality.

But the most interesting discovery? We tracked him to an ID on the underground racing network. A feat only Benny could pull off since she'd developed the platform.

Hal Pinkerton had access to a network the FBI wanted to shut down and the *Trenchant Times* would love to expose. What disconcerted me was seeing both Kaci and Trent logging onto the same server. Were they working together? Was one tracking the other? Or was it coincidence?

The next night, I raced against an overweight American, who called himself The Sliminator. Before, during, and after I beat his fat ass, her silver Ducati loomed at the forefront of my thoughts.

But when I crossed the finish line, I didn't look for her, my focus obsessively fixated on the red dot blinking at the edge of my visor display. She was fifteen miles away.

I circled the city to shake any tails that might've been following, something I did after every race. Then I went after her.

It was impulsive and futile. Dressed as Evader, I couldn't ask her the questions that were gnawing at my insides. And the puzzle surrounding her and Hal Pinkerton magnified the importance of my anonymity. Last thing I needed was for her to connect the CEO of Trenchant to Evader.

Didn't stop me from cranking on the gas and chasing the moving red dot. I would just follow her for a while, maybe steal a glimpse of her on the bike.

I caught up with her on Rogers Avenue, her red taillight a beacon against the black sky. It was after midnight, and the scarcity of traffic forced me to remain back. When she slowed on a quiet street, I pulled up to the curb beneath an overpass and used the night vision to zoom in.

Two blocks ahead, she stopped at a stoplight. Bent forward at the waist, the muscled curves of her ass wrapped in silver, her blonde braid following the line of her spine. My lips knew every bump of that spine. My palms tingled in memory of my handprints on her ass.

Her breathy sounds, her honeyed smell, and the way she touched her tongue to her teeth when she smiled, I'd memorized all of it. Every spellbinding delicacy.

All of it unavailable.

Unobtainable.

Married.

Ironic sentiment, considering I would do anything, *especially* murder, to seek revenge. Yet the thought of stealing another man's wife made me feel sick all over. I'd always believed the end justified the means. But I wasn't supposed to feel this way about the means. My longing for her was a distraction I did *not* need.

A distraction I couldn't give up.

The stoplight turned green, but instead of rolling forward, she made a *U*-turn and darted straight toward me.

Fuck, it was no surprise she'd seen me. Hard to miss the only other bike on the road. I shouldn't have followed her. It would only take a recognizable mannerism or word, and she could connect my current identity to the man who'd spent hours inside her body.

My pulse sped up. I could take off and lose her in five or six blocks.

Tuck my tail. Protect my ass. Run away. Just like the night I met her.

My insides thrashed against the idea, a strange impulse heating my veins, seething to fight. *Fight for her.*

Deep down, I knew that would never work. But I couldn't accept that. Couldn't bear the way it hurt.

I removed my hands from the grips, relaxed them on my thighs, and clocked her approach with the rapid fire of my breaths.

She stopped her bike on the sidewalk beside me. Facing opposite directions, our legs inches apart, a mantle of patient acceptance settled over us. Our expressions safely concealed beneath the visors, we took each other in. No expectations. Simply watching.

I turned off the engine, and she followed suit. The crank of a car sounded in the distance, but this stretch of Rogers Avenue, beneath the concrete arches of the elevated train tracks, belonged to us.

Her helmet tipped down as she traced a gloved finger around the cap of her gas tank. "You've got a magic key to my condo, and now you're tracking me?" She looked up. "Should I be worried?"

"I'm harmless."

She laughed. "Hearing you say that in that damned voice…" She cleared her throat. "Nice try."

Oh, if she could see my eyebrow now. No doubt it matched the twitch in my lips. "You weren't at the race tonight."

Her helmet cocked to the side. "Missing me now, are you?"

I'd told her to stop going, but yeah, I fucking missed her. So much I reached out my hand and placed it over her restless ones on the gas tank.

She jerked away, taking her entire body with it. Tension snapped through her back as she leaned forward and gripped the handlebars. Looking straight ahead, she reached for the ignition.

My hands clenched. Christ, I'd done that to her. All my bullshit had made her jumpy and distrustful, the usual heat that simmered between us gone. If she harbored any feelings for Evader, they were deeply buried beneath her hurt.

"Stay." I crossed my arms over my chest, trapping my hands. "I'll keep my hands here."

Eternal seconds ticked by. Pressure built in my head, my body thrumming to tell her who I was and why I'd done the things I did.

I couldn't risk it. Trent controlled her with threats, which meant he could extort any information I gave her.

None of that mattered, not in this moment. Right now, I was just a man, with the simple need to be near her.

"Tell me something." She angled her visor to look at me, her forward lean still poised to jet. "Something personal."

It was a quiet request, unassuming in its delivery. She wasn't prying. More like trying to connect in a way we hadn't done before.

My knees loosened around the bike, my fingers curling in the gloves. I wanted that connection. I wanted *real.*

So I gave her my most personal, most deeply-buried thought, something I had never admitted aloud. "I'm very angry with my mother."

The words resonated in my head, lingering with the vibrations of the voice modifier.

She straightened her back and folded her hands in her lap. Her silence was comforting, oddly encouraging.

I dragged a boot over the concrete between our bikes. "It's unjustified. I know this. She didn't leave me by choice. It wasn't her fault I had no family. But she left all the same. Left me with nothing but this anger." My chest tightened, my arms constricting around my torso. Pissed off thirteen-year-old boys didn't make friends in boys' homes. It was a wonder Benny put up with me. "I'm afraid it made me a bit of an asshole."

"Hmm. Is that an apology for being a dick the other night?"

I was sorry for every goddamned thing I'd done to her. "Yeah." I wanted so badly to uncross my arms and pull her against me, but I'd told her I wouldn't move my hands. "Your turn. Something personal."

Her helmet tilted back, staring at the concrete supports of the overpass. "I hate high heels. Hate the way they make me feel. Everything they stand for."

No shit? I glanced at the scratched-up black boots on her feet, considering her response. I expected her to say something about her wretched mother, but somehow her answer seemed more intimate and revealing than anything she could've said about her family.

I'd seen her glide across a nightclub, tall and confident, her sexy heels an extension of her compelling aura and beauty. I'd assumed she chose them because she loved the effect they had on those watching her. They'd certainly affected *me* on the dance floor.

"And snakes." Her voice hardened, her visor lowering to stare at her hands. "I hate snakes."

I had a very bad feeling that was metaphorical. Was she referring to Evader or the man who stole her job in the most vile way?

Fighting the swallow in my throat, I chose my words carefully. "The kind of snake who leaves a gorgeous woman unsatisfied in an elevator?"

She snorted. "No, not you. I was thinking of the spineless snake I work with. The kind that is charming to your face then unsheathes its fangs when you turn your back." Her helmet angled away, pointing down the road. "Never trust anything that swallows its prey alive and whole."

Hard to ignore that direct hit. It cut my air and scorched the back of my throat. But I swallowed it down, let it stab through my chest. God knew I deserved it.

She sucked in a sharp breath. "That just gave me an idea." Lifting her sleeve, she checked her watch. "I've got to go."

Why did I feel like I just missed a really important punch line?

She started the ignition, rolled forward, and glanced at me over her shoulder. "See you around, Evader."

Then she bolted forward, leaving me in a cloud of exhaust and confusion.

Until I walked into my office on Monday morning.

It was seven in the morning when I dragged my feet down the corridor of my very own wing on the executive floor, messenger bag strapped across my chest and coffee in hand. As much as I'd rather be on my bike than suffocating in a suit and tie, there was no sense whining about it. I'd worked myself into this position, after all.

At the double doors of Trenchant's most prestigious office, the cornerstone of power and evil, my attention caught on the plaque on the wall.

Logan Flynt scrawled in pretentious cursive, glazed in lacquer. It was official. I was the CEO asshole of dirty corporate assholes.

Once I ended the reign of corruption, what would become of Trenchant and the thousands who worked here? In a perfect world, Kaci would be innocent, and she would assume the leadership role and rebuild an ethical company. But the world was far from perfect.

As I pushed open the door and crossed the room, my attention was drawn to the ceiling. Why were the motion sensor lights already on?

Ten feet away, the desk moved. Like the entire fucking surface squirmed. I slammed to a stop, slopping coffee onto my sleeve and burning my hand. "Goddammit."

I narrowed my eyes.

Snakes. They crawled over the desk, the keyboard, and the organizer thingie that held pens and shit. A couple snakes tumbled onto the floor, and like a big pussy, I shuffled backward, spilling more coffee.

I spun in a circle, scanning the floor around my Chucks. No snakes. Releasing a breath, I took in the rest of the office, the couches, the potted plants in the corners, and the bookshelves at the far end. A few slithered at the edges of the room, but they weren't pouring out of the vents or anything.

The wriggling black bodies concentrated on and around the desk. Maybe three or four dozen, each about a foot long and thin as a pencil. I could imagine her dumping them all right on the desk and lifting that daring chin as she marched out.

More fell onto the floor, slithering beneath the desk and disappearing to God knew where. It was insane, spectacularly immature, and I really kind of adored her for it.

A smile pulled at my lips. "Well played, Kaci."

Now the question was, how much did she hate me? In other words, were they venomous? I slammed back the rest of the coffee and dropped the cup in the wastebasket. Then, while keeping an eye on the snakes, I used my phone to search the Interwebs. A few minutes later, I determined they were ringnecks. Only slightly venomous.

Did that mean she only slightly hated me? That was comforting.

Online sources said they could be handled by humans due to their tiny fangs and non-aggressive nature. I plucked one off the floor, pinching just behind the head. Given that she considered me a snake, if I died from a snakebite, it would be a poetic way to get even. I suspected she thought of that. Probably while she was talking to my other self Saturday night. If she only knew.

I needed the papers in the messenger bag, so I kept it on my shoulder as I carried the snake to Alicia's desk, holding it out of sight.

She blinked up at me, pushing out her chest in a comically obvious way. "Can I help you, Mr. Flynt?"

I'd inherited Trent's assistant along with his office. She was probably well-used by him, but I hadn't found any illegal behavior during my two days of monitoring her activities. Nevertheless, I only approached her when I needed something insignificant. "Need you to call in animal control."

Her over-plucked brows pulled together. "Sorry, did you say—?"

"Got a pest problem." I held up the snake.

She screeched, her chair rolling back and hitting the wall in her scramble to stand.

"There's an infestation." I gestured toward my office. "Make the call."

With a hand over her gaping mouth and her eyes locked on the snake, she blindly reached for the phone.

The thin, scaly body coiled around my fingers as I crossed the building to Kaci's wing. I brought the snake as an icebreaker, but the documents in my messenger bag would be the pivotal point of our conversation this morning.

If she truly wasn't involved in her family's debauchery, the details of my blackmail would break her heart. I licked my lip with cautious hope, wanting so desperately for her to be innocent. But at the same time, I loathed seeing her hurt again.

Jenna looked up from her monitor as I approached. I held the snake at my back to avoid another ear-splitting scream.

Her round face grew even rounder with a smile. "Good Morning. You're Mr. Flynt, right?"

I'd investigated Jenna, as well. She e-mailed those files to Kaci, but didn't appear to be involved in any suspicious activities. I gave her a short nod. "Is Kaci in today?"

"Yes. Right through there." She pointed, her husky voice matching her large build.

I didn't knock. I was her boss, after all. I moved the snake forward so she wouldn't miss it and opened the door.

My breath rushed from my lungs. The woman before me, with eyes of the darkest blue and silken blonde hair in waves around her arms, reclined in one of the big leather chairs in the sitting area beside her desk. Her creamy skin glowed against her black slacks and short-sleeve sweater the color of her eyes.

With a leg thrown over the armrest, her hair down, and feet bare, she stared at the laptop on her lap. She looked collected, in control of her entire being. Not tightly composed like she'd been when she watched the video.

Nothing on her face indicated strain or concealment. Her soft expression and the fluidity of her breaths seemed natural, effortless, almost at peace. It was a desirable look on her, underscoring her vivid beauty without trying. Fucking breathtaking.

She glanced up at the snake in my hand. "Now there's something you don't see every day. A carnivorous, cold-blooded reptile holding a snake."

My jaw clenched at her meaning, but my chest lifted at the sound of her lilt. I wanted to hate her for being so goddamned beautiful. I wanted to kiss her for the same reason.

I wanted to know how many times Collin had fucked her since our night together. No, fuck, I didn't want to know that.

I wanted to demand she leave him, which was ridiculous. She fucking hated me.

My muscles tensed to fix what I broke, to fight if I had to. It was a powerful need, shooting a tingle across my lips, a tingle that burned to take her mouth.

Even as I despised her for being unfaithful. I looked away, and my eyes ached with an overwhelming urge to pull back to her as my heart hammered to close the distance.

I sucked in a long, deep breath. Jesus, how could there be so much contradiction contained in my body?

Because you want her, and you know you can't have her.

The snake coiled its tail under my sleeve as I locked the door and strode toward her. Holding it by the head, I dangled the squirming body in front of her face. "I see you've been thinking about me."

She slowly closed the laptop, without a single twitch at the snake wriggling inches from her nose. "Did you know snakes have two penises?" She reached beside the chair, raised a tall wastebasket, and held it beneath the snake. "And some have spiny hooks on their dicks. You know, so they can anchor themselves inside to extend the duration of the *fucking*."

Her tone was calm. Too calm. I wanted her to scream at me.

I dropped the snake in the basket, a creature I would never look at the same way again. "Two penises?"

"It allows the snake to go from one mate to another without a period of latency in between. Which makes me wonder." She set the snake aside and leaned back, staring up at me. "How many people are you screwing to get want you want?"

I gripped the back of my neck, my stomach hardening with frustration and guilt. *Tell her. Tell her everything.*

Then what? At what lengths would she go to escape the threat Trent used against her and Collin? After what I did to her, she'd sell me out in a heartbeat, and who could fucking blame her?

I lifted the strap of the messenger bag over my head, dropped it on the floor, and looked her in the eyes. "You're asking the wrong questions. You don't even know *what I want*."

Pulling her bare feet onto the cushion and bending her knees against the armrest, she turned her head and gazed through the wall of windows beside us.

The broad shoulders of Chicago's skyline stretched over the horizon, its architecture and height spread out with room to breathe in the fiery sunrise. It was a hypnotic picture of elegance and strength, like the profile of the woman watching it.

Without moving her eyes, she said, "You want the same thing they all do. Money. Sex. Control. Life in the fast lane."

That last one was incredibly accurate, jabbing at my childhood dream of racing professionally and *legally*. But she hadn't meant it in the literal sense.

I crouched beside her chair, our faces a foot apart, and waited for her to give me her eyes. When she did, I filled mine with honesty. "You're wrong about me." Which contradicted the motivation I'd given Trent, but I didn't want her categorizing me with the assholes who controlled her. "I'm not them."

For a long moment, she studied my face. Roaming over my jaw and lips, flitting to my eyes, lingering on my right eyebrow, she blinked away, only to return to my brow again.

I stifled a smile, holding as still as possible. I seriously loved her quirky fascination with that part of me, loved that she noticed the natural arch so quickly. Other than my mother, she was the only person who'd ever looked close enough to detect it.

Something shifted in her gaze, latching on to whatever she saw in mine. "I believe you. Just like when you gave me your word in the hotel room." Her lips formed a flat line. "Why are you here?"

Christ, her expression was a heart-wrenching mix of anger and hurt. If she was innocent, she deserved to know that I planned to kill her family. But if she shared that knowledge, it could get me killed. Her, too.

I shifted back in my crouched position, needing to clear my head of her intoxicating proximity and think through this.

She slouched against the chair back, interpreting my caution as refusal. "I got your resume from HR. Is that shit legit? MIT with honors? Physics, Engineering, and Business Management?"

"Yeah."

She stared at me intensely. Despite the glow of dawn gilding her eyes in gold, her pupils dilated, a silent indicator of the complexity of her thoughts.

I needed to redirect the focus back on her. It made me nervous, her analyzing my motivations and searching for the truth. I leaned forward. "What did your husband say?"

She blinked, her eyebrows gathering.

I knelt in front of the chair and placed my forearms on the armrests, trapping her in. "Does he know about us?"

Her spine straightened, her arms wrapping around her bent knees and pulling them to her chest. "Of course he knows."

Something was missing. Something she wasn't telling me. "And?"

"And nothing. He knows I was set up."

Why hadn't the bastard hunted me down and smashed my face in? I gritted my teeth. "Does he know how much you loved it? Did you tell him how many orgasms I gave you?"

Her face hardened, and her eyes narrowed.

I was a bastard, but dammit, I needed to understand the nature of their relationship. "Did you tell him how I licked your insatiable pussy for hours?"

"I told him you licked it with a forked tongue." She smirked, but I didn't miss the shift in her breathing and the clench of her fingers on her legs.

Maybe she hated herself for enjoying our night together and would never remember it in a fond way. But I knew, *I knew*, she still wanted me as painfully as I wanted her. She was fighting it. The wounds I'd inflicted were too raw.

I could mend the damage. I *would* mend it.

Careful not to touch her, I bent over her folded frame until my chest hovered an inch from her knees. "I get that you're pissed, but you know as well as I do there is nothing hotter or more intense than the way we fucked that night."

Her head tilted to the side. "You're a world-class dick."

God, I wanted to kiss her sassy mouth. "And your soaking wet pussy loved me."

Anger tightened her eyes with a quickness that told me that was the absolute worst thing to say.

Fuck. I was going about this the wrong way. Our connection wasn't just a sexual one. There was an emotional current flowing through it, a searching kind of energy that fused on a level I didn't comprehend.

I needed to stop thinking with my cock and do the brave thing. I needed to open up my insides. Let her have a good look around. Maybe I'd learn something, too, because right now, I was operating on gut and backbone, both of which belonged to a Neanderthal.

I shifted into her space, my eyes and face exposed for her scrutiny, and infused my voice with the sincerity of my words. "It was real, Kaci. I shut off the cameras before we removed our clothes, and everything that happened after was just you and me. No bullshit."

"Fuck you." The venom in her voice sliced through the tension, a contradiction to the softening of her pretty mouth and the wet sheen forming in her eyes.

I was really mucking this up. I didn't know how to communicate what I didn't understand. But my body knew. It shook with the urge to drag her to the floor, spread her beneath me, and show her exactly how I felt.

Use your words, dumbass.

I drew in a strengthening breath. "I don't know what I'm saying here, knowing you're married, and I don't have a chance in hell." I stuffed that miserable notion into a tiny corner where it couldn't distract me. "But goddammit, Kaci, if you weren't married, I'd fight for you." I rubbed my face, felt my jaw hardening beneath my hand. "Fuck that. I'm fighting for you anyway."

Eyes of fathomless blue studied me with a fierceness that said she was listening, that she very much wanted to believe me. But her voice lashed with angry suspicion. "You started a fight *against* me. How in the hell are you going to fight *for* me?"

I wasn't in the habit of stealing other men's wives. I wouldn't fight Collin, not if she loved him. What then? What was I fighting for?

Searching her eyes, I looked past the confident glow she held at the surface and probed deep beyond the liquid blue. She stared back, seemingly content with letting me explore. I lost track of time, my bearings, and a part of my soul in the soundless intimacy of her gaze. When her arm lifted at the edge of my vision, the spell shivered.

The light touch of her hand on my cheek silenced my breaths. My heartbeat sped up. Sweat slicked my palms. And there, in the deepest reaches of her eyes and in the warmth of her hand on my face, I found what I was looking for.

It had been there all along, staring up at me in the elevator, reaching for me on the dance floor, wrapping around me in the hotel room, and right now, touching my face. Her loneliness fused into every cell of my body and made me want things I had no business wanting.

I moved my hands to the seat back behind her head. "I'm going to fight for your forgiveness." I pressed my chest against her legs, pinning her knees between our bodies. "And I'm going to fight for your happiness."

Wonderment illuminated from that lonely place behind her eyes, and a sad smile quivered at the corner of her mouth. She dropped her hand from my face and slid her legs out from between us, her feet lowering to the floor beside my knees. "Why?"

My pulse hammered wildly as I pushed her thighs to the side, keeping them together, and bent over her lap. "I don't know how to tell you. I can only tell you what it feels like." I grabbed her wrist and returned her palm to my face, holding it there.

She pulled on my grip, but I refused to let go as the sudden, desperate need for her to understand opened my mouth. "This is real. So real I feel it everywhere, like a million tiny vibrations under my skin. This…this urgency to protect you…" My breath burst in and out, and my voice thickened with the messy, unfiltered truth. "It's a crazy need inside me, driving me to be near you, to watch over you, to undo the hurt I put in your eyes. I don't fucking know what it is, but I feel it now, spinning me around—*around you*—and knocking me way the fuck off track."

Talk about ripping myself open. The sentiment that had come out of my mouth scared the shit out of me. What must she think? I sounded like a fucking creeper.

The real kicker was, these feelings weren't new. I'd buried them for nine months, pretending the silver Ducati at the finish line wasn't the reason I raced faster and harder to get there. But I couldn't tell her that.

Her fingers, now relaxed in my grip, stroked the sensitive spot beneath my ear, the movement a subconscious one that made me sigh deeply, happily. Which only added to my confusion.

I dropped my forehead to her thigh and spoke against her knee, my heart thundering. "I can't *not* fight for you."

She moved her hand through my hair, gliding her touch around the back of my ear. "You stole my job, Logan. You videotaped us having sex and gave it to my father-in-law."

Her tone was as soft and rhythmic as her touch, but the weight of her words crushed my windpipe.

She dropped her hand to her lap. "And in case you missed my reaction in his office, I hate Trent with every fiber in my body. The fact that *he*, of all people, saw that video—"

I jerked to my feet and paced to the windows, eyes on the glowing glass and concrete metropolis. "I'll regret that till the day I die." Which would be soon if I gave into this reckless urge to tell her my secrets.

My betrayal, her marriage, my revenge, all of it pressed down on my shoulders and crawled its way through me. My body itched with it, my mind pushing against the binds of our situation, searching for hidden solutions, and testing for weak areas.

I turned to face her. "Do you love your husband?"

"Yes."

Her immediate and unwavering response threatened to buckle my knees. What did I expect? That my mutilated confession of feelings had changed her heart? Didn't matter. She could sit there and watch me suffer. I wasn't going anywhere.

"The broody glare is back." She stood and closed the gap between us.

Her hands moved along the lapels of my suit jacket, straightening the creases. She seemed to be torturing me intentionally, sliding her fingers over my collar, so close to my throat I could feel the heat from them, and retreating without touching my skin.

She lowered her arms to her sides. "There are different kinds of love, Logan."

That small, unexpected addendum made it easier to swallow the knot of pain in my throat. "Okay." I strengthened my voice. "Like what?"

She stepped to the window and flattened a hand against the glass, staring into the sunrise. "There's the sparks-flying, emotionally-volcanic kind of love. You know, short-fused, explosive sex that fizzles as quickly as it ignites?" She gave me a pointed look and returned to the window. "Some might say that's not love at all."

I swallowed. "It's lust. Desire."

Was that what she thought this was between us? Fuck that. A fizzling affair wasn't what I was fighting for.

Her sigh billowed through the silence. "Desire is a form of love, however fleeting. You feel it in the moment, and holy hell, you feel the emptiness when it's gone." She breathed in, out. "It's the weakest kind of love."

She wouldn't be standing here, giving into Trent's threat, if her love for her husband was weak. The notion constricted my throat, but I pushed it away and clung to the implication that she and Collin didn't have explosive sex. "That's not how you love him."

She laughed. "No."

Sunlight reflected off her profile as she lowered her eyes to her bare feet, her dark blonde lashes resting against her cheek. "Then there's the steadfast, reliable love. A solid foundation that withstands time and hardship. The kind you protect with your life."

The absent tilt of her lips told me more than her words did. *This* was how she loved him, and I didn't know what to make of that.

A lock of hair fell against her cheek, blocking my view of her expression. I leaned a shoulder against the window, facing her, and brushed the golden strands behind her ear.

She closed her eyes and touched her brow to the glass. "The strongest love begins from a place of conflict. It's a volatile journey of committing and fighting and recommitting, but the effort is resolute and evolves into something so consuming the heart aches just thinking about it." Her chest rose and fell with the cadence of her voice. "A soul-deep fusion of two bodies where there is no room for emptiness."

Her longing was beautiful and poignant, one I felt in every painful beat of my heart, filling me with a possessive need to be the man who gave her that kind of happiness.

Her gaze lingered on mine, a flush sweeping over her face, an embarrassed smile twitching her lips. She shrugged. "You asked."

We stared at each other for a quiet moment. No words or touching, but the atmosphere hummed with all the questions that hadn't been answered.

The messenger bag on the floor held proof that my intentions were earnest and very personal. It was time to show her everything I gave her parents, and her reaction would dictate how I would proceed from there.

But I needed some questions answered first. "What are you doing with the information Hal Pinkerton sends you?"

Her breathing quickened, and tension stiffened her posture. "What?"

"You're using the schematics to attend the underground races. What else are you doing with it?"

She clenched her jaw. "How do you know about that?

"I know a lot of things about Trenchant's dirty ties. Answer the question, and I'll tell you."

Her fists went to her hips. "Obviously I'm not reporting it in the papers or turning it over to the cops. I just like to watch."

Part of me believed she used to go to watch *me*. "Why is Trent logging onto the server where Jenna is retrieving the files?"

Her eyes widened in frozen pools of blue, and seeing that loosened my shoulders with tremendous relief. Her shock wasn't only authentic, it confirmed my suspicions. She was in the dark about Trent's dealings. At least, with regard to the underground racing network.

I walked the few steps to my messenger bag. Picking it up, I gestured to the chair. "Have a seat."

She sat, watching me with a cautious expression. I lowered into the chair perpendicular to hers and removed the folder from the bag. It was harsh, but I wouldn't prepare her. I simply set the packet on her lap and studied her reaction with breathless concentration.

As she read the first page with a dazed stare, I knew Trent hadn't shared the details of my blackmail with her. Her hand shook through the next page. Several pages later, the blood drained from her face, her chest heaved, and her elbows pressed against her sides.

Fraud, laundering, embezzlement, rape, murder. The papers trembling in her fingers were bloodied with the crimes of her family.

As she flipped through the pages, I felt her pain as if it were my own. I felt her fist clenched against her stomach, the quiver in her chin, the droop of her shoulders. Aching to comfort her, I shifted forward and reached a hand toward her knee.

She flinched. "No. Just…" Her voice cracked, her palm out, warding me off. "Don't."

During that agonizing fragment of time, I saw the mother who taught me how to power through my childhood hurts. Who flew her bike over eighteen-wheelers and nearly died from a launch between two thirty-foot buildings. Who died instead from the evil that was hurting Kaci now.

Her voice cut through the dark smudge of memory. "This is what you used to blackmail the board?"

She didn't have the orange confidential envelope I'd shown Trent. "Mostly, yes."

Head down, she stared at the folder in her lap. "But they denied it, right?"

I wasn't surprised by the hope in that question. Slowly, I reached for her face, and this time she didn't cringe. I tilted up her chin so I could see her eyes. "They couldn't. The truth is all there."

She leaned away from my touch. "Are you a cop?"

I shook my head.

Angling away, she stared into the sunrise, the back of her hand trembling against her brow and shielding the glare. "This *is* personal for you."

I hadn't intended to tell her the true reason behind my blackmail, only to show her the evidence I'd given her family and evaluate her reaction. But nothing about Kaci Baskel fit into my plans. Despite all logic, I trusted her. "This is deeply personal."

Her beautiful face twisted in misery, her mouth flickering between a pained smile and a heartbreaking grimace. She was shocked, scared, haunted.

Undeniably innocent.

Which meant her definition of justice would strongly oppose mine. "We're not going to the cops. Do you understand?"

She dropped her hand and skewered me with a fierce glare. "No. I don't think I do."

The lines of her face were delicate and exquisitely shaped, even as they sharpened with anger and horror.

Maybe she hadn't leapt to the conclusion that I intended to murder her family, but some part of her must've known it was a possibility, and I needed her to understand why.

I reached in the bag and handed her the orange envelope.

I lowered the papers with frozen fingers and woodenly returned them to the orange envelope. The pressure in my chest felt as if I were being held underwater, my body weighted down by the crimes of my family, the documents I'd just read, and the connections my mind was racing to put together.

The envelope Logan had saved till last was the tipping point. Medical records, DNA tests, proof of parentage, all of it made me hyper-aware of the stillness in the man watching me.

He wasn't a man I could easily look away from, but knowing now who he was, the thought of meeting his gaze made me anxious. Would he look different to me? Would I see traits I hadn't noticed before? Features that reminded me of Trent or Collin?

I gathered my nerves, clenched my shaking hands, and raised my head.

He hadn't moved from his chair, sitting at a right angle to mine, studying me with deep golden eyes, the emerald rings around the irises intensifying his stare. Lips compressed in a line, his jaw the definition of stern. "Ask your questions."

Jesus, where to start? All the horrible things my family had done made me question my safety, made me question everything. What if they were listening? Watching us right now? The hairs on my nape bristled with paranoia. "This isn't the place to talk."

He glanced around the room and back to me. "There aren't any bugs. I already checked. If you and I met outside this office, it would cause suspicion."

Given the way he'd pulled off his blackmail, I trusted he knew what he was doing. But he wasn't making decisions based on *my* best interests. He'd lied to me from the first day we'd met. I shouldn't trust a word that came out of his mouth. But the documents he showed me? Of course, I'd verify them myself, but I knew enough about my family to know it was all true. That was something I *could* trust.

I flattened the envelope on my lap and flexed my fingers. "Your mother and Trent…" How did I ask this? He'd just given me proof that Trent had a history of rape, and I knew firsthand the kind of vile harassment my father-in-law was capable of. "Were they lovers?"

"No." The quiet fury in his voice chilled a path down my spine. "He met her in LA thirty-three years ago. I was born a year later."

Trent was already married then. I rubbed my temples, tried to massage away the rising tension. "Collin and I would've been four-years-old."

He nodded, his face tightening. "She died when I was thirteen." He looked away, staring hard out the window with so much anger etched in his rugged profile. "She kept a diary. Always had it with her. Not once did she write about her interactions with Trent. But it included journals about her lovers." He met my eyes. "My mother was a lesbian."

My chest caved in as I filled in the blanks. Then another thought, a recent memory with a different man, brushed the back of my mind. *I'm very angry with my mother. She didn't leave me by choice. Left me with nothing but this anger.*

Before I could examine that, he handed me another paper, a news article. I didn't want to look at it, unsure how much more I could handle.

When he gave an impatient nod at the clipping in my hand, I unfolded the tattered edges and read silently.

The body of Motorcycle Hall of Fame's Maura Flynt found in an Ohio hotel room.

Hotel staff discovered her body on the bed, her throat cut, and a large butcher knife on the pillow. At the time staff arrived, the body was cold and had evidently been dead some time.

There was more, but the words blurred together, forming gruesome images that bled their way into my throat, my eyes, my heart.

"I was there." His voice rasped from a couple feet away, yet he sounded so distant, lost in a different time and place. "I watched it happen, hidden beneath the bed."

I couldn't breathe as the words shaved away a layer of his coarse exterior, giving me a glimpse of the vulnerable boy in that hotel room. His shoulders curled forward, his chin tucking. It was a brief glimpse. He quickly straightened his spine, and the uncompromising set of his jaw returned.

Part of me hated my weakness for him, but dammit, I didn't want him to hide from me. I wanted to see him, the man who was so much more than a deceptive one-night stand. He'd been open about his reasons for betraying me, forcing me to look at the harsh reality without sugarcoating his role in it. But it was his regret for hurting me that weakened the wall between broken trust and second chances.

Oh, I was still hurting, and that pain was magnified by the choices I had to make with regard to my family. But I put that aside and let the thump of my heart pull me forward.

I set the documents on the floor, rose from the chair, and slid onto his lap. His arms folded around my waist with an intimacy that was familiar yet so different than our night together. It was an exchange of vulnerability, a difficult gift to give, but one that could make a person realize what it was they really needed.

Sitting sideways on his lap, I pushed my hands through the gelled-up hair above his ears and tipped his head so I could see his face. "Keep going."

He looked at me with shock then licked his bottom lip as if he wanted to kiss me. His eyes shut, opened. "My mother told me once to take her diary and disappear if anything ever happened to her." He traced a finger along my bicep, watching the movement with unfocused eyes. "So I did. Ended up on the streets in Chicago. Eventually got picked up and put in a boys' home. I'd read her diary by then and knew I had to keep my identity a secret."

He was just a boy when he watched the slaughter of his mother. Forced into a nightmare of choices *alone*. God, I hurt with him, my breath tightening around the burn in my throat.

To think Collin and I were raised by the hand responsible for his pain, yet we didn't suffer for anything except our parents love. Logan had to fight for everything. He put himself through MIT. Became the CEO of a Fortune 500 company. Though he acquired the job—*my job*—through blackmail, he'd earned the qualifications required to lead. Really fucking amazing, actually.

I lay my cheek on his shoulder, my arm around his chest, and listened to his rumbling voice as he detailed the contents of his mother's diary, the leads she'd scraped together, and her plan to go after Trenchant.

His hand moved to my leg as he talked, his thumb tracing the seam of my pants along my inner thigh. I bit down on my lip, trying and failing to ignore the flutter he produced inside me.

He shifted deeper into the chair, pulling my side closer to his chest. "Trent didn't know he had another son until I gave him that envelope five days ago. I have no idea if he shared the news with your family."

Collin would've told me if he knew. "Why did you tell him you're his son? He has no loyalties to his family. No qualms about sending Collin to prison."

The natural arch of his right eyebrow twitched. "I presented myself as the bastard son who feels entitled to his father's wealth and power. It was a motivation for my blackmail, one he relates to and therefore doesn't question."

When our gazes met, I saw the real reason he was here. The deep, angry pain beneath the shadowy lines of his brow. The need for revenge possessed him, controlled his life, and drove him to succeed.

If Trent sent Collin to prison or had him killed, how far would I go to get even? Just thinking about it made me see Logan's anger in a new light. The sense of loss I'd felt over the past five days paled in comparison.

He had no one through his childhood hardship. I had Collin through my five-day scorn.

But I didn't have Collin in the way Logan was looking at me now.

He reached up and tucked a strand of hair behind my ear, his fingers lingering on my jaw. "I'll never grow tired of looking at you."

My eyes threatened to close, so I locked my concentration on the tension in his thighs under mine, the steady breaths pushing past his lips, and the swallow crawling beneath his tie. When I glanced up, the desolation and longing in his eyes reflected my deepest ache.

An ache that he'd exploited to get what he wanted. A bitter thought whispered through my head. I could seduce him, use him for my own pleasure, and toss him away. Right now, I was the one with the power to hurt.

But I didn't want to add to the heartache in those molten-gold eyes. I'd rather challenge him. Tease him just enough then stand back and watch him burn. And maybe, just maybe, his burning need for me would turn into the fight he promised.

I shifted my body to straddle his lap. His mouth opened immediately, reaching to take mine. I gripped his face, held my parted lips an inch from his, and gloried in the push and shove of our clashing breaths. His lips were so close they heated mine, but our mouths didn't touch.

The longer I held that tenuous inch between us, the harder our breaths pumped, neither of us relinquishing eye contact. His fingers dug into my hips, my muscles wincing from the punishment. But another sensation rolled through my body, an intoxicating heat, chasing away the cold emptiness that lived inside me.

He pushed his face against the hold of my hands, trying to close that final inch. I leaned back when he shoved forward, a back and forth battle of open mouths and wet exhales, his desperation to kiss me a heady aphrodisiac. His body surrounded me with an invigorating warmth of energy, his chest so fucking hard I wanted to strip his suit and tie and worship the rough-hewn sculpture of his muscles.

But I waited, made him wait, our breaths shallow and noisy as I drew it out, teasing him mercilessly. His cock stiffened against my inner thigh, the clutch of his hands on my hips unbearable. As he tried to lick my lips, his eyes filled with a storm of emotions, and at the forefront was a wild, feral need.

When his pelvis bucked beneath me, rocking me closer, I knew I wouldn't be able to hold him off. I angled my head, smiled and, when his gorgeous eyes flashed, relaxed my grip on his face.

He fell on me, his mouth hot and wet as it devoured mine, his tongue whipping past my teeth with an urgency that had my fingers twisting in his hair, yanking him away, and pulling him closer.

Nothing about our attraction was reserved or tame. He was fire, and I was the fuel. We were angry and wanton, passionate and aching. Explosive.

And cruel.

I dropped my hands to his chest and pushed, breaking the kiss and gasping for air. "I don't trust you."

His jaw clenched, his eyes fiery flames of determination. He nodded once. Then he was on me, his tongue thrusting violently past my lips, desperately fighting for me, for *us*. He dragged my hips tight against his, the steel length of his arousal grinding along my piercing. Electric sparks shot through my clit, coaxing my inner walls to clench hungrily.

This was the man from the nightclub, the one who stole my breath with a mysterious glare, who set my insides on fire with a touch, and who fucked with his mouth and took what he wanted.

I wanted to bite him, slap him, punch him again. More than that, I wanted to make him mine. I wanted his anger, his ferocity, his pain. To claim every part of him, fuse it with all of me, and make us a singular whole.

I pulled back to look at him, but before I could catch my breath, he swooped in and stole it again with his hands on my jaw and his mouth sealed to mine. Mirroring his hold, I cupped his face, my thighs squeezing his waist. He kissed me tirelessly, tongues sparring, lips mashed together, deep-reaching and wickedly raw.

My chest heaved against his, our hearts pounding with the rush of our breaths. A curling pressure swelled between my legs, and I jerked my hips, savoring the grind of his cock, wanting more. God, I wanted him.

As his hands slid from my jaw to my neck, his mouth relaxed and a tender kiss flowed from the urgency. He took his time, his lips softening against mine, his tongue exploring with gentle licks. It was heated and thrumming with desire but also deeper, more expressive. Far more intense than any kiss that had come before it.

The path of his fingers dipped along the lines of my throat, across my collarbones, and around the curves of my breasts over the short-sleeve sweater. I slid my hips forward, thrusting my chest against his hand, my lips burning from the heat of his mouth.

I was breathless when he stopped kissing me. He leaned back, shoulders relaxed despite the heave of his chest. His hands slid to my waist, his thighs separating beneath my ass, his hard cock pressing against the throb between my legs.

His mouth was open to accommodate his heavy breaths, his lips wet and puffy, his hair tousled from my hands. I gripped the knot of his tie and re-centered it, sliding my fingers over the softly-shaven skin of his jaw. My God, he was stunning when aroused.

His half-lidded eyes darted between mine. "What are you doing to me?"

This was it. He was most definitely burning. I needed to dig up some damned willpower and step back.

Curling my nails into my palms, I pulled from his grip and slipped from his lap. His eyes narrowed as I backed up toward the windows.

He rose, prowling after me, his face reddening, his broad chest and shoulders expanding with tension. His glare pushed against me, eyes of golden-green set in an expression that seemed to prefer scowling and growling over smiling. Which only added to his intimidating disposition as he stalked closer. A foot away. "What are you doing *with* me? That kiss?" He clenched his fists. "What's going on between you and Collin?"

My back hit the glass as he covered my body with his. He grabbed my hair, arching my neck back. His other hand cupped my breast as he licked my exposed throat, sucking, kissing his way to my jaw, and groaning into my mouth. "I hate that you belong to another man. My *brother.*" He kissed me again, hard and angry, and pulled back. "I fucking hate it. So answer my goddamned question."

I whimpered, my heart hammering to tell him. Fuck! I'd known him less than a week. The bastard fucked me over. I couldn't do the same to Collin by exposing his secret.

Besides, Logan needed to earn the answer. I placed my hands on the lapels of his jacket and shoved. He stumbled back then flew forward, attacking my mouth again. Just as quickly, he tore his lips away, his eyes wide and red with so much conflict it killed me.

Don't back down. Don't give in.

I wasn't sure what he saw on my face, but he curled his lip, pulled back his arm, and slammed his fist against the glass beside my head. I jumped, restrained by the forearm across my chest, as the window wall shuddered and held.

He dropped his forehead against mine, the arm on my chest holding me in place. His other hand slid angrily over the glass, up and down, in rhythm with his short breaths.

A long moment of deadlock passed, everything left unsaid agitating between us. He seemed to be gathering his self-control. As his breathing shifted, he removed his hand from the glass and sifted it through my hair, his fingers splayed to let the strands fall between.

I raised my arm and slid my palm over his, untangling it from my hair. He let his brow sink heavier against mine, his eyes on our hands, on the sunlight that glowed around the connection. The fiery sprays of light played along our fingers as we laced them together, illuminating the beauty in the simple touch. I watched it in wonderment, filling my chest with that glow, my mouth slowly reaching for his.

He stepped back, the warmth of his touch replaced with the several feet of space he put between us. The look on his face was both heartbreaking and passionately fierce. "You can't tell Collin about my mother."

Reality crashed over me, the glow in my body zapped by a sudden chill as everything he'd shown me rushed to the surface.

He swiped a hand over his face, his eyes more resolute than ever. "I don't know what Collin's role is, but if he knows why I'm here…"

He shoved his hands through his hair and stared at the ceiling. "He can't know I want revenge. If he tells Trent—"

"Collin won't tell." I fisted my hands at my sides. "He's not involved in this. I've kept him in the dark on everything."

"What is *everything*?" He leveled me with a suspicious gaze.

I pinched the bridge of my nose and sat on the armrest of the leather chair. "Ambiguous tasks, most of which are shady, but on the surface seem completely harmless." With a sigh, I explained the nature of the board's demands over the years, like the delivery of the Timex watch, managing the direction of Collin's show, changing numbers on financial statements due to *accounting mistakes*, all of it legal but shady nonetheless.

What Logan had showed me clicked all my suspicions into place. My distrust in them was the reason I wanted to replace them when I became CEO. But what left me stunned and ice cold was the degree of their corruption. My God, I would've never believed it without his evidence.

He moved to the messenger bag on the floor beside my feet and crouched to return the documents inside. "Does Collin know you watch the races?"

"Yes." Only he and Seth knew.

"Does he know *how* you receive the schematics to attend?" His eyes were on his bag, his body stock-still. "Does he know Hal Pinkerton is feeding you that dangerous information?"

Dangerous because it was underground with illegal betting and extreme racing that often ended in injury or death. Dangerous if the wrong people discovered who leaked it to the authorities. I glared at his bowed head. "Yes."

He looked up. "Trent knows, too, which means Collin might be sharing with dear old dad."

My protective instincts bristled, hating his suspicion. Seth could've been the leak, but if I told him that, I'd have to explain who Seth was. "But *you* found that server."

"I'm looking for suspicious activity, for proof of your involvement. Does Trent have a reason to mistrust you on his own? Without someone cluing him in?"

"I don't know." Goosebumps rose along my arms, my voice numb. "Maybe he's always tracked me." Maybe Trent didn't believe I was as naïve as he always claimed.

Logan stood, strapping the bag across his chest. "When you left Trent's office, I followed you. Collin saw me across the street, and I swear he recognized me. I think he and Trent share more than you think. Which means Collin is hiding shit from you."

Bullshit. I wanted to launch at him with my claws out, but I kept my ass on the armrest and my voice calm. "Trent called Collin as soon as I left his office. And he sent a photo of you when you went racing after me. He didn't want us fighting in the streets of Chicago, making a spectacle of ourselves."

He waved a hand in dismissal. "Fine. Tell me about the threat Trent is holding over him."

Jesus, he was on a fucking witch-hunt. I gritted my teeth. "It's purchased evidence. Trent has something that puts Collin at the scene of a murder eight years ago. He's innocent."

"And you know this how? Based on faith in your husband?"

"Yes." I smiled, baring my teeth, but inside, I was picking Collin's innocence apart.

Collin told me the evidence was purchased, and I never questioned him, never doubted him for a second. My stomach twisted.

No, I refused to question his loyalties. I'd known him my entire life. My trust in him was everything. But the voice in my head reminded me that *I* hadn't been completely honest with him.

"Know what I think?" He stepped into my space, staring me down with an intensity that didn't match the gentleness in his tone. "I think he's fucking around on you, and that's why you cheated. How can you have faith in someone like that?"

I drew a calming breath and said quietly, "The relationship I have with my husband is none of your fucking business."

"I don't trust him."

The rigid tension in his face and the resolve hardening his eyes boiled my blood. "He's my best friend, the only person whose ever given a shit about me!"

He breathed in and out slowly as if working to maintain his composure. "I'm here to determine who's involved and who's not."

"Then what?" But I knew. I knew what he planned to do. My muscles tensed, and my head spun through the implications. "We need to go to the police. You have all the evidence they need to start an investigation. Let the authorities root out all the connections."

He pivoted away, pacing through the large office, his hand raking and tugging through his hair. "We can't. The evidence"—he gripped the bag hanging at his hip and shook it—"all of it will lead to *me*." He spun to face me, his eyes challenging. "I avenged those murders."

A chill tiptoed up my spine. "What are you saying?"

"Trent deals with some vile people. Assassins. Men who rape and torture and murder."

"You killed them." My shoulders tightened, self-preservation screaming at me to run, but my gut told me he'd never hurt me. Not like that. He was telling me his secrets. Very damning secrets. That was a hell of lot of trust to put in me.

"I killed rapists and murderers, Kaci. Including the man who killed my mother." His chin lifted, and the unapologetic strength of his gaze wasn't one of a crazed man. More like a battle-ready vigilante who'd lived a hard life. "I stopped them from taking more lives."

He believed he was doing the right thing, but there was a darkness in him. In the shadow of his surly glare, the turbulence of his temper, and the fierceness of his fucking.

It reminded me of the man I'd fantasized about for so long. The criminal who wore his darkness in a cloak of black leathers. Evader maimed and killed during races, a fact that hadn't deterred me during our moment in an unlit elevator.

I didn't know Logan Flynt or Evader enough to determine if they were the same man. But my mind had latched onto the idea and went searching for clues. Like the header on the news article he'd shown me. "Your mom was in the Motorcycle Hall of Fame?"

He gave a short nod, his eyes studying me from a few feet away.

I cocked my head. "You ride?"

"No."

No hesitation. No emotion. Direct eye contact. Which told me absolutely nothing.

The phone on my desk beeped. I sighed. Probably Jenna calling about the morning's schedule.

As I moved to answer it, I could feel him following. I pressed the speaker button. "Jenna?"

"Your eight-thirty meeting is waiting."

"On my way." I ended the call and turned.

Just feet apart, we stared at each other, the energy between us still there but different. The silent communication felt restricted as if waiting on certain conditions. But also hopeful and seeking.

He felt it, too. I saw it in the softening of his eyes and the slight tilt of his head as he regarded me. Then he stepped forward, erasing the gap in three slow strides. His hand went to the back of my head. His lips touched my brow and held there, coating my skin with warm breaths.

"Don't kill my family," I whispered, gripping his tie. "They're awful, but I…" I inhaled deeply. "I need some time to think."

After everything they'd done to me, I couldn't justify their deaths. Not without confirming the evidence and considering the ramifications that murder would have on Collin, myself, and especially Logan. He'd killed but hadn't murdered his own blood. *His father*. How could a person come back from that?

He cupped my face, angling it upward, his gaze searching. "While you're thinking, don't call in the cops."

If I reported what I knew, Logan would disappear. Or worse, he'd get caught. There was also Trent's threat against Collin. If I sent him to prison, he'd take Collin with him.

I nodded.

Trent had given me a month. I could wait it out to ensure Collin's protection. Then fuck this place. I'd start a new life.

But what about Collin's career? And what was happening on October twenty-seventh? Who sent Trent the watch?

God, I wanted to talk to Collin. I was keeping too many secrets from him, which meant he could be doing the same.

Logan brushed his lips across my forehead and stepped back. "Go to your meeting. I'll wait while you think. Just don't take too long."

How would I stop him from murdering my family? He could do it right now and vanish. On the flip side, he couldn't stop me from turning him in. Unless he killed me.

My nerves went rampant as I watched him leave. Our parting agreement balanced on some pretty delicate trust.

On his way out, he grabbed the trash bin that held the snake and tucked it under his arm. The muscles in his back and arms flexed as he moved through the room, stretching the wool jacket.

His hard body wasn't built for a suit. All those strong, rugged edges belonged in black leather, straddling a bike. Was I imagining this? My belly fluttered at the notion.

At the door, he glanced at me over his shoulder and pointed at the snake inside the trash bin. "You do this yourself?"

Collin had helped me find the breeder and haul the snakes in, but the rest was all me. I smiled. "I know how to handle a snake."

He returned my smile with a sad one and vanished around the corner.

As the next two weeks passed by, a miserable knot took root in my stomach. I couldn't eat, couldn't sleep, and the day-to-day demands of my job took their toll on my concentration. My jaw locked in a permanent clench, nausea greeted me with each new hour, and the shriveling feeling in my chest made every breath a goddamn challenge.

Sitting in the suffocation of the boardroom, I leaned into my elbows on the table and swallowed the rush of saliva filling my mouth. It was all I could do to not heave the anxiety writhing in my stomach.

The source of my torment filled four high-backed chairs along one side of the table. My parents and my in-laws sat in their usual them-against-me positioning with the wood surface between us. Even with my eyes averted, I could feel them. Their filth in the air, the prick of their passing glances, the blather of their voices, all of it strumming my nerves into unbearable anger.

They droned on like they hadn't committed ungodly crimes. Collin's parents bickered about the profitability of launching a new cable network. My father piped in with his technical solutions. And my mother sat silently, casting her judgment with an over-plumped sneer.

Logan and I sat on the opposite side of the table with a chair between us. A chair full of contention and looming decisions. We hadn't spoken about our secrets since the morning I delivered the snakes, yet we interacted daily as CEO and VP. He learned the ropes while I dealt with the politics surrounding his employment. Together we managed the operations as if it were our only preoccupation.

He hadn't made any moves against Trenchant and instead seemed to be settling into his new role. But his patience was a ruse. The ticking tension between us hummed over my skin during staff meetings. When we crossed paths in the halls, his cursory glances pierced me with silent questions.

We restrained from lingering looks in the presence of others. To the unknowing eye, our interactions were professional. From my family's perspective, we were enduring a forced partnership.

No one knew what I knew. Beneath Logan's suave smile and crisp suit was a murderer with a premeditated intent to finish what he'd started. No doubt he spent his free time mining the company ranks for rats while I tortured myself in deliberation, taking too long to decide, delaying the inevitable.

The inevitable was why I couldn't warm my icy fingers, why I'd lost five pounds, and why my body felt like it was shutting down. The inevitable put my family in prison or in the ground. But the part I struggled with the most was knowing once everything was brought to fruition, Logan would be gone. As a fugitive or behind bars, he wouldn't be here with me.

What the hell was I going to do about it? My severe mistrust of every damned person in my life had built a barrier between me and Collin. I couldn't come up with a convincing reason to tell him about the vile things our parents had done. What would stop him from turning them in? He didn't give a shit about the impact that would have on Logan. Or worse, what if he defended them? What if he already knew?

So I kept my mouth shut while I fact-checked everything Logan had shown me. I wasn't a journalist by any stretch, but I led an entire division of them. I verified sources, followed leads, assigned reporters to do the same, trickling out the requests and using the cautious ambiguity Trent had always used with me.

The embezzling, accounting fraud, missing employees, all of it added up, albeit hidden beneath the kind of well-placed and thorough explanations an unsuspecting person wouldn't question. The Trenchant name was stained with crime. Everything I'd unearthed soured my aspirations to lead this miserable corporation. It wasn't just the board members. The corrupted partners inside and outside of these walls were many, the layers of deceit running deep in every department.

The one thing I hadn't connected was Trent's interest in the underground racing network. According to Logan, Trent was pulling my files of the racing schematics. If that was true, why had he asked me a month ago to obtain everything I could about it? Then never asked again? He knew I was keeping that secret, and I hoped to God it was the only one he knew about.

I also investigated Logan, digging for information online, following him, and snapping photos like an obsessed stalker. He drove a Jeep Wrangler. He stopped at the Starbucks next door to the office every morning. He worked out in a gym two blocks away every night. He had no friends or family, and his address on file was a studio apartment in south Chicago. But his jeep was never in that parking lot.

Every time he slid behind the wheel of that damned jeep at Trenchant, I lost him. I used a cab to be inconspicuous, but Logan seemed to know the streets of Chicago better than anyone, knew how to whip a turn at the last second. He drove the way Evader rode his bike.

I compared the photos of Logan and Evader, studied their physiques, analyzed their heights and weights. An absurd exercise considering I'd had both of their cocks in my mouth. But my brief moment with Evader had been in the dark and the measurements of his anatomy wasn't what I took away with me that night.

Even if they were the same man, it didn't change the outcome. With each day, time wrapped tighter and tighter around my ribs. Maybe I was waiting out the month, expecting Logan to wait it out with me. Maybe I was waiting for him to fight. Not for his revenge but for me.

Sitting one chair away, he wore a black suit that sharpened the physique I knew so well and desperately missed. Always the same style with a black tie and white shirt. He must've had a closet filled with this uniform, and if I looked beneath the table, I'd find black Converse sneakers. Rebellious and sexy as sin.

His strong jaw was bare of whiskers, the cut of his dark blonde hair combed back, every strand gelled to perfection. While he rocked the clean-cut look with the smoothness of a rich businessman, I preferred him tousled and tangled and covered with scruff.

I wanted to shove my hands in his hair and muss that shit up. I wanted to kiss him until his mouth gaped for air and his eyes hooded with desire. I longed for the ruthless, sexual man who starred in my fantasies every night. Logan on a sportbike. His body gloved in black leather. His synthesized voice whispering filthy things.

This crazy need to meld two men into one made me uncomfortable. I didn't need any more complications in my life, but my body was desperate to merge them. My thighs flexed together, and the warmth between them swelled into a needy clench.

"What impact would it have on digital media, Kaci?" My father stared at me over his silver-rimmed spectacles.

I slid my hands to my lap and slowed my breathing. My open disgust with them was nothing new. I abandoned pleasantries seven years ago when they forced me into a contract. But there was no more contract, and they didn't know I knew their secrets. Didn't know I was a phone call away from turning them in. Didn't know I was considering other angles of retribution. "I don't care. Just fire me and leave Collin alone."

My mother pushed back from the table and stood to bend over it, her blue eyes sparking with outrage. "Grow up, Kaci. Get over your petty disappointment and do your damned job."

My insides winced at the viciousness in her tone. No matter how heartless she was, part of me would always crave her love.

God, I resented that. Add in my revulsion at their crimes, and I couldn't keep my mouth from curling in a hateful sneer.

They would assume my indignation had everything to do with Logan's betrayal. So I played the part. "My *job* was stolen from me by a man who blackmailed everyone in this room. Let's talk about that."

Trent lowered the phone he was constantly consumed by and leveled me with hard eyes. "Putting your nose in our affairs won't turn out well for you."

I didn't even bother looking to my parents for support. They knew the threats Trent held over me. Their greedy agendas took priority.

White noise buzzed in my ears, and my head pounded. As much as I tried to tune out my mother, her voice penetrated.

"...your thrift-store leggings, and what are you wearing on your feet? Are those biker boots? We have an image to uphold, and your disrespect will not—

"Kathleen." Logan's voice was syrupy soft, but everyone in the room stilled, my mother included. "Sit down and shut up."

A vein bulged in her forehead, and I suppressed a smile. It was impossible to dismiss the lethal edge beneath his sharp black suit, but the people in this room would respect that. They'd want that kind of danger on their side.

"*I* am Kaci's boss." Logan relaxed against the chair back. "If she's violating the dress code, or if her attitude is affecting her performance, *I* will deal with it." He gave me a dispassionate glance and returned to her. When my mother sat, he continued, "As for the cable network's impact on digital media, I believe it will gain an even greater competitive advantage in the marketplace if you used Dalton's ideas."

He carried the conversation seamlessly, even as he knew none of these initiatives would be brought to fruition. I imagined my mother in an orange jumpsuit, her face shriveled from the loss of Botox. Then I pictured her cold, dead eyes and blood draining from her lacerated throat.

I pressed a fist against my stomach and stared at my lap. When I looked up, she was glaring at me with her lips pursed.

She would never care for me the way a mother loved a daughter. She didn't give a shit about Logan's video. Hell, she'd encouraged the original setup with the male escort, Holden. But that didn't justify a death sentence. She also stole millions from charities and was an accomplice in hiring assassins. Maybe the latter justified death, but it wasn't my decision to make.

The meeting adjourned, and Logan and I went our separate ways in the corridor, headed to our own wings. When I reached the door to my office, I sensed him. I'd been so lost in my thoughts, I hadn't heard him change direction. But God, how I welcomed the heat from his body at my back, the scent of his clean soap, and the deep rhythm of his breath.

My pulse skipped, and my limbs locked up. He stood right behind me, not touching, but close enough to scramble my brain. I stepped into my office, and he stayed on my heels, shutting the door behind him.

As I turned, he caught my waist with one big hand, preventing me from facing him. His other hand traced a slow, torturous path down my arm, setting sparks of electricity through my blood.

Brushing my hair off my shoulder, he lowered his mouth to my ear and whispered thickly, "I miss you."

I blinked hazily at the skyline through the windows across the room, stunned by the amount of relief his words brought me. Two weeks of stress sloughed off my body, and I twisted to face him.

He stopped me again, his hands on my hips, fingers clamping down. "Please, don't turn around. If you do…" He inhaled deeply. "I'm trying to stay away, but if you look at me right now with those gorgeous eyes, I'll forget all about your marriage."

I nodded, my entire body focused on the hands on my hips, my skin burning for his fingers to move beneath the hem of the shirt.

His hard chest brushed against my back, and his hands tightened against the thin material of my leggings. "You're done thinking about this shit. It's taken a toll on you. You're too pale. You've lost weight." He touched his brow to my shoulder, his exhale warming my back. "There's goddamned bruises under your eyes. It's time to end this."

His nose and mouth pressed into the curve of my neck. His chest rose and fell against my back, mirroring the heave of mine. He was all around me, bracing me with his strength and chasing away the coldness in my limbs. The connection I'd missed so badly, the simple pleasure of his presence, the hope that maybe I wasn't alone, his warmth, his smell, his words, all of it snapped into place and formed a power line between us.

My heart sped up. I broke away from his grip and stepped out of reaching distance before turning to face him. "You want to know what I want?"

He nodded once. The rigid tension in his body, the cords twanging in his neck above the tie, and the fire flickering in his eyes told me he was seconds from ripping my clothes off.

I wanted more than that. I wanted his arms around me while I slept. His warm body curled around mine, sharing *our* bed and protecting me from the things I couldn't fight alone.

I wanted to be the one he fought for, to be the reason he lived and breathed. I wanted him to choose me over revenge. "If I tell you to kill them, that will make me just as evil as they are. If I turn them in, you'll disappear to evade the repercussions of your crimes. If I walk away, their greed won't end, and more people will die." I raised my chin and stared deep into his eyes. "I want the fourth option."

His eyebrows pulled together, one higher than the other. "There is no fourth option."

"You know there is. You just have to decide if you want it, too."

22 LOGAN

I paced the basement warehouse, weaving between motorcycle parts and circuit boards, hands in the pockets of my jeans, then pushing through my hair, and returning to my pockets. Restless energy skittered over my shoulders, my thoughts caught in an endless loop.

Benny was due back any minute. I should've been focused on the message she was retrieving. But my convictions, my plans, every damned thing I knew about myself and my life, shifted and pulled toward Kaci. All that mattered was her happiness.

It had been fourteen days since I'd touched her, smelled her, and talked to her on a level that didn't involve corporate initiatives. Fourteen days since I'd held her in her office, the curves of her back against my chest, my hands clinging to her tiny waist. Fourteen days since she told me she wanted the fourth option.

You just have to decide if you want it, too.

I wanted *her* above all else. I knew it then, and I positively knew it now.

Hungry, possessive desire was my constant companion, burning my chest, muddling my mind, and pulsing through my cock. So I paced. To redirect the path of my thoughts. To burn off the jealousy that gripped me when I thought of her with her husband. But the sound of my footfalls only intensified the buzz in my head.

Finally, the basement filled with the sounds of the elevator descending, the door shutting, and the squeaks of Benny's boots on concrete. A moment later, her small frame appeared in the doorway between the warehouse and the garage.

The braided pigtails of her orange wig fell over her shoulders. A blue leotard gloved her arms and chest, the rest of her covered with pink overalls. The outfit, combined with the mischievous bow of her lips, reminded me of a smurf.

She held up a dollar bill and waved it at me with a twinkle in her huge expressive eyes. "We got him."

I waited for the rush of excitement to vibrate my insides, but my breathing continued its even rhythm, and my legs strode toward her without any real sense of purpose. My body didn't feel a fraction of the energy it should have.

I took the dollar from her waiting hand and stared at the handwriting on the front, the scrawled numbers blurring into a trail of zeros. "He placed the bet." *Finally.*

"I verified it on the network. Every dollar is there." She smoothed a hand down one orange braid and flicked the end back and forth. "The fact that he sent the confirmation on the smallest bill in print adds a kind of pathetic irony, doesn't it?"

I nodded numbly and stuffed the dollar into my wallet. The final piece of the plan was complete. Trent took the bait. The months of anonymous offers I'd made through the Timex watches worked.

October twenty-seventh was only two days away. My last race. Everything was in place.

But everything had changed.

Benny narrowed her eyes, the glare dramatized by the drawn-on eyelashes that swept half-way to her temples. "Why do you look so butt-hurt?" She put her hands on her hips. "You're supposed to… I don't know, smile with crazy eyes or something."

A decade of preparations and meticulous work, and here I stood, two days before D-day, imagining a life without the finality of revenge, without finishing a plan with a gun in my hand.

Whenever I closed my eyes, I saw that life in Technicolor. Two bikes side-by-side on a racetrack. The fierceness of her forward incline on the Ducati. Her braid whipping over her back as she looked at me. That look, my God, it was searching, hopeful, demanding. The same expression she wore when she told me she wanted the fourth option. The option I felt in the deepest reaches of my soul.

But what if I was wrong? What if I let her in, gave her everything I had to give, and it wasn't enough? It was in my nature to choose the path with the most resistance, to not back down from a fight. Maybe I'd win this race, *win her*. But what if she left me down the road? What if she left me like my mother?

I scrubbed my hands through my hair. I needed to get out of my head and follow my damned heart. So what if it was half-baked, delusional, and feverishly beating like the wound-up pulse of a very tiny mammal? It was really quite simple. I wanted her, and if that scared the shit out of me, *good.* I needed to be scared. I needed to be fucking terrified, because the best rewards in life didn't come from pussying out.

The strongest love begins from a place of conflict.

I pivoted, my resolve propelling me the short trip to the workbench lined with computers. "Change of plans."

"A distraction," she snapped, clomping after me.

"No." I whirled on her, my voice ricocheting through the rafters. "A change of heart."

Her green eyes flashed, her face twisted in confusion. "You're not talking to me, Logan."

"I do talk to you." I turned back and dug through the clutter on the workbench, gathering penlights, wire cutters, and…where the fuck was the RFID reader? I shifted to the next bench. "I tell you everything."

She knew every conversation that transpired between me and Kaci. Except for the intimate stuff. That was none of her business.

"You don't tell me how you feel." She caught a bundle of wires knocked away in my aggravated search. "I know you have more than one feeling, you angry man. For the past month, I've seen grouchy, dreamy, lazy, slouchy—"

"Those aren't feelings." I glanced over her outfit, pausing on the blue-sleeved arms. "They're smurfs."

She shrugged. "I have a date with Gargamel tonight. But the connotation applies. You've been moping around, staring into your beer bottle. You haven't raced in two weeks. Which would be hard to do with that huge stick up your ass." She crossed her blue arms. "I just want to hear you admit it."

I drew in a deep breath. She didn't give a damn about the revenge business. Her employment with me ended in two days, regardless of the outcome. And with the salary I'd paid her over the past decade, she could retire on a yacht with a full staff of servants dressed in cosplay.

She was busting my balls because we shared a ten-year friendship. And that friendship was worth ten-thousand retorts.

I turned to face her and spoke through my teeth with all the frustration I'd felt for the past month. "I want to kill the loneliness inside her more than I want anything else." I gestured to the room of electronics and engine parts. "More than any of this. I want to be the one who makes her happy."

She chewed on a fingernail and shifted her weight to one foot. "She's married."

And lonely.

I pushed my shoulders back and pressed my lips together. "It's a hail Mary, Benny."

She cocked her head. "The hell with Mary." Her grin stretched from ear to ear. "You've got me. What do I need to do?"

Determination settled deep inside me. My heart thundered with purpose. I gripped the back of her head, pressed her cheek to my chest, and kissed the top of her wig. "I need you to get me into her condo undetected."

Sneaking into Kaci's condo in the middle of the night dressed as Evader wasn't a levelheaded plan. It was a balls-out declaration. Walking away from my revenge, exposing my underground identity, and standing over her bed where she slept with her husband was a reckless way to fight for her happiness. But reckless was my way of giving her everything I had to give, including the power to decide what to do with it.

And I hoped to God she chose me over him.

As I stepped off the elevator on the eighty-eighth floor, I was pretty sure the veins in my temples were going to pop, probably while the contents of my stomach hit the floor. Slipping past Trump Tower security had been the easy part.

Benny had finalized the program on the RFID reader, which gave me access to the parking garage and Kaci's floor. She shut down the cameras and the entire security grid in the tower, including the alarm systems in the residential condos. *A five-minute glitch*, she'd said. Enough time to scatter the guards as I rode one of my spare bikes into the garage, took the elevator, and stepped through Kaci's condo door.

Pocketing the metal reader, I shut the front door silently behind me and was greeted with the dark hush of the condo's interior. I swallowed back my simmering nerves and followed the display on the visor. The night vision prevented a clumsy fall in the dark, and the image of the condo's blueprints guided me to the master suite.

The helmet, however, would probably get me shot. I wasn't just an intruder. I was an intruder wearing a notorious mask. I would have to talk fast, and with any luck, Collin didn't sleep with a gun.

Straight ahead, the skyline twinkled through the windows beyond the sitting room. I was drawn to the magnificent view, but instead followed the diagram, turning down the hall on the right. My hands slicked with sweat in the gloves, and my muscles ached with tension as I forced my boots to move slowly and soundlessly.

This was the part I hadn't strategized. What if I found them having sex or their naked bodies entwined in sleep? How would I stop myself from going apeshit? I hadn't thought past the breaking-and-entering and standing-over-the-bed plan. What was I going to say? *Choose me.*

I reached the open door at the end of the walkway, my heartbeat pulsing in my throat. Time to step into the dark, murky waters of risk. Risk of being turned in once I showed them my identity. Risk of Collin bludgeoning me to death for sleeping with his wife. Risk of Kaci's rejection.

I wouldn't have to spell it out for her. She was a brilliant woman and would understand the magnitude of what I was giving her. But was it enough? Was *I* enough?

I pulled in a deep, silent breath and flexed my fingers. Then I strode through, crossed the room, and stopped at the foot of the bed.

Blankets gathered in messy lumps, but the edge-sharpening perception of the night-vision outlined the forms of two bodies, entwined front-to-back, fit together like lovers after sex.

No amount of mental readiness could've prepared me for the jealously surging through my veins. Blood roared past my ears, and my hands balled into fists. I closed my eyes, seconds from yanking him out of bed and losing all sense of reason.

Man up. Power through it.

Stretching out my fingers, I opened my eyes and searched for her toned arms, the strands of her blonde hair, something familiar in the pile of bedding.

I stepped forward, locking my spine and measuring my breathing. But when my gaze landed on the pillow, the strength in my legs threatened to melt away.

Two heads lay side-by-side. Two heads with short, black hair. My vision tunneled. Two masculine jaw lines. My ribs squeezed. Two faces shadowed with whiskers.

The shock of a thousand volts slammed into my heart, electrocuting me into a state of stupefied paralysis. Unholy mother of fuck.

He was gay.

Collin Anderson.

Right-winged commenter.

Kaci's husband.

Gay.

I wasn't sure how long I stood there. Remotely, I heard the rasp of my thinning breaths as my thoughts filtered through every interaction I'd shared with Kaci and every goddamned thing she'd said. About Collin. About love. Maybe the clues had been there all along, but Jesus, I would've never guessed this.

The longer I stood there, the lighter my chest felt. She loved her husband, but not in a way that would threaten her future with me. Her marriage was a ruse, one that had likely been forced on them in lieu of Trenchant's goddamned image. God, it all made sense now.

I backed out of the room on silent feet and strode down the hall, headed toward the other bedrooms at the opposite end of the condo. Each step ladened with guilt, every breath filling with hope. Fucking hell, why hadn't she told me? I'd treated her like a cheater. I'd judged her. *Used* her. How could she not hate me?

My gait quickened, my blood seething beneath my skin in my urgency to find her. When I pushed through the door of the second largest bedroom, the remnants of my shock fled into the stillness of the room.

The king-size bed was empty, the blankets twisted and thrown to the side. My attention caught on the couch that faced the windows, my eyes locked on the curl of blonde hair draped over the armrest.

Anticipation built in my gut. I locked the door and covered the distance, my need for her powering my strides. I needed her in my arms. I needed her to forgive me. I needed to protect her, to make her happy. My needs with her were endless and intoxicating, and I would spend the rest of my life fulfilling each and every one if she let me.

Rounding the side of the couch, I knelt before the illumination of her sleeping figure and removed my gloves. "Night-vision off."

Her lashes fluttered but remained closed. The moonlight from the window cast a glow over her golden hair and paled the smooth skin of her long legs folded beneath the tangle of her nightshirt.

The sight of her curled in the corner of the couch wrapped a painful fist around my heart. It also magnified the significance of her loneliness.

She wouldn't be alone anymore. *She belongs to me.*

I drank in every detail of her body, from her delicate bone structure and soft breaths to the curl of her fingers beneath her cheek. A steady, calm pulse of peacefulness floated through me, filling me with euphoria. I didn't want the moment to end, but I couldn't stop my hands from sliding over either side of her face. "Kaci. Wake up."

She stirred, her breath hitching and her eyes blinking away sleep. I held her face as she straightened her head and stared at my visor, her hands lifting to wrap around my wrists.

There was no surprise or fear in her gaze, her silence passing long and deep with the whisper of the vent in the ceiling. Finally, she licked her lips and released a heavy breath. "I'm not dreaming?"

I shook my head.

Her eyes widened. "You said my name."

I nodded.

She moved her hands from mine to hook a finger beneath the collar of my leather jacket. "I love the ties, but this—" Her other hand slid over the side of my helmet as her face transformed into a breathtaking smile. "This is you."

"You knew."

His synthesized voice hummed over my skin, caressing every nerve-ending in my body. Not even shock or the dregs of sleep could dull his effect on me.

Logan. A man who didn't have hairy moles, a unibrow, or bucked teeth. Maybe I was shallow, but God, I wanted *him* to be the man under that helmet so damned badly.

How many times had I imagined his thick, low timbre beneath the distortion, his golden-green eyes behind the black visor, and the sculptured body I knew so intimately stretching the seams of those leathers?

I slid to the edge of the couch, my knees bracketing his hard thighs, and gripped the sides of his helmet. "I hoped."

With his huge hands cupping my face and all his imposing strength kneeling between my legs, I couldn't stop the shiver of hopeful excitement. He was here. Damn all the consequences that would follow. He'd come for me, and Trenchant didn't seem to be on the agenda. At least not at that moment.

I only wore a t-shirt and panties. Yet the surrounding air rose in temperature, fleeing the space between us as an invisible line pulled us together. His hips rolled into the *V* of my thighs, grinding in a slow circle. He pressed me into the couch, and his jacket creaked with the movement. A tremor quaked over his body, all that leather rubbing against my t-shirt and hardening my nipples beneath the thin fabric.

My breath quickened, and his followed, faster, louder. That sound, *his need*, surged a tingling up my legs as my brain dizzily grabbed hold of reality. The commanding suit and tie, the powerfully-built muscles, the aggression exuded on a bike and in a boardroom, every masculine tool that held me captive was all wrapped-up in one destructively-sexy, badass package. And all of it was right here, vibrating between my legs, burning for me.

A spasm convulsed through my inner walls, and my thighs opened wantonly. I slid my thumbs along the seal of his visor, trying and failing to unlock it from its closed position. "I need to see you."

Bathed in the glimmer from the lights beyond the windows, he released my face and unbuckled the chin strap. His hips shifted with the movement, whispering cool air over the damp crotch of my panties. I wanted him there, and the thought produced a torrent of clenching inside me. "Hurry."

My lungs filled with air as the slow lift of his helmet revealed the cords of his neck, his strong whiskered jawline and, my God, those lips.

I launched at him before the chin guard cleared his eyes. Grabbing his wide shoulders, I captured his mouth and stole his surprised exhale. The helmet thumped somewhere behind him as his fingers shoved through my hair and his tongue curled through my mouth, claiming and fighting and claiming again.

His stubble scratched a trail of fire around my lips. Zaps of electricity ricocheted through my body. My mouth closed over his, pulled back, and attacked again, over and over, filling the room with the wet smacking sounds of our hunger.

The aggressive press of his jaw controlled the movement of mine, and the toe-curling stroke of his tongue spiraled more wet heat between my legs.

He broke the kiss, and his gaze lifted, searching my eyes. The dark blond strands of his hair stood up every which way, a delicious contrast to the clean-cut, gelled look in the office. Pale flickers of light danced over his perfectly straight nose, the etched planes of his chiseled cheekbones, and the moisture glistening on his parted lips.

I couldn't look away from those lips, and as they tilted into a gentle smile, months of anxiety and loneliness tumbled off my shoulders and scattered into the dark. Why did that smile have such an effect on me? I loved his broody, lopsided brow, but his smile? It held conviction and healing, a promise that this beaten-down connection between us would survive, despite the lies and betrayal.

He unzipped his jacket and shrugged it off. As he yanked off his shirt, his bare shoulders and biceps played and flexed beneath his smooth skin, his eyes never leaving mine. "We have shit to hash out, and we will. I'm not going anywhere." He glanced at the door and back to me. "I locked the door. I know what's going on down the hall."

I straightened, my mind piecing together his meaning and the implications. "You saw them?"

"They were asleep." His attention lowered to my lap. "Widen your legs." He leaned over me, a twitch jumping in the carved bricks of his nude chest. "Wider."

My body obeyed as my protectiveness of Collin held onto the conversation. "It's *his* secret, Logan."

He nodded, gripped my ankles, and stretched them farther apart, propping my feet on the edges of the cushion. I held breathlessly still, lost in the stroke of his knuckles as they slid along my legs, from my knees to the edge of my panties.

"Fuck, Kaci, I've missed you." He flattened his hands on my inner thighs, framing the triangle of my white panties. His thumbs traced just outside the edges of the lace, caressing the sensitive skin. "So soft here. Like silk."

I jerked my hips, my clit pulsing against the piercing and my pussy quivering to be stretched and filled.

He leaned into me, his brow resting against mine as he hooked a finger in the crotch of my panties. "What would Collin do if he walked in right now?"

I tried to form a coherent thought, but sweet fucking hell, that finger. He worked it through my folds, teasing the edges of my opening, around and around without entering. "Logan, please."

He shifted closer, his chest pressing me into the corner of the armrest, all his hard, heated flesh enveloping my senses. His mouth opened to accommodate his staggering breaths, and his hips rocked with the sudden thrust of his finger.

Shock waves trembled through my insides. His mouth closed on mine, his tongue a gentle lick compared to the violent drive of his finger. One commanding thrust followed by another, and I was completely at his mercy. Wet and needy, I melted like butter, falling helplessly, shamelessly, under his spell.

He brushed his lips over my cheek, my eyelids, my nose, returning to my mouth and kissing me again, deeper, harder. His hips rolled in a seductive grind, rocking his torso with the pace of his finger. The position of his body put his groin at the edge of the couch, and I wondered if he was rubbing his cock against the cushion to assuage the ache.

"Does he have a key to your bedroom?" His finger circled my

piercing, his mouth moving against mine. "Anything I need to worry about if he finds Evader here? Or finds me *as* Evader?"

I dug my nails into his shoulder blades and bucked against his touch. "He'd knock before using the key." I licked my lips, my heartbeat elevating with my need for relief. "He's not possessive or conniving. Not— Oh God, right there."

He shoved two fingers inside me, his head falling to my shoulder as he pumped in and out. "Not what?"

I grabbed his hair and held him against me as I flexed my hips, clenching my muscles and fucking his hand. "He's not a bad man, Logan. I *know* him."

He pulled his hand away and brought it to his mouth. "Not what I'm asking." He wrapped his lips around his wet fingers and sucked, his eyes closing. His nostrils flared, and a low moan rumbled deep in his throat.

I shuddered, mesmerized, as he opened his eyes and returned his hand between my legs.

"You need to understand…" He thrust his fingers inside, sparking a tremble along my thighs. "If Collin does anything that forces me to run, *we* are running. You and me."

A confrontation with Collin would likely result in an airing of secrets. Would Collin call the cops and turn in the notorious Evader? Would he call his father and devise Logan's death? No fucking way. Not Collin.

His hand stopped moving, his fingers curling along my inner muscles. "We'll decide what to do about Trenchant *together*. And if we have to run, we'll do it *together*. The fourth option."

Running away together. The fourth option. It sounded so fairytale-ish. But that didn't stop a very hopeful flutter from taking flight in my stomach. "And if I tell you to walk away from your revenge?"

He removed his fingers, laced them through mine, and moved our hands to his chest. "Feel that?"

The thump of his heart strummed against my palm, steady and strong. I nodded.

"It beats for you, Kaci. I choose *you*."

The last traces of tension loosened from my muscles and broke free. It was dangerous to cling to those words, to believe that regardless of what happened, he wouldn't leave me. But the risks he'd taken to sneak into my condo, not knowing if Collin would turn him in or tell his father, attested to the fact that he'd given up his revenge.

I'd lived in constant paranoia since I married Collin, always on guard about sex and relationships, but not now. Not with him. Funny that the man who betrayed me made me feel...less worried? Certain? *Safe.*

He tilted his head, his face so close his breath brushed my lips. "And if you have to trade your career for a life on the run?"

I untangled our hands and placed both of mine on his whiskered jaw. A fever of emotions coursed through me, but one sentiment burned stronger than all the rest. "I go where you go."

His face hardened beneath my palms, his eyes holding mine hostage. "Unless it's prison or death."

A swallow formed in my throat. There was definitely no *us* in either of those scenarios. "Then we fight and evade."

He rose and smacked a hard palm against my thigh, startling a gasp from my lips. "Stand up."

Evidently, he was done talking. And done waiting because he gripped my hand and jerked me to my feet. I followed willingly, a glutton for the sexy way he took charge.

Leaning into my back, he walked us toward the bed, clicking on the lamp as we went. "I've thought of nothing but you every day, every second." His hands curled around my hips, lifting the nightshirt and yanking it over my head. "It's been a month, Kaci."

Only the panties remained, and my bare skin shivered beneath the caress of the air, my nipples tightening into needy points.

"No girlfriends? Or flings?" I kept my back to him, staring at the empty bed. Why the hell was I asking this? Yet I couldn't stop. "I've seen you at the races. You damn near have to beat the women off you."

He spun me, and the backs of my legs hit the mattress. With his hands on my waist, he lowered me onto the bed and dragged me to the center on my back, the sheets soft and cool against my skin.

Leaning over my body, he propped his fists on either side of my hips. "It's only been you since our night in the elevator."

My mouth dried as I connected that night to every moment since. He saved me from the bald man in the alley. He blackmailed my family and fucked me in a hotel room five days later. He followed me on Rogers Avenue and told me he was angry with his mother. "You knew that was me on the bike? All this time?"

He straightened and released the button on the waistband of his leathers. "My helmet"—he lowered the zipper on his pants—"has night vision, among other things. I didn't know who you were until you removed your helmet in the elevator."

Okay, wow. Finding out the woman sucking him off was his brother's wife? That explained his sudden freak out. And now I was curious about the *other things* his helmet could do.

He removed his boots. His pants went next. Then he stood before me, a powerhouse of twitching muscle, all long, strong limbs and a huge, hard cock. Really hard. Long. Thick. *Distracting.*

"Keep staring at it." He gripped the base with a tight fist as his gaze roamed my body and landed on my face. "You're about to feel exactly how hard the last month has been."

His voice was casual, but the intensity of his golden-green eyes said so much more. His wide stance and the *V*-line etching his abs didn't move. Time didn't move as we stared at one another, our thoughts colliding and twisting together, our eyes communicating on a level that transcended words. In that single moment of eye contact, we fought, apologized, forgave, and fucked. Then, through that power of silent understanding, we shared our fears, desires, and hopes.

It left me trembling for more.

Lifting my hips, I slid off my panties and tossed them. He tracked my movements, his fist tightening on his cock. I planted my feet on the bed, spread my legs, and slid my finger along my slit.

A wave of twitches rippled over the tensile muscles of his torso right before he shot forward. His body covered mine, his heavy bulk crushing my air and jump-starting my heart. His ragged breaths heated my face as he lightened his weight with his arms and spread me wider with the force of his legs.

His head dropped against mine, and he looked down the length of our bodies. Hand on his cock, he positioned himself and rubbed the tip through my folds.

I flexed against him, his lips separating, our exhales merging.

Then he raised his eyes and stared intently into mine. "I'm clean. No more shit between us, okay?"

No more secrets and no more condoms? I nodded, grinning. I was on the pill. But instead of asking about that, he thrust. A hard, claiming shove to the root.

We shuddered together, joined as closely as two bodies could be. He buried his mouth in my neck, mine dropped to his shoulder, and he groaned so hungrily it made my heart pound and my pussy clamp down.

His body tensed and shook over me, against me, surrounding me.

He rotated his hips, slow and patient, dragging his cock deep inside, letting me adjust to his size.

Then he moved. Fast. Ruthless. Out of control. He was carnal need, power, and passion. I felt it in every drive of his length and the hard contractions of his ass beneath my hands.

He swept me up in his madness, overwhelming me with a thousand sensations at once. The stroke of his tongue on my neck, the leather and soap scent of his skin, the rippling packs of muscle in his back, the soft tousle of his hair, the scratch of his hard nipples against my chest, his eyes finding and locking on mine, and the sudden and mind-blowing shock of my orgasm.

I came hard and long, a moan tearing from my throat, every molecule in my body on fire with tingling pleasure. When I caught my breath, it escaped with laughter.

"There's my girl." He kissed my forehead, pulled out, and flipped me to my belly. My pussy was still pulsing from my release when he entered me in one, long slam of his hips.

He bent down and brushed a kiss over the top of my spine. Propping his upper body with one hand, his other caressed my thigh, moving higher until he reached my hip bone and lifted it to angle my ass in the position he wanted.

I rocked my hips, dragging the heated steel of his length in and out. "I don't know if I'm up for a repeat of last time."

His hand stopped my movements, gripping my thigh and yanking my butt tight against his pelvis. "Yes, you are."

With his cock still buried and his knees on the outsides of mine, he wove his fingers through my hair and lowered his hard, warm chest against my back.

Then, on hands and knees, he rode my body the way he rode his bike. *With intimidation, recklessness, and unharnessed energy.* Collin's words, and while they rang true, I shuddered at the memory of him imagining his brother like that.

The heat of Logan's body chased the thought away. His thrusts slowed, his mouth moving to my spine. He kissed every inch of my back and shoulders as he pushed in, pulled out. His cock hard, thick, and constant, his lips soft, tender, and full of adoration, it was an intense slide of flesh and whispered breaths and need.

One hand braced beside mine, his other now a dominating hold on my breast, he kneaded my flesh and tweaked my nipple with skill and possessiveness. His touch held a direct line to my pleasure centers, my nerve-endings gravitating toward the shift of his hand as it slid off my breast to caress down my ribs and over my mound.

The rub of his thumb over my piercing pulled me to the edge of euphoria. My back arched as he continued in tormenting circles. His thrusts, his thumb, his mouth on my neck, all of it moved me higher, faster, toward release until I was just breaths away.

He pistoned his hips and yanked hard on the steel ring. I exploded. My muscles clenched around his cock. White-hot bliss rippled through my blood, my gasp stretching my jaw in a frozen gape.

He leaned over my shoulder, gripped my face, and captured my lips with his. He kissed me fiercely as he pumped his hips and followed me over. His masculine groan vibrated against my mouth, the hot pulse of his seed soaking my well-loved insides. His body shook as he ground his pelvis with a final jerk.

When we collapsed in a sweaty pile of limbs, my breath left my lungs in a satisfied rush. He rolled to his back beside me, his arm falling across my ass. His chest heaved, fighting for air and glistening with his exertion.

I slid my front to his side and ran my hand over the warmth of his pecs and biceps. I wanted to kiss every inch of his glorious body, taste him, breathe him in. So I did.

As I nipped and licked from the top of his head to the curl of his toes and everywhere in between, he watched me with an intense, pensive look on his face. “Come here.”

I climbed up his body, his cock already hard and ready and brushing against my belly, and straddled his waist. He positioned my hips over his, the hands on my thighs gentle, the potency of his gaze consuming. I quivered above him. I would never get enough of this man.

Slowly, he slid me down his length, stretching my delicate tissues, holding my gaze and thrusting the final hard inch into the clasp of my body. Then he held my hips tight against him. Not moving or speaking. Simply watching. Joined in the most intimate way.

He reached up and wrapped a hand around my nape, pulling me toward him until our foreheads touched. “No matter what happens or how volatile the journey, there will be no room for emptiness. I promise.”

I sucked in a staggering breath. *The strongest love.* Maybe he was promising he’d always be with me. Maybe he was telling me he loved me. Either way, his words breathed both tenderness and honesty. With just the sound of his voice, he called me out of the nothingness

I'd lived in my entire life.

A hot lump swelled in my throat, my eyes burning with weeks of built-up emotion. I wanted him so much it hurt.

He released my neck to cup my face and claim a kiss, his tongue stroking in a slow, tender entwining. Our bodies rocked together as he made love to my mouth, to my body and soul. It was there, in a bed I once despised for its emptiness, where we caressed and explored and murmured into the early morning.

It wasn't all gentle and slow. He was a beast after all and worked me harder and longer than ever before, his face between my legs, his cock in my mouth and everywhere else. But every moment was given and received with the kind of eye contact that reached so deep it engaged the heart. The variance between his gentle moments and his demanding ferocity held me in constant suspense. And somewhere in the mix, I found myself falling, recklessly, insanely, into soul-deep happiness.

Sometime after three o'clock, we settled into a lazy cuddle, our voices whispering through the dark silence. We talked about Collin, our parents, his friend Benny, the contrast of our childhoods, the birth of the underground racing network, his dream to be a pro sportbike racer. We covered the gamut yet had only scratched the surface.

Now, wrapped in the protective fold of his arms, I listened to the even rasps of his breaths. Even in sleep, he held me as if he would never let go. And I held him right back, my cheek on his chest, our legs intertwined.

Our fierce connection terrified me, and now that I could feel it mending and locking, the fear of losing it clawed at the back of my mind. What if he slipped away while I slept? What if the connection faded by morning?

I had to believe this crazy, mercurial, beautiful thing between us was real. We began in a place of conflict, and we would be stronger for it once we overcame it.

I twisted in his arms and glanced at the clock on the table. *4:13 AM*

It was Saturday morning. We had the weekend to decide how to proceed with Trenchant. *Together*. Trent's one month ultimatum was over. I would turn in my resignation, and strangely, I felt zero remorse about leaving the company I'd worked so hard for.

What that meant for the future, I didn't know. But I did know I'd found what I needed. Happiness was right here, so alive and present in the moment. And like all things fought and won, I would protect it, *him*, with my life.

I woke to a quiet, sunlit room. My muscles ached, the tissues between my legs were sore as hell, and my eyelids weighed a hundred pounds each.

But the strong arm around my belly, the chest against my back, and the warm mouth brushing my shoulder? Best feeling ever. His comforting embrace was completely mine. A languorous smile took hold of my lips, and pure joy swished through my veins.

I stretched like a cat, arching my back and rolling in his arms to see him. His hair was a tousled mess of hotness, his eyes half-lidded and admiring. The lazy contentment on his face seemed to brighten the light spilling in the windows, warming my insides and tingling filaments of delight over my skin.

He lifted a hand and stroked his thumb over my cheekbone. His fingers slid down my face and under my chin, where he lingered with a caressing knuckle. "Christ, you look sexy in the morning."

"You should talk." I was absorbed in the dark whiskers on his jaw, the creases on his cheek from the pillow, and all that exposed muscle definition leading to the gathered sheets around his waist.

I could look at his body for hours, but my eyes kept returning to his face and the unabashed way he devoured me with his stare. We lay on our sides, face-to-face. My arm bent beneath my head to pillow my head, and his did the same. This silent intimacy was something I'd never experienced with another person, yet it came so easy with him. With just a simple look, I had everything I ever wanted.

The eye contact broke when his mouth closed over mine. A kiss that intensified as his fingers entered me. When carnality took over, it was no longer just a kiss but a merging of bodies. His cock buried deep, our tongues twined together, and our orgasms peaked simultaneously gentle and replete.

We showered, taking turns washing one another. Neither of us could stop smiling, nor could I stop kissing his turned up lips. I sampled his smile so thoroughly and frequently with my mouth I felt it burn inside me.

But as I wrapped the towel around my body and walked toward the doorway to exit the bathroom, dread trickled into my mood. It was Saturday, and Collin would be awake somewhere in the condo. The looming confrontation with him slowed my steps and lumbered my pulse.

And stopped my heart when I entered the bedroom.

Collin stood beside the bed, his arms crossed over his bare chest. Black silk pajama pants hung from his narrow hips, the same shade as his neatly-combed hair. His disbelieving glare aimed at the quiet presence behind me. "What the fuck?"

He knew what Logan looked like. Hell, every employee at Trenchant had seen their CEO's face on the company newsletter. His rigid posture had nothing to do with me bringing a man home, and everything to do with how Logan had hurt me.

But how did he know Logan was here? I adjusted the towel, trying to calm my fingers. "You used the key to my room?"

A tic bounced in his jaw. "The door was open."

I glanced at the door and twisted to look at Logan. He knotted a towel at his waist, his eyes on Collin. His lips pinched in a white slash, but his expression was…thoughtful. Had he unlocked the door before joining me in the shower? He must have, but why? Motherfucker, he was up to something.

My pulse picked up, and my hands grew restless on the towel. How would this play out? So many secrets, all of which Logan knew. But Collin… Oh God, if I trusted my gut, Collin knew nothing.

Silence stretched through the room, strumming with tension. I turned back to Collin. "Where's Seth?"

His face hardened, his blue eyes firmly locked on me in silent question. I'd mentioned Seth in front of Logan. He thought I'd told his secret. "He had a photo shoot." The cold reverberation in his tone conveyed his shock and brewing anger. "Why, Kaci? The snake used you and stole your job."

"Collin, he's not a snake." It was a weak argument considering I'd asked him to help me deliver three dozen of the slithering things to Logan's office. I could feel Logan's heat at my back, but he made no move to interject. "I didn't tell him about you. He—"

"I can't believe you crawled back in bed with him after what he did." Red splotches formed on Collin's neck as his eyes darted to my towel. "And you brought him here? *Him,* of all people?" He pushed his hands through his hair and paced through the room, his protection of me radiating from the tenseness in his body. "Goddammit, Kaci. You know what he's capable of. He'll hurt you again. He'll turn our marriage into a media nightmare."

I walked toward him and pulled his hands from his hair. "Listen, he's not interested in…"

Collin's attention caught on the movement behind me. I followed his gaze over my shoulder and watched as Logan dropped the towel and strode through the room in all his naked glory. The fluid muscles of his strong legs, the soft, heavy fall of his cock, and the flex of ass when he passed us, every inch of him gorgeous and distracting and—

Oh no.

I spun back to Collin and found his eyes tracking Logan. Anger darkened his face, but there was something else, too. Something he was trying to hide…

Oh fuck no no no.

My stomach twisted, and I grabbed his shoulders to turn him away, but his gaze swept over Logan. "Collin, dammit, don't look at him like that."

Logan walked toward the windows, stretching all those rippling muscles with his arms over his head, the sunlight reflecting off his smooth skin. Fire swept through my bloodstream and heated my cheeks. What the fuck was he doing? If Collin didn't know they were brothers…

Oh my God. Realization punched me in the gut. If Collin knew any of Trent's secrets, Logan's blood ties would've topped the list. I'd bet money that Logan unlocked the door and streaked the room to test Collin's reaction.

Really fucking sick. I grabbed the closest thing I could find—a hairbrush from the dresser—and hurled it through the room, landing a hit on the center of Logan's back. "Put some damned clothes on."

He flinched and rubbed the hurt, but when he looked over his shoulder, the bastard grinned.

Collin cleared his throat and scrubbed a hand over his jaw, but his friggin' eyes tracked back to Logan's body.

Gritting my teeth, I stepped between the two men and shouted, "Logan, stop baiting your brother!"

I had to give Collin some credit. He'd unknowingly ogled his brother's junk and didn't vomit his guts when Kaci explained our family ties. But man, his face turned a ghastly shade of white.

When I woke this morning, I made the sudden decision to meet him for the first time in my birthday suit, just to see his reaction, to find out how much he knew. Though wrong on so many levels, it proved one thing. He hadn't known we were brothers.

Which meant Kaci's faith in him might not have been misguided. Maybe his parents really hadn't involved him in their shit.

Two hours later, she finished walking him through everything we knew, including all the secrets she'd kept from him over the years, as well as my connection with the underground races. She used the flash drive I'd brought to show him digital copies of the evidence on her laptop. His family's crimes, my mother's death, the proof of our blood relation.

He responded with a whiplash of emotions. Shock that Kaci had kept so much from him. Denial that his family could commit such crimes. Disgust when he saw the evidence. And now he seemed to be settled on anger. Maybe we had more in common than just DNA.

He pushed his half-eaten plate of French toast across the kitchen table and stared at it with a clouded expression. "We need to kill them."

I coughed behind my hand to hide my smile. Wasn't he full of surprises? But Kaci wasn't amused. She glared at him, at me, back at him. Sitting at the table beside me, her hair a cascade of gold to her waist, she pulled her feet onto the chair seat and wrapped her arms around her bent legs.

I couldn't stop my gaze from roaming over her tight jeans where they stretched around her ass. That earned me another shriveling look from Kaci. Damn. Definitely still pissed about my naked walk in the bedroom.

"Okay, fine." She leaned back, hugging her knees and staring at the vaulted ceiling. "We kill them, then what? What happens to your show? Your career?" She leveled him with a glower that was tinged with exhaustion. "You would be a fugitive. And what about money? We have enough to survive for a while, but when it runs out, are you going to wait tables with me in Shitknob, Mexico?"

From there, they launched into the pros and cons of murder. I left them to it, content with watching their interactions as I cleared the table and loaded the dishwasher. I had a solution for her financial concerns, but it wouldn't placate what was really bothering her.

She slid into my vacated seat to sit closer to Collin, her hand reaching out, fingers lacing with his. The touch was familiar, the kind found in the intimacy of a lifelong friendship.

Seeing them together was reassuring in a way that defied explanation. A reassurance that had me trusting him within two hours of meeting him. His devotion and loyalty shone in his eyes. Eyes that followed my every movement when I was near her. If anything happened to her because of me, he would feed me my own dick.

Fuck, I respected that. I'd been alone my entire life, with the exception of Benny. To be here eating French toast—that *my brother* cooked—and plotting the future of Trenchant was fucking surreal. I wanted Collin in her life, in our lives.

With their fingers entwined, her other hand traced the ridiculously squared edges of his jaw and pinched the indention in his chin. "You're not a murderer. You're not *them*. And Jesus, Collin, we're talking about our parents. Our *family*. You don't just order their deaths and walk away from that without it playing over and over in your mind for the rest of your life."

His eyes flew to mine. I'd told him about the murders I'd committed, but by then, he was already overwhelmed with the barrage of his family's crimes. As he studied me now, it wasn't with judgment. Curiosity, maybe?

Were the lives I'd taken etched in my face? Shadowed in my eyes? Was he wondering if the same would happen to him? If the spilled blood of his family would creep inside him and haunt places he couldn't reach?

I justified every life I'd taken, but could Collin do the same?

I'd known about my brother's existence since I was thirteen, since the night my mother was killed and I read her diary. But I didn't know *him*. So for two hours, I watched him the way he did me, sizing him up and looking for similarities.

He took after his mother, her Italian heritage blatant in his black hair and olive complexion. His sharp cheekbones and slender face were rather aristocratic. His blunt jaw might've resembled mine, but his features as a whole—the refined way he carried himself, his charisma, his fancy shirt and slacks—all of it was made for the camera. Not for murder.

"She's right, Collin." I grabbed the coffee pot and brought it to the table. "You don't have calluses inside you, hardened tissues that will never heal. You didn't watch your mother's murder at thirteen." *And hide under a bed doing nothing to stop it.* I refilled their mugs, stifling the tremor in my hand, and set the pot on the table. "Killing isn't a part of who you are. I would gladly do the job myself, but your consent to that is the same thing as doing it yourself."

Something softened behind his eyes. Maybe it was understanding, but I didn't know him well enough to be sure.

I sat beside Kaci, and my hand instinctively went to her hair to feel the comfort of the strands between my fingers. Collin's eyes tracked the movement, his expression unreadable.

She leaned toward me and placed her hand on my thigh, stroking the leather of my pants. "We're not killing them."

Collin stared out the windows behind me. At the skyline? The clouds? Who the fuck knew? His fingers around his coffee mug looked like he was holding on for dear life. "If we turn them in, my father will make sure I go down with him."

She rubbed her brow as if warding off a headache. "We can fight him."

His eyebrows gathered as he glanced between her and me. "The evidence my father has against me… It's not all purchased."

A sick feeling curled through my gut, and Kaci tensed beside me.

He swallowed, his face pained. "You remember Brad? The artist from SoHo?"

Her hand on my thigh clenched, and she wrinkled her nose. "An old boyfriend, right? Like…eight years ago?"

She'd told me a lot about her life last night, including some of the details of her and Collin's approach to sex. As hard as it was to hear about her sharing lovers with her husband, I was grateful for her honesty. It gave me a new perspective on her loneliness as well as some insight into this conversation.

My first thought was this Brad guy had shared a bed with Kaci and Collin. But they'd only been married for seven years, and she didn't seem to remember him.

Collin nodded in answer. "We got in a fight one night. It was bad." His knee bounced, stopped. "He hit me, I hit back. His head hit..." He shoved a hand in his hair, and his knee bounced again as he struggled to maintain eye contact with her. "His head hit the wall at an awkward angle. I thought I killed him."

Fuck. I could fill in the rest, but Kaci did it for me. "You called Trent for help, didn't you? Except he didn't help you." Her tone lowered, her hand on my leg sliding restlessly. "He finished the job and used it as a threat against you every day since. Am I right?"

He rose and walked around the kitchen island with his fingers laced on top of his head and ghosts in his eyes. "He showed up at my apartment with a man I'd never seen before. By then, I'd realized Brad was still alive." Bracing his arms on the granite counter top, he stared out the window, his gaze unfocused. "The man shot Brad as soon as they walked in. Removed the body. You know the rest."

My stomach hardened. It was a murder Collin was undeniably connected to. It was his apartment. His lover. But it was Trent's assassin who pulled the trigger. And probably some purchased evidence to make sure everything pointed to Collin.

Why the fuck would Trent go to the trouble? I stood and paced out of the open kitchen and into the sitting room. Beyond the windows, the sun blazed high above the city, casting the river and lake in deep aqua.

The day was half over, and my skin tightened with edginess. I wanted a decision made, a plan devised, and a future started with my girl. But first, I had to clear out every side road. "As concerned as your parents are about keeping your sex life a secret, news that Trenchant's favorite commentator is a murderer would be much worse."

Kaci's sweet scent reached my nose before her hands slid over my t-shirt, moving up my spine and around my shoulders. "My mother cares about image, and Collin's mom despises the fact that he's gay. Each of our parents have their own agendas, and Trent balances their demands to keep them happy and loyal. But in the end, he doesn't give a shit about Trenchant's name or who Collin is fucking. He'll risk a scandal to maintain the power he holds over the people beneath him."

People like Kaci and Collin, who he'd controlled their entire lives.

My body heated, and my fingers flexed. I wanted to knock him to his knees, whimpering and begging, before I showed him the control in a six-inch blade.

That wasn't going to happen, but I did have one final ruse I hadn't shared. "I sent the Timex you collected at the nightclub."

Her footsteps shifted around me. In the next breath, she stood between me and the window, the light in her blue eyes spitting a thousand rapid questions. Fuck, she was heart-stoppingly beautiful with her teeth pressing into her bottom lip, the gold in her hair gleaming against the backdrop of the bright sky, and the heave of her irresistible tits in that tight t-shirt.

Fire leapt in her eyes as she poked a finger at my chest. "You said no more shit between us, remember?"

I couldn't tell if she was mad or just being sassy, but a delicious shiver of arousal raced through me. "No shit between us, baby." I bent my knees and stole a quick kiss. "We've been exchanging watches for months, each with a message on a chip soldered inside."

Collin leaned a shoulder against the glass beside us, his expression filled with cautious interest as he said to me, "I assume he doesn't know it's you behind the watches?"

I grinned. "I've been contacting Trent as an anonymous, influential member of the Chicago Police Department. He ignored my messages for a while until I made an offer he couldn't refuse. All he needed to do was provide me with information on the underground racing network."

Trent owned the largest multimedia company in the world. If anyone could unearth the illegal network, one of his top-notch investigative reporters could. Hal Pinkerton turned out to be that guy. And somewhere along the line, Kaci got her hands on the same information.

Her teeth were really working that sexy bottom lip, her gaze focused inward. "What does Trent get in return?"

I caressed a thumb over her mouth. "He provides the map of a race, which I don't need of course. But he thinks the police will use it to organize a raid and trap the racers. A raid that would target Evader near the finish line and hold him up long enough to let the underdog win."

Her eyebrows shot to her hairline. "Holy shit." A startled smile caught her lips. She shoved against my chest and slipped around me. "You promised him the police would fix the race in exchange for the information?" She rubbed a hand over her mouth. "Just to bait him to place a bet against you?"

Collin straightened from the window. "My father… *our* father finds the whole racing thing beneath him. Which means this bet must be a hell of a long shot with a payoff so astronomical he couldn't pass it up."

I nodded. "If I lost the race, it would be the biggest upset in illegal gambling." Pulling the wallet from my back pocket, I removed the dollar bill and handed it to her. "He gambled millions. Already transferred it to a private account on the network. It's locked down. He can't back out."

I answered their questions, but my eyes locked and held on Kaci, our silent connection braiding between us. I explained the intricacies of criminal gambling on the racing network, how it was invite-only, and how Trent had gained his invite to gamble through Hal Pinkerton. The message on the dollar bill went through a local bookie on the network, one I'd used time and time again.

Eventually, she sat on the couch and stared at the zeros written on the bill. "Since the Chicago PD isn't really involved, there won't be a raid. Evader will win, and Trent will be broke. Or at least a lot less wealthy."

Collin moved to sit beside her, his attention locked on the bet amount. "My father doesn't have this kind of money."

"Then he's pulled in my parents as well." She folded the bill, a staggered breath tumbling past her lips. "There goes our inheritance, not that we'd see a penny of it anyway at the rate they spend money."

Collin gave me a hard look, his eyes darting between Kaci and me. "Just so I understand, your original plan—before you met Kaci—was to seal his bet, place your own bet, kill them, then walk away with a lot of money by winning as Evader?"

"Yes. But we're not killing anyone. Deep down, neither of you want to give that order." My breath bottled up in my chest. "I have another idea. We put all our money on Evader, do the race, split the winnings, and turn in your parents. Then Kaci and I disappear."

An anxious look slid over his face.

Kaci tilted her head to the side, watching him with a similar expression. "What about Collin's connection to an eight-year-old murder?"

"Trent has no power without money." I crossed my arms over my chest and leaned against the windows. "Your parents will be broke, and Collin, you will still be wealthy. If Trent tries to send you to prison on false charges, you'll have the money, and therefore the legal representation, to fight him and prove his involvement. He won't have shit. Honestly, I don't think he'd even try to go after you."

Collin's lips quirked, but Kaci's face was frozen in thought.

I felt no resentment or remorse for giving up my revenge, because looking into her eyes and seeing my future there meant so much more than clinging to my past. It made my heart reach out and grab hold of her with every blood-pumping beat.

I erased the distance between us, crouched before her legs, and tilted her chin up with my knuckle. "I meant what I said about my choice. I'll walk away from the bet and everything else as long as you're at my side."

She placed her hands on my face and touched her brow to mine.

I closed my eyes, and silence settled through the room, filling the space with an impending decision. Things always felt more intense in the quiet, all the other senses working harder to perceive what wasn't heard.

When I looked up, I caught the full impact of her blue eyes, the skin around them smooth and relaxed. Her lips were parted rather than pinched in a line. I waited with my pulse in my throat to hear what she would say.

She caressed a palm over my whiskered jaw, her gaze searching. "The race is October twenty-seventh, isn't it? The date on the watch. Tomorrow."

I grinned. "He took months to place that bet. I was beginning to think he wasn't going to bite, so I laid on the pressure and put an expiration date on the offer."

"Time's up," she murmured. She chewed the inside of her cheek, exchanged a look with Collin, and they both turned to me, smiling.

A prickle of excitement surged through me as I rose to my feet.

For the next hour, we made a plan. I would race and win. Then Kaci and I would disappear while Collin turned over the evidence against Trent and the others.

"What if you don't win?" Her stunning wide eyes stared up at me, as if she were imagining the horror of Trent actually winning all that money and the damage he could do with it. "Who are you racing against?"

"I'll be racing *you.*"

27 LOGAN

Weeks of studying Kaci's every reaction in the office had taught me how to interpret her silence. Sitting on the couch beside Collin, she tightened her fingers around his hand and pulled it into her lap. Her tongue pushed against her teeth, her lips not quite lifting, but her smile glimmered in her eyes as she looked up from beneath thick blonde lashes.

She wanted to race.

My heart drummed wildly at the idea of chasing her to the finish line, but it didn't dispel my worry about the danger it put her in. The possessive, protective part of me needed her to reject the idea. She could crash the bike or get caught in a police trap or…fucking hell, all those perverts gawking at her ass? If one of those biker bastards hit on her or tried to touch her at the starting line, I'd lose my shit. A reaction that would shatter the pretense that we were racing competitors and nothing more.

Collin's initial smile flattened, and his brows knitted together. If he was realizing some of my concerns, he didn't seem compelled to voice his objection. Perhaps he knew as well as I did how much she wanted this.

I'd debated the wisdom of putting her in the race. Benny was supposed to be the challenger but her skill set would be more valuable in the background, monitoring the race and coordinating the diversion I had planned for the escape.

Kaci tilted her head, her eyes never leaving mine. "Isn't the competitor already determined?"

"Yes. The race has been billed as the undefeated Evader versus the underdog Lady Silver."

She raised her eyebrows. "Lady Silver, huh? You really had this all planned out."

"I had to. Challengers are chosen days in advance." Investors submitted their racers. There was a voting process, but in the end, money talked. "Benny and I put down a lot of cash to sponsor Lady Silver's placement."

Hype over a female challenger had already created a buzz of early gambling. As expected, the betting odds were spectacularly against her.

I sat on the couch beside her, sandwiching her between me and Collin. "If you have any hesitations about this, Benny will ride as Lady Silver. She knows the maps and the racing equipment, and she can handle a bike convincingly enough to pull it off without drawing suspicion." I touched Kaci's hair lightly and moved to the sensitive skin at the side of her neck. "You don't have to do this."

She lifted her gaze, her expression serious. "Oh, I'll race you. And I guess I can take one for the team and *let* you win." Her lips twitched. "On one condition." The power of her full smile electrified my pulse. "I want a helmet like yours."

An incredible feeling of weightlessness flowed through my veins, and I knew this was just one in a series of moments with her that would change my life for the better. She had me by the balls, the heart, and every other vulnerable bit of my body. She could have my air as well, because I couldn't breathe without her. I hoped to hell I'd never have to.

Her beauty, strong ethics, and need for love had never been factors in my plan. The last thing I expected was to find myself in desperate need of *her* love, too.

Two hours later, I left the glinting steel architecture and congested traffic of downtown Chicago and exited off I-88 to head home. The open road stretched west, the sun glaring in its dip toward the horizon.

The spare bike I'd ridden to Kaci's vibrated between my legs and filled my chest with a throaty hum. The chilly wind penetrated my borrowed clothes with a refreshing sense of freedom. But the best part of the ride was the woman hugging my back.

Her thighs squeezed my hips and her arms wrapped around my middle, and I wondered if she was the one holding me on the bike and not the other way around. Her chest pressed tight against my back, her gloved hands tucked beneath the opened buttons of my wool coat. Collin's coat. The suit, tie, thin-striped shirt, everything I wore was from his closet.

He was taller and leaner, but the fancy threads fit and saved me the headache of sneaking out of Trump Tower in my attention-grabbing leathers. The backpack on Kaci's back held my clothes and a few days' worth of hers.

We didn't discuss the possibility she might never return to the condo. Nor did we give Collin a final good-bye. After the race tomorrow night, we would make our escape to DuPage County Airport where a chartered plane would wait. Destination to be determined. All arranged by Collin, who would be there to see us off.

Forty minutes outside of the city, we were off the main roads and winding around smaller streets, headed deeper into farmland. When the traffic thinned and we hit a long stretch of empty asphalt, Kaci's hand wandered from the coat, down my abs, and cupped between my legs.

My breath caught as her thumb rubbed the head of my cock. A mile later, I strained against the wool slacks, the muscles flexing in my thighs. I moved a hand from the grips to slide gloved fingers over the tight denim leg pressed up against my hip.

She wasn't wearing her leathers, but her silver helmet lowered to my shoulder. Her hips rolled against my ass, the hand between my legs pulling on my most basic and fundamental need. I fought the urge to jerk the bike over, slide her onto my cock, and fuck her on the side of the road in front of God and everybody.

She didn't remove those tortuous fingers, and by the time we reached our destination, there was no oxygen left in my lungs.

The remodeled church where I lived was on a dead-end, country road, off the grid and hard to find. It stood sturdy and strong in an open field, with overgrown weeds between the gravel lane and the reinforced-steel front door.

As I veered around to the rear of the red-bricked rectangle, her taunting hand retreated and she sat taller. During the ride, she'd kept her helmet tilted to avoid blocking the rear camera view so I could watch for tails. Now that she'd straightened, her silhouette flashed on my visor, her helmet ticking back and forth as she drank in the surrounding pastures and woodland and the small shed that concealed my jeep.

The custom garage door in the back of the church activated when it sensed the microchip in my helmet. I pulled into the dark, single-bay garage, the steel floor rattling beneath the tires, as the automatic door shut behind us.

From an outsider's perspective, it was just a garage. A completely empty garage. For a reason.

Balancing the bike between my legs, with my boots on the floor, I hooked an arm behind me to hold her against my back and said into the mic, "Activate lift."

The voice-control in the helmet signaled the gears behind the walls. They whirred quietly, and the floor shook, then descended.

"Holy shit." Her voice muffled through the helmet, tinged with awe.

We reached the warehouse two-stories below ground. I rode the bike off the lift and parked it among fifteen others.

She slid off the seat, her long braid draped over her shoulder, her hands on either side of her helmet, wriggling it from her head. She set it on the floor and turned in a circle. Her wide eyes grew wider and brighter by the second as she took in the rows of bikes, the high-end gear boxes, the diamond-plated bike lifts, and the power tools lining the walls.

I would be abandoning all of it. Benny would sell what she could. The rest would be left behind with the remodeled church. That was always the plan. What I hadn't planned for was Kaci running away with me and everything she would be leaving behind—her dreams for making Trenchant a better company, her career, her best friend.

But she wanted the fourth option, and thank fuck for that.

I removed my helmet, setting it beside hers, and remained on the bike. I propped a boot on the frame slider and rested an elbow on my knee, wanting nothing more than to enjoy the pleasure of watching her.

She had no idea how beautiful she was. The flickering excitement in her eyes. Her tight, curvy ass in those jeans. And her abandoned smile when her attention caught on Evader's BMW S1000RR.

For a ridiculous moment, I was jealous of that damned bike. I wanted that smile pointed at me. But at the same time, it was her interest in racing that initially drew me to her. The mysterious Miss Ducati at the finish line captivated me long before I knew who she was.

Her attention shifted, and her eyes locked onto mine. She nibbled on the corner of her smile and shook her head. "So this is Evader's cave." She walked slowly toward me. "It's unreal to be here." Three more steps. "With the man I've fantasized about for so long."

I felt something press against my breastbone from the inside, and just beneath the pressure, it strummed and warmed.

Her steady gaze held mine as she approached. I couldn't look away. There was nothing hotter or more breathtaking than the view before me. Not just as a body to bury myself in or a purpose to fight for. Her beauty was in her loyalty to her best friend, her goodness amid a family of corruption, and her need for…something *more.*

It took me weeks to understand it, why I was so driven to be near her, why I wanted more than just sex with her, and why I wanted to give up everything to make her happy. She was my connection to life, my reason for fighting. She was why I felt so alive and wild and terrified. Because I felt all those things in her.

When she reached my side, she threw a leg over my lap and straddled the spread of my thighs around the bike. Face to face, she stared directly into my eyes, her body melting against mine, merging, conforming into a single beating heart.

Then she kissed me, melding her lips to mine and shoving her hands in my hair. I groaned and wrapped my arms around her back, inching her closer as I slid my fingers over the soft cashmere of her jacket. Coaxing her tongue, I deepened the kiss and flexed my hips, rocking against her and prompting her thighs to clench around me.

My pulse swished past my ears, and there was another sound, too. A voice clearing.

Kaci pulled back, and I followed her gaze to the door.

Benny leaned against the doorframe with her arms loosely crossed over her chest. She tilted her head to the side, wearing a gentle smile. In ten years, I'd never brought anyone home. She'd never seen me with a woman. I braced for some ridiculous wisecrack about my heavy breaths and the desperate way I'd been grinding my hips.

But she didn't say anything, simply smiled. She seemed oddly…subdued. Not just her mood, but her appearance. Long brown hair framed her face, her huge green eyes soft and tranquil, tan cargo pants, and a white t-shirt. This was Benny without the glitter and hair-dye and obnoxious antics.

Kaci climbed off my lap. I was reluctant to let her go, but we had a million details to iron out before the race.

I followed her through the garage, eyeing Benny sharply. "What's wrong?"

She straightened away from the doorjamb and shrugged. "It's good, Logan. It's just…" She looked between me and Kaci. "It's really good to see you happy."

After all the years she'd worked with me, navigating around my mercurial tempers, I supposed she wasn't the only one with a sudden change in disposition.

She reached out a hand toward Kaci. "Hey. I'm Benny."

Kaci accepted the handshake with a warm smile, and the reception moved into the main warehouse.

Mountains of boxes filled the basement. Benny had been busy, and perhaps that was another reason for her placid mood. After a decade of suffocating in plans of revenge, it was drawing to a close and there would be no resistance. She wanted to retire from illegal activities as much as I did. It was time to begin a new life, and I felt it take root in the softness of her eyes as she welcomed Kaci.

I took over the packing while Benny briefed Kaci on the race, the map, and the technology wired in the helmet she would be wearing. To maintain her anonymity, she wouldn't be racing in her silver leathers, and her Ducati would remain at Trump Tower.

Benny introduced her to the bike I'd selected for her. The MTT Turbine Streetfighter wasn't painted silver like the Ducati. But the chrome finish on the exhaust and bodywork suited the Lady Silver moniker. Her new helmet had a chrome-like veneer and was decked out with the same gadgetry as mine. Her excitement radiated from her pores as Benny taught her how to use it.

Several hours later, the planning and the packing were complete. Benny went home, and Kaci and I retreated to the ground floor. My living space was just that, a place to exist, to sleep, to wake and begin again. The walls and shelves were barren of personality. There were no family photos, no keepsakes collected as a child, nothing of value to take with me.

She walked through the open room, her footfalls echoing along the length of the old church. Her gaze roamed over every surface, perhaps looking for some insight I hadn't revealed. But she already knew every important aspect of my life. Time would fill in the rest.

We ate turkey and cheddar sandwiches on the bed, sitting in cross-legged positions, face to face with the plate between us. As she picked off the crust and licked the mayonnaise from her fingers, I didn't like the way her shoulders drooped or how her movements slowed with exhaustion.

The long day of planning had come at a cost. Hell, the entire past month was catching up with her. To think that all these weeks she'd been enduring in some way, working through her heartache with regards to her family, without me.

It filled me with regret, knotting my insides and swelling an ache in my chest. Adding to that was my worry about tomorrow night. My head pounded with all the details I'd painstakingly implemented. I would remain at her side every second of the race, but what if I overlooked something?

I was terrified someone would try to take her away from me. I kept imagining Trent at the finish line, waiting for her to win and shooting her as she came through in last place. Collin had set up a meeting with him during the race to ensure he wouldn't be there. But what if my trust in Collin had been squandered foolishly? And it would be a hired assassin pulling that trigger, not Trent.

I drew in a ragged breath. "We could leave tonight. Screw the race."

She reached out and ran a fingertip down my cheek. "And let Trent keep his money to hire the best defense lawyers?" Her deep-blue eyes bore into mine, searching inside me. "We'll always have races and fights and risks to contend with. As long as we tackle it together, we've got this, Logan. You and me. One race at a time."

As I considered her words, the tension trickled from my body. There was something beautiful waiting at the finish line. Something better than a winning bet or one-night with a woman in silver leathers. The finish line was the starting point of our life together.

When she swallowed the final bite of her sandwich, I moved the plate to the floor. Our clothes followed. I dimmed the lights, leaving a subtle glow through the rafters, and rolled her into my arms. We both seemed content to just lay naked in bed, fingers trailing, legs entwining, and lips touching as if our bodies were seeking the connection our hearts had already found.

After a warm, endless moment, I broke the silence. "I own a villa in Italy."

"Mmm." Her cheek bounced against my chest with her smile. "That sounds better than Shitknob, Mexico."

I traced the curve of her hip and pulled it tight against mine. "Benny can forge our identities for any country. It doesn't have to be Italy."

We didn't have to leave the U.S. as long as we maintained a low profile.

"I don't care where we go." Her voice tumbled into a breathy laugh. "Though Collin may be more inclined to visit an Italian villa than a Mexican hut."

We settled into silence, leaving my mind to wander once again through all the crazy, anxious bullshit that could keep us from reaching that Italian villa. I mentally traced every risk and concern until I found one that had never been fleshed out.

I gripped her shoulders and dragged her up the bed until her head lay on the pillow. When her gaze settled on mine, I ran a finger over her mouth and lingered on her chin. "The day Trent showed you the video"—she flinched, but I kept talking—"he followed you into the bathroom. Tell me what I walked in on."

Her eyes slid closed, and my stomach tightened. Adrenaline surged through my body, and my muscles heated. Trent was a serial rapist. If Kaci was one of his victims, there was no way I'd be able to leave him alive.

"Did he—" My voice punched through the open space, powered by dread and fury. I sucked in a breath and tried to gentle my tone. "Did he rape you?"

She opened her eyes, and they glowed in the soft illumination that reflected off the ceiling. "He tried once. I was fifteen, too young to fight him off with anything but my words."

The anger simmering in my chest exploded into a roaring fire. I was about to go fucking ballistic in a way I'd never allowed myself before. "Tell me what happened." My voice shook with a thousand fears rising to the surface.

She placed a soothing hand on my cheek, her thumb stroking my clenched jaw. "We were in my father's den. With his hand shoved in my panties, I told him *very convincingly*—her blue eyes flashed—I wouldn't be quiet about it, during or after. I threatened to tell everyone, the cops, Collin, the media."

My need to protect her seethed through my blood. My vision tunneled, and my heart banged against my ribs.

She rolled on top of me, her breasts pressed against my chest and her hands on my face. "Had I been anyone else, he would've taken what he wanted and quieted me permanently. But I wasn't worth the risk. My parents suck, but if he killed their only child, that might've put a strain on their partnership."

Her words were delivered with a shrugging kind of acceptance. It made me feel sick and helpless. I wanted to guard every moment of her life, including her past. I wanted to wipe away all the bad shit until there was nothing left but laughter and contentment. "The office bathroom…"

"He never tried to cross the line again, though he taunted me with it every chance he had. But you know what?" She touched her lips to my throat, producing a shiver that sliced through my anger. "I'll never have to see him again."

I guided her face to my chest, tucking her head beneath my chin, and we lay skin-to-skin for an eternal moment. I wished we were already in Italy with all my fears behind us.

It wasn't long before she rolled off me and dragged me with her, the brightness in her eyes begging for the one thing that could put our thoughts on hold. I crawled over her, bracing my arms on either side of her head, and devoured her with my eyes.

She looked so damned young. Her hair fell in shiny waves over the pillow, her skin flushed and smooth, yet her gaze was wise beyond her years.

Her lashes lowered, her lips parted, and her hips rocked against mine. I was instantly hard. I wanted all of her wrapped around me. Not just her pussy, but her need, her love, and her future. Our future.

And so I consumed her as she consumed me. Warm arousal replaced the chill on my spine, our bodies sliding and tangling together. When I pressed inside her, I let everything else go. Then I made love to her until all that existed was her and me and our finish line.

Four hours before the race, and the old chapel walls were closing in and thinning the air. My nerves rocked my body so hard I couldn't sit down, couldn't stand, couldn't fucking breathe. I never felt like this before a race.

But this wasn't about the race.

I strode to the bed where Kaci lay curled around a pillow, lashes spread over her cheeks, breathing steady with deep sleep. I crouched beside her and hovered a hand over her nude shoulder, her hip, her long, silky legs. Every inch of her was exposed except for the cover of her lacy black bra and panties. I wanted to touch her, *needed* to feel her. But I couldn't steal her rest.

She'd risen hours before dawn, racing the MTT Turbine up and down the gravel road, learning the nuances of the bike and the technology in the helmet. She was as ready as she needed to be. I just wasn't sure if *I* was ready.

I pushed away from the bed and paced the length of the building as the anxious voice in my head rose over the pounding of my heart.

There were a few who placed bets on her, mobsters and other vile criminals who would hunt her down after she lost the race and their money. But they wouldn't find her. Not on another continent. Not under her new identity. Hell, they wouldn't even know her true identity. I reminded her repeatedly *not* to take off the helmet, *not once* between my front door and the prearranged safe spot.

I wiped my slick palms on my leather pants and pulled in a ragged breath. The biggest threat to her was Trent. He would lose a fuckton of money at the same time that Kaci disappeared. Even if Benny raced in her place, he could connect Kaci to the scam. How hard would he try to track her down?

Fucking hell, I hated leaving that loose end. It made me feel itchy, restless, entirely too goddamned vulnerable.

The soft rhythm of Kaci's breathing changed, but it was the quiet alarm above the front door that caught my attention. A motion sensor alarm that only went off when someone or something approached the property. My stomach caved in, and my pulse skyrocketed.

Benny was in a remote location near the county airport, setting up her gear to monitor the race. No one else knew where I lived.

"Kaci. Wake up." I shook her shoulder then darted through the room as adrenaline spiked through my bloodstream.

The lack of windows meant no one could see in. But I could see out. I stopped in front of the TV monitor that hung beside the front door.

The bedding rustled behind me as I flipped through the channels, searching for the camera angle that showed the driveway. Darkness shrouded the street twenty-yards from my front door, but floodlights lit every corner of my property.

"Logan?" Her groggy voice drifted from the bed.

"There's a gun under the mattress. Get it."

The monitor showed the view of the drive and a black limo under glaring outdoor lights. My heart thundered, and ice filled my lungs.

I sprinted toward the kitchen area, grabbed my primary Glock off the counter, and checked the magazine. Fully loaded. I shoved it in the back of my pants and pulled the leather jacket over it.

Kaci appeared at my side, wearing only her bra and panties, with the gun from the bed in her hand. Her eyes widened as they locked on the monitor by the door. "Please tell me that's not Trent's limo."

The doors hadn't opened yet. It could've been Trent's or Collin's or who the fuck knew? But none of the options were good because *no one* knew my location.

I hit the button above the refrigerator, and the oak panels beside it rolled up. Then I moved her, damn near carrying her in my urgency, onto the hidden elevator. "When you get to the basement, hide. *Do not* come back up. I will come to you."

Tension snapped through her body, and her eyes sharpened into pinpricks. She shifted to step off the lift. "Bullshit. I'm not leaving—"

I kissed her, hard and fast, then gently pushed her to the rear of the lift. My heart hammered as I tapped the code on the keypad and turned my back. Behind me, the elevator whirred its descent as I sprinted to the far side of the room to the shelving unit. There, I collected my six-inch blade and slid it and the sheath in my boot.

On my way to the front door, the oak panels returned to their closed position, concealing the elevator behind the wall. I blew out a strained breath and grabbed my helmet from the back of the couch. No matter what happened, she was safe two-stories down, and both elevators required a code.

Kaci didn't have the code, but Benny did. If I didn't make it through this, Benny would retrieve her.

The monitor showed the limo doors opening, and a man in a suit was shoved out. He sprawled on the ground, his hands bound behind him. When he turned his head, the sight of his terrified eyes, black hair, and familiar face locked my jaw in a painful clench.

Who had Collin and how the fuck did they find me?

He stumbled to his feet and backed up, yanking against his restraints.

Another man rounded the limo from the driver's side, the gun in his hand trained on Collin. I knew that motherfucker. Big arms. Barrel chest. Crisp suit. Watchful eyes. The burly fucking babysitter from the office.

Trent stepped out of the limo, wearing one of his typical designer suits.

I shut down every violent emotion that ripped through me and measured my breathing. As they approached the door, I switched the camera views on the monitor.

Collin led with the burly man on his heels, the gun at his head, and his face shocked to a bloodless pallor.

I activated the intercom system, powered on the helmet to conceal my voice, and shoved it on. The facial recognition software immediately identified the gunman as Jed Williams.

They were going to threaten Collin's life to convince me to open the door. Could I trust the fear glazing Collin's eyes? Maybe he was a good actor, and this was all a ploy to get inside.

Had he told Trent I was Evader? Probably. Was Trent here to kill Evader to ensure his winning bet? Most definitely.

It was a racing rule that had never been played. The race would proceed regardless if one of the racers no-showed. Anyone who placed a bet knew this. If Trent was here to kill Evader, he assumed Lady Silver would still race. He either didn't know Kaci was the challenger or he didn't know she was connected to me.

But Collin knew. How much had he told Trent?

Trent stepped around Collin and Jed and stared into the camera lens, his voice booming through the intercom speaker. "Where's Kaci?"

Blood drained from my face. Motherfucker. I flexed my hands. Either Collin told him she was with me or he was operating on an assumption and hoping for a validation.

One I refused to give. "You've got the wrong house."

Trent glanced at the phone in his hand, his posture relaxed, his tone completely void of emotion. "Her phone is twenty feet away." He looked up. "Technology is amazing, isn't it? She uses her personal phone to log into Trenchant's private network and unwittingly installs little hidden tools on her device, like my GPS tracker."

I closed my eyes long enough to stop myself from punching my fists into the brick wall. All my meticulous fucking planning, and I overlooked the vulnerability of a goddamned smartphone.

"Here's what happens next." His hard eyes stared into the camera, his expression flat. "If you don't let me inside in three seconds, I'm going to put a bullet in her husband's head. If your weapons aren't on the floor by the door, Mr. Anderson is dead."

Sweat formed over my skin beneath the leather jacket. They couldn't get to the basement unless I gave up the code. She was safe, but for how long? They could shoot me and simply wait until she grew impatient or hungry.

Deep down, I knew what I needed to do. I should let him kill Collin for her sake and mine. Or to speed things up, I should just kill Collin myself.

But I couldn't. My chest tightened. I wouldn't.

Maybe I didn't entirely trust Collin, but Kaci did. And maybe deep down, I wanted him to live because, fuck me, he was my brother, a bond I could potentially kindle—something I'd never allowed myself to hope for.

Helpless anger boiled through my gut as I set the gun from my pants and the blade from my boot on the floor, the only weapons left in the room. Then I punched in the code and opened the door.

29 LOGAN

Trent ran a finger along the kitchen counter as he looked around my living space. His filthy fucking presence in my home made my muscles tense to the point of pain.

He'd already checked me for weapons and inspected the bathroom and closets for Kaci. He hadn't asked me to remove the helmet, and he could've shot me the second he walked in. Evidently, he was here for more than just my demise.

He lifted Kaci's phone from the counter and checked the screen. "Where is she?"

In the center of the room, I widened my stance and slid my jaw side-to-side to loosen the tension. "She's out for a jog." A believable reason for her phone to be here. Thank fucking Christ I hadn't told her to take it downstairs with her. "Soon as she sees your limo in the drive, she'll take off."

He studied me for a long moment. "We're twenty miles from the nearest town. She'll come knocking."

A few feet in front of me, Collin slumped in a folding chair. His shoulders curled forward, his hands tied behind his back, his eyes hard and bloodshot as he watched Trent. He hadn't said a word since entering, and didn't seem fazed by the gun Jed aimed at his head.

The hidden elevator was ten feet behind Collin and Jed, a comfortable reminder that Kaci was safe two-stories below.

How much did Trent know? Evader wouldn't give a shit about Collin's life. Did Trent know who I was beneath the helmet? My only concern was keeping Kaci safe, so I stuck with silence to avoid giving anything away.

Trent prowled toward me, his hands behind his back and his expression hidden beneath his tight, polished skin. "As you can guess, you won't be racing tonight." His forehead furrowed.

"Initially, I thought Kaci somehow knew about the bet I placed and had come here to warn you about the police raid. But I've checked all my connections in the Chicago PD. No one knows anything about a big race bust tonight."

Fuck fuck fuck. I didn't twitch, didn't speak.

He stepped into my space, his eyes level with my visor. "Remove the helmet."

The fucker didn't know who I was. I remained still, shoulders back, spine straight. "You may not like what you see."

He looked at the floor, grinned, and raised his head. "I've been tracking her for a long time. She attends your races. She's been here since yesterday. It's safe to assume you're sticking your dick in her. So why do you care what happens to her husband?" He looked over his shoulder at Collin and returned to me. "He's fucking clueless about what Kaci's been up to. Big surprise there."

I stifled a heavy exhale. Collin hadn't said shit.

His hand smoothed down his tie. "I brought him here, knowing she'd cooperate if I threatened him." He cocked his head. "Interesting how you seem to share her sentiment toward this man. Why not just tell me to kill him?"

His proximity gnawed at the composure I was seconds from losing. "I know who you are, Trent. You won't shoot your own son."

"You have no idea." He glanced back at Jed, who slipped a finger through the trigger guard, a command away from squeezing it. Trent's eyes flicked back to me. "Remove the goddamned helmet."

No sense delaying, and to be honest, I looked forward to his reaction. I gripped the sides, lifted it off, and tossed it onto the nearby couch.

His eyes flashed, and he took a step backward.

The refrigerator motor hummed. The clock on the wall ticked. The room waited.

He burst out in laughter. Threw his head back, barking a goddamn cackle into the rafters. The skin around his eyes wrinkled, and his over-gelled hair didn't move with his bobbing head.

When he righted himself, he sniffed, as if dismissing his momentary loss of poise. His fingers steepled against his mouth as he studied me, his gaze weighted in thought. "You sent the watches?"

Well, fuck, he was quick. I nodded. Out of the corner of my eye, I watched Jed ease off the trigger without removing his focus from Collin. Maybe I could disarm him, but he would pull that trigger before I covered the six-foot distance.

Trent walked to Collin and circled behind the chair to put his hands on Collin's stiff shoulders, giving them a squeeze without an ounce of affection. "I had this vision, Logan, that my son and I would control Trenchant Media, that I would be proud to hand the company down to him when I retired."

Collin closed his eyes, a swallow bouncing in his throat.

I had no idea if he was referring to me or Collin. I held my arms loose at my sides as I racked my brain for a way out of this madness.

Trent stared down at Collin's head. "Part of this vision was to see Kaci married to my son. Her parents are loyal partners, and I'm rather fond of her."

My stomach turned, and it took everything I had to keep my foot on the floor rather than slamming it into his face. When he met my eyes, I ground out, "Is that why you forced her to remain employed after I stole her job?"

He sighed. "I was suspicious of her interest in the racing syndicate, specifically her interest in Evader. I needed her close while I considered whether or not to place that bet against Evad—*you.*" His eyes hardened. "I knew she would eventually lead me to you."

So he could kill me and ensure the outcome of the race. Anger bubbled up, and I swallowed it back. "How did you know about her interest in the races? Who snitched about the files on the server?"

He stared at me as if he wasn't going to tell me. But if he intended to kill me, why did it matter?

Straightening the sleeves of his jacket, he met my eyes. "Hal Pinkerton was pulling the racing information for me long before he began feeding it to her. I left that trap open for her the moment I discovered she was looking for the information. Then I sat back and waited to see what she would do with it."

My fucking head swam through the what-ifs. If I hadn't sent the watches and prompted Trent's interest, Kaci wouldn't have obtained the racing schematics and gained access to the races. We wouldn't have met as Evader and Miss Ducati. I wouldn't have traded places with Holden at the nightclub. We would've began in the office as strangers without our tense yet fiercely solid connection.

"I *hoped*..." Trent removed his hands from Collin's shoulders. "That something would've evolved between her and my newly found son"—he gave me a pointed look—"so I could, as they say, keep it in the family."

My face heated. "You have a sick sense of *family,* considering the gun currently pressed against your son's head."

"I only have one biological son." He narrowed a disgusted look at Collin. "This faggot isn't him."

My lungs froze, and Collin jerked, twisting at his waist to stare up at Trent. His chest heaved as he spoke through clenched teeth. "What are you saying?"

"I'm saying, you worthless little shit, that your mother fucked one of our business partners." His tone was deadly calm. "You are not my goddamned son."

Oh, fuck. Dread curled in my stomach.

A pained expression distorted Collin's face. "Who? Where is he?"

Trent's face softened, and the gentle pat he gave Collin's back made the skin on *my* back crawl. "Your father was some gangly banker prick from Detroit. He was also a pussy. He sobbed and pissed his pants when I killed him."

Collin cringed away from Trent's hand, his face red-hot, his jaw locked with rage.

My chest ached, and my hands clenched. My empathy with Collin was met with the godawful memory of my mother's death. I pushed that away as my mind struggled through the implications. We weren't brothers. Collin wasn't his son, which was why he would send Collin to prison and why he had no intentions of letting Collin survive the night.

The distressed look on Collin's face said he was coming to the same conclusion.

Yet Trent hadn't killed us. There was more. I could feel it gathering like an approaching storm.

Trent stepped to the other side of Jed, and that movement alone ratcheted my fear. He essentially moved himself out of the path of the bullet that would exit Collin's head.

He slipped his hands in his pockets, meeting my eyes. "Frankly, I was delighted to find out about you. To have a son of my own." He smiled, but it quickly descended into a scowl. "The curious thing is, I never fucked Maura Flynt."

I breathed in deeply and spoke as calmly as possible. "You raped her."

Trent stared at his shoes as if lost in thought.

Ten feet behind him, the cabinet door beneath the sink cracked open. The barrel of my fucking Glock slowly pushed through the opening. *Kaci?*

My pulse hung in my throat, my lungs seizing. Oh God, no. How the fuck did she get in there? Did she not get on the elevator?

Every nerve in my body went on hyper-alert, and my hands shook like a motherfucker. My gaze flew to the hidden elevator and jerked away. Sweet fucking hell. She must've slipped off the lift when I turned my back. I was going to wring her fucking neck.

"I never touched your mother." Trent raised his head. "But her sister?" His smile raised a million shivering goosebumps across my skin. "She was a whore in bed."

My spine snapped straight, denial curdling my stomach and shooting tremors through my body. "My mother didn't have a sister."

"She did. Ella Flynt, who has to be your real mother, was the reporter who introduced me to Maura Flynt on the movie set." He rocked on his heels, his hands in his pockets. "Your stunt racing adoptive-mother was as gay as Collin here, though much more masculine. Butch. Very much *not* my type."

My mother was really my aunt? Who had a willing affair with him? I flexed my numb hands to keep the blood flowing. "Why are you telling me this? To make yourself seem like less of a monster because you didn't rape them?"

Trent stared at me, his expression suddenly so raw with sincerity it made the hairs on my nape stand up. "I wanted a son, Logan. My very own blood. I want you with me, on my side. To be part of my family. To run Trenchant."

Fuck, I couldn't stop shaking, couldn't escape the terrible shock. And the movement in my periphery exasperated my unraveling. Kaci's silhouette rose from beneath the cabinet. I locked my gaze on Trent, trying like almighty hell not to draw attention to her position. "You *murdered* them. I will *never* be on your side."

His face clouded, wiping away any semblance of humanity. And Kaci hovered ten feet behind them. Farthest away was Collin in the chair. Jed stood beside him, holding the gun at his head. Trent was beside Jed and closest to her. If any of them turned their heads, they would see her.

Distract them. I spun to the side and paced in a tight circle. Back and forth, step after step, I let all my fucking nerves rise to the surface. My hands shook, my muscles heated and expanded, and my breaths grew loud and labored.

And their eyes tracked my movements, waiting for me to blow a gasket. Fucking perfect.

I shoved my hands in my hair, refusing to look in Kaci's direction. "What happened to my mother's sister?"

Trent scratched his jaw. "We had a short affair. It ended when she stumbled across some things she didn't approve of."

I could fill in the blanks, considering Trent's criminal history.

"She wouldn't shut up with her threats. Hounded me for months." He shrugged. "So I had to put her down."

I slammed to a stop and swiped a hand over my face. My skin felt cold, my brain numb. He killed my mother's sister, who he claimed was my biological mother.

"I should've put it together." Trent folded his hands behind his back. "Thirteen years later, Maura Flynt picked up where her sister left off. She raised you, then she went after me."

And he killed her, too. My chest heaved, my anger boiling. I could deny everything he said about Ella Flynt, but why would he lie? If my mother's sister was a reporter, that explained the detailed evidence in my mother's diary.

Kaci shifted in my field of view, inching closer behind them with the gun trained on Jed. Blood pounded through my veins to the point of bursting. It would only take a half-second for him to redirect his aim and shoot her.

I wanted so badly to look at her, to examine her expression. Was she freaking out? Could she pull the trigger? She had maybe a seven-foot range on Jed, and Collin and I weren't in the trajectory. She had this.

Come on, baby. Don't hesitate. Don't miss.

Jed turned his head, and my heart stopped.

She squeezed the trigger, and the shot reverberated through the brick walls. Blood sprayed across Collin's face, Jed's body slumped, and I launched for my weapons by the door.

"Jesus! Fuck, Kaci," Trent yelled behind me. "Wait. Now just wait a minute."

I passed over the Glock on the floor, grabbed the blade, and turned back.

Trent inched backward with his back to me, his hands in the air. A few feet in front of him, Kaci pointed the gun at his chest, walking with him.

Collin jumped from the chair and strode toward me, his gait fueled with urgency, his arms restrained behind his back, his expression furious. I met him halfway and sliced the knife through the zip-ties, freeing his hands.

"You don't want to do this, Kaci." Trent's voice cracked. "I came here to get you, to take you back with me."

That, I believed. He would've taken her by force. After he killed me and Collin.

I slipped behind him, gripped his perfectly-gelled hair, and yanked his head back. With the blade pressed against his throat, I met her eyes.

Christ, she was stunning, standing there in her bra and panties, her dark blue eyes glowing with fierce intent. With her arms straight out, the gun didn't so much as tremble in her hands. There wasn't a hint of hesitation in her expression. If I didn't kill him, she would.

Collin leaned over Jed's body, grabbed his gun, and pressed his fingers against the man's throat. He wouldn't find a pulse. Half of Collin's face was covered in Jed's brains.

"Listen." Trent's back heaved against my chest. But his heavy breaths didn't affect the steadiness in his voice. "We can make a lot of money tonight. We'll split it between the four of us. I'll hand off full control of Trenchant. You can have all of it."

I put my mouth beside his ear, holding him still with the blade at his throat. "You killed my family, Trent. You can't replace them with money and power."

He closed his eyes. "Logan, I swear I didn't know I had a son." He turned his head, tried to meet my eyes, but the angle of the knife didn't allow it. "Ella kept you hidden from me. I wouldn't have left you without a family."

No, he would've killed me. I suspected Ella had given me to her sister when I was an infant to protect my identity. To protect me from Trent. But why didn't the diary explain Ella's relationship to Trent or the details of her death? Thanks to Trent, I would never fucking know.

"Kaci, please." Trent swallowed against the blade. "In just a few hours, I'll have billions at my disposal. You can have all of it. Just let me go."

So much for splitting it four ways.

She lowered the gun and walked slowly toward him. "No, Trent. In a couple hours, I'll be in that race, losing your millions."

His body stiffened in my hold. "You're...you're the underdog?"

She held his eyes and nodded. A sad smile tightened the corner of her mouth. Not the kind of smile that delivered revenge. She accepted his fate with strong determination, but she wasn't going to celebrate it.

Shifting her gaze to mine, she stepped back and lifted her chin with a silent *End this.*

Trent squirmed against me, begging for his life in a high-pitched voice. I tuned him out.

I'd imagined this moment for nineteen years as I drowned in the memory of my mother's blood and followed the leads she'd left behind. I thought if I gutted him while I stared into his eyes, it would kill all the cold inside me. If his life spilled over my fingers, it would chase away my anger.

But Kaci had already done those things. She warmed me with a simple look. Calmed me with a gentle touch. She replaced my revenge with a profound breath of life.

Holding her eyes, I tightened my grip on Trent's hair. It wasn't revenge that had me dragging the blade over his neck. It was my vicious need to protect her that guided my hand and opened his throat from ear to ear.

She didn't look away from my gaze as he gurgled and writhed. She stared directly into my eyes when I let him go and he crumbled to the floor. I sensed Collin beside us, bending to check Trent's pulse, but my focus was on her.

I dropped the blade beside the lifeless body, my heartbeat roaring in my head as I searched her face. She didn't seem stunned. Definitely not flipping out. Her lips parted, her shoulders relaxed, and she still hadn't looked away.

She'd killed a man. She watched me kill her father-in-law. I murdered him while she stood feet away. That kind of trauma forced itself inside a person. The blood. The darkness. The finality of a beating heart. I knew the haunting impact of that all too well.

I stepped forward and cupped her face with my clean hand. "You okay?"

She nodded once. "Relieved."

"Yeah." I moved my hand from her face and hooked it behind her, dragging her against my chest.

Her arms came around my back, and we stood there, bodies entangled, my bloody hand hanging at my side, and shared a moment of relief. Slowly, our muscles loosened, our breathing evened out, and the thump of our hearts swallowed all sound.

Too soon, she leaned back, and her stubborn chin pointed at the clock on the wall. "We have two hours to clean this up and get our asses to the race."

"Kaci," Collin and I said at the same time. Trent was no longer a threat. We didn't have to race. "You and Collin can take over Trenchant and keep your careers, live a lawful life that's not on the run."

"No. Collin can keep his career." Her eyes flickered with fire. "And he needs this win, this money to fight our parents after he turns them in."

I glanced at the gore on my hand, at the bodies bleeding out on the floor, and looked to Collin.

He stared at his shoes, his face smeared red. "Once our parents are found guilty, all control and voting rights within Trenchant will be passed to me. I may or may not keep the company, but I want to be the one to make that decision."

Kaci nodded, and I touched a knuckle beneath her chin. "I want to strangle you for slipping off that elevator."

"No, you don't."

I shook my head. "You don't want to run Trenchant?"

Her jaw tensed beneath my touch. "I want *you*."

Three words, and she owned me. Hell, she owned me the first time I saw her at the finish line.

She placed her fingers on my face. "We're so close, Logan. The fourth option. You and me."

Reckless, maddening, *perfect* woman. A sigh pushed past my lips. "There's an incinerator in the basement. Let's start there."

An hour later, the bodies were burned to ash. We'd taken turns in the shower, and Kaci and Collin sat side-by-side on the couch, deep in conversation.

I stood in the kitchen, gulping coffee and psyching myself up for the final lap. But I couldn't shake the atrocities of the night. Collin's near-death by a father who wasn't his father. The dragging of bodies to the basement. The smell of cooked flesh. The mopping up of so much blood. I was fucking tired, and I hadn't even begun to think about all the shit with my mother and her sister.

Yet as I listened to Kaci and Collin's conversation, they spoke only of the future, making plans for Trenchant, his visits to Italy, and his relationship with Seth. It was like a door swinging open, and beyond it waited a stretch of road. One that led forward, toward endless possibilities, toward my future with her.

I dumped the coffee in the sink, gave the old church one final glance. Then I grabbed our helmets and strode to the door. "Ready to race?"

She jumped up, and her smile gave me a bright fucking glimpse of what I was racing toward.

Three minutes till race time. I was trying to be cool. Laid back. Not freaked out. Cool. Cool. Cool. But the engines of several dozen racing fanatics vibrated the asphalt beneath my boots. Money exchanged hands along the starting line. Cat calls whistled through the air. And every pair of eyes for two blocks strained to get a look at my bike, the chrome-finish on my helmet, and the black racing leathers with the silver-mirrored stripes that I borrowed from Benny.

No one knew that under all this gear, I was a Trenchant executive, Evader's lover, Collin Anderson's wife, and that tonight, I'd killed a man. As I waited at the starting line, the MTT Turbine rumbling between my legs, hopefully no one knew I was seconds from puking in my helmet. Definitely not cool.

Beside me, Logan leaned into his forearms on the gas tank of his sleek BMW S1000RR, his boot kicked up on the frame slider, his black helmet cocked toward nothing and everything. Now *that* was cool.

And sexy. My God, I would never tire of looking at his ass in tight leathers, his muscular legs straddling the black-polished frame and his broad shoulders as wide as the damn handlebars. His body was built for that bike.

Beneath the dim glow of the streetlight, he and the bike were trim, smooth, and mysterious in mold and operation. From a glance, it was difficult to make out where the bike ended and he began. The strong definition of his back through the jacket, the bulge of his biceps stretching the sleeves, the creases of leather that led around his hip to the size and shape of him between his legs.

My body knew every inch of his, and it heated in memory of how passionately his hips moved when aroused, how delicious his lips tasted, and how full I felt when he was inside me.

"You're staring, baby." His syrupy voice dripped through the speaker in my helmet. His head was angled away, but I knew he was watching me in the rear camera.

Reluctantly, I turned my helmet forward. How could I not stare? "It's hard not to."

"*I* will be hard if you don't stop."

I shivered and drew in a deep breath. If he'd said that in his synthesized voice, I might've climbed onto his lap and ruined the whole I'm-here-to-kick-your-ass charade. But he'd turned off the distortion, as well as the external speakers on our helmets so our conversations wouldn't be overheard.

"How do you do it?" I turned my head just enough to see him through the side of the visor. "It's one minute before the race, and you're all casual and cool."

He unfolded from his forward recline and rubbed gloved hands on his thighs, his visor pointed toward the road ahead. "I'm terrified." He dropped his boot to the ground and adjusted his stance above the bike. "I don't know what's waiting for us at the finish line, but you can not deviate from the plan. Promise me."

The plan where I followed the map to the DuPage County Airport, no matter what happened to him, during or after the race. I wouldn't leave on that plane without him, but I'd follow his instructions to the point of departure. "I promise."

The starting line faced the entrance ramp onto I-355. We would race on the outskirts of the city, all highway, no turns. Logan designed the racing map to minimize as much risk as possible. There would be no dark alleys to hide traps. No sharp turns to slide the bike. His protectiveness of me, however overbearing, warmed me to the very deepest level.

A man with a thickset body and shoulder-length blond hair strode to the crosswalk in front of our tires. Standing on the curb beside us, he held a black flag low to the ground.

We'd only been waiting five minutes, but my lungs released a huge breath at the sight of that flag. Dozens of people had gathered. The cops would be rolling in soon.

With the map illuminated at the edge of my visor, I leaned forward, hands on the grips, eyes straight ahead. "Thermal."

The world bloomed into a rainbow of colors. The buildings and streets brightened into blue and green. Red and orange concentrated on faces and torsos and the engines of purring motorcycles.

At my side, Logan's fiery silhouette lowered into a crouch over his bike. This was it.

My heart thundered, and the flag went up.

I opened the gas and shot forward. The jet turbine engine whined as it launched me with enough torque to rattle my teeth. I reached ninety miles per hour in three seconds, dusting everything in my wake.

Except Logan. He held at my side up the entrance ramp and weaved around me as we cut through interstate traffic.

Within six seconds, I cracked two-hundred mph, and with no more pedestrians to worry about, I tucked close to the gas tank and turned off the thermal imaging.

Cars and billboards blurred into normal range of color under the black sky. The wind battered my jacket and pulled on my arms as I whipped on and off the highway's shoulder and squeezed between lanes of traffic. Adrenaline fired through my arteries. My hands slicked in the gloves, and my body shook with the force of the engine. My heartbeat was somewhere in my stomach. Fucking amazing.

"Goddammit, Kaci. Slow it the fuck down." His voice muffled above the scream of the motor.

He was right. If I wiped out at this speed, he'd have to scrape me off the pavement, piece by piece. I slowed to one-sixty, a pace I was used to on the Ducati, and focused on the openings in the heavy flow of cars.

The rear camera image showed him maneuver behind me. His body tucked so low only his wide shoulders and the top of his helmet rose above his aerodynamic windshield. Just ten more miles to the finish line, and we would be on our way to the plane, where I intended to wrap that body around mine for the entirety of the ten hour flight.

"I miss your braid." His rumble caressed my ears just as his bike passed mine and slipped in front of me.

The braid was there. I'd just tucked it out of sight in the helmet. "I miss your electronic voice."

"This voice?" His timbre morphed into the sexy, computerized overlay I remembered from the first night I met him.

I veered around a Greyhound bus and caught up with him on the other side. "Definitely that voice."

Sirens sounded in the distance. Cars honked. Chase vehicles and motorcycles with mounted cameras zipped onto the freeway. And Logan and I gave them a show.

I dodged and swerved and fishtailed the bike. He tore up the shoulder, cutting too damned close to the guard rails and gliding between cars as if they weren't there. And the entire time, he told me all the dirty things he planned to do to me, his modulated voice wrapping around me and trembling my thighs.

As we exited the interstate a mile from the finish line, he let me take the lead to make the race more convincing. I bolted away, my heart pulling to stay beside him, the air in my lungs burning with each foot of distance that separated us.

"I'm going to pass you at the finish line," he said without distortion. "But Kaci, I will follow you forever, and I will love you even longer."

I sucked in a breath as a heavy, glorious feeling filled my chest. God, I loved him. I pressed forward, pinned the throttle, and smiled. "Love you, too."

The finish line stretched over a couple blocks, bikes of all makes and styles lined up along the sides of the street. A moment later, Logan whipped past and sped over the final marker a second before I did. Swarms of people lined the street, their cheers and applause deafening. I tried not to focus on the celebration. Any one of them could've bet on me and could be plotting my death at that very moment.

We carried Glocks in the back of our waistbands, and I felt the weight of mine now as I zipped through the crowds and followed the map to the exit.

I broke free from the congestion of bikes and people just as a stream of squad cars veered around the corner. Logan appeared beside me, and I wasn't sure I breathed for the next ten miles.

I'd argued the wisdom in leaving the race together. Too much suspicion would arise. But he was spectacularly bullheaded about this part of the plan and refused to leave my side until he was certain of my safety.

A half-dozen cops chased us down busy streets, through sleepy neighborhoods, and up the ramp to I-88 as we headed west toward the airport. They couldn't match our highway speeds, and eventually we lost them in the thick flow of traffic.

I loosened my fingers around the grips and rolled my shoulders, keeping pace with the bike at my side. "Jesus, that was close."

"Take the next exit." His voice strained, his helmet aimed at the silver SUV beside him.

My pulse quickened. "What's wrong?"

Oh God, he pulled his gun out. "Stick to the plan." He held the Glock against his thigh, his visor still pointed at the SUV on his other side.

We turned off the interstate and flew down the exit, entering a quiet industrial area. The SUV followed.

Chills licked down my back, and my mouth dried. "Who are they?"

"Poor losers, Kaci. Trying to collect their debt." He slipped in behind me, his bike and his rigid posture bent over the frame, all poised to protect me. But what would stop them from shooting him?

It was so damned dark away from the lights of the city, the streets remote and barren of life. This was the part of the plan that made my stomach twist and turn.

I followed the map on the visor, cranking the bike to two-hundred mph and breaking away from Logan. My throat thickened, and my heart banged in my chest.

Approaching the brick building that matched the location of the dot on the map, I watched Logan through the rear camera. His black silhouette slowed as the SUV gained speed. He raised the gun, angling backward, his bike fast and steady.

I rounded the corner of the brick building as shots rang out.

OhGodohGodohGod. I slammed on the brakes, my head spinning and my blood frozen in my veins.

"The plan, Kaci." Logan's voice in the helmet chased away my momentary fear and spurred me into motion.

I shot forward, around to the back of the building, and found Benny in the prearranged spot behind a trash dumpster. She stood beside a blue Hayabusa sportbike and held out a blue helmet, her body covered in leathers identical to mine. I skidded to a stop and jumped off the bike.

Ten seconds later, she raced away on Lady Silver's MTT Turbine, wearing the chrome-finished helmet. Turning left on the street, she raced in the opposite direction of the DuPage County Airport.

The rumble of a speeding car approached, and I crouched down beside the Hayabusa, hidden behind the dumpster and peering around the corner.

A Mercedes zoomed past, headed in Benny's direction. Right on its tail was Logan, his arm raised, gun in his hand.

My throat swelled, and the backs of my eyes burned. I hated, hated, hated this part of the plan. As the decoy, Benny would lead gamblers, gangsters, FBI, whoever would be chasing Lady Silver to

Aurora airport. There, a plane in Logan's name would take off, without passengers, headed to Mexico.

Logan would protect Benny, I had no doubt. But who would protect him?

I shoved the blue helmet on my head and instantly despised its lack of technology. I didn't need the map to DuPage Airport flashing in my face. It was a straight shot from here. But I mourned the loss of communication I had with Logan. God, it killed me that I couldn't talk to him, that I didn't know if he was safe.

Suck it up, Kaci. You knew the risks.

I climbed on the Hayabusa and followed the plan.

Twenty minutes later, I parked the bike beside the Gulfstream private jet and removed the helmet, the shriek of the nearby jet engine ringing my ears. Walking toward the stairs of the aircraft, I stared numbly across the vast parking lot and searched the inky horizon for Logan.

I'd maintained the speed limit. Shouldn't he be here already? My insides coiled into a ball of jittery nerves. What if he'd been shot? Killed?

Collin stepped out of the cabin and sprinted down the stairs. His arms came around me, his lips pressing against the top of my head. "He'll be here."

I nodded, my boots rooted to the asphalt, my arms clinging to his dependable strength. "How are you doing with all this?"

He kissed my forehead. "I'm ready for it to be over."

My anxiety, my emotions, the lingering adrenaline, all of it bubbled up in a sudden outpour of words. "I'm sorry for keeping so many things from you. God, I'm so sorry for not warming to Seth." I blew out a breath, my fingers curling into his jacket. "I was so jealous of your relationship, but I think… I now realize that maybe Seth came along at the right time."

He stared down at me, his dark brows pulling together.

"You had Seth, and"—I shrugged—"that forced me to find what I was looking for." I scanned the dark depth of the parking lot, my fingers shaking and my wound-up heart banging for a sign of Logan.

Collin held me against his chest and attempted to distract my thoughts by detailing his plans for our parents, the company, Seth, and the billions he now had in an offshore bank account. His enthusiasm held me upright, his steadfast love kept me from falling apart as the minutes passed. Too many minutes.

I wasn't sure how long we stood there, but when a pair of

headlights emerged in the distance, I couldn't breathe, couldn't move.

The car sped toward us, some kind of cheap model hatchback, and stopped beside the Gulfstream.

Logan climbed out, and the air whooshed from my lungs. His body was still gloved in black leather, his helmet gone. His hair stuck up, messy and tousled, and his grin erased the painful distance between us. *He made it.*

Collin's arms fell away as Logan strode toward me with purpose and speed. He didn't limp, didn't favor any part of his body.

"You didn't get hit? No injuries? Bullet wounds? Blood—"

"Kaci." He laughed. "I'm fine." He picked me up, an arm under my back, the other beneath my knees, and buried his warm mouth in my neck. "But I kind of left a path of destruction. We need to go."

Then we were moving, up the stairs and into the cabin, with Collin trailing.

I combed my fingers through his hair. "Benny?"

"Safe." He set me on a long couch in the eight-passenger jet, knelt at my feet, and buckled my seatbelt. "We'll hear from her in a couple weeks. She has a few things to wrap up."

I slipped my hands behind his strong neck and gripped his shoulders. "She's shutting down the underground racing network, isn't she?"

He cupped my face, his touch as soft as his eyes. "And disposing a limo and sixteen motorcycles, among other things."

I leaned my forehead against his. "No more Evader. Your fans will be so disappointed."

Not that I would ever regret stealing him away and keeping him all to myself. He was mine, and that notion was no longer a fantasy. It was as real as my smile, as powerful as the breaths we shared.

"I've found a better race," he murmured against my lips. "Something more important to fight for." He kissed me, his tongue caressing the seam of my mouth. "A sexier prize to win."

He shifted closer, his chest resting against mine and his hips settling between my legs. I loved how his body pulled toward me so easily, the same instinctual way I gravitated toward him, as if this was the way it was meant to be. Nothing between us.

I kissed his bottom lip. "What are you fighting for now, Logan Flynt?"

He trailed kisses over my jaw, down my neck, and pressed his lips against the breast of my leather jacket, directly over my heart. "Your happiness."

All I wanted was him, just like this, his honesty, his fire, his love. "You already fought for my happiness." I lowered my face to the top of his head, inhaling his masculine scent, his soft hair tickling my nose. "You earned my forgiveness. Everything I have to give is yours."

He looked up, and the intensity of his smile and the fierceness in his eyes warmed every molecule in my body. "When I wake tomorrow, I'll fight for it again. And the day after. And the day after that. Every day, Kaci." He captured my mouth, hard and determined, and pulled back. "Every day, I'll fight for you."

His sincerity vibrated off his skin, glowed in his gaze, and powered every breath in his gorgeous body. "But we need to go." He kissed me again and stood, his attention on the cockpit. "Be right back."

I looked down at my seatbelt. Evidently, he didn't want me to move. My heart squeezed. I still needed to say good-bye to—

Collin stepped out of the cockpit, his blue eyes locked on mine, his lips tilted in a lop-sided grin. He sat beside me and embraced me in a tight hug. "We're not saying good-bye, hooker."

I hugged him back, nodding against his neck, fighting like hell to hold back my damned tears.

He leaned back and tugged on the braid draped over my chest. "I've arranged everything for your arrival. There's a change of clothes for both of you." He jerked his head at the bags on the floor by the door. "Benny took care of the passports, citizenship paperwork, and your new identities."

"Thank you," I said, my throat closing up.

He reached inside his suit jacket and removed a folded sleeve of papers. Unfolding them and flipping to the last page, he pointed at the signature line at the bottom. "I had this drawn up yesterday."

Divorce papers. I stared at his signature with blurry eyes and sensed Logan approaching from the front of the plane.

Collin handed me a pen. "This is the last of their control. We're free, sweetheart."

I accepted the pen and signed. No hesitation, despite the torrent of emotions my heart was battling. "I'm leaving you. Alone."

He slipped the papers back in his jacket and cupped my face. "I have Seth. And you're not leaving me. You're leaving *them*." He pressed a kiss to my lips and stood. "I'll see you in one month, and that villa better have decent bedding or I'm staying in a hotel."

I huffed, a smile yanking on my lips. "Love you, you fussy pain-in-the-ass."

"Love you too, you crazy bitch." He stared at me for a moment, his smile so full of love and devotion. God, I was going to miss him.

He turned toward Logan and gave him a one-armed hug. "Take care of her."

Logan nodded, his eyes burning with intensity, his jaw rigidly locked. "With every breath."

Then Collin was gone and Logan was buckled in beside me. My head fell against his shoulder, my hands reaching for his, and somewhere between zero- and forty-thousand-feet, I passed out.

I woke to a dim cabin, the whisper of air through the vents, and Logan's lips on my neck. He unzipped my leather jacket, removed my seatbelt, and helped me out of the rest of my clothes.

There was no staff on board. Only us, and the pilot, and ten hours of downtime. He'd already changed into a t-shirt and a pair of exercise pants. His blond hair hung in dark, wet strands around his ears, and the scent of soap breathed from his skin.

"Did you take a shower?"

He kissed my lips. "Yeah, it's too small for two people, but I'll help you with yours." His golden eyes glimmered in the soft illumination of the ceiling lights.

I glanced at the rear of the cabin. "No bedroom on this one."

He shook his head, his lips twitching. "There's eight chairs and a couch to try out."

I stared into his eyes, fell into them like a dream. Only I wasn't dreaming. We were on a plane. Flying to Italy. Wealthy beyond imagination. No more Trent. No more murder and revenge.

I kissed him, pressing my lips all over his face, his persistently-arched brow, his whiskered jaw, his sinful lips, and leaned back. "It's over."

He dipped his head and spoke against my lips. "No, baby. It's beginning."

A breeze drifted in through the sitting room window, warm and salty, filling my lungs with a weightless kind of peace. We'd lived in the beach-front villa for nine months, yet every time I took a breath, it was like inhaling the sea for the first time.

Life was different here. I didn't own a pair of high heels. Never slept or woke in an empty bed. I didn't work twelve hour days. Hell, we had enough money that neither of us needed to work again.

But we found something we loved. Pro racing in Italy was a big deal. Some of the most successful world superbikers were born and bred here. We didn't aspire to compete in the Grand Prix and travel the world. We just wanted normalcy and a passion to keep the mind busy. Racing in the beginner and intermediate classes gave us that.

And the really convenient part? Anonymity. We walked through the security gates wearing our helmets, we raced the circuit, declined the interviews, and left without showing our faces. The perfect job for two people who couldn't reveal their identities.

Identity was important to Logan, so much so he'd spent several months researching his biological mother. He confirmed Ella Flynt was a reporter who vanished a few months after his birth, but he couldn't find anything that linked her to a sister or a son. After a long and unproductive investigation, he decided to put his past behind him and accepted that his questions surrounding her death and his adoption to Maura had died with her.

I stood from the wicker couch and searched for the remote control as the yapping voices of news commentators buzzed from the TV. I needed to follow Logan's lead and put my past behind me, as well. It seemed like all these damned newscasts talked about was Trenchant's corrupt executives and the missing persons, Trent Anderson and Kaci Baskel.

God, how the media loved this story, constantly debating the intricacies of the scandal and tagging the company leaders as *wicked* and *evil.* The speculation about what happened to Trent and me was rampant and varying, but most believed we were killed off by one of Trent's criminal partners.

I found the remote under a throw pillow, powered off the TV, and stared at the blank screen.

The trial against Nicola Anderson, and Dalton and Kathleen Baskel began two months after Logan and I landed safely in a rural town in Southern Italy. The jury reached its verdict four months after the opening arguments.

Collin hadn't messed around, and the pressure from his legal team led to confessions by our parents and seven others within the company. Sentencing would begin next month. Each faced a minimum of life in prison.

Since arriving in Italy, I'd floundered through a flurry of conflicted feelings about how everything played out, but I had no regrets. My parents were alive, locked away, no longer hurting people. I couldn't visit them, not as a missing person. But I didn't want to. They were my starting line. Collin, Benny, and Logan were my future.

Collin was finalizing negotiations to sell Trenchant Media to its liberal, *ethical* competitor, Newswide Corp. The conditions of his sell-off was to keep his job on *The Anderson Angle* and to publicly announce his sexual orientation. I was so fucking happy for him.

I tossed the remote on the couch and strolled through the open space of the villa, my bare feet slapping on the tiles. Wide stucco archways separated the rooms, the walls and furniture in various shades of yellow and brown. Two-thousand-square-feet of cozy, and it was ours.

And we finally had the house to ourselves again. Collin, Seth, and Benny came and went frequently. Benny left two days ago after a month-long visit. She was headed to Eastern Europe in her quest to devour every corner of the world.

And now I was on a quest to devour my corner of the world and the man who occupied it. I missed him. Pathetic really, since he'd only been holed up for half a day, and that hole was a garage twenty feet from the back door.

I slipped outside, my toes sifting through the warm sand, the sun a blinding ball of fire above the endless aqua of the Tyrrhenian Sea. The nearest neighbor was a five minute walk along the beach that might as well have been five days. We never saw them or anyone on this remote stretch of golden sand. We were learning the language, but Logan preferred the privacy. His protectiveness of me required it.

I shielded my eyes with one hand and quickened my gait to the garage. The doors stood open, and the whir of a power tool droned from within. Inside, I found him bent over the seat of his new BMW S1000RR, the muscles in his back flexing with the exertion of the drill in his hands.

The whirring silenced, and he straightened, turning to face me. The drill hung from his hand, his other lifting to wipe the sweat from his brow. His workout shorts hung low on his narrow hips, his blond hair flopping in random directions of chaos. And Jesus, the cuts and ridges of his bare chest made my fingers tingle.

He looked like a sun-soaked surfer, with his lusciously-tanned complexion, his chiseled jaw covered in scruff, and the smile on his gorgeous face so easy and carefree I couldn't help but return one of my own.

"Did you get the fairing repaired?" I leaned to the side to check out his work and didn't see any cracks in the plastic.

"Yeah." He pushed a hand through his hair, the *V* of his abs contracting with the movement. "Only took four hours."

"Mm." I glanced at the silver Ducati parked beside his bike. "I fixed the cracked fairing on my bike in three hours."

"Then you can do the next one." He grinned, and his hand lowered to the waistband of his shorts. His thumb hooked beneath the elastic, dipping the black material an inch lower, taunting me.

Then it inched lower, and lower, my attention glued to the indentions in his hips, following the carved muscle with the descent of his pants. When I looked up, his eyes locked on mine, wanting me.

My body moved toward him, mindless in its need to close the distance.

He set the drill on the stool behind him and met me halfway. His hand lifted to my face, his fingertips sweeping along my jaw and down my neck. Maybe his body was mindless, too. We couldn't share the same space without touching one another.

I tilted my head back and stared into his golden-green eyes, my voice breathy. "Are you hungry? I fixed a hot mess of cheese and tomatoes and stuffed it in some bread."

He laughed, low and sexy. "You made panini?"

I shrugged. "I made something. Looks edible." Cooking wasn't my thing.

"Yeah, I'm hungry." He gripped my waist and whirled us through the garage in some kind of modified form of the foxtrot.

My hair swung around my shoulders, my hands locking behind his neck. I moved my feet in an effort to keep up, laughter tumbling from my lips. That lasted all of three seconds before he spun me to a stop with my ass against his bike. His fingers dropped to the fly of my jean shorts, releasing the button, the zipper, and dragging them down my legs. My panties followed, his eyes never leaving mine.

Warm air brushed my exposed flesh a moment before he broke eye contact and buried his mouth between my thighs. My head fell back, and my fingers flew to his hair, my body writhing against his lips. He sucked hard and licked fast, his tongue unbearable in its assault, his hands sliding up and down my legs.

My thighs trembled, and my inner muscles clenched. He caught the piercing between his teeth and sucked hard again. Licked, flicked, sucked, over and over. When his fingers entered me, the ache between my thighs burst into a cascade of rippling pleasure.

I moaned my release, pulling on his hair and rocking against his face. His lips left my pussy and moved over my hips, up my ribs, his hands lifting my t-shirt and pulling it over my head as he stood. No bra, and God, he took advantage of that, his mouth covering every inch of my chest, licking and sucking and biting my nipples.

He stepped back, his mouth wet, and the fire in his eyes threatened to buckle my knees. "Are you happy?"

Same question he asked me every day, and I always gave the same honest answer. "*You* are my happiness."

He held my gaze as he dropped his shorts, then his briefs, freeing his thick, hard cock. His smile lit up his face, the embodiment of pure, raw bliss. His and mine. I would never get enough of him.

Then he was on me, and his kiss was so fierce and deep-reaching, he had to hold me up, his arms locked behind my back and his cock prodding for entrance between my legs. He kissed me until I ran out of air. Until the world fell away. Until it was just him and me and the racing of our hearts.

Eventually, he released my mouth, shifted to straddle his bike, and pulled me into his lap. With my back to his chest, he spread my legs, bent me over the gas tank, and pushed inside me in one, long thrust. "I love you," he half-laughed, half-groaned.

The sound of his voice and the meaning of his words curled warmth through my chest. The furious thrust of hips, however, hardened my nipples and quivered my muscles around his driving cock.

"Love you too," I said with the same choked laughter.

He kissed and licked along my spine, over my shoulders, his hand in my hair, guiding my lips to his. Then he tucked us into a forward lean, my chest flat against the tank, his hips pressed against my backside. "Together, Kaci." His head dropped to my back. "Always you and me."

His hands gripped my hips, but it was his love pulling me tight against him, holding me, protecting me, giving me a life so damned full I could never want anything more in it. Two bodies fused as one.

"Always."

OTHER BOOKS BY PAM GODWIN

LOVE TRIANGLE ROMANCE
TANGLED LIES TRILOGY
One is a Promise
Two is a Lie
Three is a War

DARK ROMANCE
DELIVER SERIES
Deliver #1
Vanquish #2
Disclaim #3
Devastate #4
Take #5
Manipulate #6
Unshackle #7
Dominate #8
Complicate #9

DARK COWBOY ROMANCE
TRAILS OF SIN
Knotted #1
Buckled #2
Booted #3

DARK ALASKAN ROMANCE
FROZEN FATE
Hills of Shivers and Shadows #1
Cage of Ice and Echoes #2
Heart of Frost and Scars #3

DARK PARANORMAL ROMANCE

TRILOGY OF EVE

Heart of Eve

Dead of Eve #1

Blood of Eve #2

Dawn of Eve #3

STUDENT-TEACHER / PRIEST

Lessons In Sin

STUDENT-TEACHER ROMANCE

Dark Notes

ROCK-STAR DARK ROMANCE

Beneath the Burn

OLDER WOMAN / YOUNGER MAN

Incentive

DARK HISTORICAL PIRATE ROMANCE

King of Libertines

Sea of Ruin

New York Times, Wall Street Journal, and USA Today bestselling author, Pam Godwin, lives in the Midwest with her husband, cats, retired greyhounds, and an old, foul-mouthed parrot. She traveled the world for seven years, attended three universities, married the vocalist of her favorite rock band, and retired from her quantitative analyst career in 2014 to write full-time.

Her interests veer toward the unconventional: bourbon, full-body tattoos, and tragic villains. Equally peculiar are her aversions to sleeping, eating meat, and dolls with blinking eyes.

EMAIL: pamgodwinauthor@gmail.com

www.ingramcontent.com/pod-product-compliance
Lightning Source LLC
Chambersburg PA
CBHW020500310726
48979CB00016B/2735/J
* 9 7 8 1 9 6 6 5 3 7 1 6 8 *